Lessons in Etiquette

Christopher G. Nuttall

Twilight Times Books
Kingsport Tennessee

Lessons in Etiquette

This is a work of fiction. All concepts, characters and events portrayed in this book are used fictitiously and any resemblance to real people or events is purely coincidental.

Paladin Timeless Books, an imprint of
Twilight Times Books
P O Box 3340
Kingsport TN 37664
http://twilighttimesbooks.com/

First Edition, November 2014

Library of Congress Control Number: 2014946264

ISBN: 978-1-60619-300-6

Cover art by Brad Fraunfelter

Printed in the United States of America.

To Mum and Dad

Prologue

THE TOWER SAT ALONE IN THE MIDST OF DESOLATION.

Years ago, well before the collapse of the Empire, two powerful sorcerers had duelled each other, neither one willing to yield before it had been too late. They'd died…but the damage they'd done to the land had endured for hundreds of years, leaving wild magic to drift through the countryside and warp all the living things it touched. No one lived within miles of the Tower; no one saw the murder of crows that flew high over the tainted landscape and came to land on the battlements.

And no one saw the crows blur together and become a man.

The Sorcerer Crow smiled to himself as he pulled his dark cloak around his form. Few sorcerers could handle permanent polymorph transformations, certainly not without taking on some of the aspects of their animal form. It was far more common for their thoughts to slowly blur into the animal's mentality until they forgot that they had once been human. His solution—sharing his mind among a flock of crows—seemed to work. And besides, few sorcerers, even the most paranoid, would expect it. Any advantage was worth claiming when one was plotting treason.

His smile grew wider as he entered the Tower and saw the watcher waiting for him, standing in the shadows. As always, his employer had chosen to conceal his features behind a glamor, spelled right into the fabric of the hooded robe he wore. It was an unusual trick for a trained magician, let alone a sorcerer, but Crow could appreciate the advantages one could claim from it. If nothing else, it would be very difficult for an investigator to identify any particular magical signature.

It still bothered him that he didn't know the identity of his master. But, if nothing else, it was proof that he was working for a powerful magician.

"Greetings," the watcher said. Even his *voice* had been changed; it was spelled to sound neutral, utterly unrecognizable. "I have heard rumors from Whitehall. Are they correct?"

"Yes," Crow said, simply.

The watcher made a hissing noise, one of anger—or frustration. Only one thing at Whitehall interested him; the progress of Crown Princess Alassa's magic studies. Even the attack on Whitehall by the Necromancer Shadye hadn't interested him, despite the fact that Shadye had been stopped by a Child of Destiny. The same Child of Destiny who was now Princess Alassa's first real friend. And, to some extent, her tutor.

Alassa's early education, in everything from magic to government, had been disastrous. She lacked the ability to concentrate on anything for long, or the self-discipline she required to master magic, the key to ruling successfully. Her parents had hoped for a male child, for a prince who would keep the throne strong; they'd allowed their daughter to become spoiled before finally admitting that she was the only heir they were ever likely to have. And then it had been too late to hammer some sense into the young girl's head. Crow's employer had been delighted. An incompetent queen on the throne was part of the plan.

But then Alassa had gone to Whitehall. And everything had changed.

"A Child of Destiny," the watcher mused. "Much can happen when a Child of Destiny is involved."

"She killed a necromancer in single combat," Crow said. "Whatever else she may be, she is clearly a very powerful sorceress."

"Or a necromancer herself," the watcher reminded him. No other necromancers had been killed in duels with sorcerers; they'd been outthought or poisoned. "Do you feel that she is dangerous?"

"I feel that a capable Alassa is not in our interests," Crow said, softly. "She may well be able to take the throne without a *protector*."

It would have been easy to kill the princess, even though she was well-guarded after an attempted kidnapping in Dragon's Den last year. The chaos that had enveloped Whitehall after the necromantic attack would have provided the perfect opportunity. But a dead princess was in no one's interests, not when her death would have led to civil war.

But a princess who could be manipulated, a princess who could be *controlled...* *that* was a prize worth any amount of effort to secure. Who cared about the trappings of power when the reality was so much more rewarding?

Years ago, the Twelve Barons had managed to turn King Bryon into a cipher, powerless to prevent the aristocrats from tightening their control over Zangaria. But they'd reckoned without his son, the future King Alexis, who had turned his hobby of playing with soldiers into a deadly weapon that he had used to recover control over his father's kingdom. And Alexis's son had continued his father's policies. The barons had been forced to wait, gnashing their teeth in impotent fury, until King Randor's wife had given him a girl-child.

No one expected Alassa to be able to hold the throne without powerful support. And the price for that would be compromising her independence.

"We must act now," the watcher said, "before this...*regrettable* independence of mind the princess has developed grows worse. She is returning to Zangaria for her Confirmation. It will give us our best chance to strike."

Crow bowed his head. Zangaria was poised on a knife-edge, at least partly because of the Child of Destiny. It hadn't taken much research to realize that all the new ideas flowing around Alexis City had come from the Child of Destiny, or that Alassa was offering royal patronage to some of the merchants who used the new ideas. The nine remaining barons, stubbornly conservative, hated and feared change, suspecting that some of the new concepts would reshape their world. Crow had a feeling that they were right.

After all, reshaping the world was what Children of Destiny *did*.

But Destiny was fickle. *Nothing* was set in stone.

"Alassa will be bringing her friend," Crow said. "What do we do with the Necromancer's Bane?"

The answer was immediate.

"Kill her."

Chapter One

EMILY HAD FALLEN IN LOVE WITH WHITEHALL'S LIBRARY AS SOON AS SHE'D FIRST LAID eyes on the massive chamber. The bookshelves stretched as far as the eye could see, each one crammed with books on hundreds of different magic and magic-related subjects. Getting permission to work in the library had almost been a dream come true. It allowed her a chance to practice the local language as well as explore the shelves for anything new and interesting. She was almost guaranteed to find something.

She pushed the creaking wooden trolley between the shelves, peering down at the handful of books students had returned to the library. In many ways, Whitehall–although an academy of magic–was very much like a school from her own world, the world she tried to think about as little as possible. Magical students still returned books late, despite threats of punishment, or returned them to the wrong places. Now that the exam season was drawing to a close, the number of students in the school was dropping sharply, allowing the librarians a chance to re-sort the books properly. It was a vast project that would be completed just in time for the students to start disordering the books again.

But she had to admit that she rather enjoyed working as a student librarian. Whitehall's vast collection of books was not well ordered, certainly not by the standards of the libraries she'd used as a child. It was impossible to say what gem would be uncovered by sorting through a shelf or two; Emily had developed a habit of putting books aside to borrow and read later, even though part of her insisted that it was unfair to the other students. Not that she was the worst offender. Every time she moved a stack of heavy books, she discovered a handful of other books hidden behind them, placed there by a student who wanted exclusive access to them. It was forbidden, naturally, but it never stopped. The spells guarding the library only reacted if books were taken *out* of the library without permission.

She took a book off the trolley and worked out the title, *A Guide to Simultaneous Magic*, before carefully placing it on the shelf. The whole system was badly flawed, she'd long since come to realize. There was no single unifying system. She'd grappled with the Dewey Decimal and the Library of Congress cataloguing systems as a younger girl, yet they'd made it very hard to put a book out of place without it becoming noticeable. In Whitehall, each librarian had their own ideas about where the different books should go. A book on ancient battles might be filed under history, or under military studies. It was impossibly confusing. She'd promised herself that she would work out a system for cataloguing books, but there was just too much else to do. Recreating the Dewey Decimal System was incredibly tricky.

Carefully, she finished returning the books and wheeled the trolley back to the desk. The original librarian had left Whitehall, seemingly at the behest of the Librarians Guild, allowing his assistant to take his place. Lady Aylia was tall and elegant, with long brown hair that reached all the way down to her knees. Emily rather liked her, even if she did have the same attitude as most of the other librarians she'd met in her life. They could have kept the bookshelves in perfect order if it wasn't for those pesky users mucking up the shelves.

"One of the books you requested has been returned," Aylia said. She took a thin volume out from under the counter and placed it on the wooden table. "And I can clear you to take it out of the building, if you wish."

Emily nodded as she took the book. She'd been invited to visit Zangaria by both of her friends, once the exam season was over for good, and–naturally–she'd looked for books on the country. One of them promised to be a complete history of Zangaria, although it was remarkably slim. But then, Zangaria had been part of the old Empire until 170 years ago. It hadn't really existed until its founding monarch staked his claim to rule. And the handwritten books of this world tended to be concise because of the time and expense required to copy them.

"Thank you," she said. "I'll read it tonight and then let you know."

Aylia smiled as Emily marked the book out to herself and placed it in her handbag. "And I think that young man is looking for you," she added. "Should I start preparing the winter feast?"

Emily looked up and saw Jade waiting for her near the exit. She waved at him, and then scowled at Aylia, who seemed remarkably untroubled by her expression. It had taken Emily months to learn about the traditions in the Allied Lands; winter feasts were held to celebrate engagements.

But the thought was absurd. Emily had been sixteen when she'd come to Whitehall; by now, she was fairly sure that she was seventeen. Jade, on the other hand, was twenty-two in local years, certainly at least four years older than Emily. And he was a senior to boot, one of the stars of the school. He wouldn't even be in Whitehall next year.

And yet they were friends. They'd been forced to work together in Martial Magic, fought together to escape orcs and goblins near the Dark City, and survived the assault on Whitehall by Shadye, the Necromancer who had brought Emily to his world. Jade wasn't scared of her, unlike many of the students who knew she had killed one of the all-powerful necromancers, and he wasn't trying to suck up to her. Back home, part of her had always envied the social queens. It hadn't been until she'd found herself simultaneously feared and courted that she realized just how isolated a life they'd led.

"Go now," Aylia said. "There won't be any more books returned until after the final exams."

Emily nodded in agreement. In Whitehall, exams were actually important–and meaningful. Students had taken out thousands of books and were actually reading them, although a handful were trying to use spells to make the knowledge sink into their heads without actually cracking open the tomes. Emily had experimented with one of those spells and wound up with a savage headache that had convinced her not to try it again. There was no substitute, it seemed, for actually opening a book.

She picked up her handbag and pulled it over her shoulder, then walked over to Jade, who grinned at her. He was handsome, in a rugged sort of way, despite the nasty bruise currently marring the left side of his face. He'd taken a fall in a Martial Magic class two days ago and Sergeant Miles had refused to let him go to the healers, pointing out rather sardonically that the bruise might teach him to watch where he was going in future. In a world where dark wizards could hide the magical counterparts of landmines just about anywhere, Emily suspected he had a point.

"I was wondering if you'd like to hike up Mount Sunset," Jade said, as they walked out of the door. Outside, the corridors seemed less crowded than normal. Most of the student body had either gone home for the holidays or were currently sitting their exams. "It's been a while since we've had a proper walk."

Emily had to smile. Sergeant Miles might have been a combat sorcerer, but he was also a firm believer in physical fitness. His students ran five miles twice a week and performed hundreds of push-ups and other exercises every weekday. Once, she would have blanched at the thought of so much exercise. Now, she was stronger and fitter than she'd ever thought possible.

But Jade was right. It had been months since she'd walked for pleasure.

"Just let me put the book in my room and change," she said. "And then I'll meet you down at the side door."

Her room was empty when she entered it, unsurprisingly. One of her roommates had already headed back home to Alexis City, the other was currently sitting an exam. Emily dropped the handbag in her trunk, pulled off her robe and changed into a shirt and heavy pants, charmed to keep the wearer cool even in the hottest of summers. She stuck a compressed coat in her pocket, after checking that the spells binding it were firmly in place. Whitehall's weather was somewhat variable, thanks to the vast field of magic surrounding the building, and it was well to be prepared for anything.

The walk to the side door was uncomfortable, but she was growing used to it. Everyone knew that she had defeated a necromancer—and no one knew how, leaving a void they tried to fill with rumors and innuendo. Emily was a necromancer herself. Emily was a freakish rogue talent, with powers naturally superior to a necromancer. Emily had somehow created a spell that cut its way through the toughest of defenses. Emily had poisoned Shadye…

But there would have been no point in keeping that a secret, Emily knew. She wouldn't have been the first person to poison a necromancer; it was the simplest way of dealing with the supremely powerful and completely insane magicians. Why keep *that* a secret?

She did her best to ignore the glances thrown in her direction as she walked down the stairs, feeling—again—isolated in a vast crowd. If it hadn't been for Jade and her other friends she might have despaired, as she had back on Earth. Instead, she just carried on, knowing that she *did* have people who cared about her. She smiled as she saw Jade standing by the side door, one hand carrying a combat staff he'd been given by the sergeants. Maybe he didn't expect to run into trouble, but they'd been taught to be prepared. Trouble could appear at any moment.

"I packed a handful of combat rations," Jade said, as they walked out the door. "If we can't get back in time for dinner…"

Emily had to laugh. It seemed to be a universal law that combat rations tasted awful, even the ration bars produced by Whitehall and the rest of the Allied Lands. The bars were small, no bigger than a bar of chocolate from Earth, and they were filling, but the best of them tasted like cardboard. Sergeant Harkin had remarked that they were meant to encourage soldiers to forage and live off the land, rather than draining the army's resources by eating the bars. One of the students had asked if the bars served as an excuse for mutiny and earned himself five hundred push-ups for cheek. The sergeant had never actually answered the question.

She shook her head. "Do you want to walk all the way to the peak?"

"We can try," Jade said. "Or maybe we can just walk up to the lake instead."

The air surrounding Whitehall was pure, clear of anything that might signify the presence of a technologically-advanced society. Emily knew enough to appreciate the wonders of technology, particularly after having to live without it for several months, but there were times when she wondered if she was doing the right thing by trying to jumpstart the industrial revolution on her new world. Inhaling the air argued against it…but the sheer depth of human suffering argued for it. Those living without magic had lives that were nasty, brutal and short. Even the aristocracy, with access to magicians if they couldn't work magic themselves, lived in squalor, at least when compared to Earth.

They chatted about nothing in particular as they walked out of the school's grounds and up towards Mount Sunset. It was a strange place, even by the standards of her new world, but it was reasonably safe as long as walkers didn't stay there after dark. Emily saw strange flickers of…*something* darting through the air, hovering right on the very edge of perception. It wasn't unknown for climbers to discover they couldn't reach the peak, or that their path twisted on itself so that they found themselves starting up the mountain and then realizing that they'd reached the bottom of the path. There were even stranger tales, but none that had been verified. And if the staff had believed it wasn't reasonably safe, they would never have allowed the students to go near the mountain.

"I've been offered a chance to stay at the school as an assistant," Jade said, suddenly. "I did well enough in alchemy that Professor Thande thinks I have *potential*."

Emily made a face. Alchemy required talents she didn't have, which was at least partly why she was burning her caldron every second lesson. Thande wasn't a bad teacher, but his lessons clashed with Emily's upbringing, where precisely counting the number of times one stirred a caldron didn't matter. She was still puzzling over the fact that it *did* seem to matter to Alchemy. A numbing potion worked perfectly if you mixed the ingredients over a low heat and stirred fifty-seven times. It failed if you stirred fifty-six or fifty-eight times.

"There are a few other tutors that want a teaching assistant too, at least for a year," Jade added. He looked down at her. "Do you think I should stay?"

"I'd miss you if you left," Emily admitted, honestly. She didn't have enough friends to casually accept the chance of losing touch with one of them. But on the other hand…"What do you actually want?"

"I want to be a combat sorcerer," Jade admitted. "Helping to tutor at the school might be a step backwards. I just don't know."

Emily didn't know either. The Allied Lands seemed to consider a person's ability to do the job as well as just their qualifications, something she found rather more sensible than the focus on qualifications back home. She could see tutoring serving as useful experience for a combat sorcerer, but in truth she simply didn't know. But she knew who might be able to offer proper advice.

"You could ask the sergeant," she suggested. Miles *was* a trained and experienced combat sorcerer, one of the best. He had to be the best to be trusted to teach potential sorcerers. "He would know what you should do."

Jade frowned. "But what if he sees it as a lack of confidence?"

"I don't see why he should," Emily pointed out. Not that she could blame him for being cautious, even a little paranoid. The sergeant tested them constantly, in ways that were sometimes obvious and sometimes very subtle. "You need advice and the sergeant is the best person to answer your questions."

She shrugged. "What would you do if you refused the tutoring position?"

"Apprenticeship to a combat sorcerer," Jade explained. "He'd tutor me, supervise me…and finally put me in front of the White Council for final exams. If I passed, I'd be a qualified sorcerer in my own right."

And if you failed, you might end up dead, Emily thought.

Jade turned away from her, looking down towards Whitehall where it sat in the valley below, pressing his hands together as if he was nervous. "Have you given any thought to what you will be doing in the next few years?"

Emily had to smile. "There are five more years of schooling to go," she reminded him, rather dryly. "After that…I don't know. There are just too many things that need to be done."

"I know," Jade said. He seemed almost hesitant, unwilling to continue. That was strange and rather out of character; Emily had never seen Jade actually *scared*. He'd once casually worked his way through an obstacle course that had terrified Emily when she'd first seen it, without showing the slightest sign of fear. "Emily…have you given any thought to marriage?"

"Marriage?" Emily repeated, astonished. She'd never given any real thought to marriage, in either world. "I…"

Jade turned to look at her, his face flushed red. "There is interest," he admitted. A dozen possible scenarios flashed through Emily's mind, all rather comparable to a bad romance novel. "You're the most powerful sorceress of your generation–the most *potentially* powerful sorceress, I should say. There is no shortage of interest in you."

"People I don't know have been discussing *my* marriage prospects?" Emily sput-tered. The very thought was outrageous, too shocking for words. "Why?"

"Because your children will be powerful too," Jade explained, blushing slightly. "If you had children with a powerful magician, they might be extremely powerful. And you're the Necromancer's Bane, as well as a Child of Destiny. There are *ballads* sung about you."

Emily groaned. Years ago, back when her teachers on Earth had been trying to spark some interest in music in their charges, they'd been made to sing songs written by the Beatles. It wouldn't have been so bad if they hadn't had to sing *Michelle*–when one of her classmates had been *called* Michelle. Her classmates had teased the poor girl mercilessly for weeks. Maybe it was *karma*, but there were at least seventeen songs about Emily herself running through the Allied Lands, each one more embar-rassing than the last. Emily couldn't remember who had claimed that medieval soci-ety was genteel; he'd obviously been completely wrong. One of the songs was crude enough to make a punk rocker blush.

She collected herself as much as she could. "They just want me for my fame?"

"Yes," Jade said. His blush grew darker. "It's forbidden to approach someone in her first year, no matter how...*famous* they are. And no one is quite sure how to approach your guardian. But that will change."

"Oh," Emily said. The thought of hundreds of people she'd never met proposing marriage to her was nightmarish. She'd never even had a boyfriend, nor had she really wanted one. She'd had enough bad experiences with her stepfather to put her off the idea of dating men forever. "Maybe I should just change my face and hide."

Jade looked away, clearly embarrassed. "Emily," he said, slowly, "would you con-sider marrying me?"

A second later, his form flashed with blue-white light and he froze solid, sus-pended in time. Emily stared, wondering if her shock and embarrassment had made her work magic by accident, before she sensed the presence behind her. Only one person would have approached them in such a manner–and frozen Jade with abso-lutely no regard for his feelings.

"Hello, Void," she said, without looking around. "What are *you* doing here?"

Chapter Two

IT'S BEEN A WHILE," VOID SAID, AS EMILY TURNED TO FACE HIM. "AM I NOT ALLOWED TO visit my favorite ward?"

Emily scowled at him. Void had rescued her from Shadye, moments before the maddened necromancer would have plunged a knife into her chest, sacrificing her to an extra-dimensional force he'd called the Harrowing. And then he'd sent her to Whitehall, where she'd learned to manipulate magic and—eventually—to defeat Shadye when the necromancer had attacked the school. But she still knew very little about Void, from why he'd saved her life to why so many other magicians were scared of him.

Even his appearance seemed to be variable. Right now, he looked like a young man, with long dark hair, a sly smile—and a way of moving that suggested his body wasn't quite suited to his mind. He wore the simple outfit of a common laborer, rather than the glorious robes affected by other magicians, and carried a wooden staff in one hand. His face was too striking to be really called handsome, even if he hadn't had the smile hinting that he couldn't be completely trusted. She thought there was something aristocratic in his looks.

"He wants to marry me," Emily said, wondering inwardly if Void's appearance was a coincidence. "What did you know about that?"

"Nothing," Void said. He grinned, brilliantly. "But I can't say it surprises me."

"Well, it surprised *me*," Emily said. And yet, in hindsight, wasn't it obvious that Jade had been interested in her? He'd certainly spent more time with her than necessary. "Why does he like me?"

She hesitated, then plunged on. "And he said that there were people discussing my marriage prospects," she added. "Why?"

Void tilted his head slightly, as if he didn't quite understand why she was upset. "You know that magic is passed on through the blood," he said. "The children of magicians are likely to be magicians themselves. If you were to marry another magician, or at least bear his children, those offspring would be very powerful indeed. Quite a few of the older bloodlines would be interested in recruiting you."

"I'm not a brood cow," Emily snapped. She looked into his dark eyes, glinting with suppressed amusement, and felt her temper fray. "And are you arranging my marriage with someone I don't know?"

"You killed a necromancer," Void reminded her, dryly. "I rather doubt that *anyone* would dare to try to force you into a marriage." He paced over to Jade's frozen form and examined him, thoughtfully. "They are much more likely to try to seduce you, or to seduce your guardian."

"*You* are my guardian," Emily said. "*Have* you been getting offers for my hand?"

"I never bother to pay attention to such things," Void said. "*Should* I be arranging a match for you?"

"*No*," Emily said, sharply. "I... I don't want to marry anyone, particularly not someone I don't know. I'm too young."

"Girls can be married from the moment they start their cycles," Void reminded her. "And marriages can be arranged from the moment a girl takes her first breath. Just ask your royal friend."

Emily flushed. She'd known that Alassa would have to marry for political reasons, not for love—and even Imaiqah, the daughter of an increasingly wealthy merchant, would have to consider her father's wishes when she married. But it had never really occurred to Emily that such rules might apply to *her*. Why should they? She had no family here, unless one counted Void...

What if someone wanted to get close to *him*?

But she didn't have to take it that far. She was powerful, she was wealthy...and she was famous. There would be no shortage of people willing to court her, just in hopes of sharing the benefits she might bring to this world. The fact that an extremely powerful sorcerer was her guardian was merely the icing on the cake.

She looked up at Jade and cursed under her breath. What were *his* true motives?

"He wants to marry me," she said, numbly. "He's five years older than me and he wants to marry me."

"There are elderly men who marry very young wives," Void pointed out. He sounded bored, as if he hadn't really wanted to discuss Emily's marriage prospects at all. One thing Emily *had* learned about her guardian was that he had a very short attention span. "Five years is not that great a difference."

But it would be on Earth, Emily thought. Anyone Jade's age who courted a sixteen-year-old girl would have raised eyebrows, at the very least. It wouldn't have made that much difference if Emily had been ten years older, but sixteen...

"Why me?" Emily asked. "Does he *really* want to marry me?"

Void let out a sigh. "While I cannot deny that his family would benefit from having you marry their son," he said, tartly, "they are not well-placed to take proper advantage of it. It is therefore likely that Jade genuinely *does* have feelings for you."

He waved his hand in the air, dismissing the matter. "But I didn't come here to help you handle your suitors," he added. "There are more important concerns."

Emily shook her head. "I don't know what to make of it all," she admitted. "Does he—like—*like* me?"

Void ignored her. "Your friend the crown princess is taking you to Zangaria," he said. "Are you aware that her country is currently balanced on a knife-edge?"

Emily hesitated, then shook her head. She'd done her best to follow local politics, but they were often confusing, seeming to rely more on personal relationships than geopolitics. And there were times when the Allied Lands seemed too stupid to survive. The necromancers were still lurking in the Blighted Lands, waiting for an opportunity to break through the mountains and invade the free territories. If Emily hadn't killed Shadye, the necromancer who had kidnapped her from Earth, the war might have been over six months ago. The necromancers would have won.

And yet the Allied Lands still squabbled over petty issues.

"Alassa is the only heir her parents have," Void said. "If she fails to inherit the throne—if she fails to have children who can inherit the throne in turn—her country will face considerable unrest. Or, for that matter, if she marries poorly, her husband might become a plague on the country. There are too many issues surrounding her future—and some of those issues are your fault."

Emily blinked. "Mine?"

"You helped your friend to introduce new ideas into their society," Void reminded her. "Some of those ideas are proving quite…destabilizing."

He shrugged, expressively. "Not that they really need the excuse to start slipping towards civil war," he added. "If something were to happen to Alassa, there would be an unprecedented struggle to determine who would be the next monarch."

Emily scowled at him. "If that were the case," she said, "why would they *want* to kill Alassa?"

Void smiled, but it didn't quite touch his eyes. "Who benefits from chaos in the Allied Lands?"

The answer to *that* question was obvious. "Necromancers," Emily said. Shadye hadn't expressed any interest in capturing Alassa, but he'd been completely fixated on Emily herself. Given time, he might have seen the advantages in using mind-control spells on Alassa, or simply killing her to produce chaos. "Are they planning to kill her?"

"It's possible," Void said. "But you know how hard it is to get intelligence out of the Blighted Lands."

He carried on before Emily could say a word. "There are other threats," he added. "Do you realize that Zangaria has never had a queen?"

Emily nodded. She'd learned that from studying Alassa's country, before they'd become friends, and she'd discovered that she didn't really envy the princess. Female sorcerers weren't uncommon, but female *rulers* were unusual in the Allied Lands. Part of it was because the law stated that male heirs were always first in line to their thrones, yet there was also a sexism pervading the attitudes to monarchy. A female ruler was assumed to be incapable of displaying the thrusting vigor of a king.

But there was more to it than that. Women were expected to be subordinate to their husbands—at least, unless they were powerful sorceresses. A queen who married would find herself sharing power, even through a king would be under no such obligation. And if she chose the wrong man, the results could be disastrous. Earth's history showed that all too clearly. Mary, Queen of Scots, had chosen badly and the whole affair had blown up in her face. So too had Mary Tudor.

"You also know that Alassa was not given a proper magical education," Void added. "Do you realize that may have been because certain factions wanted her dependent upon a Court Wizard?"

Emily remembered her first meeting with Alassa and scowled. Alassa had been spoilt, surrounded by cronies who kept telling her that she was the most important person in Whitehall. The thought of someone like *that* on a throne was chilling. Later, they'd become friends, but Alassa still had a strong sense of self-importance even if she had learned a little humility. At least she'd also learned, the hard way, that sycophants were not to be trusted. When they'd come crawling back, long after Alassa had been given time to brood, she'd sent them all packing with a few well-chosen words.

But Alassa had also not been a skilled magician. Indeed, she had memorized a number of spells, rather than actually understanding the theory behind them. She'd been powerful, but a properly-trained magician would have tied her up in knots if they'd fought. It had been Emily's patient tutorage that had helped her to understand magic theory and to actually make progress. They'd passed the Charms exams together.

And, in truth, Emily had deduced that someone wanted to keep Alassa dependent on her Court Wizard much earlier. *And* there was only one logical motive.

"Because they thought a girl-ruler would be easier to handle without magic," she said, feeling vaguely insulted. All of her knowledge of her own world's history suggested that male rulers were allowed to get away with a great deal of crap, while female rulers were held to an impossibly high standard. "Why don't they just shut up and accept it?"

Void eyed her darkly. "If Alassa marries someone from within the kingdom, that person's family will be promoted above all others," he said, as if he'd expected her to know that. "The balance of power within the kingdom will be upset. If Alassa marries someone from *outside* the kingdom, a new factor will be introduced into local politics. Normally, a queen would be expected to find a strong protector, someone masculine who will safeguard her rule. Whoever Alassa chooses will become very powerful indeed."

"I can't see Alassa choosing anyone," Emily admitted. Even if her friend *hadn't* been aware of the potential dangers—her protector might start becoming her master—she wouldn't want to share power with someone else, particularly not someone who had a power base of his own, separate from her. "She'd want to rule on her own."

"And as long as she remained childless, the succession would be in question," Void said. "The White Council is very concerned."

Emily gave him a sharp look. She knew next to nothing about the White Council, apart from the fact that it meant different things to different people. Alassa had told her that it was the parliament that debated the unified response to the necromancers—and to other threats, although she had yet to hear of any more dangerous than the supercharged magicians in the Blighted Lands. But the grandmaster had hinted that it was composed of magicians, magicians who considered themselves responsible for safeguarding the Allied Lands. And Void had apparently called on the Council to discuss *Emily's* future, back when he'd rescued her from certain death.

"I see," she said, finally. "What do you want me to do?"

Void grinned at her. "What makes you think I want you to do anything?"

"You came here and interrupted me," Emily pointed out. Part of her was grateful—at least she had a chance to *think* about what she could say to Jade—but the rest of her was irked at his presumption. "I don't think you came just to tell me vague generalities about Alassa's kingdom."

"True enough," Void agreed. He cleared his throat, pretending to read from an invisible document. "The White Council would prefer that the country remain stable, with a clear line of succession to the throne. They would be very grateful for anything you do that helps ensure such a happy outcome."

Emily felt her lips twitch. "They think that *I* can help keep the country stable?"

"The White Council is not supposed to interfere overtly in the internal affairs of individual Allied Lands," Void admitted. "You, however, are a close personal friend of the crown princess, the girl who will be at the heart of the coming political turmoil. If you manage to keep her alive and reasonably independent, the White Council would be very relieved."

"Reasonably independent," Emily repeated. She shook her head. "It seems to me that independence might be difficult, whoever she picks as husband. Maybe she should just remain unmarried."

"Then the succession would be disputed," Void said, crossly. "There are *no* other direct heirs to the throne. Unless Alassa has children, there will be at least seven different noble families with vague claims—claims that will be heavily disputed by everyone else."

Emily smiled. "Why can't she have children without getting married?"

"Because such children would not be accepted as fully legitimate," Void said. "Besides, she *will* be expected to marry. The only question is who she chooses."

His eyes glittered. "If you were a man," he added, "I would advise you to court her."

Emily snorted. "And seeing you *are* a man," she countered, "why don't *you* court her?"

Void wagged his finger at her, although it was clear that he was trying not to laugh. "You should consider yourself lucky," he said. "Don't you know that there are guardians who would beat their wards for that?"

He shook his head, unable to repress a smile any longer. "A powerful sorcerer as consort might make sense—it would certainly terrify the aristocrats into behaving themselves—but it would have other risks," he added. "And besides, you *do* realize that I am over a hundred years old?"

Emily snickered. "You don't know anyone else who might be interested in courting Alassa?"

"I'd be worried about adding monarchical power to any sorcerer's already formidable powers," Void said, softly. "You already know that some sorcerers go too far in their quest for power."

"I know," Emily said.

From what she had been able to discover, necromancers rarely started out as monsters, intent on sacrificing countless innocent victims in order to boost their power. Indeed, the insanity that came with the power should have deterred all but the most foolhardy. But sorcerers who wanted greater power often took the first stumbling steps into necromancy without fully realizing what they were doing, at least until it was too late. And then they became addicted to the rush of power that came with the dark magic. As far as Emily knew, no one had ever broken the addiction. They weren't even able to understand why anyone would *want* to break free.

Void looked back at Jade, then down at the grass. "The Allied Lands have been enjoying a period of stability," he said. "That's also your fault—although no one is actually *complaining* about this one. We'd like that stability to last as long as possible."

Emily made a face. Shadye's attack on Whitehall, a seemingly impregnable fortress, had come within bare inches of succeeding. The Allied Lands had been forced to face the fact that if he *had* succeeded, the mountain range separating them from the necromancers would have been breached and the hordes would have been free to ravage the southern countries bordering the mountains. It wouldn't be long, Emily suspected, before the Allied Lands started bickering again, but for the moment the near-disaster had concentrated quite a few minds.

"I'll do my best," she promised. How exactly was she supposed to convince Alassa to pick a husband? Perhaps she should pick a prince from the other side of the Allied Lands...if that would actually work. She needed to do more reading. "And what should I do about this?"

She waved a hand at Jade. "I don't even know *why* he wants to marry me," she protested. "What should I do?"

Void grinned. "You protested at the thought of people organizing your marriage for you," he said, "and now you're asking me to tell you what to do?"

Emily flushed.

"If you want to marry him," Void added, "I will not raise any objection. Quite a few of the older pupils at Whitehall are married, along with some of the tutors, so the grandmaster is unlikely to object. And anyone else...well, you *are* the Necromancer's Bane. They'll keep their objections to themselves."

His eyes narrowed. "Do you *want* to marry him?"

Emily hesitated. "I don't know," she admitted, finally. She *did* like Jade—and, unlike so many others, he didn't seem to be scared of her. But then, he'd seen some of her early blunders in Martial Magic. The others knew her only by reputation. "I..."

"Then wait until you're sure," Void suggested. "You're a magician—the normal courtship rules don't really apply to you. You won't lose anything by turning down any other proposals that come your way. Once you actually *know* what you want, you can decide what to do. Just don't invite any demons to share your bed. That always ends badly."

"Demons?" Emily repeated. "Why...?"

"Some people are idiots who think they can play with fire without being burned," Void said. "Now if you will excuse me..."

Emily opened her mouth, but it was already too late.

Void was gone.

Chapter Three

THE SPELL ON JADE BROKE AN INSTANT AFTER VOID VANISHED.

He turned back to face her, seemingly unaware that any time had passed. Emily wasn't too surprised. She'd experienced the spell herself and had been utterly unaware of it, until someone had pointed out that the sun had moved. Jade might have noticed—they'd been taught to tell the time by reading the sun's position—but he hadn't been frozen for very long.

And what if he thought *she* had frozen him?

"I... I don't know," she said, out loud. What had they been talking about before Void had arrived? "This is all so...*sudden*."

Jade looked about as red as Emily felt. "I know," he admitted. "It's just that..."

Emily held up a hand before he could say anything else, thinking hard. On Earth, courtship was a long process, with both parties slowly drawing together. There was a great deal of plausible deniability built into the system, she realized, allowing one party to withdraw without embarrassment if they realized that the other party wasn't really interested. But Jade had come right out and declared his interest, as if he expected that would be enough. Perhaps it would be, for anyone born to this world. Emily was from somewhere very different.

What could she say? *Did* she like Jade? He was handsome, and kind, and he'd been a friend when too many others had been terrified of her—but would they really be good as a couple? Or was she being silly? This wasn't a world where couples could easily separate if they found out that they were incompatible *after* getting married. But then, Jade's family was of little consequence and Emily's was non-existent. Her thoughts spun through her head, leaving her unsure of what to do. Did she want to kiss him? Would it be easy to kiss him? She had never even kissed a boy on Earth.

No one had warned her that someone would want to court her. How had she missed even *considering* the possibility? But on Earth, she had been a social outcast and she'd just assumed that it would be the same at Whitehall. God knew she'd gone through real troubles just to make a handful of friends—and they, in their own way, were outcasts too. Hell, was *Jade* an outcast? He certainly seemed more popular than Emily had ever been.

She pushed her wandering thoughts aside and looked up at him. "I cannot get married yet," she said, finally. Void had said that there were older students who *were* married; absently, she wondered what sort of provisions were made for them. Married quarters? "I'm not saying no, but I want to wait."

Jade looked...oddly hurt. "I understand," he said, tightly. "I shouldn't have sprung it on you so quickly. I..."

His voice trailed off.

Emily felt a pang of guilt, even though cold logic told her that she had nothing to be guilty about. She hadn't played with Jade's emotions, nor had she hinted to him that she might have been interested...or had she? For all she knew, the amount of time she'd spent with him might have been interpreted as a sign of interest. Back home, male-female friendships were far from uncommon, but here they seemed to be rare. Come to think of it, the only girls she'd seen being friendly with the boys outside classes were the other three girls from Martial Magic. Or were they being courted too?

"It's all right," Emily said, although she wasn't sure if she was telling the truth. She *did* feel flattered that he'd asked, even though she'd never expected such a...blunt proposal. "I just...can you ask me again later?"

But he'd been asking her about staying in Whitehall, she remembered suddenly. Had he really been asking if she wanted him to stay with her?

And men say we women are impossible to understand, she thought, sourly. *They should try walking a mile in our shoes.*

"I can," Jade said. "I'm sorry if I was...impolite."

Emily made a face. "You weren't bad at all," she said, as reassuringly as she could. Her own emotions were spinning around in her head. "Don't worry about it. I will consider your proposal, but I have to complete my education before actually getting married."

And what happens, a dark voice at the back of her head muttered, *if he finds someone else he likes between now and then?*

Jade reached out suddenly and gave her a hug. Emily somehow managed to stop herself from flinching back, for very few people had *ever* hugged her in her life. Her mother had shown more interest in the bottle than in her only child, her stepfather had never been affectionate towards her...and the only person at Whitehall who had hugged her was Imaiqah. Now...she felt Jade's hands enfolding her and forced herself to relax. The hug didn't feel bad at all.

"Thank you," he said. It would have been easy to kiss him. "I... should we go back to the school?"

Emily winced, inwardly. "I think that would be best," she admitted. "I need time to think."

There was an uncomfortable silence as they walked back down the path to Whitehall. Emily wondered, bitterly, if they would ever recapture the easy friendship they'd had before he'd proposed to her. She'd *liked* laughing and joking with him, so much more than anything she'd had on Earth. But maybe he'd only spent time with her because he was interested in marrying her. How could she have missed it?

She grimaced as they entered the school's grounds, passing through the outer protective wards that were intended to keep out unwanted guests. Emily had always been sensitive to the wards, but ever since Shadye had invaded the school she'd had the distant impression that the wards didn't really like her. They weren't really *alive*, not as she understood the term, yet it was impossible to escape the pervading sense of *dislike* radiating out from the wards. But maybe it wasn't too surprising. Emily might have saved the school, and the Allied Lands, but her mere presence had also put them in terrible danger. Shadye had used a sample of her blood to manipulate her, using her to take down the wards from the inside.

"I'll see you at the dance," Jade said, as they stepped into the school. "Will…will you be all right?"

"Yes," Emily said, flatly. Even a blind man would have realized that she was upset. But then, Jade had done better reading her than she had in reading *him*. "I'll see you at the dance."

She walked up the staircase before he could say anything, shaking her head inwardly as she felt the school's interior twisting around her. Whitehall had been shaped by some very crafty magicians and the staircases and corridors often led directly to where someone wanted to go—or needed to go, if they were in trouble. She stepped off the stairs and found herself in front of the unmarked wall concealing the entrance to the first-year dormitories. Pushing her hand against it to open the hidden door, she stepped through the gap and into the long corridor that led down to the laundry room. Memories rose up within her as she heard Madame Razz, the housemother, angrily lecturing a first-year girl on poor behavior. Emily shook her head, wondering what had happened, then walked down to Alassa's room.

The door opened when Emily knocked, allowing her to step inside. Alassa's room was identical to Emily's, apart from the single large family portrait hanging over her bed. Like Emily, she had two roommates, both of whom had already gone home for the holidays. One of them had caught Emily, several months after she'd arrived at Whitehall, and thanked her for helping to make living with the princess bearable. Apparently, Alassa had been a right pain in the behind to her roommates, as well as everyone else.

"Don't you dare laugh," Alassa said, as Emily closed the door. "I have to wear this outfit on the journey home."

Emily looked…and had to suppress a smile. Alassa was almost inhumanly perfect, with long blonde tresses, a heart-shaped face and a perfect body. She was also wearing a blue dress that made her look rather like a peacock, complete with feathers sticking up behind her hair. It actually suited her, Emily decided, although *she* wouldn't have been comfortable showing off so much of her cleavage. But then, Alassa's breasts were perfect too.

"They expect you to wear that in the coach?" She asked, surprised. It looked as though one person would have problems putting it on without help. "Wouldn't it get crumpled?"

"My father wishes me to make a proper appearance," Alassa said. She peered at herself in the mirror, twisting and turning until she was satisfied. "It seems that there won't be anywhere to change until we actually get to the palaces and castles we're going to be staying at along the way."

Emily resisted the temptation to roll her eyes. It would have been simple for Alassa to go home using a portal, or a teleport spell. Instead, her parents insisted that she ride home in a coach, allowing her to visit a number of castles belonging to other royal families before she was formally confirmed as heir to the throne. Alassa had tried to explain why this was important, but she hadn't been sure of the details and Emily had ended up more confused than ever.

"This isn't the only dress either," Alassa added. "My mother has sent me fifteen dresses, one for each day. And I have to put them all on without help. Mother always said that I should never become dependent upon the servants to get dressed."

"Sounds like good advice," Emily said. "Anything someone else does for you is something you can't do for yourself."

Some of the more absurd royal courts on Earth had actually had protocols for who was to help the royal family dress in the morning. Some of the stories had been so absurd that she'd been left shaking her head in disbelief. At least Alassa didn't seem to have to parade around naked to convince potential in-laws that she was healthy *and* fertile. It had struck Emily as little more than an excuse for the in-laws to be perverted, although it *did* make a certain kind of sense. Several royal families had tried to conceal their ugly daughters until the marriage had taken place.

"So I have been told," Alassa said. She muttered a charm and the dress suddenly loosened and started to fall off her body. "This dress isn't even the worst of them."

She scowled. "And I won't even have my servants with me," she added. "I am to be completely dependent upon their hospitality. The Duchess of Iron thinks that it will be *good* for me. Personally, I think that *Mother* issued the orders and then blamed the duchess."

Emily watched as Alassa stepped out of the dress, then carefully placed it back in her traveling chest. The princess's underwear was almost non-existent, surprisingly. But then, every student at Whitehall was expected to wear the same all-concealing robes. Emily couldn't help noticing that Alassa had a dagger strapped to her right thigh, although she couldn't imagine how her friend was meant to draw it without tearing her dress. There didn't seem to be any slit she could use to reach it.

"There's a spell that turns the lower half of the dress to dust," Alassa explained, when Emily asked. "It shouldn't be used except in case of absolute need, when modesty is no longer a pressing concern. The dagger itself is rather special."

Charmed, Emily guessed. It would be much easier to set a spell to pop the dagger into Alassa's hand. But if the blade was charmed, the spell would be unreliable.

Alassa turned back to face Emily, holding up a long cream-colored garment. "What do you think of this?"

Emily shook her head slowly. "I think you won't be able to get into it without help," she said, finally. "How are you going to tie up the back?"

"Bet you I can," Alassa said. She lifted the garment over her head, then allowed it to fall down. A moment later, her head emerged from the top, while her hands came out of the sleeves. She muttered a handful of charms and then caught her breath as the inbuilt corset squeezed tightly. Clearly, the royal family had yet to embrace the bras Emily had introduced several months ago. Or maybe they were just impractical. "How do I look?"

"Dancing is going to be difficult," Emily said. The dress fanned out so far that any partner would be unable to do more than hold hands with Alassa. It was also surprisingly loose around the chest, concealing her breasts, while tightening around her abdomen. Emily couldn't help thinking of an exaggerated hourglass. "What is the dress actually for?"

"It preserves one's dignity," Alassa said, stiffly. It couldn't be easy to breathe while wearing that corset. "I will be meeting potential husbands on the journey home and a dress like this helps ensure a lack of scandal."

"Oh," Emily said. It shouldn't have surprised her, not after what Void had said, but it still left her feeling uncomfortable. "Because they can't reach anything more delicate than your hands?"

"That's the idea," Alassa said. She lifted up the hem and showed Emily the additional layers of cloth below. "Even the most ardent lover would have difficulty gaining access to my hidden jewel."

"Oh," Emily said. She shook her head. "Do you think I should start wearing one?"

Alassa threw her a sharp glance. "Why do you think you might need one?"

Emily hadn't meant to tell her about Jade, but somehow the whole story came tumbling out of her lips. She needed to talk to *someone* and Void, whatever his other attributes, couldn't really offer proper advice.

Alassa smirked. "I was wondering when he'd have the courage to approach you," she said. "It isn't as if dealing with your guardian would be *easy*."

"You *knew*?" Emily demanded. "You *knew* he liked me?"

"Of course," Alassa said. "Was it not obvious?"

"I missed it," Emily admitted. "Was I the only person to miss it?"

Alassa looked oddly apologetic. "You really are from someplace different," she said, as if she were reminding herself of that fact. "I should have pointed it out to you."

She muttered a charm and the dress jumped up, allowing her to pull it off her body and return it to the chest. "He always spent time with you," she reminded Emily. "When *I* was there, he still paid attention to you. How did you miss it?"

"By being an idiot," Emily sighed. But then, it wasn't as if Jade could have taken her out to dinner, or to a movie. "But what do I do about it?"

Alassa considered it as she produced the third dress. "Well, Jade's family isn't very prominent, so you wouldn't gain much advantage from being allied with them," she said. "On the other hand, his relations wouldn't have a strong motive to betray you later on. And they are tied to the Allied Lands as a whole, rather than to a specific kingdom. It could be quite advantageous to you to remain independent of the various monarchs."

"Oh," Emily said.

"Jade himself is a handsome young man, without blemishes or defects of character," Alassa continued. "He's a capable magician, with excellent prospects; he could become a combat sorcerer, or stay at Whitehall as a tutor. Maybe not particularly wealthy, but that isn't really a problem for you, is it?"

Emily nodded. Thanks to her innovations, she was actually reasonably wealthy by the standards of the Allied Lands. She wasn't anything like as rich as one of the royal families, or the long-established trading houses, but she was getting there. And besides, it wasn't as if she *needed* more money than she already had.

"So you could do worse," Alassa concluded. "But then, you could also do better. There are quite a few prominent families with strong magical bloodlines. I'd be expecting them to make Imaiqah an offer soon–she's *newblood*, with magic they'd like to add to their own. You would gain access to a whole strata of connections and influence in exchange for marrying one of their sons and bearing his children..."

She looked up, meeting Emily's eyes. "And then there's the whole Child of Destiny aspect," she added. "You have proved yourself. Lots of families would want you."

Emily stared at her. The whole process struck her as rather cold-blooded. She knew, intellectually, that marriage had meant different things throughout the years, but she had never realized that such considerations might affect *her* marriage. But then, she'd never really considered getting married at all. It certainly hadn't worked out for her mother.

She shook her head, dismissing the memories. "How did you become so good at evaluating marriage prospects?"

"My mother insisted that I should be able to understand the advantages and disadvantages of any proposed union," Alassa said. "Do you know how many people have tried to get my parents to promise me to them since I was a child?"

She shrugged. "My father may offer to arrange a match for you. For a young girl without a real family, that would be a very tempting prospect."

"And bind me to Zangaria," Emily said. Alassa's parents *had* told her to stay close to the Child of Destiny. "Do you think I should accept Jade's proposal?"

"I'd suggest waiting to see what other offers you received," Alassa said. She scowled down at the dress, then put it back in the chest without trying it on. "Of course, Jade may believe that he is doing you a favor. If you happened to be married, or engaged, people couldn't try to court you–at least, not so blatantly."

"And now I'm confused," Emily admitted. "Why can't these things be *simple*?"

Alassa took the question seriously. "Because marriage is more than just the union of husband and wife," she said. "It is also the union of two families, of combining their resources and building something greater. When a kingdom is concerned, marriage may decide the fates of thousands upon thousands of people. Such things should never be entered into lightly."

She shrugged. "Consider yourself lucky," she added. "The kingdoms we will be visiting each have a prince who may wind up marrying me. And I have to dance with them all, showing respect to all, but favor to none. *That* won't be easy."

Her lips twisted into a mischievous smile. "And by the way, my mother sent some dresses for you. Why don't we try them on right now?"

Emily groaned.

Chapter Four

THE GRAND HALL OF WHITEHALL, ILLUMINATED BY GLOBES OF LIGHT HOVERING IN THE air, was large enough to accommodate a small army. Emily sucked in her breath sharply as she stepped through the main doors and walked down the stairs into the throng, admiring the hundreds of portraits the servants had hung on the walls. Once, they had been covered with delicate carvings that had represented the many magical disciplines, but Shadye's horde of monsters had ripped the room apart, searching for hidden students. Emily privately felt that the portraits offered more than the carvings, an opinion she kept to herself.

"You look nice," Alassa muttered in her ear. "You don't need to worry at all."

Emily winced. She'd never really worn dresses on Earth, so she'd had problems learning to move in the robes worn by all students. The dress Alassa's mother had sent for her, however, was something different. It was tight around the bust and thighs, showing off the shape of her body without actually revealing any bare flesh below her neck. Moving in it was difficult and she couldn't help feeling that it was going to split open the moment she sat down, no matter how many protective charms were woven into the material. On the other hand, it was one of the more modest dresses in the hall.

The leaving dance was one of the few occasions where students were allowed to wear something apart from robes and they'd taken full advantage of it. Some of the male students wore courtly outfits—one of them had come dressed up in a robe that changed color every ten seconds—while their female counterparts wore everything from dresses to tight trousers that left almost nothing to the imagination. Emily caught sight of one girl who was wearing nothing more than a wire bikini and thong before looking away, embarrassed. Few of the guys seemed to have any compunction about staring.

"She's going to be a sorceress," Alassa pointed out. "What does she care if they stare at her?"

"They're going to be sorcerers," Emily countered.

"They still wouldn't want to make an enemy of her," Alassa said. "A sorceress is not someone to alienate."

Emily nodded and looked away, towards one of the portraits. It showed a tall man in dark robes, wearing a hood that cast a shadow over his appearance. The only thing she could make out for sure was that he had a very strong chin, almost completely devoid of stubble. Looking at the tiny nameplate underneath, she carefully sounded out the name; JACKCLAW THE STRONG. At least she was learning to speak and read the local language, although her accent was still being mocked by some of her fellow students. Translation spells were so much easier, but they tended to be somewhat unreliable.

"I see boys coming this way," Alassa muttered. She'd worn a long green dress, almost identical to Emily's apart from the gold lace that marked her out as a lady of quality. "Do you want to dance with them? It will be good practice."

"So you said," Emily said. She'd been warned that there would be a formal ball every night during the journey to Zangaria, where Alassa would be expected to dance with her would-be suitors, but she wasn't very good at dancing, if only because she hadn't danced at all until she'd come to Whitehall. "Do I have to?"

"Yep," Alassa said. She grinned. "Here is a friend of yours."

"Lady Emily," Cat said, with a florid bow. He was several years older than her, but they shared the Martial Magic class. "Would you do me the very great honor of taking a turn around the dance floor?"

Emily hesitated, then Alassa gave her a gentle push forward into Cat's arms. He caught her hands and pulled her out into the dancers, who were lining up for a new dance. Emily found herself staring around in panic—she didn't know what to do—before realizing that one of the players at the front of the hall was about to give instructions. They sounded awfully complicated, she decided as the music started to play, but as the dancers began to move she realized that it was just a matter of following the music as much as anything else. Besides, Cat made a very tolerant partner.

"I still remember my first dance," he admitted, as the tune finally came to an end. "I trod on so many toes that fifteen girls threatened to hex me."

He gave her a second bow. "Would you care for another dance? Or maybe you should let one of your other admirers take you around the hall."

Emily glanced around, surprised. Several other boys, including two she didn't recognize, looked to be angling to catch her eye. It puzzled her—surely they couldn't *all* think of her as a marriage partner—until she realized that there were more guys than girls in the hall. Every girl had a handful of admirers trailing after her. Emily found herself flushing, then summoned up her courage, winked at Cat, and headed over to one of the guys she didn't know.

"Thank you," he stammered, as the music started to play again. "I'll try not to tread on you."

Surprisingly, Emily found herself relaxing as she traded partners again and again, feeling that she could actually begin to enjoy the dancing. It wasn't the same as formal balls, Alassa had warned her, but there were fewer expectations; no one seemed to seriously expect a marriage proposal to be sorted out on the dance floor. And there was no dance card; she could dance with whoever she liked, without needing to worry about offending anyone. Alassa seemed to have no shortage of older males dancing with her either. Most of them Emily vaguely recognized as having some aristocratic ties.

She forced herself to take a breath after the seventh dance and headed over to the buffet tables the staff had placed along the wall. They were piled with food, ranging from dishes and treats that were vaguely familiar to items she had never seen or imagined before coming to Whitehall. It was funny how she never really felt homesick, not even after discovering that magic couldn't solve everything. But then, she'd never really felt as if she belonged on Earth.

I owe Shadye, she thought. It wasn't a pleasant thought.

He'd kidnapped her, tried to kill her, then manipulated her—and then she'd had to kill him. There had been no choice.

"The grandmaster has put on a decent spread," a rather snooty voice said, from behind her. "One of the man's redeeming features, if you ask me."

Emily turned, to see a tall thin man peering down his nose at her with a practiced smirk. He seemed instantly dislikeable, the kind of person who would happily condemn Emily for not being practically perfect in every way, yet...there was something about him that nagged at her mind. The more she tried to see his features, the more they seemed to slip away from her, as if something was interfering with her perception. And that meant he was hiding under a powerful glamor...

Understanding clicked. "*Void?*"

Her guardian tapped his lips, mischievously. "The grandmaster doesn't know I'm here and I would prefer to keep it that way," he said. "I'm casting a privacy ward, but do try and look a little disgusted. No doubt Sir Dogsbody here"—he gestured to himself—"has been commissioned on behalf of someone high-and-mighty to try to convince you to marry his son. Or something like that."

Emily found her voice. "What are you doing here?"

"You need a more imaginative question," Void informed her. He picked up a sausage-like delicacy and popped it into his mouth. "There have been...developments. Are you aware that Alassa's escort has reached Dragon's Den?"

Emily shrugged. Whitehall paid lip service to the claim that its students were all equal, even though some of them were definitely more equal than others. Consequently, the small squadron of troops and combat sorcerers who would be escorting Alassa—and Emily—to Zangaria had been ordered to stay in Dragon's Den overnight, before picking her up in the morning. It struck Emily as a waste of resources, but apparently it was tradition and couldn't be gainsaid by mere mortals.

"I checked them out at a distance," Void added. "Their leader is Lady Barb."

He spoke as though the name should have meant something to Emily, but it meant nothing, nothing at all. "I've never heard of her," Emily admitted finally, when it became clear that Void was not going to elaborate. "Who *is* she?"

It was hard to tell with the glamor messing up her perception, but Void looked almost...*embarrassed.* "Lady Barb has heard of *you*," he said. "More importantly, she...has a grudge against me. And you're my ward."

Emily blinked in surprise. "A *grudge* against *you*?"

"Yes," Void said. "It's a long story. And it isn't one I choose to share. But I suggest that you bear in mind that she may dislike and distrust you merely because of me."

"Why?" Emily asked. "What happened?"

"I do *not* choose to share the story," Void said. "All I can do is suggest that you watch your back. She's too...honorable to stick a knife in it without good cause, but she *will* distrust you."

He held up a hand before Emily could say anything. "I would have warned you earlier, if I'd known," he added. "I just suggest that you bear in mind that she *hates* me. Watch yourself."

Emily watched as he turned and walked off into the crowd. His glamor seemed to twist slightly; one moment he was there, the next moment she had lost track of him completely. She shook her head in disbelief as the privacy ward fell away, wondering how he'd quite managed to get into the school. It was a droll reminder that she had a very long way to go before she could match Void, or the grandmaster.

And he's just like Batman, she thought, as she started to eat her food. *He vanishes while you are finishing a sentence.*

"Good food," Alassa said, coming up beside Emily. Her small army of admirers watched her from a distance as she piled a plate high with meat patties and vegetable rolls. "Do you have something like it in your homeland?"

Emily winced. Most of the students accepted the unspoken suggestion that Void, Emily's guardian, was in fact her *real* father. It certainly seemed to make sense; Void wouldn't want to advertize that he had a daughter, but he wouldn't want to abandon her completely either. Alassa, however, had deduced that Emily came from somewhere very different, although she hadn't worked out the truth. Emily had promised that she would tell her friend on the day she was crowned queen, when she was no longer under her father's power. It would be a long time, she hoped, before she had to keep that promise.

"Something like it," she said, vaguely. In fact, she had the distant feeling that Whitehall's food was considerably healthier. "Are we going to be eating like this every day?"

"Of course not," Alassa said. She gave Emily a thin smile. "Each of the monarchs will feel the need to actually *entertain* us. Not like *him*. You think he's courting her?"

She nodded towards the grandmaster, who was standing at the head of the room, talking eagerly with Mistress Kirdáne, Head of Magical Creatures. The little man still wore the blindfold—a simple dirty rag—that he'd worn the day Emily had first met him, but there was no mistaking the power flowing through his body. Emily knew he could have cured himself easily—magic *could* repair damaged eyes—but instead he chose to remain blind. It didn't seem to slow him down.

"I don't think he will be putting on a show for us," Emily said, dryly. "And Mistress Kirdáne will happily have you mucking out the stables if you make any more veiled suggestions."

Alassa shrugged, unrepentantly. "He kept large parts of the school stable with a rampaging necromancer trying to impose his will on the structure," she said. "I could easily see someone wanting to bear *his* child."

Emily glowered at her. "You've got mating on the brain."

"*You* started it," Alassa countered. Her face fell, briefly. "But I may end up engaged before I come back to Whitehall."

"I'm sorry," Emily said, softly. "If you want to run away…"

"My parents would just track me down and drag me back," Alassa said. "And besides, if I did manage to escape successfully, there would be civil war. I couldn't have that on my conscience."

You've grown up, Emily realized, feeling an odd twinge in her heart. This new improved Alassa was her work, yet would she still need Emily? Or would they drift apart?

"I believe that someone wants to dance with you," Alassa said, taking Emily's plate out of her hand. "Go tell him that there's no hard feelings."

Emily looked up and saw Jade standing there, oddly hesitant. It was worrying to see him like that, particularly because of the bravery he'd shown when they were being chased by orcs and goblins. But asking a girl out could be harder for a boy than fighting an enemy—and Jade had asked her for something more than a casual date. Swallowing, she walked over to Jade and held out her hands. He took them and pulled her out onto the dance floor.

Jade was a better dancer than Cat, Emily decided several minutes later. The instructions were even more complicated, but Jade followed them without hesitation and Emily simply followed him. As the music changed, some of the couples went off the floor, only to be replaced by newcomers. Emily shot Jade a sharp glance and realized that he'd timed it perfectly. The next dance was a slow waltz, very romantic.

Or maybe he hadn't, she realized, as he flushed. "Don't worry," she muttered, as they moved together. His arms enfolding her felt surprisingly reassuring. "We can dance."

She felt a tingle running down her spine as Jade cast a privacy ward of his own. Unlike Void's, which had been so subtle she had barely noticed it, this one muffled the music slightly, as well as the babble of the other couples. Emily lifted a single eyebrow questioningly.

"I'd prefer to talk without being overheard," Jade admitted. Naturally; he'd taken her up the mountain so he could propose without listening ears. He hadn't realized that Void would follow them. "Emily...I'm sorry if I was too forward."

He must have talked to someone, Emily realized. But who? She assumed that the boys had housemasters—rather like Madame Razz supervised the first-year girls—but she'd never met Jade's housemaster. Or maybe he'd talked to Sergeant Miles, or one of the male tutors. He might even have approached one of the *female* tutors, hoping that they'd be able to give him good advice.

But it didn't really matter.

"It just surprised me," she admitted. And then Void had arrived and confused her. She'd been so distracted that she hadn't been able to think properly. "Jade..."

She broke off, considering what to say. "Jade, I have to finish my schooling before I consider marrying anyone," she said, finally. "And you will need to establish yourself as a combat sorcerer first, someone everyone can respect."

Jade flushed. "I hadn't meant that we should get married at once," he admitted. "I believed that we could come to some agreement and marry later, when I am ready to give you a dowry."

Emily felt her own face flush. She hadn't even *considered* a dowry; she hadn't bothered to look up how it worked in this world. From what Imaiqah had said, the parents of the girl were expected to provide her with a lump sum, although quite what happened to it after marriage seemed to depend upon the kingdom's individual laws. Some kingdoms seemed to believe the money should stay with the girl, others ruled that it went to the husband—or the husband's parents.

And if monarchy was involved, the girl's dowry might include the entire kingdom.

"I don't need a dowry," she said. It had taken her months to get used to the money system of her new world, but she was fairly sure that she already had more than Jade would make in several years. She suspected that pointing that out wouldn't help. "Look, I like you and I care about you, but we need time. I am not going to accept any marriage proposals from anyone until after I graduate."

Jade looked at her for a long moment. "You will consider mine?"

"Yes," Emily said. Just for a moment, she wished to be emotionless. Part of her thought she should say yes to his proposal. The rest of her pointed out that they might not be good together. God knew she had her problems with men and male attention. Could they come to love one another? Were they really suited to be a married couple? "I promise that I will consider your proposal."

For a moment, his lips were very close to hers. It was the easiest thing in the world to brush her lips against his, feeling a tingle running through her body as they kissed. She was suddenly very aware of her heartbeat pounding inside her chest. Her first kiss...

"I'm going to be apprenticing with a combat sorcerer," Jade admitted. "But I *will* keep in touch."

Emily felt a surge of conflicting emotions. Was he abandoning her? Or was he trying to see if they *did* have something that would last? She could beg him to stay...

"You'd better write to me every week," she said. At least she'd mastered handwriting, even though it took hours to compose a simple letter. "And make sure you keep me informed."

"You too," Jade said. He smiled—and, for a moment, Emily felt as if everything was back to normal. Except it would never be normal again. "I hope you have a good time in Zangaria."

"Me too," Emily said. Between Alassa's warnings of endless dances—and Void's rather more practical warning—she was nervous about the trip. "And I will *not* forget to write."

She kissed him again, then cancelled the privacy ward and headed to the door. The dance might have gone on until the wee small hours, but she needed rest. They had to be up early the following morning. Alassa's escort would be arriving at ten bells to take her home.

At least Void warned me, she thought, as she reached her bedroom. *But what happened between him and Lady Barb?*

Chapter Five

E MILY WAS AWOKEN BY A GROANING SOUND AS ALOHA PULLED HERSELF OUT OF BED. "The sergeant is going to kill me," she said, as she sat upright. "I drank too much last night."

She glanced over at Emily. "I'm sorry about waking you," Aloha added. "I just have to go wash before the march begins."

Emily nodded at her retreating back. Sergeant Miles had announced that the remaining students in Martial Magic would enjoy one final route march before they went home for the holidays, but Emily was excused the march on the ground she was traveling to Zangaria. She wasn't quite sure how to feel about it; she'd grown to love walking in the countryside, but route marches were never fun, even now that she was stronger and healthier than she'd ever been on Earth.

"I didn't sleep very well anyway," she said, as her roommate entered the washroom. "Don't worry about it."

She sat upright in bed and reached for her watch. It was nearly seven bells, almost time to get up anyway. Emily ran her hand through her brown hair, then swung her legs over the side of the bed and stood up. Her body felt tired, but a strong mug of Kava would make her feel better. Besides, unlike the other students, she hadn't been drinking alcohol. The others were likely to be nursing hangovers.

Jade had *kissed* her. The thought returned to her mind unbidden as she dug into her cabinet and found the traveling clothes Alassa's mother had sent for her. Jade had kissed her...and she'd let him. She hadn't even felt repulsed. It had been her first kiss and...did that mean that she was in love, or merely that she'd not wanted to humiliate him any further by pushing him away? But then, she hadn't *wanted* to push him away...her thoughts spun round and round until she felt a little dizzy. What did she actually want from him?

And everyone probably saw you kissing him, she told herself, angrily. The privacy ward might have made it impossible for someone to eavesdrop, but it wouldn't have stopped them seeing the kiss. There had been couples on the dance floor who were going much further than simple kisses, yet...this was different. Emily attracted too much attention to hope that the school had missed the kiss. By now, no doubt there would be rumors—she blushed furiously at the thought—that Jade had spent the night in her bed, even though she hadn't activated the special privacy ward that would have told Aloha to spend the night somewhere else.

Aloha emerged from the washroom looking a little better, but still hung-over. Emily reached into her chest, found one of the potions they'd been given for dealing with headaches and feminine problems and passed it to her friend, who took it gratefully.

"Thank you," Aloha said. She opened the bottle and drank it quickly, grimacing at the taste. "And I hope you have a good journey. It can be murder."

Emily tossed her a sharp look, then walked into the washroom herself. Unlike many medieval institutions, Whitehall insisted that everyone wash regularly, something that had surprised Emily when she'd first heard about it. Later, she'd realized that her new world didn't have modern medicine, but it *did* know about germs and how they spread disease. A person who washed was healthier than a person who chose to remain dirty. Shaking her head, Emily allowed warm water to cascade over her, then dried herself with a simple spell. It was so much easier than using a towel—and besides, her hair dried instantly.

Stepping back out of the washroom, she discovered that Aloha had already gone, no doubt in hopes of a big breakfast before joining the rest of the Martial Magic class. Feeling an odd sense of relief—she liked Aloha, but she didn't want to talk—Emily picked up her traveling outfit and began to pull it on. The garments felt rougher than the dresses, yet they still managed to look reasonably attractive, even on Emily. And they were charmed to protect their wearer against the weather.

Once she'd finished dressing, Emily stood in front of the mirror and studied herself, unable to avoid a smile. She looked rather like an Elizabethan gentleman, with a pair of dark trousers, a dark shirt and a belt wrapped around her lower chest. Normally, she'd gathered from Alassa, a traveler would be expected to wear a sword, but few sorcerers would ever carry one unless they were engaged in ritual magic. They knew far more powerful protections. She tested her wards to make sure they meshed well with the spells on the outfit, then headed for the door. They had been warned to eat a good breakfast.

Hardly anyone seemed to be stirring as she walked out of the dorms and down towards the dining hall. Whitehall almost felt deserted, the ebb and flow of magic that ran through the building seemingly diminished by the absence of its students. Emily felt a pang of sadness that puzzled her, until she realized that she was already homesick. Not homesick for Earth, where she'd been ignored at best, but for Whitehall—and she hadn't even left. Part of her wanted to cancel the trip and stay at the school for the holidays, if that were permitted. It occurred to her, as she stopped outside the heavy stone door leading into the dining hall, that she knew almost nothing about her tutors outside the classroom. Did Professor Thande have a wife? Or did Mistress Irene have a husband? Or...

She pushed the door open and stepped into the dining hall. It was nearly empty, apart from a couple of students she vaguely recognized. Oddly, there was no sign of Aloha. Maybe the sergeant had decided to leave *very* early and Aloha hadn't had time to grab more than a few combat rations before running down to the armory. It sounded cruel, but the sergeant had always pushed the limits.

The kitchen staff seemed to be bright and cheerful, smiling at Emily as soon as she leaned on the counter. They didn't look to have spent the night partying; Emily wondered absently just what the domestic staff did when the students were back home. Maybe they threw parties for themselves...she couldn't see the grandmaster objecting very strongly, even though she suspected that some of the aristocrats would have thrown a fit at the thought of commoners enjoying themselves. Besides, they worked in a school where the students had magic and bad senses of humor. They deserved a chance to relax after the students had gone home.

Emily took a bowl of porridge and a large mug of Kava and found herself a seat at one of the tables. Normally, they were segregated by age, but Emily had been something of an exception to that rule even before half the school had gone home. As a student in Martial Magic, which pulled in pupils from every age group, she'd been expected to join her teammates half the time, even if they were all older than her. At least they'd stopped treating her like a little girl, or someone who had pulled strings to get into the class–but then, she *had* beaten a necromancer. It was hard to argue that she was still unqualified after the demise of Shadye.

The porridge tasted bland, but it was probably the best thing for the students after drinking themselves senseless last night. Emily sipped the Kava carefully, wincing slightly at the taste, although *no one* actually drank the school's Kava to enjoy themselves. It tasted rather like ultra-strong coffee, with enough caffeine to shock anyone awake. Emily had tasted better Kava at Dragon's Den and wondered why Whitehall served such an awful blend, before deciding that the school would prefer to avoid caffeine dependency. She had never bothered to ask to confirm her theory.

She looked up as Alassa made her entrance. The royal princess looked perfect, as always, but Emily could tell that her friend hadn't slept much better than herself. Alassa picked up a jug of Kava, without taking any food, and stumbled over to sit beside Emily, muttering something about not being hungry. She sounded more nervous than anything else, even though she should be used to taking part in royal processions. But then, one of the princes she was going to meet along the way might become her future husband and consort.

"Need to get dressed again," Alassa muttered, as she slurped her Kava. "Can't go out looking like this."

Emily rolled her eyes. Her friend wore traveling clothes that were almost identical to Emily's, apart from the single golden star on the front of her shirt. It didn't even cling to her body, refusing to reveal too much of her curves, although Alassa's golden locks shone against the dark material. Maybe Alassa was just suffering from excessive nerves…Emily gave her friend a concerned look, then waved to one of the staff. A moment later, a bowl of porridge was put in front of Alassa and she started to eat automatically.

"You look lovely," Emily said.

"Liar," Alassa said, without heat. "They're going to be sending maids to help me dress. And they're all going to be reporting on me."

It took Emily a moment to realize that Alassa meant the monarchs who hoped to marry their younger sons to the princess. They would all want to ensure that Alassa was physically healthy–and they probably wouldn't trust a medical report from her parents, if such information was ever released outside the Royal Family. There was no reason they couldn't ask a healer to perform a medical check, except that would probably have been *intrusive*. Emily rolled her eyes at the thought, then finished her Kava.

"I should have insisted on bringing my own servants," Alassa continued. She sounded almost dazed. "I could have used it as an excuse to keep the others out of my rooms."

"I can help you dress," Emily offered. But she knew almost nothing about how to help someone dress, even if the dresses *were* designed to allow Alassa to don them without needing outside help. It wasn't as if she understood local cosmetics; hell, even *looking* at makeup and perfume risked running into a political and social mine-field. "Or maybe we could hire someone…"

"Probably wouldn't work," Alassa said. She finished her porridge and looked down at her empty bowl, as if she hadn't quite realized that she was eating. "They'd still insist on sending in their own people to *stare* at me."

She shook her head. "Let me try and get ready on my own first," she added. "I'll give you a call if I need help."

Emily nodded. It was funny just how little privacy Alassa had, despite having been born a royal princess. Everything from her monthly cycles to her conduct when dealing with her social inferiors would be carefully recorded by *someone*. And while her servants back home had been there to help her, Emily had no doubt that they reported directly to her parents—and all other interested parties. No doubt the prep-arations for a royal wedding included a careful inspection of her health and fertility. No wonder Alassa had turned into such a brat.

"I'll be in the library," Emily said, as she stood up. "And I'll meet you in the entrance hall at ten bells, if you don't call me earlier."

"See if you can research privacy spells," Alassa said weakly, with a ghost of a smile. "There won't be any privacy in *any* of the castles."

Emily scowled at the thought as she walked out of the dining hall. Whitehall was a place of education, yet there were secret passages that ran throughout the building, some of them allowing their occupants to peek into various classrooms and dorms. She'd never managed to convince the grandmaster to tell her why they'd been built, or, for that matter, why Shadye had known of their existence. Perhaps the students were meant to find them, or maybe the staff wanted a way to move around without being noticed. But then, given the building's mutable interior, it should have been easy to construct private corridors for themselves.

The library was dark and cold, but a touch of Emily's hand against the charmed doorknob allowed her entry. One advantage of working with the librarian was that she was allowed access at all times, although she had wondered if that would still hold true now that term was officially over for the summer. She stepped into the massive room and through the silencing wards that kept students from talking above a whisper, looking around to make sure that she was really alone. Rumor had it that the Lady Aylia slept in the library. Emily had certainly never seen her outside her domain.

Smiling to herself, Emily walked into one of the smaller rooms and inspected the graduation rolls. Whitehall kept very detailed records of its students, allowing newcomers to look up the grades of famous sorcerers…although they weren't as useful as Emily had expected before she'd actually started to use them. Sorcerers often changed their names once they graduated, ensuring that their enemies couldn't use their true names against them; it still bugged her that she had never managed to identify Void's records. Or, for that matter, the grandmaster's records. The only staff member she'd been able to find had been Professor Thande…and *his* record had included a handwritten note from his tutor suggesting that he be dispatched to a deserted mountaintop where he could practice his experiments without risking anyone else's life.

And she'd never located anything that might have belonged to Shadye…

Pushing the thought aside, Emily found the set of records that were sorted by name and looked up Lady Barb. It was easier than she'd expected; Barb was apparently short for Barbara, rather than an assumed name like Shadye or Void. But the record was of minimal use; Barb had been an excellent student, with very high marks for Healing, then she'd gone into Martial Magic in her sixth year, like Jade. And then she'd graduated and apprenticed under an unnamed sorcerer.

Void? Emily asked herself. Back when she'd first met him, Void had admitted that his history of taking apprentices wasn't very good. Indeed, he'd told her that she was safer going to Whitehall than learning from him. Could Lady Barb have been Void's apprentice at one point? But surely Void would have told her if that were the case.

Thoughtfully, Emily reread the record, trying to draw out any hidden clues. But there was almost nothing beyond the bare facts, certainly very little about Lady Barb's background or post-Whitehall life. It didn't surprise her—Alassa's records left out plenty of details, including the fact that she was a crown princess—but it was frustrating. Whitehall was primarily concerned with educating young magicians, rather than keeping tabs on them afterwards. That was someone else's problem.

Putting the graduation record back on the shelves—taking it out of the room would have triggered the wards—Emily stepped back into the main library and walked down to the genealogy section. On Earth, genealogy covered family trees; here, it seemed to include people who worked for the principle family, as well as plenty of other details that Emily wouldn't have thought needed to be included. Pulling out the first tome describing Zangaria, Emily looked for any records that might touch on Lady Barb. Unsurprisingly, she was listed as a combat sorceress, hired to defend the queen. *That* made a certain kind of sense, Emily decided. The king wouldn't want a male sorcerer looming over his wife when he was gone.

On impulse, she pulled out the blood rankings for the kingdom and studied them carefully. Alassa was right at the top; her father just below her, although a rather droll note suggested that he was no longer capable of fathering children. Reading between the lines, Emily decided that it meant he'd been having affairs and none of them had led to illegitimate children. Quite what they would have done if the only possible heir had been a bastard child was open to question. Maybe the queen would go into seclusion and then take the child as her own.

Returning the book to the shelves, she stood up and wandered through the library, glancing from book to book. She'd loved libraries back home and she loved this one;

indeed, it had a more authentic attitude than many of the ones she remembered from her childhood. There were no computers, no video games, just books…and powerful spells intended to ensure that users actually kept quiet. She caught sight of a row of books that were chained to the shelves and smiled, remembering many happy hours of standing there and studying the charms. They couldn't be taken out of the library, but she'd memorized the spells and copied them into her personal grimoire.

Absently, she picked one of the books off the shelves and glanced at it. Mentalism magic was complex and it was rare for anyone below fourth-year to try to learn it, but she'd had no choice. Shadye had invaded her mind and used her as a weapon against Whitehall. She needed a defense in case someone else managed to secure some of her blood. The memory of being moved like a puppet provided all the incentive she required. And yet there was no way to test it without actually convincing someone to try to control her, which posed dangers of its own. Who did she trust far enough to let them take some of her blood?

Catching herself, she glanced at her watch. It was almost ten bells.

Emily straightened up, returned the book to the shelf and then left the library. It was time to pick up her chest, meet up with Alassa and leave the school. And, she reminded herself, to meet Lady Barb. God alone knew how *that* was going to go.

Chapter Six

L ADY BARB WAS EASILY THE MOST *STRIKING* WOMAN THAT EMILY HAD MET.
She was tall, taller than Emily, with blonde hair cropped close to her head. Her body was incredibly muscular, reminding Emily of Sergeant Harkin; her face was not classically beautiful, but one look told Emily that this was not a person to take lightly. She wore a silver breastplate, dark trousers and a sword, even though she was clearly a powerful sorceress. Emily could feel the magic surrounding her as soon as she walked into the entrance hall.

Lady Barb was talking to the grandmaster, their voices hidden behind a privacy ward. She looked like a giant compared to his diminutive form, although Emily suspected that the grandmaster probably had the edge in raw power. Lady Barb threw Emily a sharp glance as soon as she saw her, before shifting her gaze to Alassa. She must have seen something she liked, because she nodded before returning her attention to the grandmaster. Emily wondered if they were talking about *her*, or Alassa. Lady Barb didn't seem to be the kind of person who would put up with a royal brat.

"Oh, joy," Alassa muttered. "Here comes the twisting tongue."

Emily blinked. She hadn't spotted the other man standing by the main door–Lady Barb had taken all of her attention–until he started to step forward. There was something about his movement that made her think of *crawling*, at least partly because he kept bowing in Alassa's direction, almost as if he were dancing towards her. His face, when he straightened up briefly, looked remarkably unformed, almost as if he had no character at all. And his eyes glinted oddly when he looked at Emily.

"Princess," the man said, in a breathy voice. "You are the light that knows no borders, the joy that grows in hearts, the…"

Emily's first impulse was to snicker. The man seemed to be exaggerating every movement, as well as bombarding Alassa with absurdly flattering praise…and then she realized that he **meant** every word. He seriously believed that she would be impressed by such praise, even though she had to **know** that it was absurd. Emily glanced at her friend, saw a half-bitter expression on Alassa's face and realized that she must have grown up hearing it every day. No *wonder* she had turned into such a brat. A child couldn't have known the difference between honest praise and someone flattering her because of her birth.

What a crawler, she thought, as the praise turned ever more fulsome. *I wonder how much they have to pay him for that…*

"Thank you," Alassa said gravely, cutting him off in mid-flatter. "Emily, this is Viscount Nightingale, the Master of the Princess's Bedchamber. Viscount, this is my friend the Lady Emily, the Necromancer's Bane. Treat her with respect."

The Viscount stepped forward, bowed deeply in front of Emily, then managed to look surprised and offended–and yet unbothered–in the same instant. Emily realized that she was supposed to present him with her hand to kiss and hesitated, before gritting her teeth and holding out her palm. The Viscount kissed her hand lightly and then stepped back, bowing again. Emily had to fight down the urge to wipe her hand on her trousers.

Alassa cleared her throat. "I trust that the horses and carriages are ready," she said, in her regal voice. "We have a long trip ahead of us and I wish it to be comfortable."

"Of course, Your Highness," Nightingale said. "I have organized the trip to be as comfortable as possible. We will be visiting many people who wish to admire your regal beauty."

"Good," Alassa said. Her voice didn't sound very pleased, but Nightingale didn't seem to notice. "Bring the horses to the main entrance. Now."

Nightingale bowed and backed out of the room. Emily shook her head in disbelief as he somehow navigated his way out of the door without turning his back, as turning his back on Alassa would have been a deadly insult. The princess winked at Emily, then leaned closer to whisper in her ear.

"He's very minor nobility," she said. "If he happened to displease my father in any way, he would be exposed to all of his enemies instantly."

Emily nodded, tartly. It hadn't been uncommon for medieval kings to choose to uplift men from the lower ranks, men who had no choice but to be loyal—for the moment they lost their usefulness, they could be handed over to their enemies. And if they happened to be tax collectors or lawgivers, they wouldn't have many friends *anywhere*. Maybe Nightingale had more qualifications than being able to ladle on the flattery at a moment's notice, but she hadn't been able to see them.

"Emily," the grandmaster said. He'd dispelled the privacy ward. "This is Lady Barb. She will be joining us next year as Head of Healing."

Lady Barb didn't blink, Emily realized, as she held out her hand. The sorceress just stared at her, her blue eyes unreadable. Her hand, when she took Emily's hand and shook it firmly, felt strong enough to crush Emily's to powder with ease. And she could feel the magic crackling around her, a presence more daunting than most of the other tutors.

"Pleased to meet you," she said, finally. She couldn't help feeling disconcerted; Void had been right, Lady Barb didn't seem to like her. "I hope you will enjoy working here."

Lady Barb's eyes glittered. "And you are the girl who defeated a necromancer," she said, without letting go of Emily's hand. Her voice was cold, dispassionate, almost completely stripped of femininity. Was that the price for being a combat sorceress? But Mistress Irene didn't seem so dispassionate. "How did you manage to defeat Shadye?"

"We agreed that the knowledge would remain restricted," the grandmaster said, hastily. "It is far better for the necromancers to wonder what happened than to confirm their theories."

Lady Barb looked at him, then turned her gaze back to Emily. "And you are the closest friend of the princess," she said, nodding to Alassa. "Are you capable of defending her?"

"She is," Alassa said, before Emily could say a word. "And you shouldn't question her competence..."

"It is my job, Your Highness," Lady Barb said. There was no hint of sycophancy in her voice at all. She let go of Emily's hand and stepped backwards. "Your protection from all threats is my prime concern."

There was something in her voice that made Emily start in anger. She knew all of the rumors about what had happened when she'd faced Shadye for the final time—and one of them, the most damning, was that she'd become a necromancer herself. Emily knew that she'd shown no sign of necromantic madness, the insanity that overwhelmed anyone who tried to drain the mana and life force from a sacrifice, but it could take time for the madness to become noticeable. And if someone was deeply worried, they might assume that Emily was simply more capable of keeping the madness under control for years.

But if that were possible, she thought sourly, *there would be no necromantic threat.*

Lady Barb didn't move, but Emily sensed the sudden spike in the magic field, an instant before a flickering orb of green light flashed towards her. She recognized the hex from Martial Magic, a spell that weakened personal protective wards rather than trying to break through them outright. The spell could be an absolute nightmare to dispel, simply because it was designed to be immune to standard dispelling charms. Emily reacted on instinct, reshaping her wards and deflecting the green light away from her. It flashed over the hallway and struck the stone wall, vanishing in a shower of sparks.

"Not too shabby," Lady Barb said, finally. Her eyes betrayed her irritation. "Perhaps you can protect the princess after all."

Emily scowled at her, unable to avoid the feeling that she would have *liked* Lady Barb if the older woman hadn't taken such an instant dislike to her. And the test could easily have been worse. If the hex had a chance to get enmeshed in her wards, the only other thing she could have done would have been to drop the wards completely, rendering her vulnerable to all kinds of jinxes, hexes and curses. Sergeant Miles had tested them by including a nasty transfiguration charm in the hex; anyone stupid enough to drop their wards found themselves croaking on the floor before they realized their mistake.

And then she realized the *true* purpose of the test. A necromancer might not have had the skill—or the patience—to deflect the hex. Instead, a necromancer would simply have swamped the hex with so much magic that it would have evaporated before it could do serious damage. If Emily had done that...it would have exposed her as a necromancer for sure. Few magicians her age would have had the power reserves to risk using so much magic. Emily was fairly sure that she couldn't have done it.

Of course, trying and failing would have been a pretty good sign too, she thought.

"She can," Alassa said. "But tell me—isn't protection *your* responsibility?"

Lady Barb gazed at her evenly, keeping her eyes fixed on Alassa until the princess lowered her eyes. "It is not easy to protect someone from their friends," she said, finally. "Or, for that matter, from their own foolishness."

She had a point, Emily had to admit. A husband—or a friend—would be able to get into position to hurt Alassa far more easily than someone from the outside. And it would be harder to tell if Alassa was actually in danger...Emily had a sudden vision of someone hitting Alassa, while her guards on the outside of her chambers had no idea that she was in deadly danger. Alassa would have to be *very* careful who she married. It would be easy to marry someone because of their political connections, without realizing that he was also a complete sadistic bastard. Or someone who allowed being king to go to his head.

The grandmaster cleared his throat. "Lady Emily has earned our trust," he said, his sightless eyes peering at Lady Barb. "And she is free of the taint of necromancy."

"I trust your judgement," Lady Barb said, flatly. "Your Highness—are you ready to depart?"

"There are two trunks, both sealed with protective charms," Alassa said. She looked over at Emily and winked. "Emily has a chest too, also sealed."

Lady Barb's lips twitched. "I shall inform the staff," she said. "They shouldn't go prying into your possessions in any case, but the warning should help."

She turned and strode off, leaving Emily staring after her. Lady Barb *did* look and act like Sergeant Harkin, if infinitely more attractive than the sergeant, who had been heavily scarred a long time before he'd come to Whitehall. Could she be his sister? The records hadn't mentioned her family, but Sergeant Harkin hadn't been a magician. Whitehall might not have considered his existence important enough to record.

But it was impossible to tell. Harkin's face had been so badly scarred that any family resemblance had been destroyed.

She could have been his student, Emily wondered. *He was certainly at Whitehall during her last year...*

"This will be your first holiday away from the school," the grandmaster said. "If you wish to return earlier, we will accept you."

Emily nodded. She'd been to Dragon's Den, and the Martial Magic class had been hiking around the nearby mountains, but she'd never been further away from Whitehall. The thought threatened to bring on another bout of premature homesickness, even though she knew that she could return to the school simply by using a portal. Void, of course, could teleport...but apparently the spell needed years of effort to master, to the point where only a handful of sorcerers could perform it reliably. She had no idea if the grandmaster could teleport.

"Thank you," she said, looking down at the little man. *That* was something she should know better than to think, even in the privacy of her own head. The 'little man' in question could turn her into a toad without even needing to think about it. "I'll come back if I need to."

On Earth, she hadn't really traveled very far. Her stepfather hadn't seen the value in family holidays and refused to waste money on camping trips, let alone exotic foreign holidays. And yet it could take less than a day to travel around the entire planet. Here, travel times were much greater, even with portals involved. Maybe the Allied Lands *did* have a good excuse for near-constant bickering, after all. Even the smaller kingdoms were large by their own standards. And the necromancers were a very long way away.

One of the ideas that she'd mentioned to Imaiqah's father was bicycles. What would that do, she wondered, when they were introduced? The last letter she'd had from him had said that there were problems with producing the first experimental models, although he had gone on to say that the artisans expected to overcome them fairly quickly. Emily possessed a great deal of theoretical knowledge, but it had surprised them both to realize that her practical knowledge was very limited. Even when she knew what she was talking about in great detail, it took months of experimentation before they had a working model.

"And take care of the princess," the grandmaster added. "She *is* quite important to us."

Emily surprised herself by giving the grandmaster a hug, before turning and following Alassa towards the main entrance. She'd never actually *used* the entrance hall herself; from what she'd picked up, it was rarely opened except when students were entering or leaving the school at the start and finish of term. Now, it opened out onto a courtyard, where a dozen carriages were waiting for them. Dozens of brightly-clad footmen bowed in unison when they saw Alassa, while armed soldiers raised their spears in salute. There didn't seem to be more than thirty soldiers, which seemed remarkably light until Emily realized that the only people who would risk an all-out attack on the princess's escort were the necromancers. Thirty soldiers or three hundred...they'd just be giving the necromancers more targets.

One of the carriages was painted gold, shimmering as the rays of sunlight struck it. The vehicle seemed like something out of a fantasy movie, perhaps one with a genie or fairy godmother who had turned a scullery maid into a princess for the night. Lady Barb nodded to Alassa and pointed them towards a different carriage, one that seemed far simpler than the golden coach. Emily had to smile; Sergeant Harkin had lectured them on the value of concealment and deception in war—and anyone who was targeting the princess would expect her to be in the golden carriage.

"Just for us," Alassa said, as Nightingale started to climb into the carriage. The Master of the Princess's Bedchamber—whatever that meant—looked rather discomforted, but stepped away from the vehicle. "Emily, make sure you have a book with you."

Emily nodded and held up one of the tomes she'd borrowed from the library. Alassa grinned at her and scrambled up into the carriage, without waiting for anyone to set up a proper set of steps. Emily followed her; after the endless obstacle courses the sergeants had put her though, climbing into the carriage was easy. Inside, it was light and airy, charmed to keep them both relatively cool. The glass windows - a sign of great wealth, as glass was hugely expensive—were also charmed, allowing them to see out without letting anyone else see in.

"I thought you would prefer not to ride with anyone else," Alassa said. Her face twisted into a grimace. "If you were a man, we would have had a chaperone just to make sure we didn't do anything stupid."

She glanced over at the wooden walls as the vehicle shook, before the horses started to pull it out of the courtyard. "Can you check the privacy wards? I don't trust them to have made the wards airtight."

Emily nodded and started to work. Most magicians had a specific affinity for one area of magic and hers, it seemed, was charms. Alassa had finally learned enough to qualify for second-year—mainly because Emily had been tutoring her—but Emily was still much better than her at charms. She studied the charms for a long moment, then scowled and added a further charm of her own. Why did Nightingale—or perhaps Lady Barb—think that they could spy on their princess?

"They'd say that it was their job," Alassa explained. She sounded irked, unsurprisingly. "And Nightingale takes his job very seriously."

Emily listened to the explanation, shaking her head in disbelief. She would never have imagined that anyone would appoint a *man* to supervise their daughter's bedchamber, but apparently it ran in the family. The Master of the Princess's Bedchamber held control over appointments *within* the bedchamber, which provided all sorts of opportunities for patronage, if not outright corruption. Emily could only hope that his duties didn't include watching as the princess prepared for bed.

"Each of these people need money," she said, remembering one of the reasons the French Revolution had destroyed the French Monarchy. "They must be an immense drain on your father's money."

"He grumbles about it every year," Alassa said. "They *all* claim a salary, even the Keeper of the Royal Privies, who never comes closer to Alexis than his castle on the edge of the mountains..."

Emily stared at her. "You really have a Keeper of the Royal Privies?"

Alassa giggled. "There's a position for everything," she admitted. Her face sobered, suddenly. "Blame it on Bryon the Weak. If it hadn't been for him, we wouldn't be in this mess. But he never could say no to anyone with a title."

Chapter Seven

EMILY HAD RATHER MIXED FEELINGS ABOUT DRAGON'S DEN. ON ONE HAND, IT WAS THE closest settlement to Whitehall and a place she could go to visit every month with her classmates. And it was where she and Alassa had first become true friends. On the other hand, the first time she'd visited she'd been kidnapped by a dark magician and the next few times–after Shadye had been defeated–the city fathers had insisted on fawning over her. She'd had to go under a glamor to be sure of not being recognized.

The city was independent, at least in theory; no monarch ruled in Dragon's Den. It allowed a greater degree of social mobility than any of the kingdoms, even the most progressive ones. But there *were* monarchical kingdoms nearby and they *could* have threatened Dragon's Den, if necessary. Dragon's Den would be difficult to take outright–there were a number of sorcerers living within the city, who would certainly lend their weight to the defense–but raiding parties could easily destroy most of the farms surrounding the city. It existed in a rather precarious relationship with its neighbors, which might have been why part of the city turned out to cheer as Alassa's convoy poured through the streets. Or they might just have been glad of the break from their labors.

Emily shook her head as the carriage finally pulled clear of the city and headed northwards, up a solid stone road that had been created in the days of the Empire. From what she'd read, part of the infrastructure the Empire had gifted its successor states was rotting away, despite everything the White Council could do to convince the kingdoms to maintain them. Emily couldn't help wondering if the kingdoms were merely trying to save a few gold coins, or if they were worried that the White Council might try to rebuild the Empire. Having the roads to move troops around without needing portals would be very helpful.

And besides, she thought grimly, *the necromancer armies don't really need roads.*

She turned her attention back to her book, silently cursing the writer for his reluctance to say certain things bluntly. A history book should include at least the bare outline of events, but this one–written by someone who lived in Zangaria–either fawned on the Royal Family, or barely touched on questions that Emily wanted answered. The books written by the History Monks were much more dispassionate, but they couldn't be taken out of the library. And besides, they were banned in most of the kingdoms. Possession of them was an instant jail sentence.

"This book is stupid," she exploded, finally. "What *was* the Glorious Laying of the Stone?"

"House Alexis had a gem–they called it the Soul Stone–that had been passed down from the time of legends," Alassa said. "When they became the rulers of Zangaria, they laid the Soul Stone in the foundations of the castle–my birthplace. It's been there ever since."

She shrugged as she saw the book's title. "That writer fawns even more than Nightingale," she added, rather sarcastically. "You'll notice that he skims over Bryon."

Emily flicked through a few pages and nodded. Bryon, who had apparently ruled for *forty-five years*, didn't seem to have done anything of interest. The three pages covering his period as king barely listed anything, beyond a handful of facts and figures. Emily shook her head in disbelief, unsure of just what to read into it. Few kings on Earth had ruled for so long without doing at least *something* of historical interest, even if it was just surviving on the throne.

"You called him Bryon the Weak," she remembered. "What did he actually do?"

Alassa grinned and assumed a pose that reminded Emily of Professor Locke, their history tutor. "My father insisted that I memorize it all," she admitted. "Bryon lost control over the noble families. They started raising their own armies of guardsmen, hiring combat sorcerers and other magicians, then they started pushing Byron to allow them to tighten their grip. My father said that he would have made a good scholar, but he was a poor King. He just didn't have the nerve to confront his nobles before it was too late."

Emily listened with interest. The medieval kings on Earth had faced similar problems. At worst, the king became first-among-equals, unable to impose his will on his noblemen. It hadn't been until the invention of gunpowder and heavy cannons that a monarch had been able to cow his aristocrats, even though many had maintained a limited form of independence for years. Bryon, it seemed, had disliked confrontation. His aristocrats had taken ruthless advantage of it.

She looked down at the book. All of a sudden, the silence covering forty-five years of history made much more sense.

"So," she said. "What happened?"

Alassa's smile widened. "He had a son, Prince Alexis," she said. "The prince *loved* playing with his toy soldiers, so much so that his father gave him a whole regiment of *real* soldiers to lead out on pretend manoeuvres. No one seemed to realize that the prince had watched his father's humiliation and sworn to avenge it, or that he would have the patience to build up an army bit by bit. When he took the throne, the nobles discovered that King Alexis III had a much larger force than any of them— and intended to use it. The three most troublesome noble families were completely exterminated by the King's forces."

Emily checked the next few pages in the book. They told the same story, although they also included editorials that claimed that the three exterminated families had deserved to be wiped out to the last man, woman and child. The writer didn't seem to be bothered by the fact that he'd hinted, earlier, that nothing much had happened during Bryon's reign, leaving the sudden civil war and slaughter a surprising change. Someone who read it without any other knowledge might conclude that the whole problem had appeared in the early months of King Alexis III's reign.

"I see," she said, finally. Reading between the lines, it looked as though there was much more to the story than the writer decided to tell his readers. "And since then...?"

Alassa looked down at her hands. "My father has been trying to keep the barons in check," she admitted. "I... I may not have been very helpful."

That, Emily knew, was one hell of an understatement. Even before Void had passed on his warning, she'd deduced that someone had been working to cripple Alassa's future. If she'd taken the throne before she'd met Emily, she might not have noticed that her power was being eroded away until it was far too late. The nobles might determine who she married, who became king...

...But it would be harder than that, wouldn't it? Whoever married Alassa would share her power, in custom if not in law. And if one of the nobles got into that position, he would leave his former allies behind. No, they'd be much more likely to choose a non-entity for the position, someone who posed no threat to them. They wouldn't want someone from another kingdom, who might bring allies—and armies—to assist his wife.

You don't know enough, Emily reminded herself, as she put the book to one side. *Figure out the rest first and then make your judgements.*

"Nightingale is a bit of a crawler," she said, out loud. "Why do *you* tolerate him?"

"I didn't select him," Alassa reminded her. "The post he holds is passed down through his family. It would be difficult to get rid of him unless he was caught committing treason."

Emily rolled her eyes. Who would have thought that absolute monarchy would be so difficult?

But there was no such thing as an absolute monarchy. Even the worst dictators on Earth had been at the top of a pyramid of allies and people who benefited from their rule. Those who failed to manage their inner circle properly tended to run into trouble. And Kings and queens throughout history had faced the same problem. Charles I of England had tried to rule his country personally. Even with—in theory—absolute power the result had been a slow slide to disaster. Louis of France hadn't been able to reduce the vast expenditure on the French Court before it had been too late. Those who had won rights—like Nightingale—were jealous of them, protecting them with all the force at their command.

"Maybe you need to give him the task of keeping the privies," Emily said. "Can you swap his position for the other one?"

"The Keeper of the Royal Privies has been passed down from person to person ever since King Alexis I took the throne," Alassa pointed out. "It couldn't be simply given to someone else."

"Particularly as the person holding the title doesn't have to actually do anything," Emily guessed. At least Nightingale seemed to do something useful, even if it *was* just assigning the maids and other servants to Alassa's bedchamber. The Keeper of the Royal Privies presumably didn't actually clean them himself. He might have been more willing to surrender the title if he actually had to do the work. "I think you need a cull."

"My father thinks the same," Alassa admitted. "It's making it happen that is the difficult part."

Emily leaned over and peered out of the window, watching as the farmland slowly turned into forest. She had memorized a couple of maps, but mapmaking wasn't very detailed in her new world, apart from a handful she'd seen in Martial Magic. One of the books Sergeant Miles had ordered the class to read had detailed problems with basic maps, including the mapmakers leaving off little details like contour lines and hidden sinkholes. According to the book, at least one military operation had gone badly wrong because the pass shown on the map simply didn't exist.

"We'll go hunting in the royal woods," Alassa promised. "You've never hunted before?"

Emily shook her head. Hunting wasn't common where she lived—and besides, she saw little point in chasing harmless creatures with a gun. Jade had talked about his father hunting monsters that had come over the mountains from the Blighted Lands, but those creatures posed a clear and present danger to the civilian population. Rabbits and foxes and whatever else Alassa's family might hunt weren't *that* dangerous.

"You'll love it," Alassa assured her. "Besides, you learned how to ride really quickly."

Emily nodded, ruefully. Alassa had insisted on teaching her—and Imaiqah—how to ride, at least partly to get others who could ride out with her, now that her cronies had all been scared away. Emily hadn't enjoyed the first few rides, but once she'd mastered the trick of controlling the horse she'd found herself enjoying it. And she'd watched in amazement as Alassa had taken care of her own horse. Clearly, Alassa had managed to learn more than Emily had ever realized, even when she'd been a spoilt brat.

"Just you wait until you meet Lady Cecelia," Alassa added. "She is completely horse-mad. Lives on her own, refuses to marry…spends all of her time in the saddle or in the stable. Even my father doesn't get as much respect from her as she gives to her horses. She was the one who gave me my first pony."

She looked down for a long moment. "I wasn't properly grateful," she admitted. "She swore never to allow me to buy one of her horses until I admitted to her what I'd done wrong."

Emily lifted an eyebrow, then realized that Alassa didn't want to talk about it. But Emily could guess; Alassa might not have realized, at first, that the most important part of owning a pony—or a horse—was taking care of the beast. It was easy to imagine the brat Alassa had been refusing to sweep out the stable, or brush the pony's coat, or whatever else one had to do to take care of a large animal. If Lady Cecelia was as horse-mad as Alassa suggested, she would have been outraged at such mistreatment. And she clearly wouldn't have hesitated to give the young princess a piece of her mind.

Alassa might envy Emily, if she knew the truth about her origins. No matter what she did in the future, there were people who would already remember the little brat she'd been as a child. She could never escape the shadow of her past. But Emily had left her past behind when Shadye had brought her into this world. Everything she'd done on Earth seemed almost dreamlike to her—and no one else would truly understand it, no matter how she tried to explain.

She shifted position and watched as the forest grew thicker. The trees were growing closer to the road, she realized, providing no shortage of concealment for bandits who might want to sneak up on the small procession. Sergeant Harkin, in one of his many lectures, had admitted that the borderlands between countries were often lawless, if only because neither country could patrol it without making the other suspect that they intended to launch an invasion. Besides, the poor bastards who actually lived there, he'd added, found themselves visited by tax collectors from both countries. Was it any wonder, Emily had asked herself, that they might turn to raiding?

The forest vanished suddenly, to be replaced by a wooden fort that seemed to have come out of the Wild West. Emily stared at it, unable to understand why they'd even bothered to build it when a single fire-spell would turn it into an inferno. Some of the fortress designs they'd studied in Martial Magic had been designed to force attacking magicians to waste power, but they'd been composed of stone and warded to make it harder to break them down. This fort was stupid and senseless.

"Border forts are rarely well-designed, unless they're at a chokepoint," Alassa said, when Emily asked her what the fort was designed to *do*. "They are always the first targets when someone comes storming over the borders, so no one invests much in them. And wood is cheap out here."

"That actually makes sense," Emily said, shaking her head. "How did you know *that?*"

Alassa stuck out her tongue. "My father is the King, my Uncle is a duke and one of my protectors is a Man at Arms," she said. "I often heard them talking about our borders when I was younger."

There was a rap on the door, followed rapidly by the sound of someone trying to open it. The lock clicked and the door opened, allowing Lady Barb to stick her head into the carriage. "We're staying here long enough to change the horses," she said. "If either of you want to answer the call of nature, now is the time."

Emily made a face. One thing she *did* miss from Earth were proper toilets. Whitehall *did* have plumbing, but hardly anywhere else did, particularly out in the wild. She'd lost a great deal of modesty in Martial Magic, yet she didn't particularly want to do her business in front of a horde of strangers.

"It's a good idea to go," Alassa said, standing up. "You never know when you might have the chance to go again."

Emily sighed and followed her out of the carriage. The fort smelt funny to her, a faint mixture of burnt wood and oil. And horses, dozens of horses. There was a field behind the fort where several dozen horses were kept, ready for the next courier who needed to change animals. Several of them were being led out to replace the ones pulling the carriages; Emily couldn't help but notice the stirrups the riders were using. *That* had been her idea, one of the concepts she'd introduced. They'd clearly spread further than she had realized.

The next part of the journey passed quickly, once they finished at the fort and headed back on to the roads. Emily found herself staring out of the window as the procession passed through a series of small hamlets, each one barely large enough to support more than twenty people. Or maybe there were other houses hidden away in the undergrowth. There was no time to do more than pick up impressions before they were past the hamlet and heading back down an empty road.

She felt the carriage slow down as they entered a larger town, with massive buildings built out of stone. There was a large crowd cheering them, although Emily had the private suspicion that some of them were there because they hadn't been given any choice. But others seemed more than willing to welcome the Princess of Zangaria and invite her to marry their Prince. Emily was still shaking her head as they left the town behind and headed onwards. Did they really think that Alassa would make her choice based on who shouted the loudest?

"I can't marry the crown prince of another kingdom," Alassa explained, "and Alluvia has too many other princes. If I married one and took him away…"

Understanding clicked in Emily's mind. "It reduces the risk of civil war," she said. "They'd be glad of that, wouldn't they?"

"If I had a brother, he would be the heir and I would be the spare," Alassa said. She looked oddly wistful for a long moment. "If I had two brothers, the younger might try to overthrow the older. And I would be sent off to marry someone to seal a treaty. But I am alone."

She looked up as the carriage rattled over a bridge. "But we're almost at the castle," she added. "And then we have to get dressed. *Before* we are formally presented to the king…"

They shared a groan. "You're lucky," Alassa added. "You won't have it so bad."

Chapter Eight

EMILY SUCKED IN HER BREATH SHARPLY AS THE CARRIAGE RUMBLED TOWARDS CASTLE Alluvia. It was a massive structure, seemingly larger than Whitehall, perched on a craggy rock that allowed it to dominate the city below. The city itself was much smaller than Dragon's Den, somehow giving the impression of being *compact*, as if thousands of people had been jammed into a relatively small space. It had no walls, something that puzzled Emily as the carriage started to head up the street towards the castle. But then, if someone *did* attack, the population could be herded into the castle or–more likely–told to flee into the countryside and fend for themselves.

The street was lined by cheering people, who waved at the carriage as the small procession drifted past. Emily had to smile as she realized that most of them grew less enthusiastic once the golden carriage had passed, even though *Alassa* hadn't passed yet. But it did prove that the diversion was working and no one knew where the royal princess actually was. The wards surrounding the vehicles would make it harder for magic to be used to target her. Emily settled back as the road circled the castle, before finally reaching the gatehouse. She felt a tingle as they passed through an outer set of wards–weaker than Whitehall's wards–and came to a halt in the courtyard.

Whitehall was dimensionally transcendent, larger on the inside than on the outside. Castle Alluvia was very definitely *not*; the courtyard seemed tiny, barely large enough to house Alassa's vehicles and escorts. Lady Barb rapped on the carriage's door, inviting them both to climb out of the vehicle. Emily jumped down gracefully, then turned to help Alassa climb down with somewhat more dignity. The princess looked around with interest, even as everyone from the castle's staff bowed to her. Emily followed her gaze, unable to escape the impression that Castle Alluvia was crude compared to Whitehall. But then, there was nowhere near as much magic worked into its structure.

"Your Highness," Nightingale said. He looked tired, but there was nothing wrong with his outfit, a garish mixture of purple and green. "You must change, and then be presented to the King."

Emily rolled her eyes at the little man's self-importance, although he was right. Protocol dictated that Alassa could not be greeted formally until she was presented to the kingdom's monarch, which meant that she had to be dressed for the part. Emily had wondered why the king couldn't simply meet them outside the castle, to which Alassa had pointed out that *she* was the guest and the king couldn't be seen to come to meet *her*. And besides, she'd added a moment later, they both smelled pretty rank after hours in the cramped carriage. She didn't want the King's first impression of her to be that she was smelly.

Nightingale had evidently been to Castle Alluvia before, for he led them over to a little door set into the stone walls. Inside, it was dark, without even a hint of light.

Emily hesitated, but Alassa marched inside as if nothing could stop her. And perhaps it couldn't. Emily looked up at the darkening sky, caught sight of a handful of birds flying around the castle's towers, and stepped inside. There was a second tingle—the doorway was protected against intruders—and then she was in a small corridor leading into the building.

Whitehall's corridors were massive, wide enough to allow several people to walk side-by-side at once. Castle Alluvia had corridors so thin that Emily felt a hint of claustrophobia, each one illuminated only by burning torches rather than magical lights. It made sense, she knew; anyone who attacked the castle would have to come at the defenders one at a time. Even so, it still felt odd compared to Whitehall. But then, the defenders of this castle didn't have vast amounts of magic to help them.

And if they were attacked by a necromancer, it wouldn't matter anyway, she thought. Whitehall hadn't been saved by its powerful wards, just Emily...and knowledge from a very different world.

If anything, the staircases were even worse. Alassa had to bow her head to avoid striking it on the stone ceiling, while Emily could barely stand upright. It was impossible to escape the feeling that the castle was permanently on the verge of collapse, or that the passageways would become so small that she would find herself trapped there. She bit her lip and followed Alassa, reminding herself that the King of Alluvia wouldn't want to kill or embarrass his distinguished guest.

"Your rooms, Your Highness," Nightingale said, as they came out of the stairwell. "The castle's staff will tend to your needs."

"Very good," Alassa said. She *sounded* like a princess, almost like the brat she'd been when Emily had first met her. "You may leave us."

Nightingale bowed and left the room, leaving the girls alone. Emily watched him go, closing the door behind him, and then looked around Alassa's room. It was massive, with a huge four-poster bed at the head of the room, illuminated by a chandelier filled with glowing candles. Emily couldn't help wondering how they managed to light them all, before deciding that it didn't matter. It gave the room an oddly romantic atmosphere.

There was a smaller bed placed in one corner, although it was still larger than the bed she'd had at Whitehall. It took Emily a moment to realize that they were meant to be sharing the same room, although she wasn't sure why *that* had surprised her. She'd shared a room at Whitehall with two other students and Alassa had done the same; hell, one of Alassa's roommates had *thanked* Emily for helping the royal brat turn into a decent human being.

"No windows," Alassa said. They shared a long look. "I'm sick of being in rooms without windows."

Emily couldn't help agreeing. Their dorms at Whitehall had no windows either—and *they* were illuminated by magical lights. But then, no one would want to run the risk of an assassin climbing up the castle walls and getting into the room through a giant window. And besides, the more cynical part of Emily's mind added, it would be harder for Alassa to leave without the King's permission.

She walked over to a door set in one wall and opened it, peering inside to see a wash basin and privy. There didn't seem to be any plumbing, she realized after a moment; there were vast jugs of water waiting for them to wash themselves. Whitehall's showers had been primitive compared to the ones she remembered from Earth, but Castle Alluvia didn't even seem to understand the concept of plumbing. Void had told her never to drink water that hadn't been boiled, proving that the locals understood the existence of germs—or was that just sorcerers? Could they drink the water in the castle?

"Boil it with your magic," Alassa suggested, when she asked. There was a sharp knock on the door and the princess raised her voice. "Come in!"

The door opened, revealing five young women dressed in simple black robes, with white caps on their heads. Emily remembered vaguely that white caps denoted personal servants in some kingdoms, but there were so many differences between the various kingdoms that made up the Allied Lands that it was impossible to know for sure. In some ways, the Allied Lands worked hard to prove that they were separate kingdoms, although they hadn't—yet—managed to establish separate languages. The Empire had existed long enough to ensure that everyone spoke the same standard tongue.

Four of the maids went down on their knees, facing Alassa; the fifth remained standing, but bowed her head. "Your Highness, we have come to tend to your needs," she said. "It is His Majesty's instruction that you present yourself before him."

Alassa kept her face expressionless. "Bring up my trunks from the carriage," she ordered, grandly. "And bring up Emily's as well."

Three of the girls vanished out of the door, presumably to go downstairs and recover the trunks, while the other two advanced on Alassa and started to undress her. Emily stepped to one side, wondering absently how the girls intended to bring up the trunks; it would be very difficult to get them up the claustrophobic stairwells. Magic, perhaps—or maybe there were other, wider stairwells for the servants.

The girls returned with the trunks and put them in the center of the room, then walked out of the door again. Emily opened her trunk and recovered one of the dresses Alassa's mother had sent her, silently grateful that the queen hadn't wanted to risk Emily outshining her daughter. The green dress might have been very simple, if expensive by the standards of Zangaria, but it was also easy to put on without needing help. She concealed a smile as the maids pulled Alassa's clothes off, just as the door opened again and the three maids returned, carrying a large bathtub of scented hot water.

Alassa threw her a dirty look as the maids started to wash her, as if she couldn't wash for herself. Emily wondered how her friend managed to endure it; she couldn't have tolerated complete strangers stripping her naked and then washing her thoroughly. Shaking her head, she walked around to the other side of the bed and hesitated, unable to decide if she should undress now or wait until the maids were gone. Being naked in front of her roommates had been hard enough, but she didn't even *know* the maids. Maybe it was that sheer lack of personal relationship that made it easier for Alassa accept it.

But then, Alassa hadn't been raised to think of the lower classes as *human*.

"You may use the remaining water," the head maid said. "It is still warm."

Emily wondered just what they'd been told about her; she might not have been an aristocrat, but she was the Necromancer's Bane. Did the king really want to *offend* her? It struck Emily, a moment later, that she was thinking like Alassa had thought, back when they'd first met. There was no reason to assume an insult without proof—besides, Alassa was easily more important, socially, than Emily. Even if she *had* beaten a necromancer.

"You can bring her fresh water," Alassa snapped. "*Now!*"

The maids bowed and retreated, taking the bathtub with them. Emily glanced at Alassa in surprise.

"Making you use my old water is insulting," Alassa said, simply. "The king wanted to test me, to see what I would do when they tried."

Emily was still puzzling over that when the maids returned, carrying new buckets of water and the emptied bathtub. Their leader offered a grovelling apology as her subordinates poured the water into the tub, then headed back towards Alassa. Emily rolled her eyes at their backs and saw her friend smile in return, just before she was surrounded by the maids.

The water smelled faintly of flowers and herbs, Emily decided, as she undressed and washed herself. There didn't seem to be any dedicated bathroom; the water splashed on the marble tiles, creating a slipping hazard. Emily wondered if they were just going to leave the puddles there, before realizing that the maids would probably come into the room while they were being presented to the king and clean up the mess. She made a mental note to ensure that her trunk was locked before she left the room. No doubt the king would expect his maids to search their possessions if they had a chance.

After the long journey, it felt good to wash, although she would really have preferred a shower. She found herself considering ways to convince the king to install modern plumbing, before realizing that they could have done it long before Emily had been brought into their world. Maybe someone was hoping that the king and his family would rot in the filth of their own living accommodations…it didn't seem too likely, but it made her smile as she towelled herself down and donned the dress. In the mirror, she looked rather unimpressive, almost waiflike.

She heard a muttered curse from behind her and turned to see Alassa, still being tended by the maids. Two of them were working on her hair, propping it up in a manner that made Emily think of Marge Simpson; two more were poking and prodding at her blue-white dress, fanning it out to ensure that no one could do more than hold hands with her. Emily couldn't help noticing that the dress was rather like a wedding garment from Earth and wondered if the symbolism—a virgin bride—held true for Zangaria too. *Was* Alassa a virgin? It was odd, given how much else they'd shared, they'd never talked about sex. And Alassa hadn't raised the topic when Emily had told her about Jade's proposal.

It was nearly an hour before the maids finally pronounced themselves satisfied. Emily had gone from amusement to boredom and had been reading a book, which she returned to the trunk as Alassa stared at herself in the mirror. She *did* look striking, although Emily had some difficulty understanding how she was meant to go through the corridors without brushing her hair against the ceiling. They met eyes and Alassa winked at her, then dismissed the maids with a wave of her hand.

"Remember your protocol," Alassa said, as the door opened again. Nightingale and Lady Barb stepped into the room. The Master of the Princess's Bedchamber had changed into an outfit that was even more eye-catching than the first; Lady Barb didn't seem to have changed at all. "I bow to the King; you count ten ticks and then curtsey. Then stay on one knee until he gives you leave to rise."

Emily nodded. Alassa had told her the same thing for the last ten days before they left Whitehall. Alassa *was* nervous, Emily knew, fearing that she wouldn't make a good impression. Her prospective husbands might have heard of her reputation and feared to marry her—or, alternatively, they could have thought that a royal brat would be easy to manipulate. It still struck Emily as odd, but a mistake on *her* part could reflect badly on Alassa.

"Your Highness," Nightingale said. "You look wonderfully regal."

Alassa nodded imperiously, but said nothing.

"Come with us," Lady Barb ordered. She didn't seem very impressed with Alassa's royal title, or perhaps it was just the company she kept. "His Majesty is waiting for you."

Emily stayed one step behind Alassa as they walked out of the second door and into a antechamber that housed two beds. Nightingale and Lady Barb were literally sleeping outside Alassa's door, Emily realized; absently, she wondered how they tolerated each other. Somehow, she couldn't see them being friends. Outside the antechamber, there were three soldiers on guard duty, two of them wearing the livery Emily had seen on the guards escorting the carriage. The third wore different colors.

The corridors were wider deeper inside the castle, she saw, as they walked down a massive flight of staircases and stopped outside a pair of giant wooden doors. Alassa gave her a nervous glance, then winked as the doors began to open, revealing the royal court. Hundreds of people were inside the chamber; they turned to look as Alassa strode in, staring at the royal princess. Emily almost quailed before a push from Lady Barb forced her to start walking up the aisle. It was impossible to escape the sense that she was attending her own wedding.

King Jorlem was a tall, powerfully-built man who was slowly turning to fat. He seemed to be bald, wearing a heavy crown as if it were the lightest thing in the world. Emily couldn't help thinking of Henry VIII, before realizing that King Jorlem, at least, had two male heirs. If he had any daughters, none of the genealogical tables

Emily had consulted had shown them. But he'd want daughters, wouldn't he? They could make useful alliances, particularly if they couldn't actually inherit on their own.

Alassa stopped, two meters in front of the throne, and bowed. Emily felt her heartbeat racing faster as she counted ten seconds, then curtseyed. Despite all the practicing Alassa had made her do, she still nearly tripped over herself. A moment later, she went down on one knee, feeling oddly exposed, almost humiliated. King Jorlem wasn't *her* King. Besides, no one knelt to the president.

"We welcome you, Crown Princess of Zangaria," the king said. His voice was thin and reedy, but there was no mistaking the absolute assurance of power behind it. "You are most welcome in Our court."

"I thank you, in the name of my father," Alassa said.

Emily listened as they exchanged ritual pleasantries, wondering just how long she was supposed to stay on one knee. No doubt anyone born to this world would be able to stay there as long as necessary, but Emily felt her body going stiff. To distract herself, she looked around as best as she could without moving her head too much, catching sight of a tall handsome youth who was eying Alassa with an unreadable expression. The Crown Prince, Emily decided. *He* wouldn't be able to marry Alassa. Beside him, his brother looked faintly bored by the whole affair.

One man, wearing long black robes with golden stars, was staring at her. Emily looked back at him, sensing magic spinning around his form; he had to be the Court Wizard. He would have heard of her and, like so many others, wondered just *what* she'd done to defeat Shadye without embracing necromancy herself. She felt his magic field touching hers lightly and stiffened, unsure of quite what he was trying to do. Read her mind? She tightened her defenses anyway, deliberately looking back at the King. After a moment, the intrusion faded away and disappeared.

"And so you are welcome," King Jorlem concluded. He glanced briefly at Emily, a flash of curiosity in his eyes. "You may rise."

Emily stood up.

"We shall now proceed to the Great Hall for the welcome feast," the king added. His face twisted into a grin. "We shall show you proper hospitality."

He stood up and took Alassa's hand, as if he were her true father. Emily watched as he led her towards another set of doors, then started to follow them. The rest of the court followed in their wake.

Chapter Nine

THE PROTOCOL OFFICERS DIDN'T SEEM TO KNOW WHAT TO MAKE OF EMILY. ON ONE hand, the official story explaining her origins placed her firmly in the servant class, suggesting that she should be eating with the other servants in the kitchen, at least until she was a qualified sorcerer. On the other hand, the widely-held belief that she was Void's bastard daughter meant they risked offending an extremely powerful sorcerer by giving her less than full honors. And she was not only Alassa's close personal friend—and quite wealthy in her own right - but she was also the student who had defeated a necromancer in a duel. Who knew what she would be capable of when she grew up?

In the end, they'd put her at the high table, sitting next to the Crown Prince. Lady Barb and Nightingale had been given seats at a lower table; Lady Barb didn't seem to mind, but Nightingale looked furious. He'd been effectively demoted by King Jorlem, Emily realized, after some thought. Seating was based on social class and the mere presence of a handful of guests upset all of the arrangements. It struck Emily as rather silly, although she had a feeling that it served a useful purpose. She just didn't know what it could be.

"I often thought that I would like to go to Whitehall," Crown Prince Dater said. He seemed less inclined to take protocol seriously than the junior aristocrats; besides, he could talk to Emily without committing himself to anything. "But I had to stay home and learn how to rule."

Emily found herself liking the Crown Prince, even though she had the feeling that he was a skilled dissembler. The Allied Lands had quite a few cases of young heirs deciding that it was time to take the throne by assassinating their fathers— and, for that matter, fathers killing sons because they feared their ambitions. All of them were partly covered up in the official records, although the History Monks had recorded the truth. No wonder their books were banned in most of the kingdoms.

"It was Hedrick who had the magical inclination," Dater added, a moment later. "And he is courting your princess."

Emily glanced over at where Alassa was sitting, between King Jorlem and Prince Hedrick. Hedrick was handsome enough, in a bland sort of way, but the bored expression on his face didn't bode well for any future romance. He could at least *pretend* to be interested in Alassa. His father, on the other hand, was bombarding her with questions, some of them clearly about Emily. Alassa didn't seem to be uncomfortable talking about her friend. It probably served as a distraction from having to talk about herself.

Hedrick had magic? Emily hadn't sensed anything from him, but then he might not be powerful enough for it to register—or powerful and disciplined enough to conceal his power. He didn't seem to be carrying a wand, a sure sign of poorly-developed talent, but he *was* wearing a sword…though that might have been protocol. Apart from King Jorlem and his children, none of the aristocrats carried weapons. The king could have ordered them all cut down in a moment.

She glanced at some of the aristocrats, noting that some of them were staring at her, probably wondering just what made her so special. How many of *them* had magic? Some noble bloodlines worked hard to develop their magical talents, even to the point of inviting commoners like Imaiqah—and Emily herself, she acknowledged with an internal scowl—to contribute genes. Others were horrified at the mere thought of sullying their bloodlines with commoner blood. Absently, she wondered just how many of those unions bore the required fruit. Nothing she'd read in the library had suggested much understanding of genetics; there had certainly been no mention of anything resembling DNA.

"Hedrick talked about becoming my Court Wizard, but father wants him to marry someone outside the kingdom," Dater continued. He sounded almost wistful. "Hedrick himself doesn't seem to care very much."

He glanced at his father, who was still chatting to Alassa, and then back at Emily. "So...what really happened at Whitehall?"

Emily flushed. "I beat Shadye," she said, simply. "And it isn't something I can talk about."

"I *am* a Crown Prince," Dater said. "You can tell me."

"I can't," Emily said, shaking her head. "We have to keep the necromancers guessing."

Dater gave her a sharp look. He'd grown up in a shark tank, to all intents and purposes, and had to learn how to play the great game of intrigue—as Alassa had called it—very young. If something was being kept a secret, it implied that there was a strong motive to *keep* it a secret—and the mere act of deciding what had to be kept secret often implied the motive. It would be easy for someone to draw the conclusion that Emily was *ashamed* of what she had done, or knew that it would be an instant death sentence if word got out. And that suggested necromancy.

No one seemed to believe that necromancers could conceal their true nature for very long. The mere act of sucking so much mana and life energy through their brains and into their wards unhinged them. A necromancer could easily vaporize someone who looked at him the wrong way, secure in the conviction that the act *wouldn't* give him away. His warped mind wouldn't see anything wrong with that at all. By that standard, Emily had shown no signs of necromancy.

But people would always wonder...

"Maybe the grandmaster came up with something," Dater prodded. "Or maybe he did something careless and died because of it."

"Maybe," Emily agreed.

She looked up as the servants brought in the first part of the meal. Hundreds of rabbits had been killed and cooked by the kitchen staff, before being carried upstairs and placed in front of the diners. Emily had known, intellectually, that meat didn't come out of nowhere, but she'd never truly grasped it until she'd seen the sergeants cooking animals they'd caught to feed their students. Now, it was almost commonplace to see whole animals. But they were rabbits...

And there are people who eat snails, she reminded herself, tartly. *And cats, and dogs, and insects*.

"This is just the beginning," Dater warned her, as the servants placed a slice of meat on her plate. "There will be *much* more to come."

Emily worked a charm Sergeant Miles had taught her to make sure that the food was actually safe to eat. She'd had several bouts of queasiness after eating the food at Whitehall, even though most of it was cooked properly. And then there had been the dinner Cat had cooked for them in Martial Magic, which had left the entire team throwing up. The sergeants had laughed at them afterwards. They'd been warned to make sure that the meat was cooked properly. Thankfully, the charm revealed that the food was safe.

Dater chatted to her about nothing in particular as the servants brought course after course, almost all roasted or stewed meat. There were only a handful of vegetable dishes and slices of bread to go with the meat, as well as large flagons of wine and mead. Emily took a sniff of a drink Dater called Golden Mead—apparently imported from another continent at great expense—and decided that it probably wasn't safe to drink. The last thing she wanted to do was get drunk and babble all of her secrets to listening ears.

"I had to calm down the Counting Guild after the new numbers reached the kingdom," Dater said. "They were insisting that they be completely banned. My father trusted me to come to an arrangement with them. And then the abacus made it impossible. We ended up having to disband the guild."

Emily felt a shock running through her chest. The new numbers had been her fault, one of the simplest innovations she'd suggested to Imaiqah's father. Arabic numerals were so much easier to use than symbols that made Latin numerals look simple and easy. And then there had been double-entry bookkeeping, which made it much easier for shopkeepers to do their own accounts, and the abacus. The Accounting Guild of Zangaria had been crippled, then ruined, by the innovations. They'd exploited too many people to survive the crash when they'd lost their monopoly.

Dater's face was unreadable. Did he *know* that Emily had been the one who had 'invented' the new numbers? Alassa had deduced it, but Alassa had access to some inside knowledge, knowledge that Dater might well have missed. Not, in the end, that it mattered. The first abacuses had been very basic, designed from Emily's memories. Now, there was a *sixth* generation design out there and hundreds of craftsmen were competing to come up with the seventh.

"I'm sorry about that," she said, sincerely. She'd theorized that there would be more work for accountants than ever—and there probably would be, once the first true corporations were established on this world. But the guild in Zangaria had made too many enemies to survive in its current form. She assumed that was true of the other guilds too. "But they could get work on the printing presses."

Dater's face flickered, unpleasantly. The first printing press hadn't worked too well—it had been laughable compared to one Emily recalled from school, let alone a laser printer—but the craftsmen had picked up on the idea and run with it. Now, there was a very basic system for producing paper, which would eventually lead to the mass production of books. Previously, the only way to copy a text had been to do it by hand. Now, hundreds of copies could be produced very quickly. It would be a long time before the process was mature–the craftsmen were still making improvements–but it had already started to have an impact on society.

It would continue to snowball, Emily knew. The Empire's script, which looked like a cross between Arabic and Chinese, was almost impossible to learn properly unless one started very young. Even the basic script needed years of training to master; Imaiqah had been lucky that her father had been able to afford a tutor for her. And Alassa had never been a very good student, at least before she'd met Emily. But English letters were so much easier to learn and master that they were spreading like wildfire. The Scribes Guild had not been amused.

"You're supposed to be a Child of Destiny," Dater pointed out. "Do you *know* where this is taking us?"

Emily hesitated, then decided to be blunt. "I think it will make you stronger, in the long run," she said. "What good is a newborn baby?"

Dater's lips twitched. "I have yet to marry myself," he admitted. "My father is still in the process of selecting a bride for me."

"Oh," Emily said. She'd focused on girls being pushed–or forced–into marriage, but it should have occurred to her that boys would face the same pressure to marry. But then, boys had more social freedom than girls, unless the girls happened to be sorceresses. "Do you have any say in it at all?"

"My father said that I could lie with her until she had a couple of boy-children, then give her a tower somewhere if she didn't please me," Dater said. "But I hope it is someone I will be able to talk to. It's hard to talk to anyone when you're the Crown Prince. Even Hedrick doesn't really understand."

Emily nodded. "People keep telling you what they think you want to hear," she said, remembering Alassa's cronies. "Or they tell you what they want you to hear."

"That is indeed the problem," Dater said. "Do you know that, as Crown Prince, I am called upon to investigate murders in the city? The last time, I was inundated with suspects even before I looked at the corpse."

"*You* investigate murders?" Emily asked, in disbelief. Somehow, she couldn't quite imagine the sober crown prince walking around in a deerstalker and carrying a magnifying glass. "Why you?"

"The only person senior to me is my father," Dater reminded her. "No one can refuse to talk to me."

It made a certain kind of sense, Emily decided, reluctantly. A nobleman would hardly agree to talk to a common-born investigator, or even a fellow nobleman. But the Crown Prince, the acknowledged heir, could ask questions without forcing the nobleman to lose face in front of anyone else. And besides, it was probably good publicity for the royal family, particularly if nobles were involved in the crime.

Or maybe not. "What happens if the murderer comes from a noble family?"

Dater had the grace to look embarrassed. "That depends on who he murdered," he admitted. "If it was a common-born"–he made a show of glancing around to see who might be listening–"lady of negotiable affection…"

A trumpet blared before he could finish. King Jorlem stood up, waited for silence and then spoke out loud. "My son, Prince Hedrick, Duke of Harmonious Repose, Lord of the Middle Realm, will be accompanying the Princess Alassa on her journey back to Zangaria, where he will make his suit in front of her family," he said. "Should he succeed in winning her hand, we will enjoy a close alliance with a northern land, an alliance that is in both of our interests. I call on you all to praise the gods and ask them to shine their light upon the couple."

There was a brief outbreak of cheering. Alassa's face was unreadable, but Emily could see the tension in the way she held herself. King Jorlem had talked as though it was already a done deal, as if all that had to be done was the mere formality of asking her parents to bless the match. Had Alassa given him that impression, or was he merely trying to push her into accepting Prince Hedrick as a partner?

Maybe I should send a message back to Whitehall and ask for the prince's records, Emily thought. The grandmaster might think carefully on the political implications before sending them, but Lady Aylia wouldn't hesitate, if Emily phased the request carefully. She believed that information wanted to be free. *See just what he got in his exams before he graduated.*

He was at least five years older than Alassa–more likely six, Emily realized–but that wouldn't seem to be a problem to their eyes. Age wasn't such an issue when dealing with princes; it only seemed to matter seriously when princesses were concerned. It made sense–a princess who had passed the menopause simply couldn't have any more children–but it still made Emily shudder in disgust. Did they view every princess as a brood cow? Or, for that matter, princes as stud bulls?

But he looked…*bored.*

Was he homosexual? Emily wondered. Admittedly, Alassa wasn't wearing one of the dresses that exposed most of her breasts to public view, but she would have expected a young man to show more interest in the beautiful princess. Or maybe he was simply very good at concealing his true feelings, just like his brother. And if he *was* homosexual…? James of Scotland–later James I of the United Kingdom–had been homosexual and it hadn't stopped him from siring three children. That said, his kingdom might have regretted his second son taking the throne as Charles I.

"As the princess must continue her journey to her kingdom tomorrow, we shall celebrate her arrival tonight," the king continued. "Let the revels begin!"

The noblemen stood up as a flock of servants arrived and started pulling the tables aside, while a set of minstrels started to play in the far corner. Prince Hedrick stood up, after his father had shot him a sharp glance, and held out a hand to Alassa. Emily had to smile inwardly as Alassa stood up, took the prince's hand and allowed him to lead her down to the dance floor. Unlike in Whitehall, she realized, there was an order to the dances that allowed the various unmarried noblemen to switch between potential wives. Hedrick, on the other hand, seemed to be stuck with Alassa.

A surprising number of noblewomen seemed to surround the king as soon as he stepped down from the high table. Dater leaned over and explained that ever since their mother had died, the king had been taking solace by dancing with as many noblewomen as possible. If it had gone further than dancing…no one seemed to know. Or care; a brief period as the King's mistress could set a woman up for life, or even bring honor to her family. Emily rolled her eyes and sat back, watching the dancing.

The first dance finished, allowing a balladeer to start singing a ballad. Emily winced inwardly, wondering if she could get away with making herself invisible or simply running out the door, as she recognized the song as one of the ballads about *her*. At least it wasn't one of the truly *crude* ones. She'd promised herself that if she ever got her hands on the person who had written a raunchy song implying that she'd used forbidden sex magic to beat Shadye, she'd do a great deal worse than turning him into a slug.

"He doesn't sing very well," Emily muttered, when the ballad had finally finished. "Why do you keep him?"

"Father likes his old war songs," Dater admitted. He held out a hand and stood up. "Would you care to join me on the dance floor?"

The honest answer to that was *no*, but there was a desperation in his eyes that made Emily relent. Of course; if he danced with someone, courtly whispers would have them engaged by the end of the day. And if he happened to compromise himself in any way, it might prove disastrous to the monarchy. At least he had real power to console himself for having to adhere to protocol as closely as possible.

But he could dance with Emily without upsetting anyone.

She was very tired by the time the ball finally came to an end.

Chapter Ten

W HAT A...BORING LITTLE TIT," ALASSA SAID, AS SOON AS THE MAIDS HAD BEEN CHASED out and the door firmly closed. "I cannot understand why his father was so sure Hedrick would make a good match for me."

"He knows magic," Emily pointed out. "And he's the only *spare* they have."

"I'd have to put up with him for *years*," Alassa protested. "He didn't even stare at my chest!"

Emily blinked as she started to undress. "You *want* him staring at your chest?"

"It would have been a kind of interest," Alassa said, sourly. "Instead, I didn't have the impression he cared about me or marriage at all. No liking for me, no liking for the power of being my consort...not even any thoughts of how his marriage could help his kingdom."

She rolled her eyes. "I hope that the next one is better," she added. "Because I am *not* marrying Hedrick!"

"Tell your parents," Emily advised dryly. "Come to think of it, how can we send a message back to Whitehall?"

Alassa frowned as she started to undo her dress. The maids had been distressed when Alassa had ordered them to leave without undressing her, but Alassa had been insistent. Besides, getting out of the dress was a great deal easier than putting it on. And she wasn't expected to wear it again for months, if at all. The sheer scale of waste was appalling, Emily had decided. Even by the standards of a royal family, the dresses weren't *cheap*.

"If you don't mind it being read, you can use the communications sorcerer," Alassa said, finally. "Lady Barb will have used him to inform my parents that we arrived here safely. But if you do want to keep the contents to yourself, you'll have to send it via courier in a sealed envelope. The Allied Lands work hard to keep their couriers safe from interference."

Emily nodded, sourly. "Do I have to go down to the city to hire one?"

Alassa snorted. "You're in a royal castle," she said, dryly. "Just call one tomorrow, once you've written the message. One will come."

She finished undressing and walked over to the mirror. Her skin showed no trace of the stresses of the journey, or the dancing they'd done for hours after dinner. Emily almost envied her, even though she could hear the tiredness in her friend's voice. *Her* body showed too many signs of stress, even after months of heavy exercise in Martial Magic. At least she didn't ache so badly these days.

"We have to be away early tomorrow," Alassa said. "We can't show *too* much interest in one place, or other suitors will start wondering if we've made arrangements with King Jorlem."

Emily finished pulling off her dress and underclothes, then walked over to the trunk and retrieved her nightgown. Alassa might feel comfortable sleeping without anything covering her, but Emily had never been able to sleep naked. On Earth, she had sometimes worried about her stepfather coming into the room, particularly when he'd been drunk. And in Whitehall, she'd never had a room of her own. She had always shared with two other girls.

"Good night," she said, shaking her head at Alassa's massive bed. It looked easily large enough to hold seven people without them having to be very friendly. "How do we turn off the candles?"

"You don't," Alassa said. "I can draw the curtains around the bed, but..."

She scowled. "I shall have words with Nightingale," she added. "You *have* to sleep in the light."

Emily shaped a spell in her mind and then cast it towards the candles. *Darkness* was a simple spell with a number of military applications. It created a zone of absolute darkness that was nearly impossible to see through without powerful magic, or spells attuned to the original spell. The user could easily sneak up on someone before they managed to dispel the darkness, or use it as cover for an escape.

She swore out loud as she realized her mistake. With the candles shrouded, the entire room had plunged into darkness. Alassa tittered as Emily generated a simple light globe and found her way to her bed, climbing in and pulling the sheets up to cover her body. The bed might have looked crude, but it was comfortable. Although, she had to admit, after sleeping on the hard ground more than once, *anything* would have felt comfortable.

"Good night," Alassa said. "Lady Barb will wake us in the morning."

Emily closed her eyes and...

She snapped awake, her eyes springing open and peering into the darkness. Something was wrong. She couldn't say what had woken her, except perhaps the training and experience the sergeants had hammered into her head. One of their many tests had been to have someone sneak up on the pupils while they were sleeping, ready to perform a nasty trick that would teach them not to fall asleep in hostile territory–or at least to set wards and other traps to ensure that sneaking up on them wasn't easy. Emily still remembered the humiliation of waking up to discover that she–and the other Redshirts–had been tied up and rendered completely helpless. Someone with bad intentions could have easily slit their throats while they were sleeping.

For a long moment, she heard nothing, apart from a faint snoring from Alassa. They had never shared a room together before, but Aloha snored and Emily had eventually grown used to sleeping through it. And then she'd learned how to cast silencing charms that had made the whole matter irrelevant, leaving her to wonder why she hadn't thought of it earlier. Emily listened, carefully, unsure of what had awoken her. And then she heard the very light tread of someone trying hard not to make a sound.

The sergeants had taught her how to *listen* to her surroundings. She'd been blindfolded while the other trainees tried to sneak up on her. One of them–Jade, she recalled–had the bright idea of tossing a shoe over her head to create a distraction, for which he had received a pat on the back from Sergeant Miles. Now, though, she held herself still as she listened, trying to pick out the sounds of individual people. *Someone* was in the room.

One person, she decided, after a long moment. There only seemed to be one person in the room, apart from herself and Alassa. And it probably wasn't Alassa or one of her escorts; surely, not even Nightingale would come into the princess's room while she was sleeping. Besides, he would probably have announced himself, rather than sneaking in...unless he wanted to peek at a sleeping beauty. Emily pushed the thought aside savagely as she strained her ears for other clues. Nightingale would have to be insane to try to sneak up on a sorceress-in-training.

Emily braced herself, recalling what she could of the room's layout. The trunks were at the far end of Alassa's bed; they hadn't had time to push them to one side. Her own bed was in one corner...maybe she could roll out of bed without being heard. But then, if someone *was* trying to sneak in, they'd be listening carefully for signs of trouble. Emily peered into the darkness, wondering if she dared use one of the spells Sergeant Miles had taught her. She could see in the darkness like a cat, if she used the spell, but it would also reveal that she was awake. If, of course, the intruder was sensitive to magic...

Maybe it's the Prince, hoping for a more intimate meeting, Emily thought, then dismissed it with a shrug. Hedrick hadn't shown the imagination necessary to be a royal brat, let alone a royal would-be rapist. And Alassa wouldn't have led him on like that. Could it be the other Prince? Some instinct told her that it was unlikely, although she wasn't sure why. Too many of the lessons the sergeants had taught her to trust her instincts without really knowing why she knew something.

But she had to do something. Carefully, she concentrated on the spell that had plunged the room into darkness. It was still there, still drawing on her mana; it needed so little power that she could have maintained it all night without feeling the drain. Closing her eyes, Emily reached out towards the spell and cut off the mana. It faded away rapidly, allowing the candles to shine out and illuminate the room. They weren't particularly bright, not compared to a magical light, but anyone who was used to the darkness would think that they had suddenly stared into the sun. Emily heard a curse in a feminine voice and opened her own eyes, using one hand to shield herself. One of the maids stood at the far end of Alassa's bed, holding a stone wand in one hand.

Emily threw a freeze spell, as she had been trained to do in Martial Magic. The maid lifted the wand and deflected it, somehow. Emily blinked in surprise, before realizing that someone had loaded the wand with spells and charged it with mana, allowing her to use magic without actually having the gift. Or maybe she was just a very poor magician. Her expression seemed curiously dull for someone who had been trying to break into a princess's room.

And then she plucked a knife off her belt and threw it at Emily.

Emily ducked, silently thanking the sergeants for their training. Most magicians relied on their magic, they'd warned, which left them vulnerable when their magic failed them. The knife struck the wall in a shower of bright red sparks, drawing

Emily's attention to the blade. It was stone, with a number of runes cut into the hilt, runes that helped to channel mana and life force. A necromancer? But why would a necromancer use a wand?

Scream, you idiot, she told herself. The sergeants had also told her that if an attack was about to take place, the person standing watch should make a loud noise. How the hell had she forgotten that? She bellowed "INTRUDER" as loudly as she could, while launching a second spell at the maid. The maid deflected it with her wand, just as Alassa poked her head out of the curtains. Emily took advantage of the sudden distraction to fire off a binding spell and watched the maid crumple to the ground, ropes appearing from nowhere and tying her up. It was a far more complex spell than the freeze jinx, Sergeant Miles had explained, but it was also far harder to deflect. The wand clattered to the floor as the maid let go of it, then she hit the ground herself.

The door burst open, revealing Lady Barb. She was carrying a glowing sword in one hand, while deadly balefire crackled around the other. And she was wearing full uniform...had she even slept? Part of Emily's mind wondered just what she'd been doing while a maid crept into Alassa's room—but then, the maid had been good at sneaking around. Who knew what other passageways there might be into the guest quarters?

"Get away from her," Lady Barb snapped. "Who *is* she?"

"She's an assassin," Emily snapped back, ignoring the instruction. The maid was staring up at her with wide frightened eyes, her breathing suddenly ragged and uneven. Emily couldn't tell if she was panicking or if she'd taken poison. There was no way to know. "And I don't know *who* she is!"

Lady Barb muttered a spell and the maid's robe disintegrated, revealing a small belt of knives and a couple of artefacts Emily didn't recognize. "Cursed," Lady Barb muttered, as she removed the knives without touching the blades. "And very dangerous."

"By the gods," Nightingale's voice said. "Is Her Highness safe?"

Alassa drew herself up, crossing her arms under her bare breasts, and glared at him. "Her Highness is safe," she snapped. "And Her Highness wishes you to get out of here. Now."

Nightingale hesitated, as if he were on the verge of protesting, and then walked out of the room. Outside, Emily could hear frantic demands for information from the other guards, all of whom had been bypassed. Heads would be rolling, Emily realized, and King Randor might make sure that it happened literally. If Alassa had been assassinated, the succession crisis would take place at once.

"Stay on the bed," Lady Barb ordered Alassa. She looked over at Emily. "Do you recognize the runes on the blades?"

Emily had to fight to keep herself from looking away. "No," she said, finally. "I've never studied runes properly."

A cursed blade would be lethal, even if the target was only scratched. Given time, an ingenious enchanter could produce one that would be lethal only to a single specific victim. Or the reverse, ensuring that the blade could never be turned against its owner. She'd barely studied enchanting weapons, but from what the sergeants had said she knew that some killed instantly while others inflicted a nasty curse on their target.

"Necromantic runes," Lady Barb said. "Why were they on her blade?"

Emily stood up, walked back to her bed and looked down on the knife that had been flung at her. It was stone, just like the knife Shadye had pressed into her hand six months ago, but it felt *different*. Shadye's knife had been drenched in the blood of the innocent—and Sergeant Harkin, who had insisted that Emily kill him, knowing that his *lack* of magic would give Shadye an unpleasant shock. This knife...was just a knife.

"It isn't a necromantic blade," she said. Absently, she ran a pair of testing charms over the knife, finding nothing. Of course, the sergeants had also warned her that some cursed items were very good at concealing their true nature. "It doesn't have the feel of one of their knives."

She cursed her own mistake a moment later. With so few details of what had actually happened at Whitehall confirmed—and with countless rumors spreading across the Allied Lands—she had just given Lady Barb another reason not to trust her. Picking up a pillow, she used it to pick up the blade and carry it over to where Lady Barb had put the other weapons, then looked at the maid. She was shaking with fear.

"She wasn't a magician," Emily added.

"So it would seem," Lady Barb agreed. She picked up the girl's wand and examined it. "A very basic weapon, charged with mana—not a tool for more complex spellwork. I wonder who created it."

Alassa and Emily exchanged glances, then Alassa spoke what they were both thinking. "Hedrick?"

"He doesn't benefit at all from your death, Your Highness," Lady Barb pointed out. "At best, he loses his chance to be King of Zangaria. At worst, he gets blamed for your murder and his father hands him over to your father in chains. It's hard to see who *does* benefit from your death."

She reached out, grabbed the maid by the shoulders and pulled her to her feet. "Tell me," she said, staring into the maid's eyes, "why did you try to kill the princess?"

The maid staggered, then sagged in Lady Barb's hands. "She's fainted," Lady Barb observed, with a hint of disgust. "I'd better go talk to His Majesty. Someone will have to tell him what happened before he gets it from the rumors that will already be fanning around."

Alassa nodded, although Emily could tell that she was worried. She'd been injured before—Emily had almost killed her on their second meeting, although it had been an accident—but facing assassins in the darkness was different. And the assassin had been one of the servants, the men and women who were beneath her notice. Who else might intend to pick up a knife and bury it in Alassa's back?

"I want you to ward all the doors," Lady Barb ordered Emily. "And then do *not* come out until I call you. Whoever else tries to get in, don't let them. And feel free to use lethal force if they prove too insistent."

"Understood," Emily said. She scowled as a thought struck her. "Why didn't you ward the doors yourself?"

"It is insulting to King Jorlem to suggest that we don't trust him," Lady Barb admitted. Her face twisted into a bitter sneer. "I think we're past that, right now."

She threw the bound maid over her shoulder, used a spell to pick up the knives and the wand, then headed for the door. "Remember what I said," she added. "No one gets in until I call you."

Emily watched her close the door, then started to ward it. Warding a room from the inside was simple, but it could also be dangerous when the magician wasn't keyed into the overall protective wards. It was quite possible that the Court Wizard would complain loudly–but, as Lady Barb had pointed out, they were beyond caring. And it was also possible that the Court Wizard had a hand in the whole affair. Just because neither Emily nor Lady Barb had been able to think of a motive didn't mean that someone else *couldn't*...

And if they *had* managed to blame it on the necromancers...?

"Can you sleep here?" Alassa asked. Her perfect face looked worried, almost scared. She'd known that she was a potential target from birth, but it hadn't been until meeting Emily that she'd really come to believe it. "The bed is big enough for both of us."

Emily hesitated, then nodded slowly. "Just let me finish doing the wards first," she said. "You go to sleep. I'll join you in a moment."

"If I can sleep," Alassa said. "I... why did she want me dead?"

"I wish I knew," Emily said. She finished the wards and straightened up. Sharing a bed was something she had *never* done, but Alassa needed it. "We'll find out tomorrow."

Chapter Eleven

Lady Barb had let them sleep in, Emily was surprised to realize when she was finally woken by the sound of banging on the door. Rolling out of bed, Emily shaped a spell in her mind as she padded over to the door, cancelled the ward and opened it. Lady Barb stood there, looking rather tired. Emily guessed that she hadn't slept at all since the assassin had been caught.

"Get washed and dressed–traveling clothes," Lady Barb ordered. Two maids stood behind her, carrying another massive tub of warm water. "Then we have to speak to His Majesty."

Emily nodded, then looked at the maids. "Are they…safe?"

"We searched them," Lady Barb said, "but keep an eye on them anyway."

The maids stepped into the room and put the tub down on the floor. Lady Barb followed them and assumed a watchful pose, leaning against one wall. Emily scowled as she realized that that they were going to have even less privacy that she'd thought, then turned and walked back to the bed. Alassa was waking up slowly, one hand on her dagger.

"Time to get up," Emily said. She looked over at Lady Barb. "Is there any chance of a large mug of Kava?"

"Downstairs," Lady Barb said. "If you are not rested, you can sleep in the carriage."

Emily didn't feel very rested–but then, drifting off to sleep after the maid had been captured had been difficult. The wards she'd constructed around the room weren't very strong, certainly not strong enough to stand up to a combat sorcerer for more than a few minutes. On the other hand, if someone *had* tried to break them down, she would have been alerted before it was too late. Sleeping in the rocking carriage suddenly seemed like a very good idea.

She tried to ignore the maids as she washed, then dressed herself in traveling clothes. Alassa did the same, waving away their attempts to help her. Emily had to smile as Alassa used a very basic spell to keep her hair under control, even though neither of them had been able to get the spell to remain in place permanently. A maid who was close enough to brush Alassa's hair was also close enough to cut her throat.

Lady Barb inspected them both quickly, then led the way out of the room. Outside, the guards were on the alert, clutching weapons as they eyed their local counterparts suspiciously. Emily wasn't very reassured; the maid had slipped past them without being noticed, which should have been impossible. But Sergeant Miles had taught her that someone with magic could sneak past anyone without magic, as long as they were careful and didn't make silly mistakes. And if the necromancers really were involved, the guards would last about as long as a snowflake in hell.

"The castle is on alert," Lady Barb muttered, as they walked down a corridor. Guards were everywhere, although Emily had a feeling that there were so many guards that someone with bad intentions could probably sneak through in the confusion. "And King Jorlem is very unhappy at what almost happened to you."

Emily had expected to return to the grand hall, but instead Lady Barb led them into a smaller chamber, barely larger than their room. King Jorlem and his younger son sat at a long table; they stood up as Alassa entered the room. The king looked tired, but grimly determined; Prince Hedrick, Alassa's prospective husband, didn't seem to care that Alassa had almost been assassinated. Crown Prince Dater was nowhere to be seen.

"Please, be seated," King Jorlem said. "I will have food brought in for you."

"Thank you," Alassa said, as she took the seat facing King Jorlem. "Right now, we need Kava more than anything else."

"It will be provided," King Jorlem assured her. "And I deeply regret what happened last night."

Emily leaned forward. "Do you know why she did it?"

"The Court Wizard is examining her now," the king said. If he was annoyed at *Emily* asking him a question, he said nothing. "Hopefully, we should have answers before you depart."

Emily concealed a flash of bitter amusement as the maids put steaming mugs of Kava in front of them. It was impossible to escape the feeling that King Jorlem wanted them out of his castle, which made sense if he believed that the necromancers were involved. Whitehall hadn't been able to keep Shadye out for long—certainly not with his secret weapon in the castle itself—and Castle Alluvia's defenses were flimsy in comparison. A necromancer would knock down the walls and smash the castle flat.

But then, she asked herself, *why would they try to assassinate Alassa when they could just take out the entire castle?*

Necromancers were insane. Everyone knew that—but Emily knew that they could also be surprisingly rational. Or, for that matter, delay their pleasures long enough to allow all the pieces to fall into place. And yet she found it hard to understand why a necromancer would use a maid to assassinate Alassa. Unless they wanted King Jorlem blamed for the attack...but that seemed rather subtle for a necromancer. She rubbed the side of her head, cursing the tiredness under her breath. Maybe it would make more sense when she felt better.

She sipped her Kava as the servants returned, bringing large platters of meat, eggs and bread. Once, just looking at the meal would have made her feel sick; now, thankfully, she could eat it—and be grateful for a high-energy breakfast. There were almost no fatties in Whitehall; magic was demanding, even of those who didn't take plenty of physical exercise along with their magic studies. The food and drink made her feel a little better, although the necromantic plot—if it was a necromantic plot—didn't make any more sense. But then, looking for sense in an insane mind was probably a waste of time.

Prince Hedrick still didn't seem to show any real reaction to Alassa—or anyone else, for that matter. He just sat there languidly, seemingly unwilling to do anything. Emily watched him eat with a dainty caution that seemed almost the exact opposite of his elder brother, wondering just what was going through his mind. If he had graduated from Whitehall, he couldn't be stupid—or touched in the head, as the locals said. Stupid magicians lasted about as long as it took them to mess up a spell and blow themselves to bits.

The food wasn't quite as good as the meals at Whitehall, she decided, as she finished her meal and pushed the plate to one side. On the other hand, she had a feeling that they would be grateful for it; there hadn't really been any lunch yesterday, not even combat rations. She had realized that nobles considered sandwiches to be commoner food during her first month at Whitehall, but it seemed odd that they would starve themselves deliberately while traveling.

She looked up as the door opened, revealing Crown Prince Dater and the Court Wizard. They were followed by five other men in military tunics, two of them clearly magicians even though they weren't wearing robes or carrying staffs. Emily frowned inwardly as she saw one of them looking at her, then looking away sharply when he realized that she had realized that he was staring. Was he impressed with her reputation, Emily asked herself, or was he being wary? Were the other magicians intended to back the Court Wizard up if he confronted *Emily*?

"Father," Crown Prince Dater said, with a bow. "We have completed the interrogation of the maid."

Of course, Emily realized. He'd told her that it was his job to serve as chief investigator of any serious crime. And this one *definitely* involved the nobility.

"Good," King Jorlem said. "And what have you discovered?"

"Ails was deeply in love with Hedrick," Dater said. He sounded as if he didn't quite believe what he was saying. "She believed that he was going to marry Princess Alassa and go to live in Zangaria, that her only hope for keeping him with her was to murder the princess before it was too late."

Lady Barb swung around to stare at Prince Hedrick. "And what do *you* know about this?"

Hedrick showed the first trace of any real emotion—annoyance—that Emily had seen on him.

"I know nothing about it," he said. "I certainly did not know that she was in love with me."

"And no doubt you didn't tumble her when you had a moment," Lady Barb sneered. She turned back to the Crown Prince. "I thought that all of your servants were under loyalty and obedience spells. How could she successfully break into the princess's room and come close to murdering her?"

"We believe that she convinced herself that murdering the princess was in the crown's best interest," the Court Wizard said. "As such, she could have brought herself to assassinate the princess…"

Emily frowned inwardly as Lady Barb picked away at the explanation. She'd studied mind control spells after Shadye had used one on her and discovered that they were tricky things to use properly. The more powerful the spell, the greater the risk of side-effects, including reducing the intelligence of the victim. Most servants were under spells that prevented them from knowingly doing anything to harm their masters, but if the maid had reasoned out that killing Alassa was in their best interests, she could have done it. Perhaps.

She held up a hand before the argument could grow any worse. "Where did she get the wand? And the knives?"

Dater frowned. "We are investigating," he said. "Whoever made the wand was clearly a formidable enchanter, but there are at least seven possible suspects in the city. The maid herself was not a magician. As for the knives…they're really nothing more than stone. They could have come from anywhere."

But the runes couldn't have, Emily thought. *Either they were necromantic blades that simply hadn't been used before or they were fakes, intended to convince us that we were looking at necromantic work.*

Stone knives weren't uncommon outside the nobility, she'd learned, when she'd been researching how magic interacted with materials. Professor Thande, in one of his many digressions, had explained that stone could soak up a surprising amount of magic, or channel it without turning to dust. Some metals allowed faster passage of magic, but they tended to decay rapidly. The necromancers used stone tools because metal knives would destroy themselves before they had finished draining every last drop of mana and life energy from the corpse.

But there was no point in trying to ban stone knives. They were simply too common—and besides, iron was too expensive. Emily had actually managed to dig the formula for making steel out of her mind and pass it on to the blacksmiths, but they hadn't managed to actually produce it yet. And aluminium was shockingly expensive. If Emily had been carrying a couple of cans of fizzy drink when she'd been yanked into the new world, she would have been set up for life. Aluminium hadn't become commonplace on Earth until new techniques for producing it had been discovered.

"Really," Lady Barb said. She shot Emily a sharp glance, no doubt wishing to question her further on why she knew that the blades weren't necromantic, then looked back at the Crown Prince. "I would like to interrogate the girl for myself."

"I'm afraid that won't be possible," the Court Wizard said. "I… broke her mind."

Lady Barb's eyes glittered. "Your servant should have been under spells that made it impossible for her to lie to you," she said, addressing the Crown Prince. "Why was it necessary to break her mind while questioning her?"

There was a long uncomfortable pause. "She was not quite right in the head," Dater said, finally. "Either because she fell in love with Hedrick"—he shot his brother a snide glance, which brought no visible response—"or because there was something wrong with the obedience spells. She just started to babble when we asked her questions."

"Or someone befuddled her," Lady Barb pointed out. "Did you check for that before you started poking into her mind?"

Emily shivered. A sorcerer could peer into someone's mind, if they were prepared to commit what was effectively mental rape. But it had very real effects, including causing terrible pain and—perhaps—snapping someone into insanity. What would it do to a girl who was already under an obedience spell—and, perhaps, someone else's spells too? She could easily see a necromancer pushing the first set of spells aside, then imposing his own…but why would they be so subtle? It wasn't in their nature.

But who else benefited from Alassa's death?

King Jorlem didn't benefit at all. He would have risked war with Zangaria if the princess died while in his castle. And if Hedrick didn't want to marry Alassa, he could have gotten out of it without threatening his father's kingdom.

And no one in Zangaria benefited. Without a clearly defined heir to the throne, there would be civil war once King Randor died. Such chaos in the north would suck in the neighboring nations, each one looking for its own advantage. Eventually, the necromancers might be able to take advantage of a weakened Allied Lands…maybe it was their work after all. But it was still oddly subtle. There was no reason why they couldn't achieve the same results by attacking Castle Alluvia openly.

Emily shook her head, tiredly. Maybe she was underestimating them. Or maybe she was missing something obvious.

"So we are left with a mystery," Lady Barb concluded. "A young maid who might have been so deeply in love that she risks a war between two countries, a young maid who has *never* been touched by the prince she loves. Or a young maid who was used as a tool by someone else in an attempt to assassinate Princess Alassa. I do not like mysteries."

"You go too far," Dater snapped. "We handled this investigation as carefully as we could…"

King Jorlem tapped the table sharply, silencing his son. "Her first priority is safe-guarding Alassa," he said. "Hedrick; did you know *anything* about this?"

His son shook his head. "I never even looked at her," he said. "I had no idea she cared so much."

Emily scowled, inwardly. Even without obedience spells, the maids wouldn't have been able to say no if the princes had wanted to have some fun with them. God knew that plenty of kings and princes on Earth had managed to have bastard children, often healthier children than they'd had with their wives. Henry VIII had even tried to have his bastard son put into the line of succession, although that had been before the birth of his sickly legitimate son. He had probably rolled over in his grave when he realized that both of his daughters had sat on the throne after him.

But the princes might not have *cared* all that much about the maids. It was easy to imagine one of them giving gifts to his favored maid, or simply using her and then pushing her aside. And why would the maid become infatuated with Prince Hedrick? Why not his considerably more handsome elder brother?

Maybe you're just being shallow, Emily told herself, and snorted.

"We will accept that, for the moment," Lady Barb said, finally. "King Randor has instructed us to continue with the progression, despite the fact that we are already running late. With your permission, Your Majesty, we will depart for Red Rose."

"Hedrick should be ready to go with you," King Jorlem said. He gave his son a sharp look. "And I'm sure that he will be a credit to the kingdom."

Emily doubted that, but held her tongue.

"We will leave in twenty chimes," Lady Barb informed Hedrick. "Be there—or you can catch up with us."

"I think we can forgo the full departure ceremony," King Jorlem said, standing up. His sons followed him a moment later. "It has been a pleasure seeing you again, Alassa. You were barely knee-high when I last saw you."

Alassa stood up, walked around the table and gave him a formal embrace. The crown prince wrapped her in a bearhug, then whispered something in her ear that made her giggle. Hedrick didn't even bother to hug her, although that might have been protocol. He *was* going to be traveling with them. Emily had listened carefully to all of Alassa's lectures, but she knew that she didn't have all of the protocols fixed in her head.

"And it was interesting to meet the famous Necromancer's Bane," the king added, looking at Emily. "The Allied Lands owe you a great debt."

"Thank you," Emily said. She stood up and then curtseyed as best as she could in the traveling clothes. "And thank you for the hospitality."

Lady Barb shot her a sharp look—clearly, that was pushing the limits—but the king merely laughed.

"I wish you were staying for longer," he said. He certainly *sounded* sincere, but he'd been king long enough to know how to lie convincingly. "There is so much we could have shown you—and many of the sorcerers wish to talk to you. But it is not to be."

He waved his hand in a ritual pattern. "May the gods continue to smile upon your journey," he added. His voice softened as he looked at Alassa. "And may the life of two become one."

Emily watched him walk out of the room, followed by his two sons, then looked at Alassa and raised an eyebrow.

"He's expressing the hope that I will marry soon," Alassa said. She turned and started to walk towards the door. "Come on. We're going to spend most of the day in the carriage. Again."

Chapter Twelve

NIGHTINGALE MET THEM AS THEY WALKED OUT OF THE CASTLE AND INTO THE COURT-yard, drawing Lady Barb aside for a frantic conversation. Emily heard enough to realize that he was annoyed at having been left out of breakfast with King Jorlem, although she couldn't tell if he thought he'd been insulted or if he'd thought he should be there to support Alassa. Lady Barb's response was quiet, too quiet for Emily to hear, but it managed to convince Nightingale to shut up. Emily was almost impressed.

Prince Hedrick had a coach of his own, along with a small troop of soldiers as an escort. Emily was relieved; she'd worried that they'd wind up sharing a carriage with the Prince, which would have prevented them from talking openly. She scrambled up into the carriage and watched as Alassa waved goodbye to the castle's staff, before she scrambled up to sit beside Emily. A moment later, the carriage lurched into life.

"We're several hours late," Alassa observed. "We may end up spending two days in Red Rose."

Emily shrugged. "Is your father going to be happy?"

"Probably not," Alassa muttered. "But cancelling engagements would cause diplomatic storms. I'm not just meant to make an appearance; I'm meant to dance with the princes and show myself to the crowds."

"But you were attacked," Emily protested. "Isn't your safety important?"

"So is pleasing—or at least refraining from offending—the other Kings," Alassa said, sourly. She looked out of the window for a long moment, eying the cheering crowds. "If someone like you causes a diplomatic incident, it can be smoothed over. But me? If I cause a diplomatic incident, the entire kingdom could suffer."

Emily nodded and straightened up. "That blade wasn't a necromantic weapon," she said, flatly. "I handled Shadye's knife and it felt...*evil*. The blades the maid carried were just ordinary blades, cursed to kill whoever they cut."

"And she was carrying several of them," Alassa agreed. "Not the sort of thing anyone sane would do with a necromantic weapon. Or an Object of Power."

Enchanted objects were common, but they rarely lasted very long, unless the spells holding them together were renewed on a regular basis. Those objects that *did* remain charged for decades—or centuries—were often incredibly powerful, with hundreds of legends surrounding them. Emily had been amused to discover that Objects of Power were more common in legend than in reality. Besides, there was nothing that quite matched the One Ring or the Deathly Hallows, something so powerful that nothing could stand against it.

"I don't think it *was* the necromancers," Emily said, dragging her thoughts back to the topic at hand. "And I don't see how King Jorlem benefits from arranging your death. Can you?"

Alassa shook her head.

"So," Emily said. "Who does that leave?"

She scowled, thoughtfully. "Who was next in line to the throne before you were born?"

"The Duke of Iron—my uncle," Alassa said. "But he's not much younger than my father. If he took the throne, he wouldn't be on it for very long before death took him. He did marry a younger woman, but they never managed to have children."

Emily could envisage a royal uncle killing the princess, *then* the King, just so he could take the throne, but surely someone else would have considered the possibility. And besides, presumably the duke couldn't lie to his brother. Any plot would have been sniffed out before it was too late.

"He's a good man," Alassa added. "And he spends most of his time near the border anyway. He dislikes coming in to Court."

"I like him already," Emily said. They shared a smile. "Who else is there?"

Alassa considered. "There are the Nine Barons," she said, after a moment. "They have some claim to the throne, but it is very thin. The strongest would be Baron Silver, at least by marriage; he's my mother's brother. But she was the youngest child in his family, so she wouldn't have been very important if she *hadn't* married my father."

"I'm confused," Emily admitted. She rubbed her forehead. "Baron Silver is your uncle, right? Your mother's brother." Alassa nodded. "Doesn't that give him a claim to the throne?"

"No, although he *could* try to claim a regency," Alassa explained. "The other barons would unite against him if he tried a blatant power grab."

"So your father married the baron's daughter," Emily mused. "Couldn't you marry one of their sons?"

"It would put one of their children on the throne," Alassa reminded her. "Even as consort, he'd have a disturbing amount of influence. The other barons wouldn't stand for it."

Emily rolled her eyes. Clearly, King Randor hadn't hesitated to marry a baron's daughter, but princesses had to put up with different rules. Although it *was* possible that they had a point; a king could seek his pleasure elsewhere, while a queen had to remain faithful to her husband. It all seemed absurd to her. Why couldn't Alassa simply find someone to impregnate her and then have no further contact with him?

"Because they wouldn't have been sealed and brought into the Royal Bloodline," Alassa explained, when Emily asked. "And besides, they would want to know who had fathered my child. Who knows *what* could happen in the future?"

"You could marry a commoner," Emily suggested. "Someone who..."

"You really are from somewhere *different*," Alassa said, in tones of absolute disbelief. "What do you think that would *do* to the bloodlines?"

Emily wondered just how long that would last. If commoners had been getting wealthier since Bryon and Alexis III—even before Emily had started introducing her innovations—they would eventually start demanding a greater say in how the money was spent. Or, for that matter, offering to meet noble debts in exchange for marrying into quality. Emily had no idea how stable such a marriage would be, if one had been born noble and the other a commoner, but she suspected that it would happen. And then...

Introducing new blood might be just what the nobility needed. Inbreeding had severely damaged aristocracies in the past. But they'd have to get over their prejudices first.

"So you really have to choose between marrying an outsider and praying that it doesn't lead you into trouble, or remaining unmarried," Emily said. She shook her head a moment later. "No, you *can't* remain unmarried."

"No," Alassa agreed. She lowered her eyes for a long moment. "Did you see that it was Hedrick who learned magic?"

Emily nodded.

"The crown prince is rarely trained in formal magic," Alassa said. "*I* was only allowed to go to Whitehall because I have no siblings. Ideally, I would have taken the throne and my sister would have been my magical support. People...worry about the effect of sorcery on their ruler's mind."

She smiled, ruefully. "My father isn't *that* powerful," she added, "or perhaps he would have taught me himself. As it is, people worry more about sorceresses. They think that women with power are dangerous."

Emily snorted. That had been true in her world's history, too. The Romans and Greeks had feared powerful women, while in medieval Europe the mere accusation of witchcraft had often been enough to condemn even the most aristocratic of women. But here, they might have a point. Not all of the full-fledged sorcerers she had met had been stable—and necromancers were completely insane. And she'd heard of sorcerer-kings who had allowed their lust for power to overwhelm their common sense.

"They expect a strong man to take you in hand," she said, quietly. How could *anyone* think like that? But if they'd known Alassa while she was a brat, they might have had a point about that too. A year ago, the barons had probably feared what would happen if Alassa had been allowed to take the throne. "And to rule in your stead, if necessary."

"Yes," Alassa said. Her face twisted into a snarl. "Bastards!"

Emily nodded in sympathy. Zangaria—and the rest of the Allied Lands—seemed to be governed by sexist principles. Emily found them outrageous and stupid, not least because she knew that there were plenty of queens who had governed successfully in Earth's history. But Zangaria had never had a female queen—and it did have a tradition that women were supposed to follow their husbands. Whoever married Alassa would inherit a ready-made power base he could use to make himself very prominent indeed.

And if they'd known her before she went to Whitehall—and they would have known her—they might have been right to worry.

She turned and looked out of the window, watching as farmland gave way to tiny hamlets before returning to farmland. Most farms were small, worked by hand and animal power, despite the prevalence of magic in the world. Emily had sketched out plans for steam engines that would transform Zangaria–and then the rest of the planet–along with several other ideas that craftsmen might be able to turn into something workable. But it wouldn't always be beneficial, she knew. The cotton gin had been invented just in time to make slavery economically profitable again.

A handful of peasants were working in the field, not bothering to look up as the procession flashed by. Emily wondered at their dull clothes and permanently tired expressions, wondering why magic wasn't used to help them. But she knew the answer to that; even the simplest of healing spells consumed a surprising amount of energy. If every magician in Whitehall tried to offer healing without fee, they'd drain themselves overnight and accomplish very little. And the peasants, having a very hard life, would age rapidly. Living in filth didn't help.

She shuddered as they raced past a farmhouse that was really more like a shack. Little children were running around, almost all naked. Even the ones that wore some clothes were wearing nothing more than loincloths. She caught sight of a woman working at a spinning wheel and shuddered as she realized that the woman couldn't be much older than Emily herself. Her belly was swelling with yet another pregnancy.

Jade had asked Emily to marry him at seventeen, just below legal age on Earth. It had never really sunk into Emily's mind that legal age in the Allied Lands was defined as after a girl started her first period. But then, none of her school friends had been married…the girl she'd seen, for a brief moment, hadn't won the genetic lottery. Without magic, without money, she'd simply been married off as early as possible. Emily doubted that she would live more than another ten years.

Maybe you're wrong, she told herself. But she doubted it.

She must have dozed off, for the next thing she knew was that the carriage had stopped and someone was banging on the door. Emily opened the door and jumped down to the ground, then turned to help Alassa step down. They were in the midst of a city, with mountains rising up all around them. Oddly, there were only a handful of people staring at the royal party, but Emily found it something of a relief. Alassa didn't seem to care.

"Welcome to the Republic of Tarn," Lady Barb said. "We planned to stop here for lunch, but we don't have much time so eat quickly."

She meant it too, Emily realized, as she followed Lady Barb into a small inn. There were no city fathers waiting for them, no ceremonies they had to endure; all they had to do was eat and drink. Emily checked the food automatically, then started to eat as much as she could. The meal was simple–Nightingale could be heard grumbling that it wasn't suitable for a princess–but surprisingly tasty. Besides, the inn was much cleaner than the accommodation in the last castle. Even the toilets were clean.

"The city fathers have laws enforcing hygiene," Lady Barb explained, when Emily asked. Being away from the last castle seemed to have improved her mood, although magic crackled around her protectively. "Anyone who throws their slops into the streets gets publicly beaten. Innkeepers are expected to keep their dwellings *clean*. Those who are caught flouting the law are sold into slavery and made to clean the city."

Emily shuddered. It sounded awful. On the other hand, the city fathers did have a point. Poor hygiene accounted for most of the epidemics that had ravaged the medieval world, before medical science had advanced to the point where germs were understood—although it had taken longer for everyone to accept that something as simple as washing one's hands after going to the toilet could help prevent the spread of disease. Some doctors had been surprisingly reluctant to accept it, even though they'd been *doctors*. Didn't they know that their first duty was to their patients?

And Tarn seemed to smell much better than Dragon's Den.

"The Republic sits between Alluvia and Red Rose," Lady Barb added, clearly taking advantage of the opportunity to educate Alassa about the city. "Simply put, the city can support itself through careful farming, but it cannot hope to expand into either kingdom—both are happy to leave it independent as a buffer between them. It also allows for a great deal of trade that might not be officially acknowledged."

Smuggling, Emily silently translated. And if it was a republic, was it *democratic*?

"The city fathers are the heads of the most powerful families in the city," Lady Barb said, when Emily asked how the city was governed. "The rest of the population doesn't have any say in decisions, unless the council is deadlocked and they have to put the matter to the free population. But the city fathers are themselves bound by the law."

Emily suspected that it was actually a great deal more complicated than that, but she got the general idea. Not a democracy in the sense she understood it, then, but perhaps a more lawful state than an absolute monarchy. And besides, the city fathers would know that they didn't dare push people too far. The results might be disastrous.

"Rather like Dragon's Den," Alassa said, clearly remembering their brief meeting with the city fathers after they'd been kidnapped. "The council has absolute power as long as it doesn't push too far."

"True," Lady Barb agreed. "And isn't that true of every government?"

She waved to the innkeeper and paid out a small pile of gold coins. The innkeeper carried them over to a set of scales, weighed them carefully, then totted up what they owed. Emily watched in some amusement, remembering her first experience with gold coins; none of them, even the ones issued by a single kingdom, were standardized. Naturally, their value tended to fluctuate too. It didn't help that various alchemists had actually succeeded in turning lead into gold, although it didn't last long and was easily detectable with the right spells. Professor Thande had claimed that turning gold into lead lasted longer, but apparently it wasn't a skill that was in great demand.

I'm going to have to set up a proper mint, Emily thought, as Lady Barb motioned for them to stand up and head out to the carriages. *And then standardize all of the currency.*

There was no fort blocking the road into Red Rose, somewhat to Emily's surprise, before she realized that any large raiding party would have to come through Tarn before it reached the next kingdom. The mountains would make it harder for bandits to operate, although Emily suspected that they would never be eradicated completely. But if both kingdoms were quietly leaving the mountains as a barrier between them, it was likely that they rarely patrolled the area. The mountain folk wouldn't have to turn to banditry to survive.

The countryside seemed marshy, almost completely abandoned. Emily looked out of the carriage as the sun started to set in the sky, wondering if she'd been wrong about the mountains being the only natural barrier. The marshes would provide another problem for an invading army, as well as being almost completely devoid of supplies. A small party might be able to survive—the sergeants had taught Emily what plants could be safely eaten and how to obtain water—but an army would find itself in serious trouble. No doubt the inhabitants of Tarn were quietly delighted that Red Rose couldn't really expand towards them either.

Emily sighed as the stars started to appear in the sky. There was no such thing as being able to read the future in the stars—or so she had been told—but she *had* learned how to use some of them to navigate. Several of the route marches the sergeants had taken them on had been in pitch darkness. *This* world didn't have streetlights pushing back the night. And the countryside was often infested with creatures that only came out when the sun had vanished below the horizon.

"Traveling at night isn't safe," Alassa said. "But we can't stop until we reach the Red Castle."

"As long as we can stay on the road," Emily muttered. Outside, it was so dark that she could see almost nothing outside the carriage. Even the use of one of the night vision spells didn't help much. "What happens if we drive into the bog?"

"We die," Alassa said. "Hardly anyone lives here and they're never friendly to outsiders. They normally just ignore everyone, even tax collectors. But then, they have very little to collect."

Emily scowled and closed her eyes. God alone knew how long it would be before they reached the Red Castle, but she might as well try to get some sleep. There would be dancing when they arrived and she would be expected to join in. Or would she? She hadn't had to dance at Alluvia.

Wait and see, she told herself, and drifted off to sleep.

Chapter Thirteen

W AKE UP," ALASSA HISSED. "YOU'LL WANT TO SEE THIS."
Emily opened her eyes and stared out of the window. The Red Castle was rising up in front of them, a towering fairy-tale structure that seemed too fragile to be real. It couldn't possibly be intended for war, she decided. She wasn't even sure how it managed to remain stable. It shouldn't be able to exist.

Magic, she thought, remembering Whitehall's interior. *A wizard did it.*

The castle seemed to be glowing with an eerie red light, casting an odd sheen over the surrounding buildings. There didn't seem to be a full-sized city, merely a handful of buildings and guardposts. Emily guessed that the castle had actually been designed as a place for the royal family to visit when they wanted a break and would therefore be some distance from the capital city. But they couldn't rely on it in wartime. A single mana-eating spell would cripple the spells holding the castle together and it would simply collapse under its own weight.

She felt the waves of magic as the carriage clattered over the drawbridge and into a large courtyard. There was more magic running through the air than anywhere Emily had ever been, apart from Whitehall. And it felt oddly familiar, reminding her of the nexus that existed under the school, where she'd fought and beaten Shadye. Had the Red Castle been built on another nexus? The advantages of such a position were obvious—and they might explain why the castle itself was so fragile. There would be no way to take down its wards without inside help.

Which was precisely what Shadye had at Whitehall, Emily thought. The memory still horrified her. *He had me.*

The carriage stopped and she clambered out, followed by Alassa. Neither of them looked their best, Emily realized, wondering if they would be expected to change into something more comfortable before they met the King. She glanced at her watch and realized it was almost midnight. Unless the time zone was different in Red Rose…she scowled as she realized there was no way to know. The timekeeping system here didn't seem to be as well-organized as the one on Earth.

"It has been decided," Nightingale said self-importantly, "that you will have time to change before you meet the King." He waved to a handful of maids. "Take them to their rooms and help them to change."

Lady Barb followed them as they were escorted down long crystal corridors and into a single oversized room. Like Whitehall, the interior of the Red Castle was far larger on the inside than on the outside. Someone had probably spent years mapping out the basic structure, creating a building that was effectively an Object of Power in its own right. Like Whitehall, it might even have a form of intelligence, perhaps enough to manipulate its own structure. It was a true wonder of her new world.

Emily sighed when she saw that the room had a proper bathtub, large enough for four girls to sit comfortably. Baths were rare at Whitehall; the only time she'd been able to have a proper soak had been when they'd gone swimming as part of Martial

Magic. But there was no time to enjoy it; she pulled off her traveling clothes, stood briefly under the shower to wash away the dirt and grime, and then donned the next dress. Alassa pushed the maids away, used a spell to do her hair and then pulled on her own dress.

"We're going to have real problems if this goes on," she muttered. "It's already midnight."

"Yeah," Emily agreed. "How long do we have to dance for?"

They were late at the Red Castle, which meant that they would probably leave late the following morning, which meant that they would be late at the next destination...if it had been up to her, they would either have gone directly to Zangaria through the portal or stayed a couple of days at each kingdom, just to catch their breath. The punishing schedule was going to drive her mad. Or they might wind up so tired that the next assassination attempt would succeed.

"At least an hour," Alassa said. She straightened up, glared at herself in the mirror and then marched over to the door. "My father told me that being a princess brought responsibilities as well as rights."

A pity he didn't make you understand that earlier, Emily thought, as they walked through the fairy-tale corridors, surrounded by their guards. Lady Barb walked beside Emily, glancing around suspiciously as they passed servants and other guards. She didn't seem very happy to be in the Red Castle, but Emily could understand it. A castle with a mutable interior could easily be turned against them by the person in charge.

They stepped through an arch and into the main hall. The king—King Rupert, if Emily recalled correctly—stood up and waved as they entered, rather than following any form of protocol. Emily found herself liking him on sight. He was a short fat man with a jovial smile, wearing a golden tunic that glittered as it caught the light. Behind him, there were three young men and a single woman. The woman seemed almost in awe of Alassa.

"Never mind protocol," King Rupert said, as he stepped off the dais and swept Alassa up in a hug. "It has been *years* since I have had the pleasure of your company." He looked over at Emily and winked at her. "And the famed Necromancer's Bane. I have long hoped to make your acquaintance."

Alassa smiled as King Rupert let go of her. "Thank you for your welcome, Uncle Rupert," she said. "I'm sorry about the delay."

"I'm just sorry someone tried to kill you," King Rupert said. His gaze moved to Prince Hedrick. "And Hedrick! Why you're here I will never know."

"I greet you in the name of my father," Hedrick said, sullenly. He didn't seem to cope well with the absence of protocol. "And my father sent me."

"Got sick of looking at you, did he?" King Rupert asked. "Can't say I blame him. Use some of that magic to give yourself a better face, boy."

He looked back at Alassa. "But I am forgetting my manners," he added. "You will remember Jayman, of course; I think he was ten when you last saw him. My heir now—and married to a delightful young woman. I had to bribe him to convince him to attend this reception." He held up a hand and stage-whispered. "He doesn't like these parties."

Emily looked over at Prince Jayman. It was hard to see how he was related to King Rupert, because Jayman was tall, inhumanly thin and had a rather sour face, as if he were constantly biting on a lemon. And he didn't seem to be good at hiding the fact he didn't *like* being the butt of the King's jokes. He gave Emily a brief look of disdain, as if he'd discovered her hiding under his shoe, and then returned his attention to his father. Emily felt a flash of pity for his wife, wherever she was. She didn't seem to have attended.

"And then there's Slark, who is your age, and Athol, who is actually a year younger," King Rupert continued. "Both of them are in the prime of life; Athol is going to Whitehall later this year, when term resumes. It might be good for you to be engaged without actually marrying for some time."

Emily had to fight to keep a straight face as she studied the two younger princes. Slark should have been handsome, but he had a slimy appearance that gave Emily the creeps; Hedrick, whatever else could be said about him, struck her as a far better person. Athol looked reassuringly normal, but he also seemed unformed. He wouldn't be able to marry until after leaving Whitehall, at least if he intended to marry a crown princess. And he was a year younger than Alassa. Would that actually matter?

"And, finally, my daughter Mariah," King Rupert concluded. "You'll discover that you have something in common. You were both terrible brats when you were young!"

Alassa stiffened as the king laughed, although the movement would have been impossible for anyone to see without knowing Alassa very well. Princess Mariah looked to be about twelve years old, although it was impossible to be sure. She was tall, but she didn't appear to have started puberty yet. Emily couldn't help wondering if there was a reason she hadn't started to grow breasts, unless she was just a late developer.

And Mariah didn't seem to find her father very funny either.

"But I do understand that you're tired, so we are going to have only a small formal dance," King Rupert said, after a long moment. He waved a hand towards the minstrels, who began to play a waltzing tune. "Slack will give you the first dance. And Hedrick can partner Mariah around the dance floor."

Emily stepped backwards as the throne room became a dance hall. King Rupert laughed out loud as dance couples formed up, waving cheerfully to his subjects while watching Alassa with a semi-parental eye. He seemed to be almost insane—or maybe he just enjoyed life. Emily couldn't help wondering what would happen to Red Rose when the crown prince took the throne. He didn't seem inclined to turn into a cheerful King.

"Take a seat if you don't want to dance," Lady Barb said. "If you're standing up, it implies that you're looking for a partner."

"Oh," Emily said. She'd never been to a courtly ball before leaving Earth. But then, no one knew that—and those who thought they knew the truth behind her birth considered her little better than a commoner. "You're not looking for a dance partner, are you?"

"I have to keep an eye on the princess," Lady Barb reminded her, as they sat down on the seats along the edge of the hall. "Although I'm not sure that she's the one in danger."

Emily frowned. Slark seemed to be holding Alassa more tightly than necessary, his hands inching down towards her rear. He had nerve, Emily decided; even before she'd actually mastered Basic Charms Alassa had still been able to do considerable damage. Or maybe he was just too arrogant to believe she would actually harm him. There was a considerable difference between picking on a girl without aristocratic ties and a prince.

"That prince is in danger," Emily agreed, finally. "I'm not going to waste my time feeling sorry for him."

"That wasn't what I meant," Lady Barb said. There was a hint of exasperation in her voice, as if she thought Emily was deliberately evading her. "She might not have been the target of the maid's assassination attempt."

It took Emily a moment to work out what she was saying. "You mean…me? I was the target?"

Lady Barb ticked off points on her fingers as she spoke. "The maid had some very strong spells on her that should have prevented her from doing harm to the royal family," she said. "Killing Alassa should have been unthinkable, as murdering the crown princess of a much larger kingdom is an act of war—and suicide. And I don't think that Hedrick aroused that kind of passion in *anyone*."

Emily couldn't disagree. Some girls liked bad boys—there was a whole fandom built up around Draco from *Harry Potter*, even through Draco had never shown any redeeming features—but Hedrick didn't seem to be the type to attract them. He wasn't good or bad, merely…boring. Emily could imagine a maid slipping into his bed in exchange for money or a promotion, but love? Or even a crush? It seemed unlikely.

"Maybe there's more to him than meets the eye," she said, finally. "How well did he do at Whitehall?"

"He graduated as a generalist sorcerer," Lady Barb said. "I've sent a message to the grandmaster asking for specifics, but we won't get them until tomorrow—if then."

She shook her head. "Besides, killing Alassa would not benefit anyone, certainly not in the long run," she added. "Killing you, on the other hand…"

The grandmaster had shielded her from the worst of it, but Emily did know that powerful voices had called for her to be killed while she was unconscious after defeating Shadye. They'd feared that she could turn into an even greater threat, either because she was a necromancer herself—and would therefore go insane with power—or because she had somehow managed to master necromancy without the insanity. Either one would tip the balance of power drastically.

But they didn't know the truth. Emily had beaten Shadye through use of concepts from her world, concepts that she'd powered with magic. If they had known…

They would have greater reason to want me dead, she thought. *I know too much*.

It would be relatively simple, she suspected, to create an atomic-scale blast with magic. So far, no one seemed to have thought of the possibilities inherent in cracking atoms—materials science was in its infancy, at best—but *Emily* knew that if she allowed the concept to leak out, *someone* would try to make it work. And that was one of the *minor* concepts. What about antimatter? Or kinetic-energy weapons? Or wormholes? Or...there were just too many concepts, all of which would leak out if she used them too openly. *Anyone* could run a standard analysis spell. They'd learn how to use it without truly understanding what it actually *did*.

And if they knew the dangers, they'd have a collective heart attack.

"I had never considered it," she admitted, dragging her mind back to the here and now. "If I was the target...why did the girl hesitate? And why *me*?"

"Her mind broke under interrogation," Lady Barb reminded her. "That tends to suggest that someone else had already tampered with her mind, to the point that further intrusion destroyed it. But the controlling spell would have clashed with the loyalty spell. It's possible that she hesitated because the two different imperatives were battling for control of her mind."

Emily silently damned her with her gaze. How *could* she be so clinical? A young girl was dead—no, worse than dead. No magic could repair a broken mind. If even relatively small mental problems were seen as barring inheritance, a body without a mind would be useless to society. The maid's body might simply be destroyed, or worse. Professor Thande had noted, in passing, that there were plenty of magical uses for human flesh. Most of them verged on dark magic, if not necromancy, and were thoroughly illegal, but they were practiced anyway.

"You have enemies," Lady Barb added. "And there are people who feel that you might have snubbed them when they asked for your hand..."

Emily put her head in her hands, feeling despair welling up over her. "I can't marry them all," she pointed out. "Any more than Alassa can marry all three princes..."

"You can send them a polite note explaining that you don't intend to marry yet," Lady Barb suggested, wryly. Her eyes narrowed as she studied Emily. "But your enemies could easily have programmed the maid to kill you."

The thought made Emily shudder—she'd been controlled herself and she *knew* it was horrific—but she considered it, as coldly as she could. *No one* knew how she'd beaten Shadye, not even the grandmaster or Void. And the necromancers wanted to live, even as their skin decayed and their bodies began a long transformation into eldritch abominations. Even the most insane necromancer would hesitate before challenging Emily herself. Sending in a remote-controlled assassin made perfect sense.

And it might explain why the necromancers hadn't attacked the castle directly.

"They gave her the knives," Emily said, thoughtfully. "Why advertize their involvement so blatantly?"

"Maybe they thought you'd go after them," Lady Barb suggested. "Or maybe they wanted to taunt you."

It made sense, Emily decided. If she'd been killed, the plan would have worked; if she went after them, she might stumble into an ambush manned by two or three necromancers. Could they work together that long? Not that it really mattered; without careful preparation, one necromancer would be too much for her. And if Emily just went on her way, the legend of the Necromancer's Bane would be dented. It was just the sort of over-complex plan a necromancer would devise.

She wanted to ask Lady Barb questions, to demand to know why she disliked *Emily* merely because she disliked Void. Or to ask if she really was Sergeant Harkin's sister...but if that had been the case, surely she would have said something by now. And, for that matter, just what had happened between her and Void. What had they done to each other?

The dance came to an end, with Prince Slark staggering off towards the dais while his younger brother took Alassa's hand. Emily looked at the retreating prince and recognized the signs of a very minor hex, one that caused confusion and disorientation in its target. No doubt Slark's wandering hands had reached too low and Alassa had hexed him, carefully enough that no one seemed to notice.

"Clever girl," Lady Barb whispered. "She has definitely improved a great deal since you met her. Your work?"

"Yes," Emily said.

Lady Barb shrugged. "Make sure that you ward your door tonight after you finish undressing," she ordered. "And we'll try and use the portal to get to our next destination, if the king can be convinced to give us permission. It should help us make up for lost time."

"Or maybe we should just sleep in the carriages," Emily said. "Don't we have sleeping potions?"

"You can't push horses too far," Lady Barb snapped. "Or people. Just tell your mentor to remember that."

She turned and stalked out of the door. Emily watched her go, puzzled.

Just what had happened between her and Void?

Chapter Fourteen

WHEN EMILY OPENED HER EYES, BRIGHT SUNLIGHT WAS STREAMING IN THROUGH THE clear glass window. For a long moment, she just lay there, wondering how much longer they would be allowed to lie in bed. It was clearly well after dawn. And then she remembered that she'd warded the door as best as she could, ensuring that no one could get into the room. For all she knew, Lady Barb, Nightingale and King Rupert were on the other side, wondering just what Emily and Alassa were doing.

She smiled at the thought as she pushed the covers aside, climbed out of bed and walked over to the window. Proper glass was hugely expensive—so far, she hadn't been able to recall how to mass produce it, although she knew it must be possible—and using so much of it in a single room suggested great wealth. If it was real glass, if course...Emily knew enough about the power of a magical nexus to know that someone could program the Red Castle to produce its own glass, given enough time and knowledge. She smiled again as she stared out over the countryside, catching sight of a model village in the distance. There was no sign of any other habitation.

"Good morning," Alassa's voice said, from behind the curtains. "What time is it?"

Emily looked at the sun's position in the sky. "Somewhere around eleven bells," she said. It wasn't too surprising. They'd danced until three in the morning, then stumbled into bed. Emily had barely been able to muster the energy to set up the wards before falling asleep. "I think it's time we got up."

The curtains rustled, then Alassa poked her head out. "King Rupert promised that we could use his portal," she said. "We can leave fairly late, if necessary. The trip through a portal is instantaneous."

"White Rose," Emily said, shaking her head. There had to be a story in there, probably one related to the chaos following the collapse of the Empire. "Why don't we just stay with the portals?"

"Because I am meant to be showing myself to the people," Alassa pointed out. "Besides, it is Tradition."

They shared a droll look. No one saw Alassa on her journey home, unless the golden coach also included an image generator that allowed them to *think* they'd seen her. The tradition seemed thoroughly pointless as far as Emily could tell, although there might have been a reason for it at one time. Perhaps it had been intended to allow the bards to write ballads claiming that Alassa had fallen in love with her husband's kingdom when she'd visited. But it wasn't as if the Queen of Zangaria would ever be able to stay...

"Go wash," Alassa said. She started to tug at her hair, then gave up. "And then we can call in the maids."

Emily rolled her eyes, but nodded. She would have liked to spend an hour soaking in the bath, just to work out some of the kinks from two days in a carriage, but there was no time. Instead, she washed herself quickly, dried herself with a towel and donned one of the simpler dresses. At least *she* didn't risk causing a diplomatic incident if she didn't wear the most expensive dress in the world. From what Alassa had said, wars had started over less.

There was a sharp knock at the door. Emily walked over, carefully dismantled most of the wards, then allowed the door to open. Lady Barb stood there, her hands on her hips. She didn't look happy, but it took Emily a moment to realize *why*. Emily had opened the door without thinking to check who was on the other side.

"I could have been *anyone*," Lady Barb pointed out, as she poked the remaining wards with her finger. There was a flash of light and they shattered. "And to think that you got good marks from Sergeant Miles."

Emily flushed. Unlike the other classes at Whitehall, it was difficult to tell just how well she was doing in Martial Magic. The class was designed to push the pupils to the limit, but it also often presented them with no-win scenarios to see how they would cope with them, as well as exercises that could have painful results for those who failed. If she'd been that careless in class…she remembered the experience of being tied up while she was asleep and shuddered. The sergeants would have been very sarcastic as they humiliated her in front of the entire class afterwards.

"Learn from someone else's mistakes," Sergeant Harkin had told them. She would never have thought that she could miss such an aggressive teacher, but she did. "It's cheaper than learning from your own."

"My master—the one who took me as an apprentice—would have smacked me for such carelessness," Lady Barb added. "*Don't* do it again."

She walked into the room and closed the door behind her. "The king wishes to see us after breakfast, then the Princess Mariah requests the company of Princess Alassa in her chambers," she continued. "The younger princes will be accompanying us back to Zangaria, so they are currently attending upon the gods."

"They can't *all* marry Alassa," Emily said. The plan had been to visit ten kingdoms on a slow journey to Zangaria. If all of them had at least one eligible prince, Alassa would wind up with ten suitors. And if there were more possibilities, that figure would rise rather steeply. It was a shame that Alassa couldn't simply marry *all* of them. But it would have been illegal—and impractical, besides. "Why are they coming?"

"Diplomatic reasons," Alassa grunted. She didn't look too happy, even though she still managed to look beautiful. "And to keep the rest of the world guessing until the truth is finally revealed."

"True," Lady Barb agreed. "Viscount Nightingale is currently meeting with the King's advisors, discussing their planned terms for a marriage treaty. King Randor will consider them all carefully before he makes his final decision."

Emily winced. Alassa was a royal princess, the only heir to the throne they had—and she wouldn't have the final say in who she married. Her father would make the decision for her, although Emily hoped that he would at least consult his daughter before signing her over to another man. But then, Alassa would be queen! An unhappy marriage could be disastrous for the kingdom. And she would certainly have *some* magic to use if her husband proved a poor choice. It could all end really badly.

The maids came into the room and helped Alassa into the washroom, leaving Emily and Lady Barb alone. Emily wondered if Lady Barb would lecture her further on security, but instead the woman just seemed content to study her, saying nothing. Her blunt stare was unnerving; in some ways, it felt worse than Sergeant Harkin's fury when his students made avoidable blunders. It hadn't been until after his death that Emily had realized that most of his anger was feigned. The sergeant had never really lost his temper with any of them.

"I need to ask you something," she said. "Can I carry a weapon?"

Lady Barb lifted her eyebrows, politely. "You are a sorceress who defeated a necromancer in single combat," she said, coolly. "What do you want with a *weapon?*"

Emily flushed at her tone. "I want something I can use as a last resort," she said. "And perhaps some armor. This dress"–she pulled at the material with her hand–"isn't designed to repel blades."

"Guests wearing armor and carrying weapons would be a breach of etiquette," Lady Barb said. "Besides, I have no suit of armor in your size. Have you even *used* armor?"

"Yes," Emily said, flatly. "I have."

The sergeants had provided all kinds of different armor for their students; they'd laughed at the concept of combat sorceresses wearing chainmail bikinis and nothing else. Emily had experimented with the armor, although it hadn't been as good as armor in the movies. She'd ended up black and blue after practice bouts. Some of her fellow students had been less lucky and had needed to go to the infirmary.

They'd also taught her the basics of weapons mastery. She'd used swords, daggers, bows and arrows and a number of other weapons, although it took years to qualify as a full weapons-master and very few soldiers ever did. A fully-qualified weapons-master could command his own salary, carrying out missions that ranged from outright assassination to bodyguard duties. And they were almost unbeatable by lesser warriors.

But magic will kill one stone dead, she thought, and scowled. She knew a handful of killing spells, thanks to Sergeant Miles. But she'd also been warned not to use them unless there was absolutely no other choice.

"And what," Lady Barb asked, "would your...would the grandmaster say if you carried a blade?"

"I think he'd be relieved that I was learning from experience," Emily said, tartly. Had she been about to refer to Void? "What happens if I am stripped of magic? It has happened before."

Lady Barb eyed her for a long moment, then bent down and retrieved a dagger from her boot. "I carry several concealed blades, but I'm a bodyguard," she said. "You are both a guest and a lady with...a dubious pedigree. It is unlikely that the various monarchs will casually accept you carrying weapons openly."

Alassa carries a weapon, Emily thought, but she said nothing. Lady Barb might not *know* that Alassa had a knife, or perhaps as long as it was concealed people could pretend to ignore it. Besides, after the first assassination attempt, Alassa carrying a weapon was fully justified, even though she *was* a magician.

"I shall find you a knife you can carry, but do not use it unless there is great need," Lady Barb added. "Carrying a weapon into the King's presence without his permission could result in a whipping, if you were lucky. Some kingdoms would want to put you to death."

Her lips twitched into a smile. "Do you still want to carry a blade?"

Emily nodded.

Once the maids had finished readying Alassa for breakfast, they walked out of the room and down into a small chamber. Princess Mariah was waiting for them there; she stood up, ran over to Alassa and hugged her tightly. Emily found herself momentarily uncertain of the correct protocol for greeting a princess—she doubted that King Rupert would be very happy if she met Mariah the same way she'd met Alassa—but the princess caught her hand before she could do anything and squeezed it tightly.

"I've heard all of the songs about you," she said, as she led them to the table. "How much of them are actually true?"

Alassa giggled; Emily flushed bright red. Even Lady Barb seemed amused.

"Very few of them," Emily said, finally. The only one that was anywhere near the truth, ironically enough, was one that praised Sergeant Harkin as a willing sacrifice. She would have liked it more if the songwriter hadn't gone on to suggest that Emily had somehow used a form of necromancy to win. But it was still better than the ballads that claimed she'd won through complicated sex rituals. "And the ones written by adolescent boys are the worst."

"Sit, eat," Mariah said. "The men won't be coming, I'm afraid. They never share breakfast with the women. Tradition."

Lady Barb smiled. "Most of the different kingdoms preserved the original customs of the Empire," she said, "at least at first. Later, some of them started to invent their own traditions, just to be able to claim an individuality in certain matters. But the kingdoms remain remarkably similar. Many social protocols are effectively identical."

Emily nodded. She'd loved history on Earth and, if she'd had the time and freedom, she would have loved to study the history of her new world in detail. The strange blend of medieval technology and magic had produced some very odd results, while the cultural hegemony of the Empire had produced others. Almost everyone spoke the same language, at least as a second tongue. And many of the 'individual' languages were actually nothing more than local dialects. Given time and the presence of so many translation spells, the languages would probably continue to fragment…it would be a fascinating study. Maybe she could join the History Monks when she graduated.

But the monks don't interfere, she reminded herself, and scowled. *I don't have that option.*

They ate their breakfast while Mariah bombarded Alassa with questions about Whitehall. It wasn't clear yet, it seemed, if Mariah had magic or not—and she might not be allowed to actually learn to do more than control it. As a young girl with three older brothers, it was unlikely that she would ever inherit the throne, which meant that her role in life would be to serve as part of a marriage treaty. Her husband might not like the thought of his wife being a skilled magician. Emily had a feeling that some of Alassa's suitors felt the same way, but there was nothing they could do about it. Alassa needed to be her own Court Wizard.

Alassa told the girl some stories about Whitehall, although she glossed over her own early months at the school. Mariah giggled when Alassa talked about the time when they'd rigged up a transfiguration spell in Melissa's door, keyed to activate the next time someone touched the wood. She *didn't* mention the fact that Melissa, after spending nearly an hour as a frog, had retaliated by casting a spell on Alassa's clothes that turned them transparent at unfortunate moments, or that after one exchange of spells that had got out of control they'd all been sent to face the warden and had spent the night lying on their chests.

"I hope I am allowed to go," Mariah said, her eyes shining. "If I were a magician, who knows what I could do?"

"I'm sure you could go," Alassa said. "Magic can be a very useful tool."

Mariah turned her gaze on Emily. "And you have to tell me how you defeated Shadye," she added. "A full necromancer...how did you do it?"

"Carefully," Emily grunted. She couldn't risk telling anyone, even Alassa. Her friend had duties to her kingdom. If Emily told her the truth, Alassa might decide she needed to use the knowledge in defense of Zangaria. "And Whitehall was devastated."

The grandmaster had hinted that the number of people applying to come to Whitehall for the next term had fallen. Emily wasn't sure if that was just a statistical hiccup—new first-years arrived all the time, like Emily herself—or if people were actively staying away from the school after Shadye had nearly destroyed it. But Shadye had been beaten and Whitehall had been rebuilt...surely, the necromancers wouldn't risk a second attack without knowing just what had happened to Shadye. Or maybe people were scared of *her.*

She finished the bowl of fruits and oatmeal she'd been offered for breakfast, then watched as Alassa and Mariah headed off to chat about being princesses. Alassa seemed remarkably patient with the young girl, although perhaps it wasn't too surprising. They *did* have a great deal in common, even though Alassa would probably have denied it if Emily had pointed it out. Mariah would never inherit the throne. Perhaps she would see it as a relief.

Lady Barb escorted Emily into a second chamber, where King Rupert sat on a modest throne. Emily blinked in surprise; she hadn't realized that King Rupert might want to talk to her, instead of Alassa. But then, he clearly *knew* Alassa—or chose to pretend that he did. Emily hastily curtseyed and went down on one knee as Lady Barb withdrew, leaving her alone with the King. He looked rather more serious than he had on their last meeting.

"You may rise," he said. His lips twitched into a smile, although there was no humor in his eyes. "And you may be seated."

Emily stared at him. Offering her a seat was a *major* concession in any form of royal audience, suggesting that he considered her of very high status indeed. But she wasn't–officially, she was a commoner, or a bastard. And yet she *had* defeated Shadye…was he worried that she might be offended by being refused a seat? Her mind spun while she retrieved a small stool and sat down on it, facing King Rupert.

"You're a Child of Destiny," King Rupert said, flatly. "You have already changed the world."

There was a long pause. "Many of your innovations have already reached my kingdom," he added. "Tell me…where is it leading us?"

Emily swallowed, wondering just how he'd drawn the link between Emily and the innovations pouring out of Zangaria. Maybe he'd been spying on her…or, more likely, he'd been spying on King Randor. And Alassa's father knew where the innovations were coming from. There was no point in trying to pretend ignorance.

"To a better world," she said. It was true, although not all of the nobility would agree. What would happen when wealthy commoners started objecting to taxation without representation? Or, for that matter, when everyone could read and newspapers were printed without government censorship? "And one that can resist the necromancers more effectively."

The king leaned forward. "You are a very strange person," he said. "If your father was not who he was, you would be dead."

Emily shivered, seeing–for the first time–the ruthless monster underneath the jovial exterior. King Rupert's first priority was maintaining his power, whatever the cost, just so he could pass his kingdom down to his eldest son. And if he hadn't been scared of Void, he might have ordered Emily's death, just to see if Destiny could be cheated.

"Be careful," King Rupert added. "Your…*innovations* are raising up a storm. It may destroy you." He smiled. "You may go."

Emily left, feeling as if she had barely escaped with her life.

Chapter Fifteen

Emily was still mulling over King Rupert's words when the small procession—now joined by two princes and their guards—made its way out of the Red Castle and down towards the portal. He'd *threatened* her, effectively warning her that others might also want to kill her...of course, she'd upset their kingdoms merely by introducing new elements. Emily had known that it might happen, but it had still been a nasty shock. And he'd effectively admitted that if she hadn't had Void as a guardian, she might have been killed by now.

She couldn't decide what to do about it. Tell Alassa? Her friend might understand—and then cause a diplomatic incident. Or, perhaps, she wouldn't even believe Emily. King Rupert seemed like a jovial uncle to her, a man who seemed to accept her as a young girl first and a princess second. She might not want to believe anything bad about him. And besides, if Rupert had wanted to kill Emily, he'd had opportunity. There hadn't been any threat at all in the Red Castle.

Eight more kingdoms to go, she thought, dully. *Eight more threats?*

But King Jorlem hadn't threatened her. His son had discussed the innovations without ever mentioning that he held Emily personally responsible for them—but then, he might not have realized the truth. After all, as far as most people knew, Emily was nothing more than a powerful sorceress-in-training who had defeated a necromancer. There was no obvious connection between her and the innovations, unless one happened to have inside knowledge of Whitehall *and* Zangaria. That had been how *Alassa* had deduced the truth, after all.

Her mind was still spinning as she sensed the portal coming into view. It sat in the middle of a grassy field, right in front of a fortified position that could be held for hours, even without magic. The portal didn't *look* very complex—it was nothing more than a simple stone arch, large enough to allow three or four carriages to drive through comfortably—but the magic surrounding it was hellishly complex. And it could be sensed from miles away by anyone with any sensitivity to magic at all.

The sergeants had gone into some detail on the advantages and disadvantages of a portal. On one hand, once set up, troops and equipment could be moved instantly from one part of the Allied Lands to another. A small bridgehead could be captured in enemy-held territory and then expanded with the help of troops coming through the portal. On the other hand, it was relatively easy to *disrupt* a portal, effectively destroying it, while it could take hours to set one up. A single enemy magician with a great deal of skill could get close enough to knock down the portal without being noticed until it was too late, allowing the enemy to counterattack and wipe out the bridgehead before it could be reinforced.

"Impressive, isn't it?" Alassa muttered. She could sense the portal too. "My first tutor in magic used to work on portals. He told me that only the most skillful of enchanters dared work on a portal."

Emily nodded, feeling oddly as if she were about to ride a roller coaster. The magic field just kept growing stronger and stronger. She hadn't done any enchanting herself—that was a third-year subject—but she knew enough to realize that it was incredibly difficult. The enchanter she'd visited in Dragon's Den, the one who had sold her the chest, had been one of the best in the world. Did he help construct portals?

"Here we go," Alassa said.

Emily felt the magic field twist sharply. She cried out in pain as something wrenched at the side of her head—or at least it felt that way—and then the pain simply vanished. Emily rubbed her head, feeling a headache flowering into life; she had to swallow hard to keep from vomiting. Alassa reached out and put a hand on her shoulder, an odd gesture of compassion. But then, she'd been through the portal too.

"The stronger your talent, the worse the effect," she said, softly. "You're going to be very powerful indeed."

Emily whimpered, feeling stabbing pains running through her head. The sergeants had taught her pain management spells, but every attempt to use magic seemed to set off another explosion in her head. Instead, she tried to meditate and focus her mind, yet her thoughts kept spinning around and around in her head. Alassa offered to cast a sleep-spell on her, to give her time to recover, but Emily shook her head. The mere movement seemed to make her head hurt more.

She'd wondered why Void teleported everywhere, given that it could be very dangerous if the magician's concentration slipped for even a second. Or, for that matter, if he tried to teleport into a location that was heavily warded against intrusion. Now, though, she suspected she knew the answer. Portals would cause him terrible pain and flying ran the risk of someone using their own magic to send him tumbling out of the air. And besides, teleporting didn't need someone to set up a matching portal at the far end.

"They never told me about that," she said, through sheets of pain that refused to fade from her mind. "If portals are so dangerous to magicians…"

"But only to magicians of extreme power," Alassa said. There was a hint of envy in her voice. "It hurt me, yes, but I kept going. You…you couldn't light a candle at the moment."

She made a face. "Someone could put you through a portal and immobilize you," she added. "I think you'd better refrain from telling *anyone* what happened."

Emily wasn't so sure that it would matter. Void would presumably know the dangers—and so would the necromancers, if they were the ones behind the assassination attempt. And besides, there were other ways to block her powers, at least for a few hours. Malefic, Shadye's ally, had used a potion to keep them from using their magic. If he hadn't deliberately allowed Emily and Alassa to escape, they might well have died in Dragon's Den.

"I won't," she said, finally. "Don't tell anyone either."

Her senses swam and she must have blacked out, for the next thing she knew was that someone was pushing a potions bottle against her mouth. Barely aware of what she was doing, she sipped it gratefully and felt a sudden charge of energy sweeping away the headache. It wouldn't last—she knew from experience that the potions never did—but it would allow her to survive the rest of the day.

"A nasty shock," Lady Barb observed, as she withdrew the potion bottle. "But you should be fine. Just make sure that you get plenty of rest tonight."

Emily scowled. They had reached White Rose, which meant that there was likely to be a formal reception ceremony and then more dancing—and loud music. Despite the effects of the potion, she knew it would be hours before she recovered completely and she couldn't face the thought of more music. Besides, she really *didn't* want to have to dance with the princes, particularly not Prince Slark. Alassa had told her more than she wanted to know about the prince's wandering hands.

"I can speak to Nightingale," Lady Barb said, doubtfully. "Perhaps you could spend the time examining the proposed marriage contract instead of attending the ceremonies."

"Tell him that I ordered it," Alassa said, firmly. "*Someone* has to read the contract and besides, Nightingale has been complaining that he hasn't been allowed to attend all of the ceremonies."

Emily stared at her. "But I wouldn't know what to say…"

"Don't worry about it," Lady Barb advised. "Having someone read it now is just a ritual, part of the ceremonies. King Randor will have the final say in all matters. Just let us know if they want something completely unacceptable."

"Oh," Emily said. "And what constitutes unacceptable terms?"

Alassa smiled, but it didn't quite touch her eyes. "Anything that compromises Zangaria," she said. "And, for that matter, my independence as queen."

"Go upstairs," Lady Barb ordered. "I will deal with Nightingale."

Whatever she said must have been effective, Emily decided later, because after that no one seemed to expect her to attend the ceremony, let alone the dancing afterwards. The maids brought her a large jug of water and a platter of bread and meat, which might have been intended as a subtle insult. Emily found it hard to care as she sat down in front of the fire to eat. Food and drink would make her feel better before Alassa came back from the dance.

She *had* made progress on learning how to read the local language, but the marriage contract was extremely difficult to parse out. The translation spell didn't help, representing part of the contract in old English and the rest in a style that seemed almost chatty. Emily had never been entirely sure of how the translation spells *worked*, but they didn't seem to work too well when dealing with aristocratic double-speak. Half of the passages in the contract seemed to contradict the other half.

If I ever get home, Emily thought, as she produced some parchment from her trunk and started to copy out the passages in a more understandable style, *I will never complain about internet user agreements again.*

The contract started by acknowledging that Alassa—although a mere girl, it added in those exact words—would be the Queen of Zangaria and the dominant partner in her marriage. Her husband would be styled as royal consort, rather than King.

However, she was to settle on him lands and monies sufficient to uphold the dignity of a Prince of White Rose, including a household of no less than four hundred servants. Emily shook her head in disbelief as the contract went on to specify that the royal consort would have his own manor near Alexis, although he would be living with Alassa. What exactly did he want a manor *for*?

It grew even more outrageous as she parsed out the rest of the document. The royal consort was to have a place on the Privy Council, with a vote equal to a middle-ranking lord and the same say in affairs as the rest of the councilors. Emily was sure that was contradictory too—not all lords were created equal. Besides, she had no doubt the royal consort was also expected to influence his wife while they were alone. And if, the document continued, Alassa became pregnant, the royal consort would be crowned king once she gave birth.

Maybe it made a certain kind of sense, Emily decided, reluctantly. If Alassa died in childbirth—a risk even for the high nobility—and the child survived, he or she would need a regent who would be completely devoted to the child's interests. The father would be the best person for the job, although Emily's studies of history suggested that it wouldn't work out as neatly as the contract-writers might have assumed. It was quite likely that the father would try to take advantage of the position for himself. After all, when the child became king, the father would no longer be regent.

The following clauses seemed designed to cover each and every possible eventuality. If the couple produced no children after five years of marriage, they were to divorce, but the former royal consort would still hold his position on the Privy Council. Emily couldn't see Alassa—or her father—agreeing to *that*. If the couple had a major falling out, so terrible that there was no hope of cooperating long enough to produce a child, the royal consort could return to his homeland, keeping the dowry he would be given as part of the ceremony. The wording seemed to be imprecise over the exact status of the marriage in *that* eventuality; Emily couldn't tell if they would be still married, or if it would be counted as a *de facto* divorce.

"I don't believe it," she muttered out loud, as she read the final sections. "What do they think they're getting into?"

If Alassa married the Prince of White Rose, there was to be a permanent alliance between the two powers. There would be no trade barriers or excessive taxation on passage between the two kingdoms. Remembering one of the political maps the sergeants had made her memorize, Emily thought through the implications. If someone attacked White Rose, it would risk setting off a general war throughout the Allied Lands. The necromancers would just walk in and take over once the dust had finished settling. And that would be the end.

This is supposed to be a draft, she reminded herself, as she stowed her notes away in her chest. *They're going to haggle over the exact terms. I wonder which of them is in the stronger position.*

She contemplated it for a long moment. Alassa *had* to marry, both for political and social reasons. It was expected of her, so much so that she hadn't raised any serious objections—at least not in Emily's hearing. On those grounds, Zangaria was not in a good position to bargain; they *needed* a royal consort. But the sheer prestige of having provided the Royal Consort of Zangaria and the father of the next King of Zangaria would be very useful for any other kingdom. It wasn't as if Alassa was short of suitors. And a royal consort from outside Zangaria might be able to build up his own power base—one of the clauses in the contract referred specifically to patronage—but he would never have the influence of someone who was actually born in the country. He would always be dependent, in the final analysis, on Alassa.

Poking through the chest, she found the copy of *Mental Blood Magic* she'd borrowed from Whitehall's library and carried it over to the bed. Lady Aylia had threatened all kinds of punishments if she lost the book, but she hadn't raised any serious objection to Emily taking it for study over the holidays. After what had happened when Shadye had invaded Whitehall, no one could argue that Emily didn't need to know how to defend herself. All of the standard precautions against Blood Magic had failed miserably.

The book, as always, felt faintly uncomfortable to the touch. Almost all of the books that touched on dark magic—or something that could become dark magic, given bad intentions—felt unpleasant when she touched them with her bare hands. She'd tried wearing gloves, just to see what would happen, only to discover that the effect was still there. But then, a protection that was so easy to circumvent would have been no protection at all.

She carefully muttered a disarming spell as she opened the front cover. The Librarians Guild saw itself as the guardian of forbidden knowledge; anyone who defied the first warning and looked inside without proper care would come to regret it. Lady Aylia had told her that none of the books in Whitehall—even the forbidden books—were spelled to be lethal to anyone who touched them without permission, but it was a danger when dealing with tomes from outside the school. A handful of stories Emily had read as part of her ongoing project to learn as much as she could about her new world confirmed it. Reading the wrong book could result in paralysis, unwanted transfiguration—or death. Some sorcerers *really* didn't like anyone poking into their private library.

Blood Magic was both simple and very complicated, she read. Simple, because it could be worked with a sample of the victim's blood, which retained its potency until the victim died. Complex, because using it could be incredibly difficult if the victim had any relatives; the presence of someone else close to the victim by blood tended to mess up the spell. It was at least partly why Shadye had found it so easy to use Blood Magic against Emily. In this world, she had no relatives at all.

The writer of the book had never even considered the possibility of alternate worlds. As far as Emily knew, Void, the grandmaster and Mistress Irene were the only ones who knew that alternate worlds definitely existed. Even Shadye, who had kidnapped Emily from *her* world, hadn't seemed to realize what he'd been doing until afterwards. Still, he did have some useful suggestions for blocking any further attempts at control. Emily rubbed the side of her head and concentrated on the mental discipline. It should, at least in theory, sink into her wards and provide additional protection, but it was hard to concentrate.

Giving up, she closed the book—feeling the protective hex slipping back into place—and returned it to her chest. Outside, she heard the sound of birds cawing as darkness fell over the land. She walked over to the window and peered out through the glass, catching sight of a flock of crows landing on one of the castle's towers. In the distance, she could see lights , almost certainly the nearest city. Most castles seemed to have been constructed in or near cities for ease of control.

The door opened, revealing Alassa. "Prince Hildebrand is a definite gentleman," she said, as she closed the door behind her and started to disrobe. "Very smart, very soft-spoken—and a trained weapons-master. He might be ideal. King Gama is a pain in the buttocks though. He spent half the evening talking about my dowry. Even Nightingale got tired of it in the end."

She grinned. "And Prince Slark had his face slapped," she added. "A perfect end to the day."

Emily rolled her eyes, then sighed as she started to set up the wards. Seven more kingdoms to go. How would she survive?

"You'll get used to it," Alassa assured her, when Emily said that out loud. "Besides, do you really want to go through seven more portals?"

Chapter Sixteen

T HE NEXT SEVEN DAYS FELL INTO A ROUTINE. THEY WOULD GET UP EARLY, BREAKFAST with their host in informal surroundings, then travel to the next kingdom on the list. Emily found them all beginning to blur together into a single kingdom, if only because they were so *similar.* The customs were almost identical, the dances all equally formal. She couldn't help feeling exhausted by the end of each day, to the point where she begged off a second dance at the last castle. By then, they had picked up no less than *fifteen* suitors for Alassa's hand. It was rather more than likely that all but one of them would be disappointed.

"They call these mountains the Mountains of Mourning," Alassa explained. "According to legend, there was once a Faerie city on the highest mountain, where humans would be taken by their masters and turned into monsters. It was destroyed during the war, but hardly anyone ever visits. There are just too many ghosts."

Emily shivered as the mountains came into view. They—and other natural barriers—seemed to serve as borders between the various kingdoms, which made a certain amount of sense. Projecting an army over the mountains would have been difficult for the locals, even without magic to make it harder. The handful of people who lived there generally kept themselves to themselves. If they knew that Alassa was passing through their territory to return to Zangaria, there was no sign of it.

"You spent plenty of time with Prince Hildebrand," Emily said. The temperature was dropping rapidly as they approached the mountains, even though the carriage was supposed to be spelled to keep it warm. "Do you *like* him?"

Alassa couldn't blush—for which Emily envied her—but she did look embarrassed. "Have I been spending too much time with him?"

"I'm not sure," Emily admitted. "You know how little protocol I can be bothered to remember."

"Lucky you," Alassa said, without heat. "I just happen to like him."

Emily wasn't too surprised. Prince Hildebrand was two years older than Alassa, reasonably handsome, very clever—and fourth in line to his father's throne. There would be little prospect of White Rose and Zangaria being united permanently by marriage, unless his three older brothers and their children died before Prince Hildebrand. He wasn't a magician, at least as far as Emily could tell, but he didn't seem to be intimidated by Alassa's magic. And he had some practical experience in governing that would serve Alassa very well.

Lady Barb had finally obtained a reply to the message she'd sent to Whitehall, which she'd shared with both girls. Prince Hedrick had majored in hierology, the study of how magic interacted with the gods and the faerie. It was very much a theoretical subject, which indicated a lack of great power or application. His other marks had been reasonable, but very far from brilliant—and he hadn't stayed any longer than fourth-year. There was no suggestion that he'd taken Martial Magic, or knew any killing spells.

That proves nothing, Emily reminded herself, once again.

Hedrick bothered her. He didn't seem interested in *anything*. Alassa had danced with him–by custom, she had to spend at least one dance with each suitor–and he had shown no interest in her at all. Nor did he seem to be interested in other girls–including court ladies who wore clothing that barely covered their private parts–or boys. Emily had danced with him once and realized that he seemed to be going through the motions. He didn't even seem to be involved enough to be *bored*.

She'd wondered if someone had enchanted him and raised the issue with Lady Barb, but Lady Barb dismissed the thought. Anyone who showed signs of enchantment would be checked at once by the Court Wizard–and besides, Hedrick just seemed uninterested in the world, rather than someone who might be under outside control. Emily had then wondered if he had a mental problem, but she knew too little to even take a stab at guessing what he might have. And besides, how could she begin to help him? Magic seemed helpless to deal with mental trauma.

"Well, make sure you read the contract carefully," Emily warned. She'd shown Alassa her notes during the journey from White Rose to Hallow. "And make sure your father knows that you like him–if you like him."

Alassa flushed. "It also makes the others more attentive," she added. "They all cluster around me–except Hedrick."

Emily snorted. The various princes behaved themselves when under the stern gazes of their chaperones–apart from Prince Slark, who seemed not to learn from experience–but their whispers could be very crude. Emily had overhead enough comments to know that Alassa was practically being propositioned, something that she clearly found exciting even though she knew better than to allow it to go too far. What would happen, she wondered, if it *did* go too far? Would they forgive her for turning a prince into a frog?

They might just ignore it, she thought, dryly. Diplomacy in the Allied Lands seemed to largely consist of ignoring things. *And besides, she would have to kiss the prince to turn him back.*

"Well, be careful," Emily advised. "A boy may be nice when he's wooing, but turn into the devil when married."

Alassa gave her a sharp look. "And you know this *how*?"

The honest answer to that was that Emily's stepmother had married a man who had seemed decent, who seemed to be able to provide for her and her young daughter–and who had turned into a demon after the wedding. He'd driven Emily's mother to drink and made her feel utterly unwelcome in her own home. If Shadye hadn't kidnapped her, Emily doubted that she would have lasted very long on Earth. But it wasn't something she could tell Alassa, at least not yet.

"Common sense," she said, instead. "They all want something from you. See how they act when they have it."

She looked out the window as the landscape slowly became more and more rocky. According to the map, there was a pass through the mountains wide enough to accommodate the carriages, but it wasn't an easy passage. By comparing it to some of the comments made by the History Monks, Emily guessed that the pass had been carved out by the Empire—and the successor states hadn't bothered to maintain it. Rain, snow and rock falls would have taken their toll on the road. It started to grow thinner too as they inched further upwards, with a river on one side. Given enough time, Emily realized, erosion would complete the destruction of the road.

The Romans had built their monuments all over Europe. Their roads had lasted for hundreds of years, as had some of their buildings. But their engineering skills had been better than the Empire's engineering skills; besides, the Empire had built the road in a very dangerous place. Emily couldn't help wondering, as the wind started to shake the carriage, just how long it would be before someone had a serious accident and plunged down into the river. Judging by the speed, anyone who fell in wouldn't be coming out again.

"Birds," Alassa said, suddenly. "Lots of birds."

Emily followed her gaze. There were suddenly *hundreds* of birds in the sky, flying over the carriages and heading away from where they'd been resting. She'd been told by the sergeants that if the birds appeared disturbed, something had disturbed them—and *that* suggested there was someone lying in wait. The carriages stopped—Lady Barb had evidently had the same thought—and guardsmen rushed past to take up defensive positions. And then a thunderous noise split the air.

The creature crashed down in front of the guards, beady eyes fixed on the puny humans confronting it. Emily couldn't believe her eyes. At first, she thought she was looking at a baby dragon, and then she saw the rooster's head grafted to the lizard-like body. A cockatrice, she realized, remembering the magical creatures she'd seen in the zoo surrounding Whitehall. It was a hybrid created by the Faerie, just because they could; they'd *lived* to make the mortal world suffer. The creature had to be in terrible pain every moment of its existence.

"Get out," she snapped. She'd *ridden* on a dragon—and if the cockatrice was even a quarter as powerful as the dragon she'd met, it would be devastating. There were close to a hundred armed men facing the monster and Emily knew with a cold sinking certainty that it wouldn't be enough. "Now!"

She jumped down from the carriage, then moved away to allow Alassa to jump down and join her. The various princes were drawing their own swords, although none of them looked very enthusiastic about trying to fight the cockatrice. Emily found it hard to blame them; even at a distance, the monster was daunting. Maybe it could be reasoned with…dragons were intelligent, even though they rarely took interest in human affairs. But what could they offer the creature?

Lunch, Emily thought, sourly.

The cockatrice threw back its head and produced a horrible crowing noise—almost as if it were trying to roar, but didn't quite know how—then lunged forward, blowing fire towards the guardsmen. They stumbled backwards as the archers opened fire, hitting the creature with a dozen arrows, all of which bounced off the scales. Part of Emily's mind noted that it didn't seem to have the fire-blowing powers of a full dragon, or the guardsmen would have been incinerated in the first seconds of combat. But it's natural armor more than made up for the lack.

It half-hopped, half-crawled forward and lashed out at the guards. Powerful claws sliced through their armor as though it was made of paper, tearing them into bloody chunks. The creature's beak snapped down on a guardsman who was trying to escape, biting him in half, only to spit out his upper body seconds later. It didn't seem to be bothered by a second flight of arrows, even one that barely missed its evil eyes. A guardsman struck it with a sword, only to see the sword glance off the creature in a shower of sparks. Seconds later, the cockatrice ripped him apart and tossed the remains in the river.

"Get back to the end of the convoy," Emily snapped at Alassa. The princes seemed eager to escort her to the rear. "Hurry!"

She took a step forward as Lady Barb threw a powerful hex at the monster. It crowed again and lashed out at her. She barely managed to save herself as its claws ripped the first carriage apart, scattering luggage trunks into the air. Two of them splashed down in the river to be lost forever. The creature advanced on Lady Barb, who somehow managed to hold her ground, firing off a second hex. Bright red balefire flared to life around the creature, making it howl in outrage, but it kept coming.

Everything has a weakness, Sergeant Harkin had said. *Everything and everyone. Sometimes you just have to find it. And then hit the weak places with your hand and the harder places with a utensil.*

Emily gathered herself and threw a cutting spell right at the creature's eye. Arrows hadn't managed to discourage it, but maybe a direct hit…the creature crowed so loudly that Emily's ears hurt, rearing up in pain. For a moment, Emily thought it would retreat, before it came forward with deadly intent. The look in its eyes held her frozen until a second blast of balefire raged over them. Lady Barb yanked Emily back as the cockatrice thrashed around, breathing puffs of fire into the air. The best they could do was injure it.

Mistress Kirdáne hadn't told them anything about killing cockatrices, or dragons. Hell, everyone believed dragons to be damn near invincible, at least while they were on their guard. Most of the dragons who had been killed by humans had been asleep at the time, according to Mistress Kirdáne, and the other dragons hadn't taken their deaths lightly. But then, they'd also operated on a completely different timescale to humanity. One town had been devastated seventy *years* after a dragon had been killed nearby.

"Get the princess out of here," Lady Barb snapped. "And then tell the princes to run too."

Emily shook her head. The cockatrice could *fly*. Alassa wouldn't be safe unless Emily managed to teleport her out—and she'd been warned, in no uncertain terms, not to try teleporting until she was considered ready for it. Alassa might escape the cockatrice, only to be killed by her incompetent friend's experiment with teleportation. And no one would ever know what had happened to them.

Lady Barb threw three more hexes and a curse in quick succession, trying to keep the creature distracted. The hexes were designed to burrow their way through wards—more powerful versions of the spell Lady Barb had used to test Emily—and might have an effect on a creature that drew on the magic field to fly. It howled as bright magic flickered around it, then shook it off. All of the reports claimed that magical creatures didn't have any proper control over magic—their magic depended on instincts rather than actual control—but Emily couldn't help wondering if that was actually true. The cockatrice had beaten the hex with remarkable speed for something that didn't really know what it was doing.

"I told you to run," Lady Barb snapped. She shook Emily, violently. "Run, damn you!"

"Not yet," Emily said. An idea was slowly flowering into her mind. It had worked in a book she'd read once…of course, not everything she'd read in fantasy books really applied in a fantasy world. "Give me a moment."

The mirror charm was one of the simplest spells taught at Whitehall—indeed, Emily knew that most of the pupils had memorized it long before they actually came to the school. Emily modified it, working at frantic speed, and then cast it in front of the cockatrice. It saw its own reflection and reared back, staring in disbelief. And then it settled down, crooning slightly as it kept its gaze fixed on its own reflection. It seemed to have forgotten about its prey.

"It's admiring itself," Lady Barb exclaimed. For once, she sounded almost respectful. "I do believe that it is admiring itself."

Emily wasn't so sure. Some creatures, if confronted with a mirror, would assume that they were facing a rival male and attack. The mirror charm probably wouldn't last long if the cockatrice tried to rip the imaginary creature apart, leaving them to face a maddened—and understandably angry—creature. There was no way to know just how intelligent the cockatrice actually was. Dragons were intelligent, if *alien*; chickens didn't seem to be any more intelligent here than they were on Earth.

"We have to do something more permanent," she said, grimly. She didn't know any curses that would burn through the creature's scales; tunics made from dragon skin were highly prized simply because hardly any curse could get through them. "How do we kill one of these things?"

"Drown it," Lady Barb said. They turned to look at the fast-flowing river, then back at the cockatrice. "How do we get it into the river?"

Emily scowled. The river would have killed a human quickly, but the cockatrice was much larger and tougher than any human. It was likely to come raging out of the water, intent on killing its tormentors. She wondered, briefly, if they could slip around the creature before it realized that the mirror was an illusion, but it would be just too risky. Even distracted, it was still blocking the road.

She could try something she'd been thinking about for months, a spell that destroyed the bonds holding matter together. The cockatrice would literally collapse into dust. But using the spell so close to Lady Barb—and Prince Hedrick—would give them a chance to analyse it. The secret would be out and the consequences would be incalculable. Given enough power and knowledge, someone could reduce an entire castle to atoms…

And then she had a thought.

"Watch it," she ordered, and then sprinted back to the carriage. The coachman had run to join everyone else, unsurprisingly, but her chest had been made for her. She needed no help to pull it out of the coach. Once it was out, she touched her hand to the magical seal and concentrated hard, trying to program in a complex series of commands. The chest was bigger on the inside than on the outside, but the original designer had limited the access to whatever could fit through the hatch. But with a little tinkering...

Should have done this with something disposable, she thought, realizing her own mistake too late. The chest had cost a sizable sum of money—and it contained things she didn't want to lose, including the library's books—and her grimoire. And the book Void had given her before she went to Whitehall. Cursing herself, she carried the chest back to where Lady Barb was standing and winked at her.

"What are you...?"

Emily grinned and ran up to the cockatrice before she could think better of it. Up close, the air around the beast was hot, hot enough to make her sweat. Opening the chest, she activated the access point to the pocket dimension inside, praying that her modifications held. If not, the cockatrice would either destroy her possessions or break free. Neither one was a good thought. The beast stirred as the pocket dimension opened up, then vanished in a flash of light. Emily sat back, suddenly aware that she was shaking. The cockatrice was now confined within her chest.

Very carefully, she tested the spells and relaxed as she realized that they were holding. Time didn't pass inside the chest, at least in theory. But she'd never confined a cockatrice inside a chest before—as far as she knew, no one had. And she couldn't simply blink the dimension out of existence without destroying everything.

"You...are...crazy," Lady Barb said. "Do you realize that getting it out is going to be a nightmare?"

"Yeah," Emily admitted. "But for the moment, it's trapped."

They shared a long look. "Let's go," Lady Barb said, finally. "The king and queen are waiting for us."

Chapter Seventeen

E MILY SUCKED IN HER BREATH AS THE CITY OF ALEXIS FINALLY CAME INTO VIEW. THE city was more impressive than she'd expected, larger than Dragon's Den and sundered by a river that ran down from the Mountains of Mourning and poured into the sea. Small boats floated on the river, some recognizable as fishing boats, others with purposes she couldn't identify. In the center of the city, she saw a castle rising up on a small hillside. Like many of the others she'd seen, assaulting it would be difficult, almost impossible.

Or at least it would be without magic, she thought. *Or a dragon or two on your side.*

"You get to ride in the open coach from here," Alassa said, as the procession stopped, briefly. She'd changed into a white dress while they'd been traveling, which hadn't been easy even with Emily's help. There just wasn't enough room in the carriage to dress someone properly. "Just keep waving as we move up the Royal Mile."

"I'll try," Emily said. She'd become used to people staring at her, ever since she'd defeated Shadye, but having thousands of people watching as she passed was too much. "You sure you want to ride?"

"Tradition," Alassa said. They'd picked up a white horse for her when they'd stopped at the first fort inside Zangaria. "But it is much better than riding in a coach."

Emily stepped out of the carriage and walked over to the open coach. It was large enough to hold Emily and six of Alassa's suitors; the remainder had a coach of their own. Not that *they* would be cheered much, Alassa had told Emily, very quietly. The common folk were not always enthusiastic about their royalty marrying outsiders. Even when the local was the dominant partner, it often meant trouble.

She caught sight of the chest—and of the coachman eying it suspiciously. The cockatrice was in stasis—she couldn't imagine how it could break free—but if it did, the expansion would destroy the carriage as well as the chest itself. She honestly wasn't sure what to do with it; Alassa had suggested giving it to her father as a gift, although Emily rather doubted that the king would *want* a cockatrice. The alternative was keeping it in the chest until they got back to Whitehall, whereupon she could unload it into the zoo. A great many creatures had escaped in the wake of Shadye's attack—she had nightmares about where the mimic might be hiding—and they might be grateful for a cockatrice. Or maybe its relatives would turn up fifty years later, demanding revenge.

Lady Barb climbed up behind her and nodded to the driver. He cracked his whip and the carriage began to move down the road towards the city—and the crowds waiting for them there. Lady Barb sat back, eying Emily out of the corner of her eye. She'd even asked, rather sarcastically, if Emily had trapped *Shadye* in her chest, which was alarmingly close to the truth. Emily had pointed out that Shadye was dead—it certainly seemed impossible for him to have survived—and refused to talk about the matter further. In hindsight, perhaps she should have tried to drown the beast instead.

Alexis had walls, but the city had expanded to the point where the walls only really protected the inner city. The first building they saw were small hovels, made from waste material and mud, just like the other shacks they'd seen on the journey. And yet there was an air of...*hope* that surprised her. The people who had moved to the city thought that they were working towards a better life. There were fewer children than she had expected, unless they were at school. Did Zangaria insist that everyone go to school? It seemed unlikely.

The street was lined with cheering crowds and armed guards. Most of them were shouting for Alassa, welcoming her home with varying degrees of enthusiasm, but a small number were cheering Emily. Only a handful of people in the Allied Lands could claim to have killed a necromancer and most of them had cheated, normally by poisoning the necromancer or luring him into a killing ground.

Alassa lifted her hand and waved grandly towards the crowds. Emily honestly couldn't see how she maintained her balance on the horse, but Alassa had been riding since she was a little girl. Horses seemed to love her, even if no one else had been so kind before Emily had almost killed Alassa for trying to bully Imaiqah. Emily had at least mastered the basics of riding, but she did intend to learn to teleport as soon as possible. She always had the feeling that the horses were plotting to tip her off and run away.

"Wave," Lady Barb hissed. "Show your appreciation."

Emily nervously obeyed. She could *feel* thousands of eyes on her, staring and judging...the roar grew louder as she waved, although she couldn't tell if they were cheering her, or Alassa, or even Lady Barb. The princes were waving themselves, she realized as she glanced behind her; they were clearly enjoying the parade. They didn't seem to be getting many cheers, but they didn't seem to care either. Of course they wouldn't; the person they needed to approve of them was Alassa's father, not his subjects. Zangaria didn't have a parliament which had to give a seal of approval to the royal wedding.

The people themselves ran the gauntlet from very poor to respectable middle-class, like Imaiqah's father. Emily wondered if *he* was somewhere in the crowd, but she'd never laid eyes on him before and wouldn't have known him if she'd seen him. Or what about Imaiqah herself? Surely her father would have wanted her to show herself to Alassa, although it sounded absurd. Emily couldn't have picked a specific face out of the crowd to save her life. She caught sight of a large group of teenage girls, being watched by a handful of older mothers, and smiled inwardly. No doubt they saw the whole procession as a break from their work - and a chance to catch the eyes of young men.

Most of the poorer people wore drab clothes, little better than sackcloth. The middle-class wore brighter outfights, almost certainly individually tailored, although they didn't seem to wear gold or silver cloth. That made sense; the noblemen she'd seen had often worn gold or silver, which suggested that wearing it *without* being an aristocrat might be illegal. Or maybe it was simply too expensive, even for up-and-coming merchants. Emily still had only the haziest idea of production costs, but she knew that Alassa's discarded nightdresses–the ones she wore at Whitehall–cost more than Imaiqah's entire wardrobe. Some of them had been made from silk imported from the Western Isles.

Maybe I should have spent more time shopping for clothes, Emily mused, then dismissed the thought. She had never enjoyed shopping for clothes on Earth; she'd never had the money to keep up with fashion and she'd been mocked for her choices. Certainly, her mother had never taught her how to shop, let alone what she should wear. Besides, the robes they wore at Whitehall were free and convenient. And she had never really envisaged leaving the school until Alassa had invited her to visit Zangaria.

The roar died away slightly as they reached the gate leading into the inner city. Emily suspected that the wall surrounding the original city would have been a formidable defense at one point, but it had been badly weakened when so many houses had been built close enough to the wall to allow someone to scramble onto the battlements without having to climb up on siege ladders. And one side of the inner city opened onto the river–someone on a boat might be able to sneak into the inner city without being noticed by the guards. She couldn't understand what the monarch had been thinking when he'd allowed it to happen, unless it was an unintended consequence of something else. Maybe Bryon the Weak hadn't been able to say no to his commoners either.

Or maybe the nobles encouraged it to weaken Alexis, she thought. The gate looked tough–Emily could sense magic crawling over it, making it stronger–but if the walls couldn't be held, the gate and gatehouse were effectively useless. She watched with interest as they passed through the gate–a small line of soldiers bowing to their princess as she passed–and into the inner city. The city certainly smelt cleaner that some of the others she had visited; it was quite possible that they even had basic plumbing. Or maybe they just put it all into the river.

The outer edge of the inner city seemed to be composed of tower blocks, each one with at least five floors. They looked tiny compared to the skyscrapers Emily recalled from Earth, but she rather doubted that anyone in Zangaria could build a skyscraper without using magic to hold it upright. The sergeants had told their students about buildings held up by magic–floating in the air or perched on the head of a needle–but they all had the same weakness. If something happened to the magic, they came tumbling down and smashed to pieces on the ground. Only a nexus could provide enough magic to keep the building safe.

Most of the population looked rather more prosperous than the people outside the walls, she realized, as she started to wave again. Their cheers seemed somewhat less heartfelt and more calculating, although she was probably imagining it. Being able to live in the inner city was something of a status symbol, according to Imaiqah; the successful commoners were the ones who could afford to live there. The apartments might be small, unless they had vast amounts of money, but they brought an astonishing amount of prestige.

There were a handful of larger buildings, all guarded by armed men. It took Emily a moment to realize that they were banks, storing money and records for the locals, or contract rooms, where contracts were stored. From what she'd heard, a large contract between two merchants could only be legally enforced if it was recorded and witnessed by the King's bureaucrats, a service that cost a bronze coin from each of the participants. Emily had puzzled over that until she'd realized that it gave the king and his servants a neat way to keep track of what the merchants were doing, although it didn't work as well as they might have hoped. Someone who broke an agreement that *hadn't* been witnessed would still be blacklisted by the merchant community.

The banking system itself was fundamentally flawed, Emily knew. It charged money for everything, including saving money, which meant that only the very wealthy were able to use it. Most people just kept their money at home, under their beds or in a magically-secured chest like Emily's. It was impossible to get a loan without having enough property to guarantee the loan, which put a freeze on economic activity. One of Emily's long-term plans was to create a bank that *would* allow small amounts of credit, just to see what other ideas people would come up with if they had a little support. But it would be difficult to start one in Zangaria.

She smiled when the tower blocks became houses as they moved closer to the castle. Some of the buildings belonged to noble families, passed down through the generations to ensure that their families would have a place to stay while they were in the city. Being able to maintain such an establishment was yet another sign of wealth; the older buildings never changed hands, but the younger ones were often traded between aristocratic families as one family tried to rise and another finally admitted defeat, at least for the moment. Given enough time, the merchants might also try to muscle their way into the very highest levels of society. Who knew *what* would happen then?

"That's the Speaking House," Lady Barb muttered, pointing towards a long low building that had been built in the shadow of the castle. One half of the building looked like a noble mansion, complete with golden paint; the other half looked plain and unadorned. "The painted half of the building houses the Noble Estates, where noblemen meet to discuss the kingdom's affairs; the unpainted half of the building houses the Assembly, where the commons meet. But no one pays much attention to them."

Emily scowled, but nodded. Reading between the lines, Alexis III had made a deal with the wealthier commoners, offering them a share in political power in exchange for their help defeating the rebellious and over-mighty nobles. He'd won the civil war—after killing three of the worst barons and exterminating their families, just to make the point—and he hadn't exactly broken his word, but as long as the king and noble families controlled most of the wealth in the country, the Assembly could be safely ignored.

But that was going to change, Emily knew. Even without her innovations, the merchants would probably have continued to grow in wealth and power, giving them influence—unless the king tried to tax them into submission. But heavy taxes would simply kill the goose that laid the golden eggs. France's failure to match Britain as a merchant society had certainly been made worse by a taxation program that actually penalized success. And, for that matter, allowed vast numbers of wealthy noblemen and clergy to escape paying taxes altogether. How many of those problems did Zangaria have?

And if it went on, what might happen? Charles I hadn't known. Emily did.

Lady Barb pointed out a handful of other landmarks as they approached the castle. There was a colossal temple dedicated to Lokane, the patron god of the royal family. This world had never spawned a religion dedicated to worshipping a single god, somewhat to Emily's surprise; the concept had never really occurred to them. All of the gods existed, somewhere, they believed, even if not everyone worshipped them. According to some of the books Emily had read, there were over two *thousand* major gods and goddesses—and uncounted minor ones, including household gods who were spawned when a new household was created. If one state happened to overrun another, the losers would still keep their gods.

There were a handful of other temples, including a small temple that seemed almost completely unadorned. Emily frowned in puzzlement, wondering why the temple was so *plain*, before realizing that it had to have been a deliberate decision. Even a temple would have to pay colossal rents to remain in the inner city.

"That's the shrine to the Crone Goddess," Lady Barb explained, when Emily asked. "Do *not* go inside unless you are accompanied by one of their sisters."

Emily blinked. "Why not?"

"There are *very* powerful spells woven into the building," Lady Barb said. "They don't like intruders—you have to be welcomed into their mysteries before you can enter safely, unaccompanied. And men are not welcome at all. Those who walk in come out as women."

She snickered. "The writing on the front door says that no man shall walk out of this temple, if he be foolish enough to enter," she added. "They mean it too."

Emily shook her head in disbelief. Every time she thought that she was used to the strange new world, something else happened to remain her that the locals often had very different attitudes from the people she'd known on Earth. Transforming a man into a woman—or vice versa—would cause all sorts of mental problems, but they seemed to be completely comfortable with the idea. Maybe she should be relieved; if Alassa could have been transformed into a man safely, she had no doubt that her parents would have done just that.

The castle rose up above them as they passed over a drawbridge and into the courtyard. It was more confining than she had expected, with hidden murder holes in position to rain down arrows and sorcery on uninvited guards. She remembered the sergeant's lessons and shivered. Alexis Castle had been designed to stand off a siege for as long as necessary. And as long as they didn't face a necromancer, the castle was almost completely impregnable.

Or it will be until they invent cannons, Emily thought. After kings had mastered cannons, noble fortresses had suddenly become a great deal less impregnable. It had started the process that had bound Europe into proper countries.

"You wait at the rear of the room until the king calls you forward," Lady Barb informed her. "Alassa must greet her father on her own, then the princes will be presented, one by one. You come last."

Emily felt an odd flash of irritation, but nodded. Alassa was her father's only child, after all, and the princes were royal guests, even if they would be largely disappointed. Emily was nothing on that scale, although she *had* beaten a necromancer *and* a cockatrice. She watched the footmen unloading the boxes, handling her chest with extreme care, and smiled inwardly. Anyone would think that they thought the pocket dimension would burst at any second and a very angry monster would be freed. But the dimensions should hold. She'd assured them of that a dozen times over.

She glanced upwards as she heard birds cawing overhead. There were dozens of birds flying around the castle's towers, from a single snowy owl to a huge flock of ravens. She had to smile, oddly touched by the sight, before Nightingale caught her arm and dragged her into the castle. His touch felt unpleasant and she shook him off, unable to understand why he was panicking. The king wouldn't mind a short delay, would he?

Inside, she saw a large stone door, slowly opening to reveal a grand hall. Bracing herself, she took one look at Nightingale, who looked surprisingly worried, and then followed Lady Barb into the hall. The king was waiting for them.

Chapter Eighteen

A LASSA'S FATHER WAS STRIKING.

It shouldn't have surprised her, Emily realized. Alassa had been literally *programmed* to be beautiful, to the point where she was physically perfect, at least in appearance. Why shouldn't her grandfather have done the same to her father? King Randor of Zangaria was astonishingly handsome, with long blonde hair, a beard and brilliant blue eyes. He wore a simple red and purple tunic that didn't do anything to conceal his physique. Emily couldn't escape the absurd impression that he was a character from a bad cartoon series come to life.

Queen Marlena, Alassa's mother, stood beside the throne. She looked surprisingly frail for the wife of such an intensely masculine man, but Emily recognized an iron determination in her eyes that reminded her of Mistress Irene. This was not a woman to take lightly, she realized. Unlike her husband, Marlena was starting to go grey at the temples, yet she carried herself with a poise that only added to her aura of determination. The red dress she wore neatly matched her husband's tunic.

The throne was surrounded by a throng of noblemen, all wearing their finest outfits. Some of the barons were wearing robes that matched their names, others stranger outfits that showed off their simple lack of concern for society's approval. The lesser lords wore simpler outfits made out of expensive materials, showing off their wealth as well as their humility. Emily wondered just how many of them faked it, using cheaper materials or magic to give the appearance of wealth. There was no way to know.

From what Alassa had said, the noblemen argued amongst themselves as often as they argued with King Randor. Her father quietly encouraged it, on the grounds that it kept the noblemen from uniting against him. Emily wasn't sure that was a good idea for the long-term stability of the kingdom; if Alassa died suddenly, perhaps in childbirth, there would be no strong coalition of noblemen to enforce peace. But then, the coalition probably wouldn't last very long in any case. The prize—the kingdom itself—was simply too tempting.

The guards lining the walls carried staffs, rather than bladed weapons. They also wore masks that concealed their identities. From what Alassa had said, the disputes between aristocrats sometimes turned violent, with fists flying and magic not too far behind. And then the guards would move in and separate the combatants with as much force as necessary. It was often the only opportunity a low-born guard would have to manhandle a nobleman and they tended to enjoy themselves while doing it. Alexis I had ruled that his court would not become a battleground and he'd enforced it brutally. And every king since then—except Bryon—had done the same.

Emily watched as Alassa made her way up towards her father, looking almost like a bride on her way to the altar. The nobles drew aside to allow her to pass, although some of them were watching with ill-concealed calculating expressions. They knew that the kingdom had never had a ruling queen before and suspected that she would be weak, perhaps as weak as her great-grandfather. And they knew that she'd been a brat before she went to Whitehall. Someone like that would have been easy to manipulate.

Alassa stopped in front of the throne and knelt before her father. King Randor waited one long moment, just long enough for silence to fall, and then stood up and took Alassa's hands in his, helping her to her feet. The assembled nobles cheered lustily at the silent acknowledgement of paternity, although the calculating ones didn't seem to be cheering very enthusiastically. But they had to wonder if the guards were also monitoring them and if a lack of cheering would be reported.

"Our daughter has returned for her Confirmation," King Randor said. He seemed to speak quietly, but the words echoed through the Great Hall. "We welcome her to her place amongst us."

The nobles cheered again. Emily wondered just what they were thinking about the new Alassa—and about Emily, who had made the change happen. And about the fact that she'd effectively gotten away with nearly murdering the heir to the throne. It would have been an accident, but that would have been no consolation to anyone caught up in the inevitable civil war. And if they knew that *she* was to blame for the new innovations...

"We also welcome twenty-two princes who have come to bid for her hand," King Randor continued. There was no trace of doubt in his voice—but then, *his* marriage would have been arranged for political reasons too. He saw nothing wrong in the practice, even though he could have ignored his wife and Alassa would have found it hard to ignore her husband. "Give them great honor, as they deserve."

Twenty-two? Emily glanced back and saw that the princes had been joined by a handful of others, princes who *hadn't* come with the procession. But they hadn't had time to visit *all* of the prospective princes in their natural environment. Emily wondered absently if that meant that those princes had a poor chance of winning Alassa's hand—or the exact opposite. Alassa had already declared that there was absolutely *no* hope of spending the rest of her life with Prince Slark, even if she had to kill him herself. And Prince Hedrick just didn't seem to care.

The herald stepped forward as trumpets blared. "Your Majesty, Your Excellencies, Your Lordships...Prince Hedrick of Alluvia, son of King Jorlem!"

Prince Hedrick ambled up to the throne as if he were an actress on a catwalk. Emily had to conceal her own amusement and noticed that several of the lords were doing the same, although others were looking calculating. If Prince Hedrick was touched in the head, it would ensure that he wouldn't be able to supply Alassa with a backbone—although if they thought she didn't have one, they didn't know her very well. Given time and experience—and magic—she was likely to be formidable.

King Randor's face showed no trace of his true feelings as he accepted a bow from Prince Hedrick. Emily watched as the prince stepped to one side and waited as the herald announced Prince Slark, who swaggered forward and bowed grandly to King Randor. Some of the younger members of the court looked interested, but the older ones still looked calculating. A slimy prince might be easy to manipulate too.

He wouldn't force her to marry him, would he? Emily asked herself. But who knew *what* Slark would bring to the match, apart from his own personality? What sort of calculations might cross the King's mind? And yet Alassa was determined to refuse him.

One by one, the princes bowed to King Randor and joined the line beside the throne. Emily realized that the whole purpose of the ceremony was to introduce them formally, ensuring that everyone would know who they were. But there were so many princes that she felt her head beginning to hurt just trying to keep track of them. Maybe Alassa could do it—she'd been memorising aristocratic genealogies since she had been old enough to read—but Emily couldn't. It was hard enough remembering the spells she'd memorized since coming to Whitehall.

The line of princes finally came to an end. It was difficult to read King Randor's feelings—he was far more skillful than his daughter at concealing his innermost thoughts—but Alassa looked both relieved and worried. Emily realized, as heads turned back towards the doors expectantly, that *she* was next. She wanted to run and hide—this was going to be worse than any of the other kingdoms—but somehow she held herself in place. And then the herald read her out.

"Your Majesty, Your Excellencies, Your Lordships…Lady Emily, Necromancer's Bane."

Emily had to force herself to walk forward, feeling all eyes on her. She had no real title—*Lady* was a courtesy title offered to a sorceress—but she *had* killed a necromancer. And if she'd tricked Shadye, no one would have kept it a secret. The mystery only added to the potency of her growing reputation, as well as suggesting that no one should mess with her. In hindsight, she wondered about King Rupert's veiled threats. Should she have been snarkier to ensure that he *knew* she was powerful?

But even the most powerful of necromancers could still be poisoned.

The back of her neck felt hot as she approached King Randor. Alassa hadn't been entirely sure of the correct protocol for *Emily*; officially, she was common-born, but she *was* a close friend of the princess and that effectively conferred aristocratic status. And then she *might* have been the daughter of an immensely powerful sorcerer, powerful enough to cause huge amounts of devastation if he felt that his daughter had been insulted, and she *had* killed a necromancer. All of the factors, added together, could only cause confusion. Who knew *what* the correct protocol should have been?

She curtseyed, very carefully, and then went down on one knee. It was the standard protocol used by sorcerers and sorceresses, who were generally considered honorary nobility. They were powerful, but not too powerful. There was a long pause, just long enough for her to wonder if she'd messed it all up, and then King Randor stepped forward and helped her to her feet. Up close, the impact of his presence was astonishing. If Emily hadn't faced Shadye, who had also had a powerful presence, she might have swooned at his feet.

The cynical side of her mind pointed out that such a presence would be a power-ful asset to any monarch. Or, for that matter, to any man. Love potions and spells didn't last very long, unless one deliberately brewed one of the forbidden recipes, but glamors to make someone more attractive could be quite potent. And not, for some reason, forbidden, at least outside Whitehall.

"Lady Emily saved the life of Our crown princess," King Randor said. He hadn't let go of Emily's hand. "When she was kidnapped, it was Lady Emily who rescued her. When an assassin tried to murder her, it was Lady Emily who saved her life. When a cockatrice tried to kill her, it was Lady Emily who tricked and captured the beast. She is welcome in Our kingdom."

Emily shivered. The true target of the first kidnap had been Emily herself, with Alassa as the innocent bystander—although she couldn't blame King Randor for thinking otherwise. Apart from the grandmaster, Void and Emily herself, no one knew the truth. And then Lady Barb had raised the question of just *who* had been targeted by the charmed maid. And there was no way to know if the cockatrice had deliberately targeted the royal procession or if it had just been hunting for lunch.

King Randor pulled her close, close enough for her to feel his beard pricking against his skin, and whispered in her ear. "We'll talk later," he said, too softly for anyone else to hear. "And you *are* welcome."

He sat back and motioned for Emily to stand on the other side of the throne from the princes. Alassa's face remained expressionless, but Emily read her relief as she relaxed slightly. Emily's first meeting with her father could have been disastrous and they both knew it. The king looked up, his gaze sweeping the hall, and then smiled at his nobles. It was a smile that suggested a certain amusement at their expense.

"It is Our wish that We shall hold a proper dance to welcome the princess home," King Randor said. "And all of you are welcome to stay."

And he will carefully note the names of whoever doesn't stay, Emily thought, as the minstrels came from a side door. The throne room was easily large enough for a dance, although it struck her as odd to combine the two functions. But then, perhaps the castle simply didn't have too many large rooms. She looked up at the curtains propped against the wall and realized that someone could hide the throne without too much effort. Maybe the mere act of hiding it turned the throne room into a simple hall.

A maid caught her hand and pressed a piece of parchment into it. Emily stared at it blankly, seeing a list of dance names and nothing else. There were twenty-three dances listed in all; she realized, as King Randor clapped his hands and dispelled the formal atmosphere, that Alassa was meant to share one with each of the princes, and then perhaps use the final dance to imply favor. Or perhaps share it with her father or uncle instead.

"Ah... Lady Emily," a voice said. Emily looked up to see a young man, barely a year older than her, looking at her nervously. He was handsome, in a bland kind of way, wearing a simple black tunic. "I am Brain, apprentice to Court Wizard Zed. Can I ask for the honor of marking your dance card?"

Understanding clicked. In order to avoid the embarrassment of choosing a new partner between dances, the men would come up to the women and mark their cards for each dance, reducing confusion during the actual dancing. Alassa was already surrounded by princes, each one trying to put their name in as quickly as possible. It didn't seem as if Alassa was allowed to decline, but then she *did* have to share a dance with each of them. And they were all begging for the second dance too.

"You may," Emily said. Brain didn't *look* like a nobleman who thought he was god's gift to womankind. Besides, she had no idea of who she could and couldn't dance with, at least according to standard protocol. Some of the barons couldn't dance with the daughters of the newly-created Earls, although the logic escaped her. "Would you like the first dance?"

He marked his name on the card, then waited beside her as several other young men came up to add their own names. Emily felt oddly flattered and yet flustered by the whole experience; how many of them wanted to dance because they liked her and how many of them were just eager to tell their friends they had danced with the Necromancer's Bane? She caught sight of the Court Wizard standing beside the throne and shivered inwardly as Zed stared back at her with a hint of abiding dislike. Had *he* been the one who had bungled Alassa's early magical education?

And, if so, had he done it deliberately?

"You'll have to point people out to me," she said, as the music started to play. "Who is the stone-faced man beside that young girl?"

"That's the Duke of Iron," Brain said, as they took their places. "He's the King's younger brother and chief defender of the realm. The woman is his wife."

Emily nodded. The Duke of Iron didn't seem as handsome as King Randor—he had a nasty scar on his face that he seemed to have decided to keep, despite the existence of spells that could have removed it—but there was something about him that Emily couldn't help liking. His wife was clearly younger than him, yet she was obviously devoted to the duke. Her bright red hair spilled down over a gown that was clearly held in place by magic, or the stares of every young man in the hall.

The other princes had had no trouble in finding other partners, mainly the daughters of rich and powerful noblemen. Brain identified a handful of them for her, including Baron Silver—the queen's brother—and Baron Holyoake, who was apparently famous for great voyages in his younger days. Zangaria had not been able to set up any colonies away from the main continent—the natives had been too tough—but apparently it had turned a fading baronetcy into a powerful family once again.

"Zed wishes to talk to you later," Brain added. "He wants to know how you beat a necromancer."

Emily scowled as the dance—a formal waltz—started. *Everyone* seemed to want to know the answer to that question, but all of her reasons for keeping it to herself continued to apply. Given someone with enough magic to experiment—and the basic concept—the results could be disastrous. Emily knew that magic could be used to split atoms. Who knew *what* else could be done when a magician started to poke around with the whole idea?

"I'd be more interested in talking to him about other subjects," she muttered, using a privacy ward to ensure that no one could overhear them. "What sort of magician is he?"

"An Alchemist," Brain explained. "His whole career has been spent studying and improving the Royal Bloodline."

He leaned closer. "But I can't tell you anymore," he stage-whispered. "Big secret that, very big secret. Unless you have something to bargain with."

"We'll see," Emily said. She *did* want to know just what went into the Royal Bloodline, but she might not have to bargain to find out. "And thank you for the dance."

"You're welcome," Brain said. "Feel free to come visit us at any time."

Emily had to smile. "I will," she said. She allowed her smile to get wider as he flushed. "And *thank you* for the dance."

The dancing lasted until very late, unsurprisingly, but eventually it was all over and Emily was escorted up to her bedroom. This time, she wouldn't be sharing with Alassa; Emily had been given guest quarters suitable for a royal princess. She kept her private thoughts–that any hotel on Earth that showed such lack of concern for hygiene would be closed down–to herself and stumbled into bed. At least the punishing journey was over. And tomorrow she could begin to explore in earnest.

And with that thought, she went to sleep.

Chapter Nineteen

Eᴍɪʟʏ's ᴇɴᴛɪʀᴇ ʙᴏᴅʏ ᴀᴄʜᴇᴅ ᴡʜᴇɴ sʜᴇ ᴄʀᴀᴡʟᴇᴅ ᴏᴜᴛ ᴏғ ʙᴇᴅ ᴛʜᴇ ғᴏʟʟᴏᴡɪɴɢ ᴍᴏʀɴ-ing. One thing that was rarely mentioned in the historical novels she'd read was that carriages had almost no suspension—and, despite the spells that made the ride smoother, it always took a toll on the passengers. She stood up, glanced at her watch and then headed for the washroom. It might have had cold running water—the king-dom didn't seem to have hot water on tap—but she could heat it up using magic. She just needed a soak.

Thirty minutes later, she pulled herself out of the bath, used another spell to dry herself and reached for the chest before stopping, appalled. There was a *cockatrice* inside! It should have been sealed in its own private compartment, held firmly in stasis, but she'd weakened the charms holding the pocket dimension together when she'd altered the entrance to snatch up the creature. She would probably have to open it very carefully in a zoo and then try to snatch the chest away before the out-raged monster could destroy it—and her.

Opening one of the wardrobes, she found a handful of courtly dresses and a cou-ple that she suspected were for daily use. The material felt odd to her fingers—it took her a moment to realize that they were made from something completely unfamil-iar—but she had no difficulty pulling one of the dresses on. Glancing in the mirror, she smiled at her own reflection and then jumped as the door opened. She'd been too tired to ward it before collapsing into bed. Emily spun around to see two maids, both looking young and alarmingly cheerful. And, she realized grimly, bound with loyalty and obedience spells.

"We're here to do your hair, Milady," the lead maid said. "The queen insisted on it."

Emily swallowed the objection that came to mind. The maids had their orders and they would carry them out, or die trying. It was *easy* to fix her hair using magic—and she'd certainly never been interested in spending hours in the salon back when that had been an option—but having servants was a sign of wealth and power. Besides, magic *did* have its limitations.

"You look lovely, Milady," the maid said, twenty minutes later. She'd braided Emily's hair so it fell down her back in a single long plait, then rubbed something on her skin that had made it paler. "The young men will be fawning over you."

"I doubt it," Emily said. All of the princes would be fawning over Alassa. But then, she *had* been warned that she would be getting marriage proposals from people who just wanted her for her genes, literally. And Jade had proposed to her. "But thank you."

She'd barely had time to notice the interior of the castle when she'd been escorted to her chambers. Now, with the maids leading her down to the breakfast hall, she had a chance to see chambers filled with strange artefacts and endless rows of suits of armor, positioned neatly against the wall. She'd seen something similar in Whitehall, but they'd been charmed to act as part of the school's defenses. Were these suits of armor also charmed, or were they just part of a historical display? Although she could imagine someone stopping to take the swords or the maces and using them as real weapons.

The breakfast hall was almost identical to the others she'd seen along the journey, apart from the massive coat of arms hanging from the wall. Zangaria's official crest consisted of a pair of swords crossed over a magic wand and a crown, implying that force of arms had won the kingdom and force of arms would keep it. Alexis III would probably have agreed wholeheartedly with the sentiment. Alassa was sitting in front of her parents, talking to them too softly for Emily to hear. Her father stood up and beckoned Emily to a seat.

"Please, eat," he said, as he sat down again. "We do not need to stand on ceremony here."

"Thank you," Emily said. It was a great concession, even if she *was* Alassa's friend. But then, royal protocol had never really been designed for someone like her, someone who could fit into so many different categories. "And thank you for the dresses in the room."

Queen Marlena smiled. "I was told that you had few dresses," she said. "You are welcome to borrow or take any of them."

King Randor smiled affectionately at his wife, then looked at Emily. "Lady Barb informs me that you have a cockatrice in your chest," he said, bluntly. "Is it safe there?"

"I think it probably needs to be decanted, sooner rather than later," Emily said. The enchanter who had created the chest had told her that it would last indefinitely, but that had been before Emily had started fiddling with the spells to trap the monster. And if it did somehow burst out...what would happen? At best, it would be trapped in Emily's chambers. "Would you like it?"

"Zed wants it for his experiments," King Randor said. "You are aware, of course, that blood from such creatures is among the most powerful magical substances in the world?"

Emily nodded, then scowled. "It's a living creature," she said. "Do you really want to kill it? *Can* you kill it?"

"Drowning works," King Randor said. "And there are some spells that befuddle the creature long enough for it to be killed by other means. You may have invented a new one."

He shook his head. "Still, the creature is yours," he added. "Sell it to Zed, if you want, or keep it as a nasty surprise for anyone who breaks into your chest. You wouldn't be the first sorceress to do something like that."

Queen Marlena spoke into the silence. "I've heard a great deal about you, Lady Emily," she said, nodding to Alassa. "Tell me about yourself."

Emily hesitated, then gave her the bare bones of the story the grandmaster had cooked up to explain her existence. It was understandable, he'd told her, that she'd want to skirt around the subject of her father, particularly if her mother had been unfaithful. Bastardry was a touchy subject among the nobility, and among the wealthy merchants. The queen didn't sound if she believed Emily completely, but she said nothing. Besides, she would think she knew what Emily was lying about.

"My daughter and my wife will be looking at clothes for the Confirmation," King Randor said, after they finished breakfast. "Perhaps, Lady Emily, you would give me the honor of your company?"

It wasn't a request, Emily knew. She said goodbye to Alassa, who didn't seem too pleased at the prospect of spending hours with the tailors, and followed the king through a set of passageways that seemed barely wide enough to accommodate his form. A set of wards barred their way, only to be banished by a word from the king himself. Others protected his privacy, Emily realized, as she felt the familiar muffling presence. She hadn't really been aware of Whitehall's wards after the first few weeks; in time, she assumed, she would get used to these too.

"This is my private study," the king said, as he led her through a stone door. "It's location is unknown to everyone but myself and my daughter. Even my wife doesn't come in here."

Emily wasn't sure if she should believe him or not. He'd certainly been casual about showing her to the study, but then—the wards would make it harder for her to retrace her steps later. And there were plenty of rooms in Whitehall that could only be accessed by people with the right level of permission—the female dormitories, for one.

The study itself was a comfortable shambles, illuminated by a single magical light. Two chairs were positioned beside a heavy desk, covered with parchments and a handful of quills. A large sofa was positioned against one wall, underneath a bookcase that held a handful of elderly tomes. Emily couldn't help taking a look at them, only to scowl in disappointment as she realized that most of them were written in the same ancient script as the book Void had given her. The ones that were written in the standard speech seemed to be nothing more elaborate than family trees.

"Alexis II started a project to calculate those among the nobility who might be able to join the Royal Bloodline," King Randor explained. He picked a set of parchments off the nearest chair as he spoke. "His idea was that eventually the nobility would be cleansed of all imperfections and be as close to the Faerie as mortal flesh and blood could be. We are still working on it today."

He stepped back and motioned for Emily to take the seat, then sat down facing her. "Do you know just how much trouble you have caused?"

"Yes," Emily said, her mouth suddenly dry. The wards pressed down on her mind, interfering with her ability to think clearly, or work magic. "I know."

"You almost killed my daughter," King Randor added. "Do you know what the penalty is for causing the death of the heir apparent?"

He went on before Emily could shape an answer. "Death by slow torture, then hanging," he informed her. "Accident it might have been, but there's nothing in the law about it being an *accident*."

She *had* gotten off lightly, Emily knew. By almost any reasonable standard, she should have been expelled, or handed over to Zangaria for trial. The thrashing she'd received from the Warden had left her sore for several days, but it had been pitiful compared to what she should have been given as a punishment.

"And then you saved her life. And you helped her become a better person," the king added. "And yet you have also caused upheaval in my kingdom. Where is it going to end?"

Emily winced. King Rupert had asked the same question.

"In a better world," she said. She hoped desperately that the king would believe her. "Everything I have introduced has been for the best."

"Not everyone would agree," King Randor said, mildly. "You may be amused to discover that the recent...disagreement between Baron Holyoake and the city of Watertown was made worse by broadsheets written and published by people using the ideas you invented. Or, for that matter, that slander about the baron's wife was turned into a paper attacking her and freely distributed around the city. And all of them were written in your new letters. Which are spreading like wildfire, by the way."

Emily didn't trust herself to say anything. English letters were so much simpler than anything the locals had invented for themselves that they would definitely spread like a fire, transforming everything they touched. It took *years* for a reasonably intelligent person to learn the basics of the Empire's written script; English letters could be learned in a few months. There was no reason why farmers, even serfs on the land, couldn't learn. And it lent itself to transliteration easily, even if there were several different ways of spelling the same word in standard use. Sooner or later, someone like Dr. Johnston would try to codify them all, but for the moment everything was in flux.

"The Scribes have done better than the Accountants," King Randor added. "They, at least, were quick to embrace the printing press. There's more work for them now than there was a year ago and they're pleased about that. But tell me...how long will that last?"

"There will always be people too lazy to work for themselves," Emily said, finally. "And there will be plenty of other jobs for them as the new letters spread."

"They're already beyond my borders," King Randor said. "And some of your other ideas have spread too. Stirrups, for example. They have spread to the other kingdoms already."

Emily nodded. Imaiqah's father had told her as much, in one of his letters. Stirrups were simply too obvious an idea, once someone actually made the breakthrough. They too would have spread, no matter what King Randor had done to try to keep them a state secret. One person taking a look would probably be able to guess the basic idea.

"I'm informed that there are other ideas taking shape in the workshops," the king added. "These...steam engines. I am told that one of them should be ready for testing any day now. New kinds of metal. And knowledge. Knowledge is spreading faster now. What will that mean for us?"

"A better world," Emily said. "One where more people achieve their potential."

For some reason, people tended to take knowledge more seriously if it was written in books. One particular leaflet had talked about basic hygiene, starting with the concept of always boiling water—which was widely-known—and going on to discuss basic cleanliness as the key to good health. Emily was no doctor, but even *she* knew the importance of good hygiene.

This world *didn't* know it. Outside of the very wealthy or well-connected, very few people could afford a healer to attend them when they were ill. Or giving birth; Emily had listened to an account of a childbirth in Dragon's Den and had felt utterly disgusted. Didn't they *know* that a dirty bed was almost certain to infect either the mother or her child? A clean delivery room, clean tools to cut the cord, boiled water to wash the mother and child…such little things could make all the difference between life or death. As the knowledge spread, most midwives—there was a midwives guild, the only one that was exclusively made up of women—would either adapt or start losing business. Emily found it hard to care about their feelings.

But she knew she should. The midwives would have to spread the innovations to women who couldn't read.

"But also one where your innovations will put new stresses on society," King Randor said. He might have had a point. If health levels grew better, Zangaria would have a population explosion during his or Alassa's reign. Eventually, it would reach the limits of the kingdom's ability to feed it and collapse, but it would take years to reach a new balance. "What will it do to us?"

"Make a better…"

"And what else?" King Randor demanded, suddenly angry. "Do you know how many nobles have come to me and demanded that I ban the printing press?"

His eyes narrowed. "Or, for that matter, that I banish the people responsible for introducing your innovations," he added. "But what would *that* do to my kingdom?"

"There is a legend about a man who found a goose that laid golden eggs," Emily said, feeling her heartbeat starting to race. King Randor *could* banish Imaiqah and her family, or simply kill them and destroy the new workshops. "Every day, the goose would lay an egg and the man would spend the money, enjoying whatever he bought with it. Until the day he decided to kill the goose and see what was inside it."

His eyes bored into her as she continued, forcing her to fight to meet his gaze. "He found nothing, but…but whatever one normally finds inside a goose," she continued, waving her hand in the air. "And because the goose was dead, there were no more golden eggs for him and he died a pauper."

There was a long uncomfortable pause.

"My daughter will inherit a kingdom shaped by the decisions I take," King Randor said, coldly. "I do not know where these innovations will lead. Why should I allow them?"

"They will build up the wealth of the kingdom," Emily said, quietly. "If you are wise enough to keep the tax levels low, you will still have a flood of golden eggs from the merchants and craftsmen to come. The more ideas are shared, the more innovations there will be. The more innovations, the wealthier your kingdom—and the more you can claim in tax. Eventually, you will become far wealthier than any of your barons."

"And a class of merchants who will demand a greater say in government," King Randor said. He'd spotted the sting in the tail, all right. The Assembly would eventually grow to the point where it would want a say in political affairs, as well as wealthy commoners marrying into poor, yet haughty noble families. "Who knows where *that* will lead?"

Parliamentary democracy, Emily thought. But it wasn't a concept she could explain, not without having to tell him where it came from. And that was only the best possible outcome; the middle class managed to gain the levels of power and co-opt the upper classes, effectively replacing them. In much of Europe, the upper class managed to co-opt the middle class, creating poorly-managed states that eventually went fascist. And in Russia and China, revolution from below eventually led to communist states.

"I would like to make use of your innovations," King Randor said, "but I fear where they will lead us."

"They will make your kingdom far more powerful compared to states that *don't* embrace them," Emily offered.

"Yes," King Randor said. "You do realize that you've already lost control?"

"I never really had it," Emily admitted. The moment she'd sent the letters to Imaiqah's father, the matter had been out of her hands. They were already designing printing presses and steam engines that were—so far—only theoretically possible. Materials science had barely even entered infancy. "But too much control can be a bad thing."

"So can too little control," King Randor said, softly. "But that was my mistake with Alassa. I gave her too much freedom because I resented my father directing my every waking moment. Does she have time to rebuild her reputation before she takes the throne?"

He shook his head. "We will talk about that later," he added. "For now, I believe that Lady Barb is waiting to see to you."

Emily couldn't help a shiver.

Chapter Twenty

"Y̲OU APPEAR TO HAVE SURVIVED," LADY BARB SAID. "THE KING WAS QUITE PLEASED with you."

Emily flushed, feeling unsure of her own emotions. The king hadn't sounded pleased with her–and if she hadn't saved Alassa's life and soul, she had the feeling that the king would have wanted her dead. Maybe he *did* want her dead, but the complex network of obligations that underwrote a monarchy insisted that he should keep her alive. Failing to reward someone who helped him would not have encouraged others to do the same.

"Pleased," she repeated. "I don't think I want to see his displeasure."

Lady Barb snorted. "*They* will see his displeasure," she said, nodding towards the princes at the far end of the hall. "Just look at them."

Emily concealed her amusement. While they'd been traveling, the princes had worn traveling outfits that weren't too dissimilar; indeed, they'd looked almost identical. Now they were in Zangaria, they were able to wear whatever they wanted, just to show off their powerful bodies. Prince Hildebrand wore a golden tunic that was tight in all the right places, Prince Slark wore a suit of silver armor–Emily was surprised it didn't push the limits of the permissible–and Prince Athol wore a set of green robes, cut like the robes students wore at Whitehall. The only prince who didn't seem to be interested in showing off was Prince Hedrick, who wore a simple black suit.

They hadn't just concentrated on their clothes either. Their hair had been styled in different patterns, with several of the princes actually opting to dye their hair purple or green. Emily couldn't help thinking of them as more than a little effeminate, although social customs from back home didn't always apply in Zangaria. But they still looked a little absurd to her eye.

"Peacocks," she said. "What happens if none of them win her?"

"They go back home," Lady Barb said, simply. "And besides, even if one of them did get to marry her, the marriage wouldn't take place at once."

But they would exchange binding vows, Emily thought. Historically, royal engagements had been made and broken with the greatest of ease. Here, though, both parties would swear formal oaths, enforced by magic. If Alassa refused to marry the prince later in life, the results might be disastrous. King Randor was probably working hard to ensure that all kinds of weasel words were worked into the contract, just to allow his daughter to break it without suffering for it.

Lady Barb rose to her feet. "The princes will spend the day entertaining the court," she added. "They won't be seeing the princess again until tonight."

Emily blinked. "Entertaining the court?"

"They will be calling upon powerful nobles and seeking their support for their suit," Lady Barb explained. "If they manage to convince some of the nobles to support them, the king will take it into consideration when he makes his final choice."

Emily scowled. She'd had a vision of the princes playing football or something to show off in front of the court, although it was a silly thought. Or maybe not. There were enough princes to make up two football teams and it would give them a chance to show off in front of Alassa. But mere skill at football–or fighting–wouldn't be enough to win her hand.

Lady Barb led her down the corridor and into a small suite of rooms. They had to be hers, Emily realized as she looked around; they were almost uncomfortably bare, even though they were in a royal castle. A handful of weapons hung on one wall, including a metal object she didn't recognize; a set of books lay on a large wooden table that looked to have been hand-carved from a tree trunk. The walls were bare stone, utterly unmarked.

"Take a seat," Lady Barb ordered. "We have a great deal to talk about."

Emily frowned. There were no seats in the room. She opened her mouth to ask, then realized that she was meant to sit on the stone floor. It felt uncomfortable under the dress as she knelt, unsure if Lady Barb was trying to irritate her or if it was merely the way she always acted. The sergeants had disdained luxuries too. But a simple wooden chair wouldn't have been too much of a luxury, surely.

Lady Barb sat cross-legged, facing her. "There will be another dance this evening," she said, rather dryly. "Nightingale will no doubt wish to ensure that you meet some of the younger noblemen in the court."

"Why?" Emily asked. She hesitated, then asked the question that had been bothering her since the fourth castle they'd visited. "Why are there so many dances?"

"They're intended to prove that the dancers are physically healthy," Lady Barb said. "There is no way that the happy couple"–her lips twitched into a very brief sneer–"will be able to inspect one another naked prior to the ceremony. Dancing…is a way of proving it–and not just to the prince and his family. And besides, it allows Alassa to meet them in controlled circumstances."

That made sense, Emily decided. Most customs made sense, at least in context. It was when people kept them after the original purpose was no longer required–or forgotten–that cultures and nations tended to run into trouble. Alassa's own impressions of the princes would be important, even if she wouldn't have the final say on who she married–and she'd want to see how they behaved in the castle. Prince Slark had already put himself out of the running, thanks to his behavior. And, as he had a younger brother, there wouldn't be any diplomatic repercussions from a blunt refusal.

Lady Barb cleared her throat. "How much do you know about cockatrices?"

"Very little," Emily admitted. The one she'd captured had been the first one she'd seen. "I know that they were created by the Faerie, but little else."

"We're not sure how they breed, or even if they *do* breed," Lady Barb said. "Roosters might not last very long, but dragons are effectively immortal. But we do know that they prefer to stay away from humans. They know that we can kill them."

"We didn't kill the one we encountered," Emily pointed out. If she hadn't had the idea of distracting the beast with its own reflection, then putting it in the chest, who knew what would have happened? The most likely answer was that the cockatrice would have eaten them all and destroyed the carriages—or she would have had to use the disintegration spell. "How many magicians does it take to kill one?"

"At least ten, working in unison," Lady Barb said, grimly. "But they normally stay away from all humans, unless someone does something incredibly stupid, like walking into one of their lairs. This one shouldn't have been anywhere near the mountain pass."

Emily saw the implication at once. "Someone pointed it at us," she said. "Just like they used the maid."

"Indeed," Lady Barb said. "Which brings us back to the original questions; who did it and what were they really trying to achieve?"

"I have a different question," Emily said. "What does it take to control a cockatrice?"

"A great deal of magic or an uncanny relationship with animals," Lady Barb told her. "But most magicians with a strong connection to the animal kingdom are unlikely to get themselves involved in political struggles. A necromancer, on the other hand..."

Emily shivered. Shadye had raised an army of monsters to attack Whitehall, controlling them through his magic—but he'd been trying to lay siege to the most heavily defended building in the world. A necromancer wouldn't have *needed* the cockatrice to wipe out the entire procession; he could just have swooped down, blasted the carriages with raw magic and killed everyone before they even realized that they were under attack. But then, the necromancer would have had to come far into the Allied Lands, where hundreds of magicians could be rallied to fight him.

If Lady Barb was right—and the cockatrice had been pointed at them deliberately, just like the murderous maid—it suggested that their enemy was afraid to confront them directly. And that implied...what?

And who was the real target?

"The cockatrice could have easily killed everyone," she pointed out, finally. "If they needed Alassa alive, their entire plan could have failed spectacularly."

"Unless the beast had orders merely to kill you, then leave," Lady Barb countered. She rubbed her forehead. "Or unless there are actually two separate parties trying to get at us."

She ticked off points on her fingertips. "The necromancers want you dead—and if Alassa dies too, there will be chaos in Zangaria. That's something they'd want, because it might lead to a general war that will weaken the Allied Lands. And you have other enemies who also want you dead, but who wouldn't want to kill Alassa as the chaos might sweep over their countries."

Her eyes narrowed. "And then, you *have* been a good influence on Alassa—and you are responsible for many of the changes sweeping the Allied Lands. There are some among our own nobility who would want you dead for that alone."

Emily shivered. She still wasn't used to the idea of strangers wanting to kill her. *Then get used to it*, she told herself. *It isn't going to go away.*

"But it is possible that our neighbor kingdoms are actually hoping that Zangaria *will* fall into civil war, so they can pick up the pieces afterwards," Lady Barb continued.

"And the power balance might be altered if Alassa married the wrong person. They'd have a motive to kill her, even though the chaos might spread over their borders and into their kingdoms. It would also be an act of war."

She looked up at Emily. "If *that* is the motive behind the assassination attempt, *Alassa* was the target," she concluded. "But they just *had* to destroy the girl's mind. We don't know *what* she was thinking."

Emily nodded. "Could King Jorlem have ordered the girl to assassinate Alassa—or me—himself?"

"It would have been a complete disaster if it had gotten out," Lady Barb said. "You will have noticed that Alassa traveled with only a handful of servants, none of whom were personal attendants? The whole protocol for such visits states that the host kingdom will provide those services, just to show off how they can pamper royal guests. Just by one of the maids being controlled by an outside party, King Jorlem lost a great deal of credibility in front of his fellow monarchs. It would have been far worse if she'd actually died while under his care."

Emily *hadn't* noticed—and cursed herself for the oversight. Of *course* Alassa would have had servants accompanying her at all times; certainly, the old Alassa would have insisted on it. But Emily hadn't been raised to have servants and she hadn't really noticed their absence; besides, Alassa had made a big issue of being able to dress herself. She hadn't realized that Alassa had been preparing for royal visits where the servants would be strangers, strangers who would almost inevitably report on her to their masters.

"But that raises another problem," she said, finally. "What if the whole idea was to embarrass King Jorlem? Or to precipitate a war with Zangaria?"

"Too many possibilities," Lady Barb said. She stood up and started to pace around the room, finally stopping in front of the small collection of weapons. "All we can do is work hard to keep Alassa safe."

Emily worked the problem, trying to recall everything she'd read about assassins who had killed—or tried to kill—monarchs. Killing Alassa would be dangerous, simply because of the risk of civil war, but what about taking control of the kingdom through her? A powerful nobleman might just be able to get himself appointed regent if King Randor died, allowing him to be king in all but name. But Alassa was seventeen, not *seven*. How long would such a plan last?

On the other hand, it might not have to last very long. Whoever married Alassa would have a claim to the throne—and if someone happened to hold most of the physical power, they might be able to force Alassa into marriage. And if they *did* have the power, the other nobles might grit their teeth and go along with it, particularly if the largess was distributed with an open hand. If...

"The barons are not supposed to have more than two hundred personal guardsmen," Lady Barb said, once Emily had outlined her reasoning. "The Royal Army outnumbers them all twenty to one."

That wasn't reassuring. The sergeants had pointed out that countries with large armies had been defeated by smaller armies in the past, armies that had known what they were doing. It wasn't just manpower that determined the winner, but having that manpower where it was needed at the right time. Emily wouldn't have been surprised to discover that most of the Royal Army troops were positioned along the borders, several days march from Alexis. A quick strike at the city might allow the mastermind to present the Royal Army with a done deal.

"Twenty thousand cooks," she muttered. "How many retainers are they allowed in all?"

Lady Barb lifted an eyebrow. "Twenty thousand cooks?"

Years ago, Emily had read a science fiction story set on a world caught between modernity and a barbaric past. One nobleman, barred from having a large army, had raised a force of 'cooks,' armed very carefully with knives, spoons and ladles, all utensils that just happened to have a military application with a little imagination. The ruling monarch hadn't seen the joke and crushed the ill-disguised attempt at rebellion. In hindsight, after months spent training with the sergeants, Emily doubted that the idea would have worked very well. The cooks would still have faced a small army of men with real weapons.

But it *did* have a real-life counterpart, although much less dramatic. Napoleon had barred the Prussians from raising a large army, suspecting–correctly–that it would be used against him. Undeterred, the Prussians had conscripted men and trained them for a year, then released them and conscripted a second batch of men. When the time came to throw off the restrictions and expand their armies, they had a much larger force than Napoleon had expected at their disposal, simply by recalling all the trained men.

"It's possible that one of the barons could have tried something like it," Lady Barb said, once Emily outlined her thoughts. "And they have plenty of lands to build up their forces without being detected. But they'd still have to get the army into Alexis without being detected."

"Shadye managed to get an army close to Whitehall without being detected," Emily pointed out.

It was still a mystery how the necromancer had managed that feat. Sergeant Harkin had speculated that Shadye might have dug a tunnel–a portal would have been detected–under the massive mountain crags barring his path, but none of the exploration missions that had been sent out after Shadye's death had found anything. Emily had privately worried that they might stumble over something else while searching for the tunnel, yet nothing seemed to have happened. The grandmaster, the only other person who knew that there was a reason to be concerned, had certainly said nothing to her about it.

"None of the barons are necromancers," Lady Barb said, flatly. "If they were, we'd know about it by now."

"I hope you're right," Emily said, softly. "What about the lesser nobility?"

"The barons are the only ones who could hope to build up an army without having it noticed," Lady Barb said. "Besides, the smaller nobles tend to support King Randor–and they'd support his daughter, if there was no other choice. The barons pushed them around during the Age of Bryon and the lesser nobles *hated* it. That was how Alexis III was able to get them to support the Assembly."

Emily blanched as another thought occurred to her. Lady Barb had assumed that an aristocrat was behind the plot, if it was aimed at Alassa. Killing Emily might just be part of the plot. But what if the plotters were in the Assembly? Someone might just believe that killing Alassa would lead to democracy, or at least rule by the Assembly, rather than the nobles. It sounded insane, but revolutionaries had never been particularly sane…

But it wasn't something she dared mention. The consequences could be disastrous.

"Here," Lady Barb said. She plucked a small dagger off the wall and held it out, hilt first, to Emily. "King Randor has granted you special permission to carry it, but he would rather you didn't call attention to it."

Emily nodded. No one, apart from the royal guardsmen, carried weapons in the castle. Even the princes wore empty scabbards. Giving her a weapon might well be seen as a calculated insult to everyone else, even though she suspected that most people would never even recognize that it was a possibility. The kingdom had accepted the existence of sorceresses, but it didn't seem to really understand that a woman could carry a mundane weapon just as easily as a man.

Better to be underestimated, she told herself, as she hid the dagger in her dress.

"Alassa will be busy for hours," Lady Barb said. "Everything has to be absolutely perfect for her Confirmation."

Emily nodded. "I was invited to visit the Court Wizard," she said. "I wanted to ask him about the Royal Bloodline."

"Just don't sell him your new pet for less than twenty thousand gold," Lady Barb advised. "The scales alone could bring him enough money to set himself up as a wealthy nobleman in his own right."

"I don't want to kill it," Emily protested. The thought was appalling. "Perhaps I should just keep it as a pet."

"And then it will eat you, if it breaks free," Lady Barb warned. "Be careful. Be *very* careful."

Chapter Twenty-One

ALCHEMY WAS THE CLOSEST THING TO SCIENCE EMILY HAD DISCOVERED SINCE SHADYE had kidnapped her, although it seemed to follow rules that would have either perplexed or infuriated scientists from back home. It didn't divide neatly into subsets either; research into the magical proprieties of certain materials could lead neatly into biological research, or send a researcher haring up towards a dead end. Most of the alchemists she'd met had been rather strange, even by the standards of Whitehall; they tended to spend most of their time in the lab, fiddling with new experiments. It was very rare, according to Professor Thande, to encounter one serving as a Court Wizard.

Zed's lab was large, larger than the workrooms they used at Whitehall, crammed with tables, caldrons and glass containers holding various kinds of brightly-colored liquids. Emily could smell a multitude of different scents from the moment she stepped inside, although unlike a born Alchemist she couldn't separate them out and identify the different materials. Zed himself wore white robes inside his lab, rather than anything that identified his rank. Emily realized, in a sudden flash of under-standing, that part of the reason Zed had been given the position of Court Wizard was that he wasn't personally ambitious. He wasn't inclined to turn it into a power base for future expansion.

"My Lady Emily," Zed said, with a half-bow. Technically, she should have bowed to *him*—she was still a sorceress-in-training, rather than an independent magician—but Zed didn't seem to care. "Welcome to my lab."

Emily had to smile. The room was as chaotic as King Randor's private study, almost as bad as the alchemical workrooms Professor Thande had made her clean after a particularly disastrous lesson in alchemy. She suspected that she would be doing a lot of cleaning in the next three years, if only because she lacked the sin-gle-mindedness that was part and parcel of a good Alchemist. Brain emerged from behind a towering pile of glass tubes and gave her a shy smile.

"Thank you," Emily said. She waved cheerfully at Brain as he retreated back behind the test tubes. Glass was so expensive, she realized, because alchemists bought up most of the supplies. Professor Thande's lessons always included at least one or two test tubes being broken by unwary students. "This is a remarkable place."

Zed beamed. It had clearly been the right thing to say. "Alexis I actually started this lab," Zed explained. He turned and led her towards a small side door. "You wouldn't believe that someone who spent most of his time governing a kingdom could be an Alchemist, but he actually made a very good start on the Royal Bloodline. We've done a great deal more since him, of course, yet he laid very strong foundations. He would have been the greatest Alchemist in history if he'd been able to devote all of his time to his studies."

They stepped through the door and into a smaller room, with a table, several chairs and a single glowing light high overhead. "I don't let any of the maids come in here to clean," Zed explained, as he waved Emily to a chair. "My old master used to say that you could never let anyone else clean your lab, or it will be contaminated. He was a little strange in the head, but he was right about that."

Emily concealed a smile. All alchemists were a little strange in the head.

Zed seemed to read her mind. "Oh, he believed all sorts of nonsense," he added. "Would you believe that he actually thought that *women* radiated a field that disrupted magical vibrations? He had a daughter and an experiment that never fully worked and he thought the two of them were connected. And then he set out to find an apprentice who liked *men* on the grounds that it might reduce the disruption."

"Oh," Emily said. Maybe *she* was a poor Alchemist, but Alassa and Imaiqah were both near the top of the class in Alchemy. The whole concept sounded more than a little absurd, although not unprecedented. There had been plenty of people who believed that women couldn't do science, or were unable to cope with higher education...all eventually debunked, of course, but it had still done a great deal of damage. "And did it?"

"No," Zed said. "The problem was that he had mixed up the formula slightly, so naturally it didn't work. And then his daughter pointed out what he had done wrong and he almost had a heart attack. She went on to be one of the greatest alchemists of her era."

He picked up a large jar of water and poured it into a container, muttering a spell under his breath. "If you've been at Whitehall, you'll probably have developed a Kava habit by now," he said, without looking around. "Every student does, unless they're too stupid or too lazy to breed. I think that one of them actually married a pregnant woman because he was so lazy."

"I drink it," Emily said, wryly. "Did he *actually* marry a pregnant woman?"

"Oh, there was some sort of mix-up," Zed said. "Long time gone now."

He put the container down on the table and passed her a mug. "Pour to suit yourself," he said, seriously. "I just need to check on Brain."

Emily shook her head as he left the room. It was odd to have a magician serving anyone drinks, but perhaps it made sense. No Alchemist liked the thought of someone tampering with his experiments, even a trusted apprentice. Professor Thande had bawled out one student for touching an experiment on the table, a rare display of temper for him. She poured the Kava into the mug and tasted it, carefully. It was strong, sour and would probably keep her up half the night, no matter how much she danced.

"I hate having apprentices," Zed said, when he came back into the room. "They can never be fully trusted...but I need someone to take my place. The Royal Bloodline demands a steward."

He sat down facing her and poured himself a mug. "So tell me," he said. "How did you beat Shadye?"

Emily flushed. "I can't really talk about it," she admitted, finally. Zed seemed harmless, but alchemists were *never* truly harmless. Professor Thande had told the class—and he hadn't been joking—that the true alchemical geniuses were told to do their experiments on mountain tops or the middle of deserts, well away from civilization. "It is something I have to keep to myself."

"The grandmaster was always a secretive bugger," Zed said. "But I wonder why a defense against a necromancer would be considered a secret."

He made a show of stroking his chin, thoughtfully. "Maybe there's something about it that can't be easily duplicated," he added. "Or maybe you just got very lucky."

"Luck had a great deal to do with it," Emily admitted. "Were you the one who taught Alassa how to use magic?"

Zed gave her an odd look. "I tried," he said, finally. "But the princess refused to learn. In the end, I taught her a handful of spells and returned to my lab. I told her father that she was unlikely to be able to learn more."

He shrugged. "Those were not pleasant days. Her father would be wise to choose a more capable magician for her husband. Even *with* the Royal Bloodline, Princess Alassa was unable to learn what she needed to learn."

But she learned more at Whitehall, Emily thought. Maybe Zed had just been a poor teacher, or a bad match for Alassa. But then, Alassa *hadn't* started learning properly until she'd almost been killed. She'd been so ignorant that she'd actually tried to cheat in Basic Charms, without realizing that it would be immediately obvious to her tutors, or anyone else who actually knew the subject. It had taken months of work with Emily before she'd finally passed the exams that had barred her path to the more advanced classes.

Zed probably wasn't allowed to discipline Alassa, she thought. *How could he have been?*

"I meant to ask you about the Royal Bloodline," she said, changing the subject slightly. "What does it actually *do?*"

"Now *that* is one of the great achievements of the century," Zed said. He took a long swig of his Kava, than looked at her. "But it is also one of the great secrets."

Emily studied him. "I am a close personal friend of the princess," she said, finally. "And the king himself invited me to this kingdom."

King Randor *hadn't* said anything about studying the Royal Bloodline, but the implication was there. Zed eyed her for a long moment, then nodded. It was clear that he wanted to boast a little about his success. After all, if he was as old as he looked, he might have been working on the Bloodline for decades. Who else could he talk to?

"You are aware, of course, that magic can be used to improve a person's body and mind," Zed said. "In the short term, there are potions that can improve muscles, endurance, memory and even intelligence. Unfortunately, as you should have been told at Whitehall, such potions often have side-effects, particularly when taken regularly. Those effects can be disastrous."

Emily scowled. One of Mistress Irene's lectures had covered all of the dangers in great and somewhat repetitive detail. The potions could fail if the brewer had made even a single mistake, or turn poisonous. Or, even if they worked, the effects could be dangerous. There were stories of girls who had drunk so many memory-enhancing potions that they were literally incapable of forgetting anything, boys who had tried to *improve* their genitals and students in Martial Magic who had injured themselves, unable even to realize it because they'd blocked their sensitivity to pain. There *were* potions for Martial Magic, but Sergeant Miles brewed and distributed them personally, with dire threats about what would happen to anyone stupid enough to ignore his instructions.

"Alexis believed that certain traits could be handed down from generation to generation," Zed continued. "His mother was a keen breeder of dogs, you see, and he suspected that you could do the same to humans. If one happened to pick the right people to breed with, one would end up with superior children. It would just need a great deal of luck and research. And then it occurred to him that such traits could be engineered into his bloodline to emerge in the next generation."

Emily was surprised that Alexis had actually managed to get that far—but then, people had been breeding animals and plants for centuries before anyone had heard of DNA or genetic engineering. Given enough time and patience, it was probable that one *could* engineer humans, but she doubted that many people could wait for the generations it would take to produce results. Or, for that matter, that they'd have any real understanding of what they were doing, particularly if they combined it with their belief that noble birth meant that someone was inherently superior to a commoner. Sooner or later, inbreeding would take a deadly toll.

"He experimented, then started preparing the potions for himself," Zed said. "They were strong, even by the standards of those days; his notes suggested that they caused him and his wife terrible pain. But they managed to have four children who were healthy and handsome and keyed in for magic. Alexis II continued the experiments by appointing a Court Wizard who was primarily an Alchemist. Since then, there have been constant improvements made to the Bloodline. I have added a number myself."

His face twisted into a grin. "Do you know that the Royal Family—at least those in the direct line—have never been ill?" He asked. "Or that permanent control spells simply don't work on them? Or that you cannot even transfigure them for more than a few days? How many others, even trained sorcerers, have that kind of protection?"

Emily frowned. "But Alassa has been transfigured," she said, remembering one encounter with Melissa. Her friend had been turned into a rat. "How…"

"Not permanently," Zed said. He scowled, suddenly. "Which is at least partly why she couldn't be turned into a man."

"I'm sure that must have been annoying," Emily said, dryly. *She* wouldn't have liked to change sex, although if she'd been born in a world that seemed to have the idea that women were automatically inferior to men she might have changed her mind. But it would have confused her mind. "How…how did Alexis know that his experiment would work?"

"Oh, he experimented on commoners first," Zed explained. "They were tested and tested again until he had something that could be passed down through the generations. I read his notes of those experiments very carefully and…"

Emily barely heard him. Alexis I, the founder of the kingdom, had experimented on unwilling commoners, twisting their genes just to see what would happen. The odds would be immensely against succeeding the first time, particularly not if they didn't realize what they were actually doing. God alone knew how many monsters had been created before they'd finally found something that actually worked. Maybe Alexis's experiments had paved the way towards creating orcs and goblins...

How many had died? How many had been warped? And what had happened to them afterwards?

"Most of the experiments produced nothing, of course," Zed continued. "Some produced disastrous failures. And some..."

"What happened to them?" Emily snarled. Magic seemed to be boiling under her skin, demanding release. It would have been so easy to throw it at him. "What did he do to them?"

Zed threw her a surprised look. "I'm sure that their monarch took care of them," he said. "Those who showed no sign of ill effects were released. The others were..."

"Killed," Emily snapped. The magic inside her was responding to her anger and horror, growing stronger and stronger. Unless Zed was blind, he would be able to sense it. "They were killed after being used as test subjects."

Control yourself, she thought. It was hard to concentrate, but somehow she managed to tame the magic, absorbing it back into herself. *Remain calm.*

"The experiments produced a successful result," Zed pointed out. There was an edge to his voice that hadn't been there before. Alchemist or not, he had definitely sensed the surge of magic. "We have a Royal Bloodline."

"I know," Emily said. She forced herself to focus. "What does someone have to do to join it?"

"They need treatments," Zed said. He nodded towards the door leading into the lab. "I am brewing up the first batch now. The prince who wins the hand of our fair princess will drink it and begin the shift into the Royal Bloodline. It is *not* a pleasant process. We actually had to tie Queen Marlena down to force her to drink."

Emily winced, then a thought struck her. "You said that Alexis I had four children," she said, suddenly. "Where are *their* descendents?"

"The daughters married into other royal families," Zed said, as if it wasn't particularly important. "The king's younger son went to command the army that tried to liberate Gondar and died there, without issue. I think there was a big argument among the Allied Lands after that, because the liberation was a complete failure and cost thousands of lives..."

"Oh," Emily said. Something was nagging at her mind. "I assume you keep a copy of the Royal Family tree?"

"Of course," Zed said. "We have to know who might have been touched by the Royal Bloodline."

Emily scowled. She didn't want to ask the next question, but there was no choice. "After Alexis I, how many of the reigning kings had more than one child?"

"Alexis II had five; two legitimate and three bastards," Zed said. "Bryon had only one legitimate son and a dozen bastards. Alexis III had only two children; Randor has only one daughter, Alassa."

"A dozen bastards?" Emily repeated. It seemed excessive, although if the barons *had* wanted to keep Bryon from realizing that they'd turned him into a puppet, giving him unlimited access to women might have worked. "What happened to them?"

"Most were killed when Alexis III took the throne," Zed explained. "A handful might have vanished, but the records have been carefully sealed or destroyed."

Emily stared down at her hands, unable to fully comprehend the scale of the disaster facing Zangaria. It should have been obvious to her, if not to anyone else. Living close to other girls had made her sensitive to their monthly cycles, even though the potions they were given at Whitehall helped to keep them under control. But she'd never seen Alassa having a period.

I could be wrong, she told herself. *I don't share a room with her…*

But it was hard to deny the evidence. The number of legitimate births had fallen sharply in the Royal Family; hell, it was possible that King Randor had tried and failed to produce a bastard son. Or Alexis III, for that matter. What if Alassa *couldn't* have children at all?

A king could sleep around as much as he liked—and if he slept with an unmarried noblewoman, he might just be able to convince his aristocrats to accept the child as a heir to the throne. Or maybe he could con them into believing that the bastard was the queen's son. Alassa wouldn't have that luxury…if the prince she married couldn't give her children, the Royal Bloodline would come to an end.

They don't know what they're doing, she told herself. Or was it deliberate? No; no one, not even a necromancer could hatch a plan that would take centuries to work. *And they've knifed themselves in the back.*

"I need to talk to Alassa," she said, suddenly. Her friend might be able to put her mind at ease. "Thank you for the Kava."

Chapter Twenty-Two

Alassa's rooms were much larger than Emily's and *crammed* with servants, half of whom seemed to be doing nothing more than standing around trying to look attentive. Unlike the maids she'd encountered on the journey, there were clear hierarchies amongst them, with one of the maids firmly in charge of the others. Alassa herself sat in the middle of the room, waiting patiently while the maids fixed her hair. The fact that she was wearing nothing more than a shift in the middle of a crowd of people didn't seem to bother her.

"Take a seat," she said, when Emily arrived. "They'll be done in a few minutes."

The servants turned to face Emily and curtseyed, almost as one. Emily flushed brightly; somehow, she suspected that she would never get used to the regal treatment. At least they weren't staying on their knees this time, she told herself, as the maids turned back to watching Alassa. She couldn't imagine how her friend could tolerate having so many people around her at all times. Did they even sleep at the foot of her bed when she finally went to sleep?

She looked around the room, shaking her head at the sheer luxury of it all. The walls were painted bright blue, decorated with portraits of royal women throughout the ages, starting with the first Queen of Zangaria. She had been a determined woman, from the look in the picture's eye, but it was hard to see how she was related to Alassa. But then, the Royal Bloodline practically defined the looks of those who were born with it. Queen Marlena didn't look anything like her child either.

One large window looked out over the castle grounds. Emily walked over to it and peered down to see a group of workmen constructing a small stadium on the grounds far below. It took her a moment to realize that it was actually being set up to allow the princes to joust, although she honestly wasn't sure why King Randor would allow it. If one of the princes felt humiliated, what might happen next? They should have been warned to be on their best behavior, but they were royal *princes*, unused to anyone telling them *no*.

Emily wondered just who they expected to impress. Alassa hadn't been any more amused by team sports than Emily herself, though she'd had different reasons. Maybe the commoners from the city would be invited to come and watch...no, that was unlikely. There was no reason anyone would invite people who had nothing to contribute. The thought was absurd.

"You are all dismissed," Alassa said, from behind her. "Go."

Emily turned, just in time to see the servants filing out. Few of them looked happy at being dismissed, even though they'd had nothing to do. A handful even threw cross glances at Emily, as if she was personally to blame for their misfortunes. Did they actually think that *she* had ordered them out? But then, it was safer to blame the visitor than the royal princess.

"I used to *like* having them around," Alassa complained, once the door was firmly closed. "And now I feel crowded. When I am queen, I am going to tell Nightingale to get rid of half of them before I have a child myself."

Emily snorted. It probably wouldn't be that easy. With only one royal child in the castle, there would be an immense struggle if anyone's patronage was cut—and it would have to be cut, if Alassa wanted to reduce the number of attendants. Maybe most of the servants were low-born, although even *that* was questionable, but their patrons would be noblemen. Hell, most of them probably owed their positions to Nightingale.

"Sit on the bed, but don't let them see you doing it," Alassa added, mischievously. "They will *talk*."

"Oh," Emily said. "How many servants do you have?"

"My own household, which isn't actually under my control, has three hundred people," Alassa said. "And it seems to have expanded while I was at Whitehall."

She smiled. "But thank you for coming," she added. "It gave me an excuse to chase them all out without resorting to threats."

Emily smiled back, then started casting privacy wards into the air. Alassa's eyes opened wide, but she said nothing as Emily completed the spells. She had no idea if it was rude or not to use them in the castle—they weren't blocking anyone's way into the room—but Alassa could probably approve it for her. Besides, she didn't want anyone overhearing their conversation.

"Let me guess," Alassa said. "You've discovered that one of the princes secretly likes *boys*."

"Worse than that." Emily said. "Can I ask you a rude question?"

Alassa frowned. "Ruder than the ones my father asked me before you came to join us for breakfast?" She asked. "They were *very* rude—and personal. And I had to answer them."

Emily felt a moment of pity. One of the odder traits of the Royal Bloodline was that anyone who was sealed to it—either through birth or marriage—could *not* lie to the prime member, the ruling King. Alassa could never have lied to her father, nor could she have knowingly misrepresented the truth. If her father had decided to question her about potential boyfriends, she would have had to answer. It was easy to imagine that one of the questions might have been about her virginity.

"I'm not sure," Emily admitted. "Do you…do you *bleed*?"

"Irregularly," Alassa said, after a long moment. "Why do you ask?"

Emily took a long breath and explained what Zed had told her, starting with what Alexis I had done to establish the Royal Bloodline and about the decline in royal births that seemed to follow the modifications woven into the Royal Bloodline. There was no way she could ask if her father had a bastard son, but given Alassa's sex and her behavior prior to Whitehall, it seemed unlikely. Surely, the king would have tried to put such a son forward as a potential heir.

Alassa stared blankly at her when she'd finished. "What exactly does that mean?"

"Your family needs, in every generation, at least two children," Emily said. "Ideally, they want two *male* children, an heir and a spare. Right now, your family isn't getting what it needs."

Alassa nodded, impatiently.

"So what happens if you *can't* have children?" Emily asked. What did it actually mean if someone bled irregularly? A weak fertility cycle or something else, something worse? "What happens to the kingdom then?"

"Disaster," Alassa said. Her entire body tensed. "Do you think that it's likely?"

"I don't know," Emily admitted. "I'm not sure that the alchemists really knew what they were doing."

Alassa stood up and rounded on her. "Explain," she snapped, in a tone that would have gotten her in deep trouble at Whitehall. "What is happening to us?"

Emily hesitated. How did one explain genetics to someone intelligent but completely ignorant of the fundamentals? And if she did, she'd have to explain where the knowledge came from in the first place. She might have promised Alassa the truth, when she took the throne, but what would happen if Alassa told her father about Emily's words? King Randor wouldn't be satisfied with vague evasions, not on a matter so fundamental. He'd want definite answers.

But there was no choice.

"Imagine…*cooking*," she said, finally. Alassa didn't take Martial Magic. She'd probably never cooked in her life. Still, it was the best she could do. "You mix up the ingredients, cook them and produce…whatever you wanted to cook. Making a baby works on similar principles. The man contributes, the woman contributes…and the baby is the combination of both of them."

"I learned that from my mother," Alassa said, sarcastically. "So what does that mean for us?"

"If a couple has five children, they are all made from the same ingredients," Emily explained, as patiently as she could. Maybe she should have studied genetics, as well as a hundred other subjects that would have been more useful at Whitehall than on Earth. "The only thing that's different is the mixing."

Alassa giggled.

Emily shot her a sharp look and continued. "The problem is that some of those ingredients are bad ones," she said. She knew enough to explain about dominant and recessive genes, but that would have taken too long. The analogy was simpler. "If you have a bad ingredient, it can be overshadowed by the other ingredients, but it isn't actually *gone*. If those children actually happened to marry *each other*, the bad ingredients would be strengthened."

"But if those people happened to be perfect," Alassa said slowly, "wouldn't perfection reinforce itself? That's why the high nobility refuses to even consider marrying commoners. Their blood is purer than their social inferiors."

"Except the bad ingredients would combine and grow stronger," Emily said. On the face of it, Alassa's logic was perfect, as well as making perfect sense for her world–but it just didn't work that way. "Incest is an extreme example; the bad ingredients would definitely find partners and grow stronger. Depending on the exact mixing, the bad ingredients might be the ones in control. However, even if you had a larger population without overt incest, the bad ingredients would still be there. Sooner or later, they would be reinforced when two carriers meet, marry and produce children."

"I think I understand," Alassa said, doubtfully. "The nobility has only a handful of people it can legitimately marry, so any bad ingredients will eventually pop up into the open."

"Close enough," Emily said. She held up a hand before her friend could say anything. "The problem is that the alchemists started fiddling with the Royal Bloodline to engineer traits they found desirable, without fully understanding what they were doing. It's quite possible that one of the traits they created had a side effect that reduced fertility. Or that they tried to select for male children and simply failed to get it quite right."

"If they had, I wouldn't have been born," Alassa snapped. "But why did it even happen?"

"They didn't know what they were doing," Emily reminded her. "It's possible that they never noticed until it was too late, if they noticed at all. Your father has a brother, remember. The real problems might not have appeared until your father took the throne."

She hesitated again, then plunged on. "Your mother had to be treated to join the Royal Bloodline. Is it possible—now—for someone without the treatments to bear royal children? Or could you get pregnant if your partner wasn't treated?"

"I do not know," Alassa said, after a moment's thought. "My mother told me *never* to experiment with boys, not even a mere kiss."

Emily noticed that she didn't say that she'd *obeyed*, but kept that thought to herself.

"It could get worse," she said, instead. "The Royal Bloodline might be destroying the vigor you need from outside families. Instead, it may be folding over and over itself. In the long run, it could destroy your family."

"My Uncle has no children," Alassa said. "His wife never took the treatments."

Emily reached out suddenly and hugged Alassa as tightly as she could. Who would know about the problem? The aristocracy probably paid close attention to the king's child—and to the king himself, who might be seeking comfort in the arms of a mistress. Would they notice that he'd only had one child, legitimate or otherwise? It was certainly possible to prevent conception—there were potions that could do that—but King Randor might not have used them, not if he *needed* a male heir. And yet he'd failed to produce one.

It struck her that they could have simply given the treatments to other women—a short-term solution, at the very least—before she realized that might have given their children a claim to the throne. Or perhaps a stronger claim…she shook her head, wondering why someone had deliberately set out to make such a complex system. No; it was more likely that it had grown up over the decades, as the Empire was slowly replaced by successor kingdoms. Every time she tried to follow the lines of quasi-logic that marked the difference between legitimate and illegitimate children she felt her head starting to hurt.

"They don't know what they're doing," Alassa repeated. There were tears in her eyes. "Where is it all going to end?"

"You should be able to do something about it," Emily said. "Maybe I'm wrong. Or maybe there are ways to make someone compatible with you without giving them the rest of the bloodline. It needs research…"

It crossed her mind that she should call Professor Thande. He was younger than Zed, but very well thought of in the alchemical field. Maybe he would be able to offer suggestions.

But it wasn't her call to make.

"I shall discuss it with my father," Alassa said, finally. She pushed Emily away gently and walked over to the chair, sitting down on it with a sigh. "I hope you're wrong."

"So do I," Emily said.

But she had a feeling that she *wasn't* wrong. Royal families on Earth had suffered badly because of inbreeding, most notably the Hapsburgs. Charles II of Spain—the last of the line—had been a suffering animal, unable even to chew his food properly. And he'd been impotent, unable to continue the line. Perhaps it had been something of a relief. Other branches of his family had had similar problems, even if nothing quite so extreme. She'd worried about Alassa before she realized the true nature of the Royal Bloodline.

Alassa straightened up. "There will be another dinner tonight," she said, changing the subject. "And then a dance. A number of young noblemen have requested the pleasure of your company, but as most of them are really boring I have arranged for you to be escorted by Sir Xavier. Officially, he's a diplomat who has represented Zangaria to the White Council several times in the last four years."

Emily frowned. "Don't I get to choose my own escort?"

"I thought you hated having men trying to court you," Alassa said. She stuck out her tongue, then smiled, brilliantly. "I can arrange for you to be escorted by Prince Wandering Hands, if you like, or Baron Ambitious, or even Sir I-Want-To-Be-A-Lord. You're my best friend—just how many of them want to get close to me through you?"

Her smile died. "This way, you get a reasonably entertaining companion and I get to look like I control your life," she added. "They'll draw the right conclusion and leave you alone."

"Thank you," Emily said, finally. "Do I still have to dance?"

"Dance the first dance," Alassa advised. "After that…if you don't want to dance, don't let them fill out your dance card. It's a major insult to refuse a dance once the name is on your card. Unless you're injured, of course. They'd be expected to understand that."

Emily snorted. Far too many rules in the aristocratic world seemed to depend on everyone being perfectly aware of when the rules were ignored, but paying no attention as long as the formalities were observed. Alassa's arrival at each of the castles in a grubby carriage and traveling clothes could be construed as an insult, but no one *royal* had actually met her at the door. They knew perfectly well what she'd done—and why—yet they said nothing. The implied insult could be ignored.

"Or ask Sir Xavier to fill out every dance," Alassa added. "He hates these balls too."

"I like him already," Emily said. "Is there a reason for that?"

"Officially, he's a diplomat," Alassa repeated—and winked. "Unofficially, he's a Black Sword—one of my father's spies. But I didn't tell you that. I'm not actually meant to know."

Emily had to laugh. "How did you find out?"

"I have sharp ears," Alassa admitted. "And I was often presented to guests when my father was hosting meetings. They all pretended to admire me—and then ignored me from that moment onwards." Her face fell. "I should have been paying more attention. And I should have been more...like a princess."

"You have plenty of time to make up for what you didn't learn," Emily said. No *wonder* King Randor had been so worried. His daughter should have started learning how the levers of power worked right from birth. Instead, he had allowed her to become a brat. "And besides, you have friends who will help you."

"I should give Imaiqah a title," Alassa said. "I *will*, when I'm queen. Is it wrong of me to enjoy her company?"

She shook her head before Emily could answer. "Tomorrow, we're going hunting in the game preserves," she added. "You are welcome to come, as are the ladies of the court." Her lips twitched. "Although most of *them* will stay back and pretend to faint if they see even the slightest splash of blood. The prince who brings back the most carcasses will be honored by being allowed to sit beside me at table."

"I thought you had to treat them all equally," Emily said.

"I do," Alassa agreed. She gave Emily a droll grin. "But I can choose which one sits beside me tomorrow."

There was a knock at the door. "Time to get into something less comfortable," Alassa said, with a sigh. "And to think that Imaiqah is having *fun*."

The door opened, revealing a small army of maids. "Go to the library," Alassa added. "The maids will find you when it is time to get dressed. And if Nightingale complains, feel free to turn him into a toad."

"I think your father would object," Emily said.

"I *know*," Alassa said, with a sigh. "He certainly complained enough when *I* did it."

"You turned him into a toad?" Emily asked. "Why didn't they change him back?"

Chapter Twenty-Three

T HE CASTLE'S LIBRARY WAS NOTHING LIKE AS INTERESTING AS WHITEHALL'S LIBRARY, although it did manage to have quite a lot of information on the royal and noble family trees. Emily traced Alassa's line backwards, wondering if she was actually right after all; there was no direct evidence to *prove* that the Royal Bloodline was reducing fertility. But it was impossible to deny the fact that there were fewer and fewer children in each generation, until Alassa had been an only child, without even a half-sibling.

She sat at a heavy wooden table and made notes on a piece of parchment, trying to figure out what—if anything—she could *do* about it. But the problem seemed largely insolvable, unless someone could figure out what they were actually doing and how to fix it. There was nothing in the library on the precise techniques used to create the Royal Bloodline, yet in the absence of knowing anything about genetics, she doubted that they could deal with the problems they had created.

Most of the time Earth science is superior, she thought, ruefully. *Now there is something here that is superior.*

She was still mulling it over when the maid entered the library and curtseyed to her. "Begging your pardon, Milady, but it is time to dress for dinner," she said. "There is water already prepared in your rooms."

"Thank you," Emily said, gravely. She would *never* get used to having servants, let alone being pampered all day. Besides, it was only for the summer. If Whitehall had refused to allow Princess Alassa servants, the grandmaster would certainly not allow Emily to hire a maid. "Just let me return the book to the shelf."

She put it back and then allowed the maid to lead her back to her rooms, wondering just how long it would be before the printing presses started to mass-produce proper books. Probably not too long, she decided, although it would take several years to master the concept. And then who knew what would happen? Most of the books King Randor kept in his private library were rare, but largely uninteresting. What would happen when they started experimenting with public libraries?

The Librarians Guild will be pleased, she decided. *More work for them.*

It seemed futile to argue with the maids as they fussed over her, washing her in scented water and then fixing up her hair into a neat ponytail. That too was something she definitely didn't intend to grow to enjoy; how could *anyone* survive being pampered to the extent that they couldn't put on their own clothes? Hadn't there been a royal court on Earth where each and every article of the king's clothing was supposed to be presented to him by its own set of servants? Given a couple more generations, Zangaria might be like that.

"You look lovely, Milady," the maid said, when they had finished. "The young men *will* be impressed."

Emily rolled her eyes as she walked over to the mirror and inspected herself. This time, they'd given her a dress of blue silk that shimmered around her, charmed to remain warm even in the coolest temperatures. Emily dismissed the maids and drew Lady Barb's dagger out of her previous dress, trying to decide how best to wear it. The sergeants had taught her how to use a dagger, but not how to conceal the weapon. And she knew she couldn't wear it publicly. The king would have to take official notice of *that*. Eventually, she strapped the blade to her lower leg and practiced ducking down to draw it.

There was a knock at the door. "Come in," she called, after a quick check to ensure that she was definitely decent. Alassa might be so convinced of her own superiority that she didn't care about being naked in front of her inferiors, but *Emily* knew better. "The door is unlocked."

The door opened, revealing a tall man dressed in a simple suit. He looked...average, somehow, the sort of person one might pass in the streets and never truly notice. Even his age was hard to guess, although that was true of almost anyone in a world where rejuvenation potions, glamors and hard work could make anyone look older or younger than they actually were. He had brown hair, a shade of two lighter than Emily's own, and a simple neat goatee, like many of the young men in the court. And he also looked completely harmless.

"Milady," he said, in a surprisingly deep voice. "It will be my pleasure to escort you to the dance."

He smiled at her and Emily found herself smiling back. "Thank you," she said, seriously. Maybe it wouldn't be so bad after all. "You will have to tell me all about your service as a diplomat."

"I'm sure we can find something to talk about," Sir Xavier agreed. He nodded to Emily's trunk, sitting in the center of the room. "Does that *really* contain a cockatrice?"

"Yes," Emily said. "But it is perfectly safe."

Word had spread through the castle almost as soon as they'd arrived, with the net result that the maids refused to even *look* at the chest, let alone try to move it. The spells holding the pocket dimension in place weren't *that* weak, Emily knew, although she would have to have the chest checked when she got it back to Whitehall. She'd probably invalidated the warranty, insofar as there was such a thing.

"I'm glad to hear it," Sir Xavier said. "Do you intend to turn it into your own personal transport?"

Emily shrugged.

"Maybe," she said, finally. "I haven't quite decided."

Sir Xavier held out his hand. "We can walk down to the hall now, if you please," he said, politely. "I'm afraid we can't be fashionably late for a dinner with the Princes."

Emily had to smile. Royal protocol for a formal dinner insisted that it had to start at a specific time, when the royal family entered. After that, doors would be closed and no one else would be allowed into the hall, whatever the excuse. And King Randor would carefully note the names of those who didn't attend, marking them down for future attention. From what Emily had picked up, invitations to the various balls in honor of the princes were in high demand. King Randor was using them as a way of showing favor or disfavor to the lesser nobility.

She took Sir Xavier's hand and allowed him to lead her down to the grand hall. It looked very different from when she had first seen it; the servants had brought in tables and chairs for the guests. King Randor's throne had been concealed behind a curtain; a high table had been placed at the front of the hall for the royal family. Emily realized absently that there were twenty-one tables, each one with a larger chair at its head. The princes would sit there, apart from the lucky one who would be sitting next to Alassa. She wondered if they found it insulting, before realizing that it didn't matter. They couldn't *all* sit at the high table, let alone next to the princess.

There were little nameplates on each of the tables, instructing the guests where to sit. Sir Xavier must have checked before he came to pick her up, for he headed to their seats without bothering to scan the rest of the tables. The room was filling up rapidly with nobility, including a handful of barons who were apparently seated just below the high table. Emily shook her head as she realized just how carefully the King's staff had organized the ball. The barons couldn't be seated anywhere lower or they would take it as a grave insult. Their wives and children, on the other hand, could sit anywhere. One of the children loudly whined about being seated at the rear of the room until his father told him to shut up and take his seat.

Trumpets blew twenty minutes later, just as Emily was starting to feel bored. The guests rose to their feet as King Randor walked into the room, followed by Alassa and Prince Hedrick. Alassa wore a long white dress, almost like a bridal gown, her blonde hair spilling down her back and shining under the light. Emily couldn't help wondering if there was a reason protocol insisted she looked like a bride. She couldn't marry *all* of the princes...was it just intended to tantalize them? Or was she completely wrong?

"Be seated," King Randor ordered. The guests sat down. "We shall now begin."

Sir Xavier proved to be a fascinating dinner companion, somewhat to Emily's surprise. He didn't say anything about his real work for the king, but he was quite willing to chat about diplomacy in the Allied Lands, allowing Emily to pick up more about the White Council and its role in the war against the necromancers than she'd learned at Whitehall. Apparently, he told her, the near-disaster at Whitehall had concentrated a few minds. All of the Allied Lands would be sending troops to help reinforce the border, while the haggling over who would actually *command* the force had been much reduced.

"Not that it will ever go away entirely," he admitted. "They will always fear giving someone too much power."

Emily frowned. "Will troops alone be able to stop the necromancers?"

"I don't think so," Sir Xavier said. He didn't seem reluctant to talk bluntly to her, unlike some of her other dinner companions. "But if they decide to send monsters raiding over the mountains, we can use troops to intercept them and preserve our magicians for the real threat."

Emily nodded. The books at Whitehall hadn't said much about how the Faerie had created the orcs and goblins, but they *had* gone into great detail on how the shambling parodies of humanity had been programmed to breed and bow the knee to magicians with enough power to terrify them. Once terrified, they were too stupid to do anything, but *remain* terrified; Shadye's forces had launched human wave attacks against Whitehall because they feared the consequences of disobeying him more than they feared death. They hadn't broken and fled until the necromancer had been defeated.

But each female orc gave birth to multiple children in each pregnancy. Their society—such as it was—had a permanent overpopulation problem, which was at least partly why the necromancers could make such free use of them. There was no reason why one of Shadye's fellows couldn't encourage a few thousand orcs to cross the mountains and ravage part of the Allied Lands, just to remind the local nobility that they existed. If the necromancers didn't spend so much time fighting each other, Emily knew, they would have won by now. Orcs and goblins were brutish creatures, barely capable of carrying out a plan more complicated than picking a target and charging at it, but there were a *lot* of them. Human wave attacks worked when the defender couldn't hold them back any longer.

"I really can't stand these balls," Sir Xavier admitted, changing the subject. "All of the real negotiation happens elsewhere."

"And yet the kingdoms hold them anyway," Emily mused. "Why do they hold them if they're not important?"

Sir Xavier grinned. "Because it allows the princess to meet her suitors in a controlled environment," he said. "Because it allows the nobility the chance to pretend that they have a say in who the princess marries. Because it allows King Randor, long may he reign, an opportunity to show off his daughter."

He shrugged. "I was once part of a mission to Heartbreak—that's one of the smaller islands off the coastline, ruled by a single aristocrat," he added. "We spent two weeks there and every night we were wined and dined in greater style than here. And it ended without any agreement."

Emily winced. The sheer cost of food and drink alone had to be staggering. And then there was the gold and silver plates, the jewelled goblets filled with expensive mead, the fancy clothes worn by the social queens...how could anyone afford even *one* ball, let alone fourteen of them? Zangaria was a rich country, but was it *that* rich?

But would it matter if the country couldn't afford it? She asked herself. *The king needs to put on a show.*

"So," she said. "How *are* the negotiations going?"

Sir Xavier gave her an odd look. "The king and his Privy Council are handling them personally," he said, as if he had expected her to know that. "Right now, they are keen to preserve as much of the country's independence as possible, while the other kingdoms want to secure considerable influence for their prince. King Tonal actually wanted to send a few thousand soldiers to serve as the prince's guard of honor. Completely unacceptable, of course."

Emily nodded. No kingdom would be completely happy with *any* foreign troops on its soil, certainly not enough to make a stand against the kingdom's army. On one hand, it *would* give the prince some teeth he could use to support his wife, but on the other hand it would fatally weaken her position. Alassa would be better advised to keep the royal army strong and loyal to her, which might be tricky. A queen couldn't lead armies into combat, which meant that the army might develop loyalty to her commanders instead of to her personally.

"Two other princes are being offered without any strings at all," Sir Xavier added. "That looks too good to be true, so we are left wondering if they have an ulterior motive."

"Apart from wanting to get rid of the Prince," Emily guessed.

"They don't say *that* on the proposed treaties," Sir Xavier agreed. He nodded towards Prince Jean, who sat at the head of the table. "There's another reason for these balls, Milady. It allows the king a chance to evaluate their behavior for himself. If they can't control themselves in a formal ball, they probably shouldn't be allowed anywhere near the seat of power."

Emily shrugged. It made sense—but what stopped the princes from pretending to be nice until they had won the princess?

"But enough of such talk," Sir Xavier said. "Tell me about Whitehall?"

He would have made a skilled interrogator, Emily decided, as she did her best to answer his questions. Some of them touched upon the final battle with Shadye—he wanted to know precisely what had happened, just like everyone else—while others seemed designed to learn more about Emily and her relationship with Void. Emily answered briefly, wondering just who had *really* organized her companion for the evening. Had it been Alassa, as she'd said, or King Randor? There couldn't be many people better at drawing information out of an unwilling donor without needing interrogation spells.

But then, a skilled diplomat—or a spy—would be able to read her expression...and drawing conclusions from the questions she chose not to answer.

I should have spent more time playing poker, she thought, ruefully. She had a feeling that she'd told him far more than she'd intended. Kingmaker—the local version of chess—didn't require someone to keep their face blank, at least not unless one player knew that disaster was looming and the other was ignorant of the opportunity that had been dumped in their lap. Maybe she could introduce poker...no, it was impossible. She didn't know the rules.

The meal finally came to an end, with bowls of ice cream being distributed along with the dance cards. Emily was puzzled by the large portions—ice cream had been a luxury item in medieval times—until she realized that cooling and freezing spells had probably been used to produce it, instead of icehouses. It tasted better than any she'd had back home, she decided, and managed to finish it all despite having eaten a full meal. Maybe there was another reason for the dancing, she decided finally. They needed to burn off the food they'd eaten.

Sir Xavier winked at her. "I was given to understand that you might not want to dance all of the dances," he said. Alassa *had* to have told him that. "If you like, I can mark your card for every dance and we can withdraw."

Emily grinned. "You don't learn anything useful from dancing?"

"Not really," Sir Xavier admitted. "Nothing ever gets decided on the dance floor."

"Please," Emily said, after a moment's thought. It was unlikely that he had an ulterior motive, apart from wanting to escape the ball. She held out her card and watched as he neatly signed his name in each box. "I just want to go to bed."

"Hunting tomorrow," Sir Xavier said. He gave her a rather droll smile. "All of the princes will be trying to show off in front of a princess who happens to be an enthusiastic hunter herself. It should be fun to watch from a safe distance."

Emily made a face. She hadn't liked the idea of hunting, even though she'd eaten meat from animals the sergeants had caught during expeditions. Sergeant Harkin had made a remarkably tasty venison stew. But Alassa had been keen for her to come, pointing out that most of her attendants couldn't keep up with her. The alternative was being permanently surrounded by the princes.

"Yeah," she said, as the servants started to move the tables to one side. "I suppose it will be fun."

Chapter Twenty-Four

Sergeant Harkin would have exploded with rage, Emily decided, if any of his students had shown such a…lazy…attitude to departing the castle. They'd been told that the hunt would begin at ten bells, after breakfast; the princes and their various retainers hadn't been ready at eleven bells, with the sun rising ever higher in the sky. Alassa's growing impatience had been contagious, with the effect that many of the huntsmen and the maids in waiting were growing equally annoyed. By the time the princes—seven of whom were clearly suffering from hangovers—joined them, a large part of the day had been wasted.

"Maybe we won't bother to dress for dinner," Alassa muttered. "Do you think Father would allow us to eat in our hunting outfits?"

"Probably not," Emily said. Besides, it was hot—and she was already starting to sweat. They'd be dirty and smelly by the end of the day. "Why don't we eat down there?"

"Father wants a dance every day," Alassa explained, quietly. "I think Mother wanted to make sure she got a good look at the princes before he made his decision. She will insist on having a say."

"Good for her," Emily said. She looked up as the grooms brought their horses over to them, already saddled with the new stirrups. One of the grooms helped her onto the horse, which snickered unpleasantly at her. She could tell that the beast was wondering if she really knew what she was doing. "Is this horse a safe one?"

"I told them to give you the most docile horse we have," Alassa assured her. She scrambled up into her saddle without apparent difficulty. "And compared to this one, that one is a lazy old nag."

She smiled, then raised her voice. "Open the gates!"

The gates opened. Alassa's horse cantered forward, passing through the gates and heading down the long road towards the forest outside the city. Emily shivered as her own horse started to follow Alassa, praying that the citizens had heard they were coming and made sure to get out of the way. The last thing she wanted to do was watch a child crushed by her horse's hooves. She clung on tightly as the horse picked up speed, the princes cantering past her and closing in on Alassa. Behind them, the retainers and huntsmen followed at a more sedate pace.

I will learn how to teleport, she promised herself again. Maybe she could convince Void to teach her the moment she was old enough to channel so much power. Or maybe there were potions that boosted one's power…no, that was dangerous. Several necromancers had started out that way. But anything would be better than riding a horse. No matter how many times she rode, she doubted she would ever grow used to it.

The buildings started to fade away as they passed through the gatehouse and headed towards the forest. From what Alassa had said, it was clear that the forest had been preserved by royal authority and kept well stocked with game. Commoners were not allowed to hunt in the forest, at least not without special permission. Reading between the lines, Emily suspected that obtaining permission required a huge bribe for the royal gamekeepers. No doubt there were hundreds of poachers who risked killing deer, boar and whatever else there happened to be in the forest. They needed the meat to feed their families.

They paused just outside the forest. The huntsmen advanced forward, into the gloom, while the retainers handed out weapons. Emily was offered a long spear and then a bow, both of which she declined. Alassa winked at her and stuck out her tongue, then accepted a spear and a sharp knife that looked almost large enough to be a small sword. Emily made a face in response. She might give chase, but she wasn't going to kill the poor animal.

"They're all going to try to impress me," Alassa muttered, the moment Emily was close enough to her for the princess to whisper without being overheard. "Just watch them."

Emily rolled her eyes, causing her friend to giggle. Most of the princes were swapping stories about hunting creatures in their own kingdom, including a handful of beasts that had been touched by wild magic. Emily had some problems accepting that the story of a rabbit carrying a knife—and proving extremely difficult to defeat—was actually true, although she had heard of stranger things. Other princes bragged about the number of boar or deer they had taken in a single day, reducing the entire population to nothing if all of their claims were true. Was it actually possible, Emily wondered, to kill two boar with the same spear, at the same time?

A horn blew from the gloom. Alassa let out a hunting cry and spurred her horse forward, the dogs yapping as they raced ahead. The princes followed, cheering loudly as they trampled their way through the undergrowth; Emily sighed and grabbed tight hold of the reins as her horse gave chase. She leaned down and pressed her head into the horse's neck, praying that she wouldn't run smack into a branch that would knock her off the horse's back. A fall at such speeds might result in serious injury.

The trees started to blur into a confused mass of green light as the horse moved faster. Hundreds of birds and rabbits fled from the hunters, although the hunters largely ignored them. They were after bigger game. Emily could barely see anything past the Princes, all of whom seemed to be trying to cluster together as they chased Alassa. Alassa herself was almost hidden behind them, only her long blonde hair visible as it streamed out. The maids hadn't tied it up very well.

Emily shuddered as the horsemen started to split up, the trees growing thicker and thicker. Just for a moment, she caught sight of a brown shape ahead of them, ducking and weaving in a desperate attempt to escape before it was hidden again behind one of the pursuers. The deer was moving too fast for her to get a clear look at it, but there was no mistaking it for what it was. Emily felt a brief stab of guilt, remembering the movies she'd watched as a child, before the deer was cornered. It came to a halt and stared around, looking for an opportunity to jump past them and flee again. But between the hunters and the dogs, there was no way out.

No, Emily thought, as Alassa dismounted. But there was nothing she could do.

The deer hissed at the princess as she advanced with a spear, pawing the ground in its helpless fury. It couldn't seem to decide if it wanted to attack Alassa, or the dogs, which were hanging back. They were well-trained, Emily decided; no one was holding them in place. She looked away as Alassa braced herself, then heard the howl from the animal as she drove the spear into its head. A moment later, the retainers were moving forward to pick up the carcass and carry it back to the castle.

Emily felt sick as she saw the blood on the ground. She knew—of course she knew—that people hunted for food. Hell, she knew that meat came from animals, rather than simply appearing out of nowhere, as some of her old acquaintances had seemed to believe. The price of roast beef or a simple hot dog was a dead animal. But knowing it and actually believing it were two different things.

But is that really what's bothering you? She asked herself. *Or is it that they turned the hunt into a blood sport?*

She considered it as the huntsmen headed off in search of the next deer. The sergeants had hunted deer, rabbits and fish—and she hadn't felt disgusted, even when they'd made their students help prepare the meat for cooking. Gutting a fish was thoroughly disgusting and yet she hadn't felt so sick...

Maybe it was because she'd *been* hunted.

"The hunt often affects people that way," Lady Barb said. "At least on their first true hunt."

Emily turned to see Lady Barb sitting on her own horse. She hadn't even realized that Lady Barb was accompanying them, but it shouldn't have been surprising. Alassa's retainers needed someone in charge—and Alassa herself needed a chaperone. Emily wasn't sure why they bothered when her father could simply interrogate her if there was any doubt about her conduct, but maybe they just didn't want the question to arise.

"Oh," she said, finally. "How many more are they going to kill?"

"All of them will want a turn," Lady Barb said. "Right now, they're trying to decide who gets to go next. Then they will split up into smaller groups and start charging through the forest."

"Alassa said that there would be a reward for the prince who kills the most," Emily muttered, resentfully. It was stupid—and yet she couldn't help it. "Why don't they just flip a coin to determine who gets to sit next to her every day?"

Lady Barb shrugged as the horns blew again, in the distance. "Protocol," she said. "Besides, this keeps them out of mischief."

Emily scowled as the horse started to move again, following Alassa and the princes. Lady Barb was probably right; if they were hunting, they weren't trying to make agreements with King Randor's nobility. It would be easier for the king to decide who his daughter should marry if the aristocrats weren't trying to bring pressure to bear on him.

This time, the creature they were hunting looked nastier than the deer. Emily caught glimpses of a large black shape crashing through the forest; for a moment, she thought she was looking at a panther. Were there panthers in Zangaria? It didn't seem too likely. And then the creature turned and threw itself at one of the horses, knocking Prince Jean off the back of his mount. The other princes laughed as Jean hit the ground with a thump. He didn't seem to be badly hurt, but his dignity had been bruised.

A mortal wound, Emily thought, and smiled.

Alassa kept her face under control, but Emily could tell that she was amused. "The black boar is a cunning foe," she said, deadpan. "He's slipped off while we were laughing."

Prince Jean got to his feet, muttering in a language Emily didn't recognize. It had to be old, Emily guessed, old enough to be unrelated to the Empire's official language. Or maybe it was something from his kingdom. It was quite possible that the various kings would encourage their people to start speaking in a different dialect, even though it struck Emily as absurd. Unless, of course, they didn't *want* their people talking to people from neighboring countries.

Alassa didn't bother to enquire after the prince's health. "We split up," she ordered, imperiously. The princes didn't try to argue. "I'll lead one party that will give chase; I want two more parties to try to outflank the boar. The creature is too fast to be caught easily. *Then* Prince Hildebrand can take his shot at him."

The sergeant would probably have approved of her manner, Emily decided. They'd had lectures on command presence, but it wasn't easy to learn, particularly for her. There was no easy way to avoid the simple fact that she was the youngest and least experienced student in Martial Magic—and would remain so for at least two years, unless someone else from her age decided to try to join in second-year. Jade had been able to command with ease; Emily had been morbidly convinced that her teammates were laughing at her when she took command. It had always seemed harder for her to get them to do what she told them to do.

She sighed as her horse started to follow Alassa's horse when the hunting party broke into a gallop. The black boar was definitely a wily foe, even though the creature should have been easy to see against the greenery. It *was* black, Emily realized, as black as the night—and very fast. It rounded on Alassa, ran between her horse's legs and past Emily before she could do anything. Alassa winked at her as she pulled her horse around and gave chase again. The princes thundered past Emily in hot pursuit, ignoring her completely.

Two more of the princes had suffered small, but humiliating accidents by the time the black boar was finally cornered. Up close, it looked fearsome, with nasty tusks ready to leave their mark on its tormentors. Its eyes were disturbingly humanlike; mouth lolled open, revealing very sharp teeth. The creature snarled, a long sound that made Emily's blood run cold. If it hadn't been for the dogs, Emily realized, it might have been able to nip past the hunters again and vanish into the undergrowth.

But it was cornered.

Prince Hildebrand dismounted, sword in hand. The boar eyed him maliciously as he stepped forward, the growling dogs shifting aside to let him pass. Emily stared, unable to look away, as he lifted his sword...and the boar moved backwards at terrifying speed. The other princes tittered as Prince Hildebrand's first swing missed the boar completely. Behind him, the dogs started to bark. And then the boar lunged forward.

For a heartbeat, Emily was *convinced* that Prince Hildebrand was dead. Who knew *what* would happen if a prince happened to be killed while hunting? And then he stepped to one side, lashing out at the boar as it crashed past him, through the dogs and into the forest. Emily saw a trail of red blood from where Prince Hildebrand had managed to wound the creature, although it wasn't immediately fatal. The dogs yapped, scenting blood, and gave chase. Alassa and the princes followed in its wake.

This time, following the boar was easy. There was a trail of blood leading right towards its final resting place. Emily was tempted to ask if they could let the beast go to die in peace, but she knew it wouldn't happen. They'd eaten roast boar at two of the kingdoms they'd visited and it had presumably come from the hunting parties. Besides, Prince Hildebrand wanted to have a trophy, his first kill of the day. There was no way he was just going to let it go.

The boar had come to rest in a hollow, turning to face its tormentors one last time. There was a desperation on his face that made Emily's heart wince in pain. Prince Hildebrand dismounted again and advanced forward, not bothering to be careful. It was clear that the beast was weakening fast; he would only be able to claim a kill if he actually killed it directly. A wound that caused the beast to bleed to death might not count, although the logic escaped Emily. Maybe it just wasn't as heroic as killing the beast with a swing of the blade.

Prince Hildebrand lifted his sword and the beast stopped, almost as if it welcomed the final swing. Emily stared, unsure of what she was seeing, as the sword swung down and bit into the beast's head. It emitted a long growling sigh and then lay still. A moment later, Emily felt a burst of magic twisting through the air. It seemed to be coming from the boar...

Her eyes went wide with horror as she saw the boar *change*. She'd seen enough animal transfigurations to know what they looked like, but somehow this was different. The magic that trapped someone in beast form snapped the moment they died. She stared, realizing just why the boar's eyes had been disturbingly human. There was a shimmer, then a middle-aged man was lying on the ground where the boar had been. And he was very definitely dead.

One of the huntsmen dismounted and stepped up to the body. "Black Andrew," he said, after a cursory look at the dead man's face. "He deserved his fate."

Emily stared at Alassa, unable to speak. What the hell had they done?

The huntsman didn't seem to notice her shock. "I will record you as his killer," he said, to Prince Hildebrand. He sounded businesslike, as if it were all in a day's work. Perhaps it was, to him, but it was still horrific. "There will be many people who will wish to thank you."

Emily made a strangled sound. Alassa's head whipped around to stare at her. Had she known? Of course she'd known, Emily realized; Alassa had been hunting since she had been a little girl, barely tall enough to carry a small knife. She had to have known that they were hunting humans...after months, perhaps years, as a boar, the humanity would be almost gone, but the beast would still be intelligent. It would have proven—it *had* proven—challenging prey.

"How...how could you?" Emily asked. She barely recognized her own voice. "That was *human*."

There was a snicker from one of the princes. Emily felt her magic start to boil up within her, ready to lash out at him. A single thought would be all that was required to blast him into fire, to wipe him completely out of existence...she'd thought that Alassa was her friend, but how could she do that to *anyone*? How many others had died in the hunting grounds, killed by noblemen for their sport?

She had known that permanent transfigurations were possible, certainly when the victim had no protections, but...she'd never realized where it could lead. How could she? It had been unthinkable. How could anyone be so evil?

Fighting her rage, she wheeled the horse around and dug in her spurs. The horse broke into a gallop, taking Emily away from the hunters, even though she had no idea where she was going. But it didn't seem to matter.

All that mattered was getting away.

Chapter Twenty-Five

Someone was following her. Emily heard the second horse coming after her, even over the noise her own horse was making. One person, as far as she could tell…Alassa? Or one of the princes, coming to laugh at her. Raw magic crackled around her hand and she forced it back into her wards, trying hard to calm down. But it was so hard to think. She just couldn't escape the final horrific view of the dead man.

She reined in her horse and pulled it around. Lady Barb was cantering after her, her face twisted with concern. She slowed to a halt as she realized that Emily had stopped and looked over at her. Oddly, Emily had the sense that the concern was genuine. Maybe Lady Barb wasn't as bad as Void had hinted. Or maybe she knew better than to allow her dislike for Void to contaminate her relationship with the princess's best friend. If she still *was* the princess's best friend…

"Are you all right?" Lady Barb asked, finally. "You gave everyone a scare."

Emily stared at her. "I…no," she admitted. Fresh tears welled up as she realized that she was on the verge of crying. She *never* cried. "How can anyone *do* that?"

Lady Barb studied her for a long moment. "Would it help if I told you about his crimes?"

"*No,*" Emily said. She slipped off the horse and leaned against its flank. "It would have been kinder to kill him outright."

"He robbed and murdered travelers leaving the city," Lady Barb said, ignoring her. "One of them was a young girl, about the same age as yourself. The guardsmen who found her were hardened men, but they all felt sick when they saw what he had left of her. And when he was dragged in front of the judge, the judge felt that hanging was too good for him."

Emily felt her entire body shaking. How could *anyone*, even the brat Alassa had been, do that to a human being? But it should have been obvious; if transfiguration was common, why *not* use it as a punishment? Why *not* create new game to hunt by transforming criminals into animals? And with truth spells, they'd know who was guilty and who was innocent. The innocent had nothing to fear.

And yet it was still horrifying.

The horse shifted as she shivered against its bulk. She heard Lady Barb climbing off her mount, then felt her wrapping her in a hug. Something broke inside her and she started to cry openly, great heaving sobs that tore through her as tears fell from her eyes. Lady Barb patted her on the back, holding Emily until she finally regained some control. And then she reached into her pouch and produced a small gourd of water.

"Drink this," she ordered, flatly. "Water helps calm people down."

Emily scowled at her, but obeyed. The water tasted oddly flat, as always. It would have been boiled, along with the gourd itself, just to kill all the germs.

She wiped her eyes, suddenly aware that she'd broken down in front of Void's enemy. "I'm sorry," she mumbled. "I…"

"Don't worry about it," Lady Barb said, briskly. She loosened her grip and stepped back, leaving one hand resting on Emily's shoulder. "You're a teenage girl. No teenage girl is ever stable."

Emily flushed, angrily. "I've messed up Alassa's wedding plans, haven't I?"

"I don't think so," Lady Barb assured her. "Prince Jean made a snide remark, which made Alassa give him a piece of her mind. But he didn't have a very good chance of winning her anyway. They cantered off in the other direction while I went after you."

"They're all going to be laughing at me," Emily said. She'd made a mistake...simply by not bothering to think through all of the implications. The princes might not say anything out loud to Alassa, but they would certainly snigger amongst themselves. "I..."

"The world doesn't revolve around you, Child of Destiny or no," Lady Barb pointed out. "What makes you think they *care?*"

She was right, Emily realized. If Alassa could ignore the presence of a lower-ranked man in her bedroom while she was dressing, the princes certainly wouldn't consider *Emily* to be very important, even if she was Void's daughter. And even though they had seen her trap a cockatrice, they might still not take her seriously when they were here to court a princess.

"You've upset enough kingdoms already," Lady Barn added, a moment later. "Give them a chance to get used to the last set of changes, hey?"

Emily found herself giggling helplessly. They thought the changes she'd introduced so far were upsetting? She couldn't wait to see their faces when they saw the steam engine. Maybe it would take years to produce a working locomotive, but the basic theory was easy to describe and spread around the Allied Lands. And steam power led to all kinds of useful applications, from steamboats to railroads. What would happen to the Allied Lands once there was a network of rails binding them together?

And if they worried about the roads having military applications, she thought to herself, *they will panic when they realize what the trains can do.*

Lady Barb squeezed her shoulder, hard enough to hurt. "That isn't funny," she snapped. "Your changes have put one guild out of business already and risk damaging others..."

Imaiqah's father had told Emily that the Accounting Guild—or at least some of its members—had been corrupt. Even those who hadn't been outright thieves had used their advantages ruthlessly over those who couldn't read a balance sheet. Or at least one of the old balance sheets. Double-entry bookkeeping, Arabic numerals and abacuses had made it laughably easy to spot the fraud. The Accountants might have survived—there would certainly still have been a place for them—if they hadn't been so unwilling to punish their guilty members.

"They could have adapted," Emily muttered. Sooner or later, *someone* would have stumbled on something comparable to Arabic numerals, something so useful that it would have spread like wildfire. "The world changes all the time."

"You're *just* like your mentor," Lady Barb snapped. "Doing something without ever bothering to consider the long-term consequences."

Emily flinched. She wanted to defend herself, but Lady Barb was right; she *hadn't* considered the long-term consequences of what she'd introduced to Zangaria, let alone the rest of the world. Some innovations–like stirrups–would have been adopted by the various armies without dissent, but others...the printing press alone was likely to cause problems. And, on Earth, some of those problems had become the bloodiest times in the planet's history.

And she'd been wrong. Lady Barb still disliked her because of her connection to Void.

She stared down at the muddy ground, her thoughts churning around and around in her head. If she did nothing, if she went native and allowed her knowledge to die with her, what would happen? The world would remain stuck in a rut that would last until a native produced similar changes, or until the necromancers came over the mountains and destroyed the Allied Lands. No, that wouldn't happen. What she'd done already had ensured that change would come. The only real question would be just how much chaos it would bring in its wake.

What should she do? What *could* she do? It hadn't been her who had perfected the first printing presses, or produced the increasingly advanced designs. Local crafts-men had done that, working from her ideas and then improving on them as their experience grew. They'd done the same with the abacuses and would probably wind up doing the same with steam engines, once they produced a working model. Come to think of it, they could combine science and magic to make it work; a binding spell on the locomotive might stop it leaking or exploding if metallurgy wasn't quite up to the task.

"Tell me," Lady Barb said. "Where is this leading?"

She'd told King Randor that it was leading to a better world, a simple answer that hadn't really told him anything useful. It certainly didn't include the troubles that were going to come, when education was widely available and merchants were mak-ing more money than the aristocrats could extract from their estates. The king might side with the Assembly and use them to weaken the barons, or he might side with the barons and try to strangle the changes in their cradle. Either way would almost certainly lead to civil war.

It was easy to say that the aristocrats needed to be removed, but what would happen then? France had fallen into civil war after the revolution, eventually leading to dictatorship; Britain and Russia had gone through similar phases. And she *knew* Alassa; she was Emily's best friend. If they were still friends...and how well had she known her, if Alassa was capable of killing a man? But she came from a very different culture. It was easy to forget that at Whitehall...

"I asked you a question," Lady Barb said, a hint of steel in her voice. "Where is this leading?"

Emily swallowed hard, then tried to answer. "The vast majority of the population never has a chance to use its full potential," she said. It was true enough. "The changes

I have introduced will allow more of them to attempt to realize their potential, allowing them to produce greater wealth...which in turn will make the kingdom wealthier."

Lady Barb studied her for a long, thoughtful moment. "Do you really believe that?"

"Yes," Emily said, simply.

"So you do," Lady Barb observed. "Explain."

Emily blinked at her, then realized that a combat sorceress would have ways to tell if someone was trying to lie. Or at least lie deliberately. Sergeant Miles had talked about the various levels of truth spells, although he had only taught them to the more advanced students; there was one that could detect a spoken lie, without compelling the speaker to talk. Ideally, the speaker would be completely unaware that the spell was even in place. *Emily* certainly hadn't realized that Lady Barb might be testing her words for truthfulness.

"Money is useless if it is tied up," she said, carefully. She'd worked out the basics of economic theory at Whitehall, but she suspected that theory was going to prove insufficiently close to practice. Plenty of fine-sounding theories had run into unsuspected rocks and shoals in real life. "Those who have money can simulate the economy by spending it."

She grinned suddenly as she used concepts that few others in Zangaria would even have considered. "If a man makes two gold coins by...selling tunics, he can use that gold to buy food from a farmer's stall, passing the gold on to the farmer. The farmer in turn can use that gold to buy farming tools from a craftsman, who needs to dress himself so he goes to the tailor and buys more tunics."

"Craftsmen don't wear tunics," Lady Barb said.

It took Emily a moment to realize that she was being teased. "Or whatever craftsmen wear," she said, tiredly. "The point is that the money keeps going round and round. Every stop on its journey means that someone new can have the power to buy something for themselves...and so on. In the meantime, the authorities can tax a little from each person, which gives the state the funding to produce things that help stimulate the economy further."

Lady Barb frowned. "Really?"

"Yes," Emily said. "Projects like...producing a new harbor, or making roads, can be expensive, too expensive for small businessmen. But if the authorities have the funds, they can do something that benefits everyone—better roads mean faster transport between the farms and the cities, while better ports mean that there can be more shipping heading out to the rest of the world. All of which will bring in more wealth."

"And your changes help people to do their own accounts, and to read," Lady Barb said. "How does *that* create wealth?"

"The more they know, the more they can do," Emily said. It had actually been the motto of a college that had been trying to recruit students back home, although she'd never been convinced that the collages were worth the mountains of debt she would have had to assume to go there. "Sharing information leads to greater progress. That's why we have places like Whitehall."

"How true," Lady Barb mused. "And do you think that the barons are going to be happy when they realize their peasants are moving off the land?"

Emily hesitated. Zangaria's lowest class—apart from the slaves, who were treated as animals—was tied to the land, forbidden to leave the noble estates on pain of death or enforced servitude. Unsurprisingly, their treatment was horrific, even by the standards of most of the world. Equally unsurprisingly, many of them had been slipping off the land and fleeing to the cities, or learning to use the new letters and alphabet. Emily couldn't understand how anyone could expect the peasants to be grateful when they had no reward at all for their labor, but it wasn't unprecedented. The slaveholders of the American South had believed the same thing.

And what would it mean for Zangaria?

"I wish I knew," she admitted. But she had a feeling that she *did* know. There would be repression, and resistance, and outright war...just like in Russia, prior to the Revolution of 1917. It had been the Bolsheviks who had finally crushed resistance from the peasants. "Maybe the king can do something..."

But what? The barons would resist any attempt to strip them of their power. Given time, it was quite possible that the Assembly would be able to create enough wealth to support King Randor's military—or produce an army for itself—but would the barons realize the danger in time to stop it? They seemed pretty sure that they'd gelded the Assembly...

"I think you'd better think about it," Lady Barb said. She looked into the forest, then back at Emily. "Do you want to go find the hunters?"

Emily shook her head. Whatever else happened, it would be a long time before she forgot the dead body. "No," she said. "I want to go into town and find Imaiqah. I need some space."

"Most people wouldn't give the princess *any* space," Lady Barb said. Her tone was so artfully neutral that it was impossible to tell if she approved or not. "But you would be well advised to return to the castle and go visit your other friend tomorrow. Send a message, tell her that you're coming, and I will accompany you to her home."

"That isn't necessary," Emily objected. "I..."

"Oh?" Lady Barb interrupted. "You know how to find her house?"

Emily flushed again, cursing herself. She should have realized that it would be impossible to find Imaiqah's house without a street map, or a local guide. Come to think of it, did they even have numbered houses? All of the letters Imaiqah had sent home had been mailed directly to her father. Lady Barb was right. She *would* need someone to help her.

"Point," she admitted, grudgingly.

Lady Barb motioned for Emily to mount her house, then mounted her own. "For what it's worth, I agree with you," she said. "Transforming someone—anyone—into a different form is not amusing...and hunting them for sport is unpleasant. But I cannot change it."

Emily looked at her, sharply. There had been something in her voice…

"The Kings believe that punishment must be horrific in order to deter," Lady Barb added. "And you will agree that the punishment is horrific?"

Cruel and unusual, Emily thought. But what did that mean *here*? And was it even unusual?

"Who judges?" She asked. "Does King Randor pass sentence?"

Lady Barb snorted. "The king hear every case in Alexis, let alone the rest of the kingdom?"

She shook her head. "Most cases are heard by a Town Councilor," she added. "Anything involving the nobility is judged by the Noble Estates—the noble part of the Assembly. Anything involving magic is the problem of the Court Wizard. Thankfully, Zangaria doesn't have many magicians. Zed is more interested in alchemy than actually carrying out the duties of his post. I've often ended up dealing with them myself."

Emily listened as Lady Barb outlined what happened at court. A criminal case was always conducted under truth spell, with everyone involved bound to speak the truth. Civil cases tended to be less simple, with—Emily guessed, reading between the lines—a great deal of bribery involved. The person with the most money probably won. At least there was no chance of sending an innocent man to be hunted to death. By the time Lady Barb had finished speaking, they were almost back at the castle.

"I'd suggest that you make an appearance tonight," she said. "Most of those cocksure men think women are too frail to be sorceresses. They'll take your departure as proof they're right. You owe it to Alassa to look strong this evening."

Emily winced. "How often do they give you trouble?"

"The first day I came here, I had to whip three Royal Guardsmen in a bare-knuckle fight to convince them that I had earned my rank," Lady Barb said. "You can't fight the Princes, any more than Alassa can. So you need to look strong."

"I'll do my best," Emily said, finally. She didn't want to attend the dance at all, but Lady Barb was right. She *had* weakened Alassa's position, even though Alassa probably looked strong compared to her. But then, most of the princes probably didn't think of her as the fearsome Necromancer's Bane. "And tomorrow you can take me into town."

Chapter Twenty-Six

IThink the Court Wizard is annoyed with you," Alassa said, the following morning. "You might not want to visit his lair alone."

Emily winced. King Randor would have had time to talk to his daughter—and then to the Court Wizard. It wouldn't have been a very pleasant discussion. Even if Emily was wrong—and she had to admit it was a possibility—the long-term effects of the Royal Bloodline could be disastrous. And that would be bad enough for anyone, but Zangaria's political stability depended upon a line of succession.

"Very annoyed, I should say," Alassa added. "The last I heard, father had to speak to him quite severely about not threatening guests."

Alassa's eyes narrowed. "*Are* you sure about this?"

"I don't know," Emily admitted. "It just seems odd to have a fertile line start to have fewer and fewer children until you wind up an only child."

She looked around Alassa's dining room, shaking her head inwardly. What sort of mentality suggested that a young girl needed her own place to eat? But she was glad of it—and of Alassa's invitation to a private breakfast. The last thing she wanted to do was face King Randor, or the princes.

What if she *was* wrong? There would be panic, perhaps some paranoia, but no serious harm. But if she was right, the Royal Family was in deadly danger. It would simply come to an end. Emily wished she knew more about genetics, but for once Zangaria and the Allied Lands seemed to be capable of doing more than Earth. As far as she knew, it was impossible to produce children to order, at least outside science fiction.

It took generations for inbreeding to produce a catastrophic effect, particularly if the original matches weren't between brothers and sisters. Introducing newcomers should dilute the bad genes and add vigor to the family line. But Zangaria was altering the genes of any newcomer as well, preparing them for inclusion in the Royal Bloodline...what did *that* do to any new genes? Were they just turned into copies of native-born royalty? Did they actually introduce anything new at all?

"I should have spent more time with Professor Thande," she admitted, out loud. "If I knew more..."

"The day I am crowned, you and I are going to have a very long talk," Alassa said. "I don't think my father knows what to make of you."

She smiled. "I know you don't mean anyone any harm, but you can make mistakes," she added, a moment later. "And I love you for it."

Emily grinned. "When did you become such a good judge of character?"

"I think I always was," Alassa said. "It just happened that my idea of what made a good character changed after I met you."

"How true," Emily said. They shared a long smile. "What is your father going to do?"

"I think he was talking about calling in other alchemists and asking them to inspect the Royal Bloodline," Alassa said. "Unlike his brother, he isn't a trained magician;

someone independent should be able to provide proper answers. And then they can decide what they want to do to retrieve the situation."

If it can be retrieved, Emily thought.

"Mind you," Alassa added, "he will be *very* upset with you if it turns out you are completely wrong."

"I wouldn't blame him," Emily admitted. "Alassa..."

"He does want you to remain involved in the kingdom," Alassa interrupted. "But he also needs to ensure that there is a certain degree of stability. And you have a habit of turning the world upside down."

Emily nodded, miserably.

"But I do need to ask," Alassa said, changing the subject. "Why did you flee from hunting?"

"You killed a man," Emily said, after a long moment. She'd had nightmares about it after going to sleep. Animal transfiguration was one of the common jokes played at Whitehall, but it had never occurred to her that it could be used as a permanent punishment, let alone to create semi-intelligent creatures for huntsmen to chase. "I...I hated to see that."

She found herself groping for words, but none came. How did one explain to someone from a radically different culture that their culture was wrong? Emily found it hard to oppose the death penalty for truly awful crimes, particularly if a person's guilt could be conclusively proven, but hunting humans for sport? She'd been hunted herself by orcs and goblins—maybe *that* was why she found it so appalling. Or maybe it was just her culture's morality clashing with Zangaria's morality.

What would Zangaria make of Earth, if the two cultures ever met?

"I wish I understood you better, sometimes," Alassa said, softly. "And then there are times when I am merely glad you're on my side."

She shook her head. "I've got to spent most of the day in court, hearing petitions from various noblemen. The princes are supposed to see my spontaneous responses to their requests for help."

Emily lifted a single eyebrow. "And how *spontaneous* are they going to be?"

Alassa smirked. "We—my father and I - are going to be spending the morning discussing the petitions," she said. "Every one of them will be answered properly, by me. I won't actually have to think at all."

"You mean your father wrote the petitions himself," Emily guessed. "And he picked topics that would allow you to shine."

Alassa winked at her.

"Clever," Emily said. "What happens if someone asks a question you *haven't* prepared for?"

"My father will be very unhappy," Alassa said. She looked down at the remains of her breakfast, then back up at Emily. "I wish I could come with you."

"You could," Emily said, suddenly. "We wrap a glamor around you and no one would ever realize that you were the princess..."

"My father would be furious," Alassa said. "Maybe after the Confirmation, when we can all relax a little. Oh, and Nightingale will be briefing you on your part later in the week. I'm supposed to tell you to pay close attention to him."

Emily stood up and walked around the table. "I'll do my best," she said, as she gave Alassa a hug. The thought of being bored stiff for an hour as Nightingale droned on about etiquette wasn't appealing, but it was better than hunting. "And if you don't mind, I'm going to change."

"Lucky you," Alassa said. "And give Imaiqah my love."

Emily nodded and walked back to her rooms, where she changed into the clothes she'd convinced one of the maids to find for her. The outfit looked simple—a shirt and a pair of trousers - yet it was made from fine materials, suggesting that she was nothing more than the daughter of a wealthy merchant. It was loose, but allowed her to move easily, just like the uniforms they wore in Martial Magic. Emily hid her knife in the belt and checked her money pouch, then strode down to the hall. Lady Barb was waiting for her.

"You look acceptable," Lady Barb said, after a long moment of inspection. "There are plenty of young women who dress like that."

"Good," Emily said. "Will I attract attention?"

"You shouldn't be connected with Lady Emily, Necromancer's Bane," Lady Barb said, dryly. "On the other hand, you *do* look an attractive middle-class girl. There will be men who will ask for your father's name."

Emily flushed. Was it ever going to end?

She didn't *feel* attractive. She'd always been too thin, her breasts too small, her face too plain to be conventionally attractive. And what little male attention she'd received had been largely unwelcome. But now...having admirers made her feel strange. And the thought of total strangers trying to court her, just because of her looks, was terrifying.

"However," Lady Barb continued, a mischievous glint in her eye, "you may tell them that your father has already betrothed you to another young man. They should know better than to press you if they believe you to be engaged."

"Thank you," Emily said, tiredly. Maybe she should start wearing a wedding ring. Did women in Zangaria *wear* wedding rings? "How do you tell a married woman from an unmarried woman?"

"A married woman of the lower classes will cover her hair with a scarf," Lady Barb explained, "at least until her hair turns grey. The upper classes are less formal, but everyone is supposed to know everyone anyway."

She led Emily away from the main gate, somewhat to her surprise, and down a long flight of stairs that seemed to go a very long way down. Finally, they reached a dank set of dungeons, seemingly completely empty. Emily shivered as she remembered the prison cell Shadye had dumped her into, back when he'd first kidnapped her, and looked away when Lady Barb headed towards a stone wall. She pushed her hand against a particular place and the wall clicked open silently. Emily sensed the

presence of a powerful silencing charm as Lady Barb stepped into the darkness, con-
juring a light ball to illuminate their path. Without the charm, she realized, the noise
would have been heard on the upper levels.

Inside, there was a second set of stairs leading into the darkness. Lady Barb pushed
the light ball ahead of them as she walked, picking her way down a flight of stairs
that seemed dangerously thin. Emily followed her, carefully placing her feet so that
if she fell she'd fall upwards, rather than down the winding staircase. She sensed the
presence of more spells as they went lower, a thin cobweb of wards that watched for
unwanted intruders. It was hard to escape the feeling of claustrophobia.

Lady Barb stopped at the bottom of the stairs. "We're deep under the mountain
now," she said, softly. Her voice echoed oddly in the confined space. "Very few people
know there are tunnels under the inner city, let alone where they lead. The king
granted me special permission to show them to you, but you are *not* to attempt to
explore them on your own. If you do—and you are caught—you will be lucky if you
are merely hung."

Emily swallowed. "How many others know about these tunnels?"

"The king and his family, as well as a handful of trusted retainers," Lady Barb said.
"I swore a binding oath that I would never reveal the secret to anyone, without his
permission. And I may not use them for my own purposes."

She led the way forward into the tunnel network, the light ball flickering oddly as
it brushed against the wards. Emily took a deep breath, tasting the dryness in the air,
then followed Lady Barb, catching sight of dozens of passageways leading off under
the city. It was impossible to tell how old the passages were, but they might easily
have been hundreds of years old, predating Zangaria's time as an independent kingdom. A handful of tunnels seemed to be dead ends, as if someone had been altering
the network in the years after it had been constructed.

Emily found herself wondering just how far the tunnels actually went. Was there
a secret passageway that opened up outside the city? Or did one go even further? The
Royal Family would definitely want a private bolthole…or did it have more mundane
uses? If King Randor had a mistress, he might want to sneak her in and out of the
castle without anyone actually seeing. The strange laws of etiquette that governed
the kingdom might prohibit anyone from taking notice of the mistress as long as the
king didn't show her too publicly.

"I will never understand," Emily muttered.

"Few people do," Lady Barb said. She looked back, a faint smile on her face. "What
are we talking about this time?"

"The etiquette and protocol," Emily said. "Why are there such strange rules?"

"Sometimes they serve a useful purpose," Lady Barb said. "And sometimes they
just exist so the upper class can detect an imposter from the lower classes. It *has*
been known to happen."

"I see," Emily said. She stopped as she caught sight of a handful of bones on the
ground. "How…how long have they been there?"

Lady Barb shrugged. "Years," she said. "People are not supposed to find their way into the tunnel network, Lady Emily. If they do, they don't come out again. Try widening your senses."

Emily concentrated, reaching out with her mind to sense any nearby source of magic. She *was* talented—all of her tutors said so—but it still took her several minutes to detect the charm woven through the stone walls. It was so subtle that it seemed to fade away the moment she looked at it, as if it was capable of adapting to hide itself from anyone. Someone who wasn't looking for it would miss it completely, unaware that it was gently confounding their senses and ensuring that anyone who stumbled into the network without permission would never come out again. They'd keep on walking in circles until they collapsed and died.

Magic, she'd been taught, could be flashy, with effects that ranged from animal transfiguration to giant castles floating in the clouds. Or, for that matter, a school that was literally much larger on the inside than the outside, designed to alter its interior to suit the school's requirements. But the subtle magic spells could be more dangerous. Someone could be influenced into doing something stupid, or trapping themselves, without ever realizing what was happening. Even a very low-level magician with little formal training had to be taken seriously. He might just be capable of tying someone with more power, but less experience, up in knots.

"That spell"—even as Emily spoke, she could feel it trying to fade from her awareness—"that spell is very dangerous."

No, it was not *just* trying to hide. It was trying to make her forget that she'd ever sensed it.

"You have no idea," Lady Barb said, softly. The tunnel suddenly widened, revealing another set of stairs heading upwards. "And believe me, this place isn't very dangerous compared to sneaking into a dark magician's lair. It was easier sneaking into a necromancer's tower."

Emily looked over at her. "You sneaked into a necromancer's tower?"

"It was actually depressingly easy," Lady Barb admitted. "Necromancers rarely bother to take elaborate precautions, like subtle wards and tripwires; they just create the strongest defenses they can and then rest comfortably. It never occurred to Dark that I could simply dig a tunnel *under* his wards and pop up inside his tower. He didn't even bother to have a general scan underway for intruders. Once I was inside, I was safe as long as I didn't attract his attention. I watched him for months before withdrawing as silently as I'd come."

"You could have poisoned him," Emily said. "Why didn't you?"

"Another necromancer was heading towards him," Lady Barb said. "I hoped that one of them would kill the other, so I slipped away. And then their fight tore up the environment so badly that I had to throw caution to the winds and *run*."

They reached the top of the stairs and stopped in front of a blank wall. "The tunnel entrance is covered with a charm that ensures no one who isn't already clued into the secret will notice it, even when it opens," Lady Barb explained. "Still, those tricks have their limitations so don't do anything to attract attention. The king will not be happy if he has to seal up this tunnel."

She smiled, grimly. "And *don't* bring any male friends here."

Emily realized where the tunnel had to come out just before the stone wall slide to one side, revealing white marble walls. She stepped through the gap and into the shrine for the crone goddess. No one seemed to be around, but she could hear voices muttering in the distance as the tunnel entrance closed behind them. Lady Barb winked at her, then led her down the corridor and into a larger room. A tall woman dressed in white robes looked up and nodded to them, before giving Emily an almost maternal smile. Emily found herself liking her on sight.

"Use the side door," the woman ordered. "And don't forget to tell her about the sisterhood."

"I won't," Lady Barb promised.

They walked out the side door and into the streets. Emily wrinkled her nose at the smell, although it was better than some of the other cities. No one seemed to take any notice of a pair of women coming out of the temple, which didn't seem too surprising. In a society where worship was largely a matter of personal choice, why would anyone feel the urge to monitor who worshipped where? One idea Emily had no intention of introducing was religious war and genocide.

The buildings clustered closer and closer together as they walked into the outer reaches of the inner city. Emily rapidly found herself becoming lost, despite all that the sergeants had taught her—although she was sure she could have walked back to the castle, if necessary. Some of the darkened alleyways looked as threatening as they had on Earth, despite the presence of men in the uniforms of city guardsmen. They didn't look quite as corrupt as the guardsmen of Dragon's Den.

"The buildings here are small and expensive," Lady Barb commented. "Even renting a tiny apartment can cost upwards of ten gold coins a month. But few people would seriously consider renting an apartment on the other side of the wall, even if it *was* cheaper."

She nodded towards a shop. It was larger than Emily had expected, with great boxes of fruit and vegetables outside, allowing passers-by to inspect them. Emily felt her mouth opening into a smile when she saw Imaiqah sitting at the counter inside. A moment later, she ran inside and gave her friend a hug.

"It's good to see you," she said. "I've missed you."

Imaiqah smiled back. "I've missed you too," she said, as she hugged Emily in return. Her accent still sounded faintly rustic, despite Alassa's tutoring. "Come and meet my father."

Chapter Twenty-Seven

T HE BACKROOM OF THE STORE WAS CRAMMED WITH BOXES, A PAIR OF TABLES AND SOME-
thing that looked like an insanely large abacus. Several smaller ones sat on the
tables, surrounded by pieces of paper covered with scribbled notes. A young man—
two years older than Emily, if she guessed correctly—waved shyly to her and then
returned to his counting. Emily recognized the bookkeeping system and smiled to
herself. The Accounting Guild would never be able to rebuild itself now.

Imaiqah led her through another door and into a small dining room. It was tiny,
compared even to Alassa's private room, but it felt much more comfortable. A short
and rather stout woman turned to grin at Emily, before picking up a large bowl of
soup and putting it on the table. Imaiqah's mother, Emily guessed; they shared the
same basic features, even though Imaiqah's were somewhat diluted by her father.
Both of them looked vaguely Arabic, but her mother's features were sharper, hinting
at her character.

"Imaiqah has told us a lot about you," Imaiqah's mother said. She half-bowed to
Emily, as if she were unsure of Emily's precise standing. "You may call me Lin."

"And I am Paren," a deeper voice said, from behind them. "We owe you a great
deal."

Emily turned and smiled at Imaiqah's father, liking him on sight. He had a shrewd
face, with a short beard and twinkling brown eyes. And he wore a long silver chain
that hung around his neck, glittering under the light. Imaiqah had told Emily that
her father had been appointed to the City Council; Emily guessed that the chain was
his badge of office. It wouldn't be long before he became wealthy enough to merit a
promotion to lower nobility, if it were possible. If sons of wealthy merchants could
marry daughters from noble houses, why not have a rich man raised to the nobility?

"Thank you," she said. She hesitated, then remembered her manners. "Lady Barb
is waiting outside. If you could…"

"Of course we can invite her," Lin fussed. "Johan, go tell the lady that she is welcome to join us."

Another young man—one of Imaiqah's older brothers, as he shared the same basic
features—stood up and walked outside. He returned a moment later to report that
Lady Barb seemed to want to stay outside, rather than join them for dinner. Lin
shrugged and started to hand out bowls for the soup, while barking orders at her
sons to cut the bread. *She* didn't seem to consider herself automatically inferior to
the men.

Emily sensed Imaiqah's embarrassment as her father bombarded Emily with questions, some of them alarmingly perceptive. He'd built up a business from almost
nothing a long time before he'd ever heard of Emily, or realized what she could offer
him. Paren was very far from stupid and Emily suspected that the only thing stopping him from pushing any further was concern about Emily deciding to take her
ideas elsewhere. If Alassa could deduce that Emily was importing mature concepts

rather than inventing stuff for herself, no doubt Paren could draw the same conclusion. And he would have been right.

She brushed aside another question that came too close to the truth and countered with one of her own. "How did you become a councilor?"

"It's really very simple," Paren said.

Emily and Imaiqah shared a glance. Professor Thande said the same thing almost every lesson, generally before launching into a complicated explanation that left his students more confused than ever. Emily understood that following theory was important if she wanted to progress further, but it would have been easier if the theory had been broken down into bite-sized chunks. Once the printing presses were a mature technology, she intended to have proper textbooks produced for Whitehall. Even having a second copy of some of the books in the library would have been a great advantage for the students.

"There are twenty-five districts in the city, twenty inside the walls and five outside," Paren explained. "Everyone who pays taxes gets a vote. I urged my fellow merchants to vote for me—or, if they lived in other districts, to stand for election. In the end, we won around nine seats. We would have had more if the nobility hadn't started bribing the voters."

"They tried to bribe us too," Johan said. He seemed torn between staring at Emily and half-shying away from his sister. "You told them that you couldn't be bribed."

Emily had to smile. "And what do you intend to do with it?"

Paren smiled back. "Well, the five councilors from outside the walls are willing to work with us in exchange for some help," he said. "So we have a majority on the council, which allows us to push through new laws and—more importantly—cancel some previous legislation. Right now, we're funding a project to clean up the outer city and spread education as far as possible, as well as building up the City Guard. There were just too many footpads on our streets."

He shrugged. "The Great Charter allows the king the right of veto, but so far His Majesty has done nothing," he added. "We can't decide if he is supporting us, or simply doesn't care about stopping us."

Emily shrugged. On one hand, the City Council wasn't actually very powerful, not when compared to King Randor and the aristocracy. But on the other hand, someone with ambition and determination—and money—could turn it into a power base, complete with its own military force. Fighting crime on the streets was a good excuse for building a police force that was stronger than anyone would realize, at least until it was too late. And that force would be loyal to its paymasters, rather than the King.

She mulled it over as Imaiqah chatted about her life in the city. It seemed her parents didn't really believe in school holidays; they'd put her back to work the moment she'd stepped out of the portal, either working at the front counter or doing the accounts. By now, Paren owned several shops and had hundreds of people working—directly or indirectly—for him, but he seemed to want to keep his first shop in the family. Emily couldn't help wondering if it gave him some legal advantage, or if he merely wanted to keep his daughter where he could see her. But then, Imaiqah was the only magician in her family. What would he do if she decided she wanted to live elsewhere?

The soup was simple—and tasted far better than much of the food she'd eaten on the journey to Zangaria. Sergeant Miles had made snide comments about anyone who developed expensive tastes, but Emily hadn't really understood; she'd simply never had the money to develop expensive tastes before coming to Whitehall. And now, naturally, most of the expensive foods she'd admired on Earth were beyond her reach. She took another bite of the bread and thought she understood what he'd meant. Expensive tastes sometimes overshadowed good food.

"I have to show you the workshop," Imaiqah said, as soon as they were finished. "Father, can I take her?"

"Of course," Paren said. "Johan can mind the store for you."

There was no sign of Lady Barb as they emerged onto the streets. Emily glanced around, seeing only a handful of pedestrians, before Imaiqah led her off towards the riverside. Most of the citizens didn't seem to be taking any specific interest in her, although they did seem to be glancing at Imaiqah. But then, her father was wealthy; they probably considered her to be above their station. Or maybe they just knew that she had magic and wouldn't be safe to court.

"Johan used to bully me," Imaiqah admitted, as they walked. "I was the youngest and the only girl, so he picked on me. And when I came home, I turned him into a frog."

Emily had to smile. When she'd first met Imaiqah, she'd been picked on daily by Alassa, unwilling to lift a hand against her tormentor. Now, Imaiqah seemed to have picked up more self-confidence as well as magical knowledge. Turning a bullying brother into a frog might have turned her into a bully herself, but she seemed to have avoided that fate. In some ways, Emily had to admit, Imaiqah was more mature than either Alassa or Emily herself.

The smell of saltwater—and fish—grew stronger as they walked down towards the waterside. Hundreds of boats, most of them small fishing boats, bobbled in the water, avoiding the handful of larger sailing boats with ease. A number of bigger ships were positioned in the middle of the river, with smaller boats transporting their crews to and from the shore. Hundreds of birds flew overhead, sometimes darting down to snatch a fish from the boats or right out of a fisherman's hands. Emily ducked as one almost brushed through her hair after scooping up a piece of fish from the ground.

"My oldest brother went into fishing," Imaiqah said. "He used to bring us all fish, back when I was a child. It was all that kept us alive. Now, he has a small fishing fleet under his command and plenty of people following him."

Emily nodded. Scraping together the funds to buy a fishing boat would be difficult for a newcomer in the field; most of them would have a boat passed down from their parents, or try to hire on to one of the bigger boats and earn enough money to buy a share. But if someone loaned the fisherman the money to buy a boat, then allowed them to repay it over years…they would have a good investment and a great many friends. And, best of all, it *hadn't* been one of Emily's suggestions. They'd thought of it for themselves.

"And now he wants to build the world's largest fishing ship," Imaiqah added. "But I ran the math and it would be too expensive to build and maintain, particularly if he doesn't find a buyer. He was talking about something bigger than those boats out there."

"And is he going to build it?" Emily asked. "Or…"

"Father said that he could fund it for himself," Imaiqah said. She giggled. "That shut him right up."

She pointed to a long set of low buildings just behind the docks. "Those warehouses normally belong to traders," she said. "They use them to store goods for transhipment to the rest of the Allied Lands. Now, however…"

They walked up to a door and Imaiqah pressed her hand against a panel. There was a click and the door opened, allowing them both to step inside. The sound of screeching metal blasted Emily's ears before she managed to cast a protective charm to block it out. Imaiqah shrugged, her lips moving soundlessly. It took Emily two tries before she could widen the charm enough to hear her friend's words.

"I built the wards," Imaiqah admitted, once they could hear each other again. "Father thought that if we placed the main factory here, fewer people would come visit. So he told me to construct wards to keep our work hidden."

Emily rather doubted that the trick had fooled anyone, which did raise the question of just what Imaiqah's father thought he was doing. She pushed the thought to one side and allowed Imaiqah to lead her through a corridor and into a massive room, where several dozen craftsmen worked on a number of projects. Several of them were putting together a new version of the printing press—one that might allow printing in the local language, without using English letters—although it looked incredibly cumbersome compared to the original models. But it might make it easier for the printing press to be adopted by the nobility.

Most of the craftsmen were men, she noticed, but there were a couple of young girls working at their own tables. One of them was a woodworker, slowly putting together a child-sized abacus; the other seemed to be working beside an older blacksmith who watched her with a gimlet eye. It took Emily a moment to realize that the girl was working charms into the metal, making it safer to use. They hadn't quite solved all of the problems presented by inferior metals just yet.

"You'll want to see this," Imaiqah said, pulling Emily over to a large machine at the far end of the room. "It was built from your designs."

It seemed to be nothing more than a giant metal container hanging over a fire, which was carefully tended by two young men who glanced at the girls whenever they thought they weren't looking. The container was connected to a smaller set of containers, which released puffs of smoke at regular intervals. She couldn't help smiling as she realized that it was a working model of a steam engine. Another one was being put together by a team of blacksmiths and craftsmen.

Imaiqah was wrong, Emily saw, as she studied the half-completed model. Her original design had been badly flawed; the theory had been right, but local science and metalworking was simply not up to the task of turning it into a working model. But she'd given them ideas and some genius had outlined one that was actually within their capabilities. They might still have needed spells on the boiler to ensure that it didn't burst, but it should be capable of powering a locomotive or steamboat.

The craftsman waved at Imaiqah. She pulled at Emily's hand again, tugging her into a small side room. It had a large bathtub of water positioned right in the center of the room. Emily frowned, puzzled, before the craftsman dropped a small boat into the water. A moment later, it began to move of its own accord. The locals would take it for magic, she knew, but instead it was nothing more than science. There was a tiny steam engine inside the boat. If Boy Scouts could build them, why not skilled craftsmen—once they'd gotten the idea?

"I've been showing this off to fishermen and traders," the craftsman said. His accent was different to Imaiqah's, suggesting that he came from a different country. "Most of the smaller operators don't like the idea of abandoning their sails, but the bigger traders think that it will be brilliant, once we manage to build a full-sized steamboat."

Emily nodded in agreement. Steamboats would transform the world, making it much easier to build trading networks with the other continents. The necromancers would have real problems stopping them, which suggested that—in the long term—the Allied Lands might be able to build up a position away from their interference. And then, if they built new weapons, they might even be able to cleanse the Blighted Lands.

But millions of people would still be at risk, she thought. It would be impossible to evacuate the Allied Lands; even her own world, with far higher levels of technology, couldn't have evacuated a whole continent. Maybe new positions could be built up overseas, eventually producing the reinforcements that would beat the necromancers. Or maybe it was just a pipe dream.

"Building the rails is proving harder, but we're working on it," Imaiqah explained, as they walked back into the main room. "The real problem is obtaining enough iron to make them—most of the mines are owned by the barons and they're not keen to sell, unless we pay them vast amounts of money. My father has been trying to look for other sources in the mountains, but that will raise its own problems. The nearest kingdoms might object."

Emily smiled inwardly, wondering if her friend—or anyone else—truly understood what was being born in the converted warehouse. The whole world would be transformed by steam power—and how long would it be, she wondered, before they made the jump to electrical power? She hadn't been able to work out how it had been done on Earth, but she knew it was *possible*. Perhaps she should have spent more time studying the latter parts of the industrial revolution. And then there was nuclear power...

"Your father has good reason to be proud," Emily said, finally. "How far are these ideas spreading?"

"Well, the basic technique is already out," Imaiqah admitted. "We've heard rumors that Drake—one of the free cities—is working on producing its own steam engine design. Other kingdoms have been quiet on the matter, but we have had quite a few visitors. If something happens here, the idea will still be out in the world."

And someone will use it, Emily thought.

Imaiqah led her back outside, into the bright sunlight. "I'd prefer not to go back to the shop," she said. "Would you like to explore the city?"

"Why not?" Emily asked. She grinned at Imaiqah 's expression. "You don't want to go back to work?"

"It's just *counting*, and minding the store," Imaiqah said. "Just because I have magic...well, no one dares to steal from us, but it's *tedious*. And Johan keeps glancing at me oddly. And sometimes other magicians come in and offer to marry me."

Emily started to laugh. "You too?"

Imaiqah stared at her. "You *too*?"

"Yes," Emily admitted. She hesitated, then plunged on. "Jade offered to marry me."

"That was nice of him," Imaiqah said. "But are the two of you really suited to be together? You come from very different backgrounds."

Emily snorted. Her friend didn't know the half of it. "I don't know," she said. "Do *you* want to marry him?"

"I could do worse," Imaiqah said. "If father hadn't become so rich, I might have been pushed into marrying one of the other magicians. But right now he's holding out for another match."

She grinned up at Emily. "And that is all your fault," she added. "So...*thank you!*"

Emily had to laugh. "There have been quite a few other suitors," she said, changing the subject. "And poor Alassa has twenty-two princes after her!"

Chapter Twenty-Eight

IT FELT WRONG TO ADMIT IT, BUT THERE WERE TIMES WHEN EMILY FELT MORE COMFORT-able with Imaiqah than Alassa. The royal princess could be overbearing and thoughtless at times, both character flaws that could never be ascribed to Imaiqah. And besides, Alassa had to act more like a princess when she was at home. Alassa was fun, but Imaiqah was steady.

They compared notes on marriage proposals as they walked through the streets, exploring the city. Imaiqah, being a new-Blood Magician, had had quite a few offers, all from local magicians interested in using her blood to boost the vigor of his children. Some of the offers had been relatively good ones; she would have no other obligations, apart from bearing children. In a sense, she wouldn't even be the magician's wife. As long as she was careful, the magician had assured her, she could take lovers.

"I was warned that it would only get worse as we grew older," Imaiqah said. "Second-years can be approached directly, rather than talking to parents and guardians. If someone makes a magical oath…"

Emily winced. She *had* made an oath, one that she suspected would return to haunt her in the future. If someone swore to marry someone, or bear his children, they risked the oath rebounding on them if they broke their word. A young girl like Imaiqah would be in particular danger…but then, she *had* been warned of the possibility. No one had ever told Emily that people might try to marry her, just because of her genes.

They probably assumed that Void told me, she thought. Or perhaps it was simpler than that, more fundamental. The boys she knew always affected a peculiar deafness when anything approaching women's matters were mentioned. They'd been too embarrassed to even *think* about it. But then, it was much simpler for the guys.

She looked over at her quiet friend and shook her head. "Do you *want* to marry?"

"I don't know," Imaiqah said. "I do want to have children one day…but I haven't found anyone I would actually like to marry. And father would insist on having a say."

"He does seem to boss you around and keep you working," Emily observed, neutrally. "I'm surprised he doesn't have you putting up wards everywhere for money."

Imaiqah shrugged. "Basic wards that keep out mundanes are easy," she said. "*You* ought to know that, after all those lessons in Martial Magic. No one wants to hire me for that. Keeping out another magician, let alone a sorcerer…my wards won't stand up to them for more than a few seconds. You could break in simply by applying enough force to the ward.

"But I could be worse off," she added. "Poor Alassa will have to put up with her husband for the rest of her life, no matter how horrid he is."

They walked through the middle of a vast market. No one paid them any attention, apart from a handful of children who ran up and begged for money. Emily felt something twisting inside her heart, but she knew better than to actually give them anything. Mistress Irene had made it clear, on her second visit to Dragon's Den, that it merely encouraged the beggars—and the children rarely managed to keep their gains.

Their older masters would take the coin and give them scraps, if anything, in return. Any objections would result in a beating.

"Your father should adopt some of these kids," she muttered, as the beggar children ran on to seek other victims. "Why are they even here?"

"Richer folk come to the market," Imaiqah explained. "And some of them are quite happy to give the children coin."

She hesitated. "Why would my father want to adopt them?"

"Buy a large house and turn it into an orphanage and school," Emily suggested. Some orphanages could be awful, but surely they could find a staff willing to work without treating the kids like monsters. "They'd have enough of an education to be able to repay him when they were adults. And he'd have a small army of loyal servants, willing to support him later on."

Imaiqah shook her head. "It's not that easy to escape a life on the streets," she pointed out. "The street children are always seen as thieves and murderers—or worse. Not many people would give them a chance."

Emily shook her head in dismay, but said nothing. Instead, she allowed Imaiqah to buy a handful of oddly-shaped fruits from a stall and pass her a couple to eat. It was hard to figure out how to eat them—the skin was leathery and looked inedible—until she saw Imaiqah use her fingernails to tear one open, revealing a juicy white mass inside. The fruit tasted unfamiliar, but nice.

One of the later stalls was selling abacuses, ranging from very crude designs to one that had been decorated by the craftsman who'd produced it. The stall *next* to it was offering lessons in using an abacus, with a handful of young men and women signing up for tuition. Emily looked up and saw a lesson in the alleyway, with one young man showing the others how best to use the devices. It didn't take long to master the basics, Emily knew, and then they could advance on their own.

She picked up the decorated abacus and studied it. Back home, it would probably have been mass-produced, but here it would have been designed and produced by a master craftsman. It was covered in a numbers motif, suggesting the triumph of Arabic numerals over the old system. Emily couldn't help admiring the skill and dedication that had gone into the work. What would happen to the craftsmen, she asked herself, when the techniques for assembly-line production were worked out? Somehow, she knew it would be almost as disruptive as the new numerals had been for the accounting profession.

"I think I'd like to buy this," she decided, suddenly. A quick glance revealed that the seller wanted one gold piece for the abacus. "Maybe…"

"Let me do the bargaining," Imaiqah said, quickly. "I've *seen* you try to bargain."

Emily flushed. Bargaining wasn't a skill she had managed to acquire; she always wound up paying more than strictly necessary for almost everything. Imaiqah stepped forward and sweetly pointed out that one gold piece was excessive unless the gold piece was very small; surely the seller could see that no one would buy it at that price. Twenty minutes later, they finally came to an agreement; Emily could buy the abacus for three silver pieces. She produced the coins from her pouch, watched the shopkeeper check them carefully, then picked up the abacus. Imaiqah had to remind her that it needed to be wrapped up first.

"I can deliver it," the seller offered. "Where do you want it to go?"

"My home," Imaiqah said, before Emily could mention the castle. She gave him her address and accepted a receipt, then turned back to Emily. "You can pick it up when you next come to visit me, although if there really *is* a cockatrice in your luggage…"

Emily snorted as they walked onwards, passing several other stalls offering various forms of tuition, including one—run by an elderly lady—who offered various alchemical potions for young women. Several of them looked to be comparable to the ones she'd been given at Whitehall, others seemed to be love potions—and one promised a healthy baby boy to the girl who took it before conception. Love potions were banned at Whitehall, even the ones that only lasted long enough to do no real harm. But then, the effects might wear off, but the embarrassment would be eternal.

"The strongest of fixation potions, of which love potions are a prime example, can cause permanent effects," Professor Thande had said. "Anyone who drinks one may become permanently fixated on a person, whatever their prior feelings. The only way to deal with such permanent effects is to redirect the fixation to something harmless, which can cause its own problems. A victim may never be the same again afterwards. If any of you experiment with them while you study here, you will *wish* that you had merely been expelled."

"Those never work," Imaiqah said, following Emily's gaze. "If they did, that woman would have to explain herself to the Court Wizard. All they really do is give someone the courage to make the first move, confident that it will not be rejected."

Emily gave her a sharp look. "How do you know that?"

"I… one of my friends, before I came into magic, wanted to use one," Imaiqah said. "She had a boy she fancied. My father yelled at me for being stupid when he heard about it, then told me that the potions were useless and that we had wasted our money. And then everyone else found out about it and they laughed at us."

She nodded towards one of the temples as they drifted back into the upper parts of the city. "My father worships there; he donated a large chunk of money to the priests in exchange for the favor the gods had showered upon him," she said. Her face twisted into a droll smile. "But the priests favored him in future; they backed his candidacy to the council and offered him support among the holy orders. They wanted more money, you see."

Emily nodded. It wasn't an uncommon racket; bribing the priests convinced them to support you, whatever their gods were supposed to have said. If the gods were actually real…this world had had the Faerie, vastly powerful entities composed of raw magic. Why *not* gods? Or demons? Certainly, there were people who claimed to have visions of the gods, or pick up messages from the higher realms, but she'd always assumed that they were just deluding themselves. But here, who knew what might be true?

She listened politely as Imaiqah told her about the major gods. Most of them seemed to represent a single aspect of existence, although there were actually several different gods of war. Emily enquired if they were actually different names for the same entity and Imaiqah shook her head. They were apparently separate gods. Emily decided that there must have been a great deal of cross-contamination when the Empire was at its height, but there was no way to know. The History Monks didn't seem to touch on religion.

"There's a shortcut back this way," Imaiqah said, leading Emily through a tight alleyway and down to a flight of stairs that headed back towards the docks. "Father insisted that I explore this part of town thoroughly. One day we're going to be living here."

"Then you won't be very wealthy for long," Emily pointed out, dryly. The higher addresses might be a symbol of wealth, but it was clear that the junior nobility couldn't maintain them indefinitely. Only the barons—and the Royal Family—could maintain themselves permanently in the upper reaches of the city. "Or does he think he can parley it into something more permanent?"

"I've said as much to him," Imaiqah said. "But he wants to make it…"

Emily held up a hand. Something was wrong…she glanced around in puzzlement, then saw a single shadowy form advancing towards them from out of a darkened alleyway. She wondered, for a moment, if it could be Void…and then realized that the figure was not alone. Cold ice ran down her spine as she glanced back up the steps and saw two more figures blocking their line of escape. Emily reached for her magic and felt it, shimmering just below her skin. If they were ordinary footpads, they were in for a nasty surprise.

One of the men drew a sword as he advanced. Emily noted, absently, that he'd obviously had some training. Sergeant Harkin had taught his class how to use a blade and he'd pointed out a number of the more common mistakes made by amateurs. Standing up and striking a dramatic pose was a good way to have a knife shoved between your ribs while you were posing, or so he'd said. The other men were drawing their own weapons. They didn't need to threaten two harmless girls with swords.

And she'd let them get too close. She shaped a spell in her mind, one that Sergeant Miles had hammered into her head, and cast it towards the men. There was a blinding flash of light—Imaiqah yelped in shock—and their armor glowed, but they didn't stop. Emily blinked in surprise—the spell should have sent them all tumbling to the ground—and threw a second spell at the first man. His armor glowed again, absorbing the magic harmlessly. It had been enchanted to provide some protection for the man inside.

Emily's hesitation almost killed her. She was only vaguely aware of the man behind her until there was a crash and he hit the ground, his sword jangling as it fell down beside him. A half-seen form advanced forward and slammed into the second footpad, knocking him down with ease. Magic flared out of nowhere and blazed over two more forms; Emily saw their armor glow with bright light before it failed. The two men let out horrific screams before their skin caught fire and they vanished in towering flames.

Pushing her fear aside, she scooped up the fallen sword and used it to block a swing from one of the remaining men. The sword was heavier than the one she was used to using and she winced as his blow sent the weapon twisting in her hand, but she managed to use it to hold him off long enough for the shadowy figure to cut in from the side. There was another blast of magic, causing the man to drop his sword and raise his hands in surrender. The newcomer cracked him on the head with the flat of their sword and he fell to the ground, stunned.

And then the shimmer faded away completely, revealing Lady Barb.

Emily fought to gather her breath. She'd relied on her magic to protect her—why hadn't she thought of enchanted armor? And then she'd come too close to panic, freezing up at exactly the wrong moment. Sergeant Harkin would have laid her flat on her back, then made an example of her in front of the entire class. Why not? He hadn't hesitated to point out everyone else's failings.

And she would have deserved it. She could have been killed.

"You should have seen them from the start," Lady Barb said. Irritatingly, she didn't even seem to be breathing heavily. But then, she had ten years of experience—*after* graduating from Whitehall. "Or did you assume that raw power alone would suffice?"

"Who... who are you?" Imaiqah asked. "Who were *they*?"

"Interesting question," Lady Barb observed. "Enchanted armor is *not* cheap. How many rich and powerful men has your father pissed off?"

She leaned down to examine the stunned men. "The key to beating enchanted armor, Lady Emily, is to keep hitting it with different spells," she added. "You will no doubt be aware that organic wards can be adapted on instinct, as it were, but material wards are much harder to configure against general threats. Your wide-paralysis spell was insufficiently powerful to overcome them; you needed to hit them with other spells too."

"Thank you," Emily managed. Her body was starting to shake. She was a powerful magician, a potential sorceress…and yet she'd come very close to dying at the hands of men in enchanted armor. "Who sent them?"

"That is indeed the question," Lady Barb said, sarcastically. "Let's see; if you were the target, there's no shortage of enemies. If Imaiqah was the target…oh, *she* has no shortage of enemies either. Or at least her *father* has no shortage of enemies. But we know this wasn't a random attack; they knew they were facing magicians and they came prepared."

She pointed a hand into the sky and muttered a spell Emily didn't recognize. There were no visible effects, but Emily *felt* a tingle of magic and saw a flock of birds take flight, no doubt scared by whatever Lady Barb had done. Sergeant Miles had told her that some animals had better senses for magic than humans; dogs, in particular, were often good escorts for soldiers when there was no magician accompanying them. She wondered if some birds had their own sensitivities to magic.

"And enchanted armor is also quite rare," Lady Barb added. "I wonder who made it."

Several soldiers appeared at one end of the alley, carrying weapons and looking alert. They must have been summoned by the signal, Emily realized. A properly configured spell would have been largely undetectable save by the magicians watching for it.

"Take these men back to the guardhouse and have the magician freeze them," Lady Barb ordered. "Take the bodies back too, along with their weapons. I want them held until I arrive. If they're missing, I'll turn you all to mice and feed you to the cat!"

Emily glanced at her, shocked.

"Whoever did this has connections," Imaiqah muttered, drawing Emily's attention back to her. "If they were after me…they might have friends in the castle."

"I'll escort you home, then take Lady Emily back to her rooms," Lady Barb said. She hesitated, then gave Emily an odd look. "Or do you want to witness the interrogation?"

"I…" Emily hesitated. She *didn't* want to witness anything of the sort, but she knew that she would have to learn how to conduct an interrogation, sooner or later. It would be counted towards her final grade in Martial Magic. "I think I should."

Lady Barb frowned, leaving Emily with the odd feeling that she'd failed some kind of test.

"We'll take your friend back home," Lady Barb said. "And then I have to report to King Randor. He is not going to be pleased."

That, Emily was sure, was an understatement. One of his guests had just been attacked–and the nature of the attack proved that the attackers knew who they were attacking. The king would be furious.

Chapter Twenty-Nine

EMILY FELT THE WARDS THE MOMENT SHE WALKED INTO THE DUNGEONS. THEY CRACK-led through the air, an invisible web of power that threatened to suffocate her—even though she wasn't a prisoner. The dark walls, illuminated only by tiny balls of light drifting in the air, were marked with powerful runes, each one channelling magic around the cells. No one could escape without help from the outside.

Lady Barb met her at the bottom of the stairs. "You froze up," she said, bluntly. "If I hadn't been there, you and your friend could have been killed."

Emily flinched at the cold contempt in her voice. She wanted to object, to fight back—but Lady Barb was right. If they hadn't had an invisible escort, they might have wound up dead—or kidnapped, again. But she hadn't expected any form of enchanted armor. Magic should have provided more than enough protection for both of them and yet it had failed. She could have died.

She forced her hands to stop shaking, drawing on the mental disciplines she'd been taught. There was no time for fear, not now. But her mind kept reminding her that she could have died.

"You've been in Martial Magic," Lady Barb pointed out, her eyes never leaving Emily's face. "Don't you know how to cast *Berserker?*"

"We're not supposed to use it without permission," Emily mumbled, although she knew that it was a poor excuse. The truth was that she'd simply forgotten she could use it. "And…"

"And nothing," Lady Barb snapped. "I think you and I are going to spend the next week practicing both magical and mundane combat. You could have been killed today."

Emily winced. The sergeants had been firm believers in the school of hard knocks. Each practice bout had left the students feeling sore, even if there had been no per-manent injury. And they'd been *good* at what they did, to the point that they mea-sured their blows so that they were always just a *little* ahead of their students. Jade had once asked Sergeant Miles why he held back and Miles had pointed out, after ordering Jade to perform a hundred press-ups, that they wouldn't learn anything from just being knocked out time and time again. Emily couldn't help feeling that Lady Barb would be just the same.

"Thank you," she said, finally. She *did* need the experience, she told herself, and besides it would provide an excuse not to attend the endless round of hunting, sport-ing and suchlike that were giving the princes a chance to show off. Maybe Lady Barb should offer Alassa the same training. "I just…"

"Don't make excuses," Lady Barb said. She turned and strode into the dungeons. "Just learn from your mistakes before the next one kills you."

Emily followed her, thinking hard. Why had Lady Barb chosen to follow them invisibly? Had she *known* that Emily and Imaiqah were likely to attract trouble or had she just wanted to know what they would talk about when they were alone? And she was *good* at remaining undetected; Emily had never even sensed her presence until she revealed herself. It wasn't easy to sense an invisible person in the crowds, but still...

And how long had she been following them?

The wards around the warehouse-workshop wouldn't have kept out a hedge wizard, let alone a combat sorceress. Lady Barb could have slipped inside behind them and watched as the craftsmen showed off the steam engine and the other long-term projects. What would she make of them all? And what would King Randor make of them, when they were finally revealed? Steam technology would change the world.

She pushed the thought to one side as Lady Barb stopped in front of a solid metal door. It looked utterly impregnable even without the runes carved into the metal. Lady Barb gave her a sharp glance—she had been rather doubtful about allowing Emily to come with her, even though she hadn't forbidden it—and then pushed her hand against the door. Emily sensed a brilliant shimmer of magic as the cell unlocked, allowing Lady Barb to pull the door open and step inside. It was as dark and shadowy as the grave.

Lady Barb created a light ball and directed it forward, into the cell. It was a dark chamber, with a single chair sitting in the exact center of the room. Heavy manacles kept the chair's occupant almost completely immobile; Emily realized that he was weighed down with so many chains that he would have had problems moving even if they weren't secured to the metal chair. More runes had been carved into the chair itself, shaping the wards that added an extra layer of security. It struck Emily as rather excessive.

But Sergeant Miles had lectured them, more than once, on keeping prisoners secure. It was easy to believe that a person without magic would be unable to escape a magical prison, but overconfidence was a gross weakness. Besides, warding each and every cell in a prison would be expensive. Matters only grew worse when the prisoners included actual magicians, who had to be drugged to keep them under control. Most of them, the sergeant had said, were kept in pocket dimensions, where they could remain secure. And a really skilled magician might even be able to escape from there.

The prisoner looked up at them as Lady Barb fixed the light ball over his head. Emily had barely had a chance to look at him when she'd been attacked; now, she realized that he was a young man, almost certainly younger than Jade. His armor had been stripped from him, leaving him dressed in nothing more than a long undershirt that revealed scars covering his body. Emily looked away, feeling a flicker of shame, as she realized that some of the wounds were new. The Royal Guard would not have treated him with kid gloves.

"We checked him for signs of mind control," Lady Barb said, to Emily. "We found none."

She leaned down to look at the prisoner. "Good evening," she said. Her voice was so cold that the prisoner flinched. "Let me start by explaining just how much trouble you're in."

She leaned closer to the prisoner, her eyes boring into his skull. "You and your friends attacked a personal friend–*two* personal friends - of the crown princess," she continued. "And you clearly knew who you were attacking, because you had enchanted armor to cope with their magic. And, given the weapons you were carrying, you intended to cause serious harm–or death. Your actions were effectively treason. Do you know what happens to traitors?

"You couldn't have afforded that armor on your own. Someone provided it, along with the intelligence that allowed you to plot your attack. Cooperate with us and I will petition the king to have mercy on you. Refuse to cooperate and I will be forced to extract the information from your mind. That may well break you, destroying your mind and leaving your body a helpless mess. Whatever is left of you will be ritually tortured to death, the fate reserved for traitors. What do you choose?"

There was a long pause. The man looked almost…hopeless. Emily couldn't imagine how he was feeling, although she knew what it felt like to be trapped. She'd been held prisoner before, by Shadye and Malefic. But she couldn't feel any sympathy for the prisoner. He'd tried to kill her and her friend.

"You don't get to change your mind once I begin," Lady Barb said, gently. "This is your last chance to cooperate."

The man sighed. "I will not talk," he said. His accent marked him out as coming from Zangaria. "I *cannot* talk."

Lady Barb shrugged. "If someone has charmed you into keeping your mouth shut, I will break it," she said. "And if I break you…well, I will have learned enough to ensure that I don't break your friends when I interrogate them. Your mental integrity is not one of my concerns."

Emily frowned. If *she'd* been a hired footpad facing ritual torture or permanent transfiguration as punishment for treason, she would have tried to make a deal. The man should have been trying to bargain–it was his only hope–and yet he was refusing to even consider the possibility. What did that mean? Someone fanatical enough to believe that he couldn't be forced to talk–or someone who believed that his masters would punish him for confessing, even though he was safely in the royal dungeons.

She considered it, working through the various options in her mind. The first attack might have been aimed at her or Alassa; the second attack might have been the same. This attack had been specifically aimed at Emily herself, which implied that she'd been the target of all three assassination attempts. If the cockatrice had actually *been* an assassination attempt…

The barons, she thought, and shivered. She'd upset the Kingdom's apple cart, unleashing forces that would eventually destroy the aristocracy if they didn't learn how to cope in the brave new world she'd created. They would want a little revenge, perhaps believing that killing Emily would allow them to get the changes under control. Didn't they realize that life didn't work like *Atlas Shrugged*? Eliminating Emily wouldn't eliminate the changes she'd already introduced, let alone the craftsmen who had taken her ideas and run with them.

But they might not have realized the truth. How could they?

It made sense. A baron might have the clout to get someone out of the dungeons—or to have him killed, if he opened his mouth. And if he *knew* it, he would be caught between two fires, unable to appease the king without risking the ire of the baron who'd hired him.

"This is your final warning," Lady Barb said. Her voice had, if anything, grown colder. "I will break into your mind and…"

Emily touched her arm. Lady Barb turned and looked at her, sharply.

"Let me talk to him," Emily muttered, after casting a privacy ward in the air. The spell reacted oddly with the wards securing the prison, but it seemed to work. "I think I can *try* to convince him to talk."

Lady Barb gave her a sarcastic look. "And you have extensive experience in interrogating prisoners?"

"No," Emily admitted, "but I do have an idea."

She outlined her thoughts. If the prisoner could be convinced that he *would* be protected, he would talk. And then they could decide what to do without having to break into his mind, which would avoid the risk of killing him.

"Interesting," Lady Barb said, finally. She sounded unconvinced. Good cop, bad cop wasn't something that existed in her world. "And are you sure that it will work?"

Emily felt a flash of irritation that she fought down. "If it fails, you can dig into his mind anyway," she pointed out, crossly. Did Lady Barb have to question *everything* Emily did? "We lose nothing by trying and gain much if we succeed."

"Very well," Lady Barb said. She stepped backwards. "Good luck."

Emily cancelled the privacy ward and leaned forward, allowing the prisoner to get a good look at her face. He cringed back the moment he recognized her.

"You're in trouble," she said, bluntly. It was very much an understatement. "Your master is powerful enough—or so you think—to reach into the prison and kill you if you breathe a word of his existence to anyone. But we can hide you, and protect you, if you talk to us now. If not, we have to break into your mind and that might kill you. Talk—or risk death."

There was a long pause. "How…" The man said. He coughed and started again. "How can you hide me?"

Emily grinned. "I'll turn you into something and hide you in my room," she offered. "I can rig the spell to make it impossible for anyone else to find you—and you won't even be aware of time passing."

Lady Barb gave her an unreadable look. The students at Whitehall had been told, quite specifically, that they were *not* to perform any spells that risked permanent transformation, or spells that could only be undone by the caster. If Emily had cast one within the school's wards, it would have meant instant expulsion from Whitehall, if not worse. Permanent transformation was *not* a joke.

But if the man was unable to sense time passing—if he simply couldn't think at all—he would never be able to work the spells that would allow him to break free. If he *could* work the spells. He didn't seem to have any magic at all.

"The king will not treat with me," the man said. He looked up at her, then at Lady Barb. "Are you going to defy him?"

Lady Barb stepped forward. "If someone paid you to attack Lady Emily," she said, "the king will be more interested in knowing who ordered the attack, rather than simply punishing you. I believe that I could convince him to give you a lesser punishment. Besides, a few years of slaving in the mines would be better than spending the rest of your life as a hunted animal."

"My name is Trajas," the man said, slowly. "I am a Guardsman in the Iron Guard."

It meant nothing to Emily, but she saw Lady Barb's eyes open wide with shock.

"I don't believe you," Lady Barb said. There was a harsh note in her voice. "If you are trying to trick us…"

"The duke himself issued the orders to kill Lady Emily," Trajas insisted. "I saw him personally!"

Lady Barb lifted her hand and cast a privacy ward of her own into the air. "The Iron Guard is the personal guard of the Duke of Iron, King Randor's brother," she said, by way of explanation. "If *he* issued the orders…"

Emily shivered. King Randor's brother, Alassa's uncle…and a man without children of his own. If he was attempting to make himself King, it wouldn't last past his death, unless he thought his wife could still have a child. Even if not…the power would be tempting. He might just take power, rule for the rest of his life, then let the kingdom fall into chaos. Or maybe he thought he could become King, then allow Alassa to succeed him.

Or maybe he just wanted to be rid of Emily, the girl who had turned his world upside down.

"But he cannot lie to his brother," Lady Barb said. "I do not understand how he could lie–he's part of the Royal Bloodline. He cannot lie to the King!"

Emily looked down at the stone floor as she realized that Lady Barb was right. Alassa had told her that she couldn't lie to her father, even through omission. She was *compelled* to tell the truth. Maybe someone with more experience could dissemble…but if it worked anything like a standard truth spell, it would be very difficult to dissemble while under the influence. But then, a powerful sorcerer could push a truth spell aside. Perhaps the duke was an unregistered sorcerer.

Lady Barb cancelled the privacy ward and glared down at Trajas. "I want to verify your words," she said, as she touched his forehead. He flinched back from her touch, but the manacles kept him from moving too far away from her. "Do *not* try to resist me."

Magic flickered around Lady Barb as she probed into his mind. Emily shivered; she'd been warned never to try any form of mental spell until she was older, with the discipline to keep her thoughts under control. A single mistake could be disastrous. Or, for that matter, someone could have buried a nasty surprise in the target's mind, just waiting for someone to come along and stick their head into the trap. If the duke *was* a sorcerer…

But how could he be, without training?

Lady Barb stumbled backwards, deeply shocked. "It *was* the duke," she said, in disbelief. "He saw him personally!"

Emily swallowed. How did one arrest the most powerful nobleman in Zangaria?

"I will have you transferred to my own personal custody," Lady Barb said to Trajas. "Lady Emily shouldn't have to take care of you. For what it's worth, I won't surrender you to anyone until after the whole matter is sorted out."

She looked over at Emily. "You do realize that this is *disastrous?*"

Emily nodded, mutely.

"All of the barons are in Alexis, ready for the Confirmation," Lady Barb added. "If they realize that the Duke of Iron has turned into a traitor...they could jump either way."

They might be involved, Emily thought, sourly. The barons had strong reasons to oppose the changes Emily had brought to the kingdom. What would happen if they decided that the duke was in the right? If it truly *was* the duke...but Lady Barb had confirmed it. And yet...how had the duke managed to get around the Royal Bloodline's effects?

"Go to your rooms and wait there," Lady Barb ordered. "I will speak to the king, then he can decide what to do. And watch your back. If the duke ordered your death, he could influence the servants in the castle as easily as his own guardsmen. He's keyed into the spells binding them."

Emily stared at her. "Why...?"

"Because he would have been regent, if the king died before Alassa reached her majority," Lady Barb said, tiredly. "Go now. I will send for you when we know what we're doing."

Emily nodded once and left the dungeons. Behind her, she sensed a faint surge of magic and hoped that Lady Barb would ensure that Trajas was safe. He *had* tried to kill her, but he'd been obeying the orders of his superior. And that *was* a workable defense in a medieval society. The duke's men were sworn to obey his orders, even if they were unpleasant or outright crimes against humanity. Hell, they didn't even have a concept of crimes against humanity.

Alassa is going to hate me, she thought numbly, as she walked up the stairs. A handful of maids caught her eye and curtseyed, then looked surprised as Emily ignored them. *I keep turning her country upside down.*

Chapter Thirty

L ADY BARB CAME FOR HER TWO HOURS LATER.

"The king has summoned his brother to the grand hall," Lady Barb said, as soon as she stepped inside. "You will be there when the duke is challenged."

Emily nodded. She'd spent the time working on personal protective spells, wrapping them into the wards that surrounded her. They were more complex than the standard wards she'd been taught to ward off practical joke hexes and jinxes, and they drew on her power, but there was no real choice. The next attack might be lethal. And if the attackers used enchanted blades, it might still be lethal.

Lady Barb looked her up and down, then nodded. "In the event of anything unexpected happening," she added, "follow my lead. If it really *is* the duke, he'll have a contingency plan to deal with early discovery."

"Understood," Emily said, although she had no idea what they would do then. The duke was the only nobleman allowed more than two hundred personal armsmen. And he was the commander of the Royal Army. If he'd decided to rebel, it could get very nasty. "Is he coming?"

"Apparently," Lady Barb said. She walked over to the door and stopped, her hand on the handle. "And *don't* talk to *anyone* about this, apart from the royal family and myself. They need to show a united front to the barons."

Emily rolled her eyes at that as she followed Lady Barb down the stairs and into the Great Hall. *Someone* had been making frantic preparations in a hurry, for there were several dozen guardsmen outside and a handful of magicians. Zed stood at their head, looking annoyed at being dragged away from his work; there was no sign of Brain anywhere. The Court Wizard gave Emily a nasty look as he caught her eye, then ignored her as Lady Barb led her into the throne room. Alassa was standing beside her father's throne, looking worried.

"Stand over there," Lady Barb ordered, pointing to the corner nearest the throne. "And keep your mouth shut, unless you are spoken to."

King Randor looked badly worried. His expression as he saw Emily was unreadable, but she couldn't help wondering if he blamed her for the upheaval too. If his brother *was* plotting against him, the plot might be on the very verge of success; armed guards, loyal to the duke rather than the King, might be on their way to secure the castle. Emily was the bearer of bad news rather than the bad news herself, but would that really matter? It was only human to blame the messenger.

She pulled herself upright and waited, concentrating on the pose the sergeants had hammered into their heads. Remain calm, they'd ordered; don't waste a single motion. She clasped her hands behind her back and steadied her breathing, quietly readying magic just in case it was necessary. This time she was *not* going to freeze up, or be taken by surprise.

"Your Majesty," the herald boomed. "His Grace the Duke of Iron!"

The Duke of Iron looked formidable, Emily realized, even though he also looked thoroughly unhappy. His scabbard hung loosely from his belt, demonstrating that he was unarmed; Emily wondered, absently, just how carefully the guards had searched him. Sergeant Harkin had carried nearly thirty different weapons on his body, she'd been told, and most of them had consisted of devices that were not immediately recognizable as dangerous. His tunic could conceal anything from a knife to a length of steel wire, ready to use as a makeshift garrotte. And if he *was* a sorcerer…

He didn't *feel* like a sorcerer, Emily decided. There was no sense of barely restrained power, or the hints of instability she'd sensed on other powerful magicians. But magic *was* woven into the Royal Bloodline; Alassa could become a sorceress, if she had the time to concentrate on studying magic. Could her uncle have studied magic in secrecy?

His wife accompanied him, her eyes glancing from side to side nervously. She looked as if she couldn't decide if she should be holding her head up high or throwing herself on the ground in front of the king, begging for mercy. Emily felt a flicker of pity for the young woman; she simply seemed too young to really understand what was going on. Her husband was in deep trouble and she didn't understand why.

"Your Majesty," the duke said, in a surprisingly deep voice. "You have summoned me and I have come."

Emily frowned. It didn't *sound* as though the duke knew he was in trouble, but anyone who had spent years in a royal court would be a skilled dissembler. He could make his voice suggest whatever he wanted it to suggest. And yet there was a hint that suggested innocence, and puzzlement, and…

If the duke is innocent, she asked herself, *what does it mean?*

"We have called you here to address a difficult situation," King Randor said. "Word has reached Us that several of your guardsmen were implicated in an attack on the Lady Emily. When interrogated, the guardsmen claimed to have been given instructions by you personally, even though you are aware that the Lady Emily is Our guest and therefore protected by Our will."

His voice darkened. "We must ask you now," he continued, "if you issued such orders. Did you order your men to kill the Lady Emily?"

The duke threw Emily a sharp glance, then looked back at his brother. "I issued no orders to kill the Lady Emily," he said. "I issued no orders to injure her, or to scare her."

King Randor studied his brother for a long moment. "The Lady Emily was with her friend Imaiqah, Daughter of Lin," he said. "Did you issue orders to bring any harm to her or her family?"

"No," the Duke of Iron said. There was a cold note to his voice. "I do not sneak around like a common footpad. My opinion of the changes the Lady Emily has brought to your kingdom is well known, but I would not order anyone assassinated to forestall change."

"Which leads to the next question," King Randor said. He never took his eyes off his brother. "What do you think of the Lady Emily?"

Emily flushed, despite herself.

"I think that she has meddled in matters that are none of her concern," the Duke of Iron said, coldly. "I think that she is a most unsuitable companion for the crown princess. I think that she is dangerous; she defeated a necromancer and refused to tell the Allied Lands how she did it. I think that she should be sent back to Whitehall where she belongs."

The Duke of Iron didn't look embarrassed at having the truth dragged out of him. "I have always been loyal to you, my brother," he said, crossly. "Why are you interrogating me like a common criminal?"

"The report had to be checked," King Randor said. "Are you planning to usurp Our throne?"

"I am not," the duke said, simply.

There was a long pause. "We are sorry for interrogating you," King Randor said, finally. "We trust that you understand Our position in such matters."

He looked at the duke's wife. "Lithia, Duchess of Iron, We thank you for your presence here," he said. "You and your husband may depart."

"I wish to face my challenger," the Duke of Iron said. There was a harsh note to his voice that made Emily cringe inwardly. "This is slander against a member of the Royal Bloodline and, as such, punishable by death. I will face him or her"–he threw Emily another unreadable look–"on the field of honor."

"The investigation has yet to be completed," King Randor said. "You may go."

The Duke of Iron bowed–his wife curtseyed–and backed out of the room. He couldn't turn his back on King Randor, Emily realized. She watched him go, then looked up at the King. He didn't look happy at all.

"He was telling the truth," he said, addressing Lady Barb. "I could *feel* it within the Bloodline."

"The truth spells agreed that he was telling the truth," Lady Barb agreed, coolly. "I checked..."

The king glared at her. "You cast truth spells on my brother?"

"Technically, I cast them into the air," Lady Barb countered. "And I swore to protect you and your family. Protecting you from him and protecting him from false accusations are part of the oath."

"I see," the king said, dangerously. "And what of your guardsman?"

"He was also telling the truth," Lady Barb said. "He genuinely believed that the duke had sent him with orders to murder Lady Emily."

"They cannot *both* be telling the truth," King Randor pointed out.

Emily frowned, remembering a comic strip she'd once read. Captain Kirk had been stabbed–and, when he'd recovered, he'd blamed one of his crewmen. The crewman had denied the charge–and the telepath who'd investigated had claimed that he was telling the truth. They'd *both* been telling the truth...eventually, the crew had discovered that a shape-shifter had impersonated the crewman, ensuring that no one would look for him. Only sheer coincidence had allowed the real assassin to be uncovered before he could try again.

And then there had been Harry Potter's attempt to impersonate one of his fellow pupils.

"The guardsman wouldn't be familiar with the duke," she said, slowly. "Could someone have impersonated him?"

"That would be against the law," Lady Barb said, deadpan. "You mean someone could have used a glamor to pretend to be the duke?"

Emily nodded. "And perhaps a hint of compulsion as well, to override any doubts they might have," she added. "Besides, if the guardsmen were junior enough, they wouldn't question his orders anyway. They'd believe that they were following orders from legitimate authority. The truth spells can only tell what someone *believes* to be true."

"It's possible," Lady Barb said. "And yet...if the guardsmen were issued their orders in the barracks, whoever issued them had to be capable of breaking into the castle."

"Or was invited," King Randor said, darkly. "One of the barons, intent on taking the throne for himself, might have managed to issue the orders while waiting for an audience."

"A simple glamor might well have escaped notice," Lady Barb agreed. "How many noblewomen have glamors to hide unsightly features?"

"You will continue to investigate," King Randor ordered. "And... Lady Emily?"

Emily gulped. "Yes, Your Majesty?"

"The confirmation ceremony takes place in a week," King Randor said. "Try not to upset anyone else before then."

"Yes, Your Majesty," Emily said, flushing.

"And several of our young bucks have made known their interest in you," the king added, clearly enjoying Emily's discomfort. "If you want to get married..."

He laughed at Emily's expression. "Refer them to your guardian," he suggested. "After all, you are clearly not yet ready to carve out an independent life."

Emily nodded. Anyone who tried to negotiate with Void would find it a maddening task. At best, he'd just tell them that he couldn't approve the match—after making them waste time trying to convince him to support their proposal. Alternatively, he'd simply ignore their letters in the hopes that they'd go away.

"And Nightingale wishes to brief you on the etiquette for the Confirmation," the king concluded. "You may speak with him in the library."

Emily curtseyed and backed out of the room, silently grateful for the times Alassa had made her practice. Walking backwards wasn't easy; she had no idea how Duchess Lithia had managed to walk in a dress without tripping over herself. Once the door closed, she turned and walked towards the library, mulling over what she'd heard. If the mastermind behind the assassination attempts wasn't the Duke of Iron, who *was* it?

He should have asked the duke if he was a sorcerer, Emily realized, as she reached the library. *We could have checked that too.*

Could the duke have found a way to defeat the Royal Bloodline? The king placed a great deal of faith in it—and why not? He had presumably been unable to lie to his father too, just like Alassa. What if the truth-telling effect no longer worked once the previous Bloodline Prime had died? Could there be an exception to the rule and the alchemists had simply missed it?

And yet that seemed too simple to be missed easily.

Why not? She asked herself sourly. *You forgot to use Berserker.*

Nightingale was sitting at a table inside the library, reviewing a set of parchments that looked old enough to date back to the Empire. He looked up as she entered and then stood up, bowing to her. Emily walked over to him, nodded once and took the seat facing him.

"You are aware, no doubt, that the Confirmation is the most important part of the crown princess's path towards the throne," he began, as self-importantly as ever. "While she was the acknowledged heir as soon as she was born, she was not formally presented to the barons as their future monarch. Custom decreed that the Confirmation had to wait until she was seventeen years old, capable of ruling without out a regent."

Emily nodded, impatiently. Zangaria prioritized male heirs, just like medieval Europe; a younger brother would have automatically taken Alassa's place as heir. But a child, male or female, would not have been expected to be able to rule. Someone else would have served as regent…and, given enough time, have been able to build up a powerbase they could use to replace the heir. Or, perhaps, push Alassa into marrying him.

"The Confirmation will prove to the assembled nobility that the princess is capable of ruling them, that she is healthy and of sound mind as well as sound body, that she can take her father's place when he dies," Nightingale said. "It must *not* be allowed to go wrong."

"I understand," Emily said, sharply. "What do you wish me to do as part of the ceremony?"

"The crown prince is assigned a knight to accompany him," Nightingale said. "But the princess is female and it would not be appropriate for her to be accompanied by a male knight. King Randor has therefore consented to allow *you* to serve as her knight."

Emily blinked. Could a woman be knighted? She'd certainly never heard of it.

But she was sure that she *wasn't* a knight.

"There will be other noblewomen, surely," she said, finally. "Why me?"

"You don't have any relationships within Zangaria, apart from your friendship with Alassa," Nightingale pointed out. "Any noblewoman would have her own interests at stake, or those of her husband."

He didn't seem to realize that Emily's other best friend *also* came from Zangaria, but Imaiqah *was* a commoner. Maybe she just didn't count.

"Alassa will go into seclusion the night before the ceremony," Nightingale informed her. "She will be expected to pray to the goddess that she will have a long and happy and fruitful reign, once she takes her father's place. You will be there with her. The following morning, you will bear witness as the baronesses inspect her, making sure that she is healthy. Once they certify her, you will join her for breakfast and then proceed to the Assembly."

Emily wondered what would happen if the baronesses *refused* to confirm that Alassa was healthy. It made sense, particularly in a medieval environment, but she couldn't help feeling a moment's pity for Alassa. The baronesses would poke and prod at her entire body, just to make sure that she was completely healthy. They couldn't just hire a healer to do it?

"The king will present his daughter to the Assembly," Nightingale droned on. "Once they have acclaimed her, the Duke of Iron will formally abandon his right to be regent and accept her as the crown princess, the first in line to the throne. She will in turn confirm him as her heir, to become the monarch in the event of her death. After that, the barons will come forward, one by one, and swear to be loyal to her when she assumes the throne. They will be followed by the lesser nobility and finally by the assemblymen."

He took a breath. "And after that," he concluded, "the competition for her hand begins in earnest."

Emily gaped at him. "It hasn't already begun?"

"There is a difference between a crown princess who has not been Confirmed and a crown princess who *has* been Confirmed," Nightingale said.

Emily shrugged. It seemed a matter of semantics to her; Alassa had been her father's heir from the moment she had been born. But the whole ceremony was clearly important to the locals. Confirming that Alassa was healthy—and presumably fertile—would give them the promise of an heir to replace her when she died. But that really required her to marry…

Nightingale leaned forward. "There is another reason for your role," he added. His voice grew tighter as he spoke. "You must ensure that she remains awake overnight while in seclusion, to honor the traditions. And you will have to swear that she has done so."

"I see," Emily said. The sergeants had pushed them to the point where Emily could get by on little sleep, but Alassa hadn't been in Martial Magic. And it was cruel to force her to remain awake the night before she was Confirmed. How long would the ceremony even last? "And what am I supposed to do if she falls asleep?"

"Keep her awake," Nightingale said. He looked oddly reluctant to speak further, even though he knew he had to specify. "Whatever it takes, keep her awake."

Emily snorted. "How many people volunteered for this job?"

"None," Nightingale admitted. "But then, everyone who could have taken the role had…other commitments."

"Answer me a question," Emily said. "Why am I not surprised?"

Chapter Thirty-One

EMILY SHIFTED UNCOMFORTABLY ON HER SEAT AS BARON BRONZE DRONED ON AND ON about how much he loved King Randor, his crown princess and his country. It would have been a more impressive speech if the baron, who seemed never to have to pause for breath, hadn't kept jumping back to the topic of his own services to the kingdom. But then, every dinner since the duke's interrogation had included one of the barons having a chance to talk. Emily couldn't decide just who, if anyone, was meant to be impressed.

Lady Barb hadn't been joking when she'd promised Emily that they were going to be practicing magical and mundane combat. Every day, once Alassa had finished breakfast and taken the princes hunting or jousting, Lady Barb had sought out Emily and brought her to a training room. There, she'd forced Emily to practice and practice and practice, often sparring with her at the end of the session. She didn't allow Emily to use any sort of painkilling potions either, leaving Emily aching for the rest of the day. Like the sergeants, Lady Barb seemed to believe that pain was the ultimate teacher. Emily had looked in the mirror every night and been astonished to see how many bruises were covering her body.

She looked over at Alassa, sitting beside Prince Hedrick, a faintly bored expression on her face. This was the night before her Confirmation; Alassa had chosen Hedrick as her escort simply because he *wouldn't* say anything to her. Emily swallowed, not looking forward to the evening at all. The records Nightingale had found for her—after some persuasion—suggested that some previous princes had spent the night in 'silent contemplation' that was so loud that no one could sleep. Alassa might not be much better.

But then, there will be just the two of us, Emily thought. She had toyed with the idea of inviting Imaiqah, but Lady Barb had talked her out of it, pointing out that the nobility would see her presence as an insult. Emily had asked why *she* was acceptable—after all, the standard account of her birth placed her as barely above a slave— and Lady Barb had pointed out that she *had* killed a necromancer. And *that* put her ahead of even a fully-trained sorcerer.

The baron finally came to an end and sat down, much to everyone's relief. There was a pause, then King Randor stood up and announced that there would be no dancing; instead, everyone was urged to spend the evening in prayer for the crown princess. Several guests looked surprised, although it had been announced days ago. Every last detail of the formal dinners was carefully choreographed by the King's staff. Perhaps the guests simply hadn't bothered to find out what was actually going on.

"You are all welcome tomorrow," the king concluded. "And I thank you for your acclaim."

He walked behind the curtain. Protocol dictated that no one was allowed to leave before the monarch; his departure signalled that the revels were now over. Emily stood up, following Alassa as she walked out the door and headed up towards her chambers. She saw Zed scowling at her as she passed, clearly considering throwing a spell at her before thinking better of it. The alchemists King Randor had summoned to investigate Emily's concerns about the Royal Bloodline were poking their noses into his work.

But you'd hate it too if someone did it to you, Emily thought, ruefully. Magicians disliked *anyone* messing with their workspaces, to the point where it was common for them to scatter trap spells over their books, papers and equipment. Every day, Whitehall saw a handful of students trapped by spells set by their fellow students. She'd heard enough stories to know about what could happen to someone who broke into a magician's house to understand that anyone who tried would be a candidate for the Darwin Award.

Alassa grinned at Emily as she stepped into her rooms. Most of the servants seemed to have been banished, leaving only a trio of maids to help Alassa undress and don a long white gown that looked faintly odd to Emily's eyes. It took her a long moment to realize that it seemed to have been designed for an older women, rather than a young princess. The maids caught hold of Emily before she could object and undressed her too, then passed her a black gown that was the same cut and style as Alassa's gown.

"The supplicant before the goddess always wears white," Alassa explained, as soon as the maids had left the room. "Anyone who comes with them to bear witness wears black."

"Tradition," Emily guessed.

"Symbolism," Alassa countered. She stepped over to one of her chests and opened it with a touch of her magic. "The goddess will only grant one's prayers if the formalities are honored."

Emily frowned as she saw Alassa pull a book out of the chest. "What is the book?"

Alassa smirked. "Most of the men in the city do not approve of the crone goddess," she explained, as she passed Emily the book. "The book is charmed to appear like an ordinary textbook to any man who happened to gaze upon it. Those who look inside find themselves blinded."

Emily looked down at the book. Some of the letters on the front were recognizably part of the Empire's language. Others were unfamiliar, yet she couldn't help feeling that she'd seen them before. She ran her finger down the spine, feeling an odd tingle as she sensed the magic buried within the pages, then opened it to the first page. The insignia that stared up at her was instantly recognizable. It was the same as the one on the front page of Void's untranslatable book.

"The crone is the ultimate representation of womankind," Alassa said. "Her sisters—the mother and the maiden—are transient. The crone is eternal. But men fear her deeply, even though she is not unkind. They believe that those who follow the goddess think for themselves."

"Oh," Emily said. Alassa hadn't done much thinking for herself before she'd met Emily. "What happens to those who follow her?"

"Nothing," Alassa said. She smiled at Emily's expression, then rolled her eyes, suggesting that she wasn't entirely serious. "Those who tinker with the rites of a goddess come to bad ends. *Everyone* knows that."

She walked over to the far corner of the room and knelt down, facing the blank wall. "I am going to read from the book," she said, "and then try to meditate. You can kneel behind me while I read, then you can move around or read one of the other books"—she waved a hand at her bookshelf—"while I meditate. Just don't let me fall asleep."

Emily grinned. "What would you like me to do if you *do* fall asleep?"

"Feel free to wake me up," Alassa said. "My father told me that my uncle never even let him get a *wink* of sleep."

She scowled. "I feel bad for him," she added. "Being interrogated like that is *not* pleasant."

Emily nodded. Lady Barb's investigation had gotten nowhere, even though she was convinced that the true suspect was someone with access to the castle. Indeed, her suspicions seemed to have focused on Prince Hedrick, simply because he was the only trained magician amongst the princes. And the maid who had tried to kill Alassa—or Emily—had come from his kingdom.

But why would he risk summoning a cockatrice? Emily asked herself. *It could have killed us all.*

Alassa began to read out loud from the book, using a language that Emily didn't recognize. Could it be that she should have asked Alassa how to read Void's book from the start? It had honestly never occurred to her...but what *was* the language the book's authors had used? Why was it the same as that belonging to the crone goddess's followers?

Emily concentrated, then cast a translation spell.

"...Of all we see," Alassa said, her words suddenly understandable. "You bring us into the world, you marry us, you lay us out when we die..."

Her words died away suddenly. Emily watched as she closed the book, folded her hands in her lap and then started to meditate. Silently, Emily rose to her feet and walked over to the bookshelf, examining the books the young princess had been allowed to read. Several of them looked to be storybooks that were surprisingly Victorian—complete with fixed gender roles, a hefty dose of orthodox morality and heroes so brave, noble and true that they were effectively Mary Sues—one of them detailed the Empire's views on how a princess should behave and two final ones were books on magic. Emily opened one of the magic books and skimmed through it, only to conclude that the writer had been writing a book for dummies.

Alassa could have used this to grasp the basics, she told herself, sourly. *But she stayed with her memory instead.*

The other magic book was, if anything, even worse. It was merely a listing of minor spells, ranging from practical jokes to a handful of spells for domestic purposes. One of them promised to clean tables, if used by someone with enough mana to work it. Judging by the handwritten notes next to the words, the person who had originally owned the book had gotten frustrated with the spell and warned his successors not to bother trying to get it to work. A final spell was a very basic lie detector. Emily had a feeling that she knew who had given Alassa the books.

She started to read the storybooks out of boredom, while glancing up at the meditating princess to be sure that she hadn't fallen asleep. Alassa seemed to be coping with the vigil much better than Emily would have done, although there were hours to go before first light. Emily had been forced to stay on watch for a couple of hours on camping trips with Martial Magic, but she'd always been relieved before she'd dozed off. The sergeants had a number of brutally effective punishments for anyone who *did* fall asleep, pointing out that a sleeping sentry was an invitation to murder.

Emily was still reading when morning came and the maids started to knock on the door. Alassa rose to her feet and grinned at Emily, then walked over to the door and opened it. A small army of maids appeared, carrying jugs of water and a bathtub. Alassa was undressed, helped into the tub and scrubbed clean. Emily watched with some amusement as her golden hair was washed, then left to hang down her back. Emerging from the water, as naked as the day she was born, Alassa looked almost like a goddess.

"The baronesses are coming," one of the maids said, as Alassa wrapped a towel around herself. "Should I show them in?"

Alassa made a face. "May as well get this over with," she muttered to Emily, then raised her voice. "Show them in, by all means."

Emily had been introduced to the barons and their wives during the first couple of dinners, but she couldn't really say that she knew them. They all seemed to share the same disapproving expression when they looked at her, although Emily couldn't tell if they disliked her because of her official origin story or because they hated and feared the changes she had brought to their country. This time, they seemed content to ignore her and clustered around Alassa, their black dresses making them seem almost like a flock of crows surrounding a dove. They poked and prodded at Alassa, their fingers exploring every inch of her body, testing every last muscle. Emily wanted to curse them as Alassa yelped in pain. One of the women had just pinched her in a sensitive spot.

"Healthy," Baroness Silver said, finally. The other women echoed her. "You should be capable of living long and bearing many children."

Alassa watched them go and then muttered a curse, barely loud enough for Emily to hear. "When I am queen," she said, "that one will *not* be welcome in court."

Emily shook her head, unable to avoid feeling anger at the red marks on Alassa's skin. They were fading quickly–quick healing was part of the Royal Bloodline–but it proved just how badly they'd mistreated her. Maybe, if she were lucky, Lady Barb would uncover proof that the baroness who'd poked her worst was the one whose husband was behind the plot. The woman deserved to suffer before she died.

The maids returned. Two of them were carrying a white dress for Alassa, the others were carrying more jugs of water. Emily found herself being stripped and pushed into the bathtub before she could object, then felt hands scrubbing all the dirt and sweat away from her. By the time she was pulled out and dried, Alassa was in her dress and the maids were working on her hair. Emily's own dress was blue; the maids helped her into it and then did up her hair.

"I could just use magic," Emily protested, as the maids started to insert hairpins. "It will stay up."

Alassa laughed, sweetly. "Tradition," she said. She struck a dramatic pose in front of the mirror. "How do I look?"

"Like a blushing bride," Emily said. "What are you going to wear on your wedding day?"

"Oh? Green, probably," Alassa said. "That too is tradition."

Emily puzzled over that as the maids finished fixing up her hair. White symbolized purity—and virginity, which was why it had been adopted for wedding dresses. But green was often taken to symbolize regeneration and rebirth. Perhaps it did make sense; marriage was often a step away from one's parents and into a whole new world.

Once they were ready, the maids escorted them downstairs into the Great Hall. Emily hung back as Alassa walked up towards her father, seated on his throne, and bobbled a curtsey to him. King Randor rose to his feet, embraced his daughter and then looked at Emily.

"Lady Emily," he said. "Was she checked and certified as healthy?"

"She was," Emily said. As she had been told, she dropped a curtsey of her own. "Your daughter is fit, healthy—and ready."

The breakfast was small, nothing more than small fruits. Emily was silently grateful—she couldn't have eaten much and she wasn't the star of the show. Alassa's face was expressionless—most of the nobles in the room were watching her like hawks—but Emily could see her tension in how she held her body. She was more nervous than she wanted to admit. If the ceremony went wrong, it would be taken as a bad omen. God alone knew what would happen then.

King Randor rose to his feet and announced that the march to the Assembly was about to begin. He took his wife's hand and led her out of the hall; Alassa hesitated, then followed him. Emily walked by her side as the rest of the nobles came after them, heading out of the castle gates and down towards the Assembly. The streets were lined by cheering crowds, all waving banners or yelling encouragement to the princess. Emily wondered, rather cynically, if the armed guards were there to protect the nobility or to encourage the population to cheer.

Up close, the Assembly was larger than she'd realized. The elected assemblymen were lined up outside, bowing to King Randor as he walked past them and into the main hall, followed by his court. Inside, there were two long rows of seats for the nobles and elected assemblymen—and three golden thrones, placed at one end of the hall. One for the king, Emily remembered; one for the heir and one—left empty, with a sword placed nearly on top—for the Emperor. But the Empire was gone.

Tradition, she thought. But it was an odd tradition, one that puzzled her. Zangaria was trying to demonstrate that it was an independent kingdom, yet it was honoring the days when it had been part of a mighty empire. Or was it a reminder of why the Allied Lands were so important? Unity was strength; disunity meant weakness—with the necromancers lurking in the Blighted Lands, ready to swoop down on the Allied Lands if the defenses ever weakened.

King Randor sat on his throne and waited for the assembled guests to find their seats. Emily herself had been given a chair near Alassa's throne, one half-hidden in the darkness. But no one would be paying attention to her anyway, not when a princess was being Confirmed as heir. Alassa herself stood in front of her throne, waiting for permission to sit. She couldn't sit down until the ceremony was completed.

The trumpets blared as the heavy wooden doors closed with a loud thud. "MY LORDS," the herald shouted. "STAND FOR YOUR KING!"

Everyone rose to their feet, including Emily. King Randor studied the guests for a long moment and then stood up himself, motioning for the guests to sit down. They obeyed slowly, keeping their eyes on their monarch. Here, he was supreme.

"King Alexis I found this kingdom in a state of chaos," King Randor said. His voice was quiet, but amplified so that everyone could hear his words. "He brought it order. He founded the monarchy while his followers became the core of the aristocracy. Successive generations of royalty have honored the pledge Alexis made to his people. Strength, unity, order and protection!

"Now, my daughter Alassa, Daughter of Marlena, comes to take her place as heir," he continued. "It is time for her to be certified as the rightful heir, so that she may take my place when I leave this world..."

The Duke of Iron fell to the ground, like a puppet whose strings had been cut.

A moment later, all hell broke loose.

Chapter Thirty-Two

EMILY CAME TO HER FEET AS A THUNDEROUS IMPACT KNOCKED THE HEAVY WOODEN door off its hinges and sent it falling onto the people at the rear of the hall. Armed soldiers—and men carrying wands—crashed into the chamber, shouting for everyone to remain still. No one seemed interested in paying attention; noblemen were jumping up, shouting for their guards, while others were hitting the ground. A handful of guards appeared and were ruthlessly cut down by the newcomers.

A spell struck King Randor and he froze, then toppled over and hit the ground. Emily jumped forward and knocked Alassa down as another spell crackled over their heads. The entire situation seemed to have dissolved into chaos; Emily couldn't tell what was going on or who was attacking. She rolled off Alassa and readied her magic, just as a trio of men carrying wands approached the thrones. Her wards deflected their spells, then Lady Barb crashed into them, lashing out with her magic. None of them stood a chance.

"Get Alassa out of here!" Lady Barb shouted. Magic crackled around her as the newcomers attacked, trying to overwhelm the combat sorceress by sheer weight of numbers. "Now!"

Emily hesitated for a long second. King Randor was down, clearly frozen in place; his wife, the queen, was on the ground beside him. And the newcomers were getting closer...Emily caught at Alassa's arm and pulled her towards the rear of the hall, where there should be a way out. The princess seemed dazed, but followed, keeping her head low. Emily took one last glance at the fighting, realized that the newcomers seemed to have won, and then pulled Alassa out of the hall. They found themselves in a small corridor heading deeper into the building.

Sergeant Harkin had said that a situation could go from placid to absolute chaos in less than a second. Emily had never really understood what he'd meant until now. Someone had launched a coup, attacking King Randor and almost all of the senior nobility at the same time...but who? Why would one of the barons risk their own death in the crossfire? Could it be that the true enemy was a commoner? Maybe there *was* a commoner wealthy enough to buy enchanted armor...

She pushed the thought aside as she pulled Alassa down the corridor. Simple logic suggested that the intruders, whoever they were, would try to block all exits, but they couldn't have risked doing that before they burst into the main hall, or they might have alerted King Randor's guardsmen. If they could get out of the building before they managed to secure the grounds, they could escape into the city and then...Emily didn't know, but they would at least have some time to consider the next step.

They turned the corner and ran into four men wearing armor and carrying swords, perfectly placed to block the escape route from the main hall. Emily gritted her teeth as they advanced towards her, casting three separate spells towards them in hopes of overloading their armor. Magic flared around them, but seemed unable to touch them until Alassa started to cast spells of her own. The guards screamed in pain as their armor flared bright red and failed, then the spells took effect. Emily felt a moment of pity for them as she scooped up two of the dropped swords and passed one of them to Alassa. So many spells combining would produce results that were almost impossible to fix.

"Traitors," Alassa seethed. "Who *are* they?"

Emily shrugged. The duke had collapsed first—what did that mean? She couldn't escape the odd feeling that she *should* know what had happened to him, but her conscious mind refused to provide answers. Had he broken his oath and suffered the consequences? But if he *was* behind the coup, he'd lied to his brother despite being part of the Royal Bloodline. How the hell had he done that?

"Down here," Alassa said. "We can get into the tunnels and escape underground."

"But the duke would have known about them," Emily protested. He'd been his father's spare and his brother's military commander. The duke would know *all* of the secret passages; he, like the students at Whitehall, would have had ample time to explore the building and locate them all. "We can't risk using them."

Alassa stopped and stared at her. "I... I don't know how he did it," she said. "If he *did* do it."

There was a shout behind them as two armed guards appeared. "Stop," one of them bellowed. "You are our prisoners."

Both girls cast spells at once, directing them at the guards. One guard's armor overloaded, sending him falling to the floor; the other kept coming, balefire crackling around him without touching his skin. For a long moment, Emily stared in disbelief before realizing that the guardsman was actually a magician in disguise. He lifted one hand and threw a powerful paralysis spell at the two girls. Emily parried it with an effort and threw back a blast of raw power. The magician would have no trouble deflecting it, but he'd be blinded for a handful of seconds. Emily lunged forward, sword in hand, and lashed out with a more focused spell she'd learned in Martial Magic. The magician's wards failed, just for a long second, long enough for Emily to bury the sword in his chest. He let out a grunt and staggered backwards, toppling to the ground. Emily pulled the sword out and then beheaded him, just to be sure.

There was no time for horror and revulsion at what she'd done. Emily turned and rejoined Alassa, leading her rapidly down the corridor towards the tunnel entrance. They rounded a corner and stopped dead. Seven heavily armed men and two magicians were standing in front of the tunnel, clearly ready to prevent anyone from escaping into the underground network. Alassa used a vile word and lashed out with her magic, but the two magicians deflected it from their companions. Emily caught Alassa and yanked her backwards as the magicians started throwing spells back at the girls. One of them struck Emily's wards with something that almost knocked them down before they got out of range. Oddly, the guards didn't seem interested in giving chase.

They have to guard the tunnels, Emily thought, grimly. *Can't risk having King Randor or his family getting back to the castle.*

Alassa led the way through a pair of wooden doors and into a smaller chamber that was less ornate than the main hall, but built along the same general principle. The commoners had to sit here, Emily decided, as they ran through the middle of the hall and out towards the commoner exit. There would be guards outside by now, she knew, but if they failed to break out they might as well surrender...no, that couldn't be risked. Alassa would probably be forced into marriage to one of the barons, assuming the barons were actually behind the plot; Emily herself would be executed. Unless Void came to the rescue...

"Wait," she said, before Alassa could run out of the building. "We need to disguise ourselves."

Alassa gave her a blank look, then nodded in understanding. Every girl at Whitehall—and at least half the boys—learned how to use glamors to change their appearance. Some were simple illusions, designed to hint at larger breasts or cleaner faces, others were suffused with tiny compulsion spells which insisted that no one should look too closely. It would be easy to place a more powerful version of the charm on themselves, but it was too likely that they would run into another disguised magician. He might well spot the glamor and then wonder what it was concealing.

Emily recalled the first set of guards they'd encountered and carefully shaped the glamor spell, casting it over them both. As always, it felt faintly odd to be wearing a glamor of any kind; she hadn't been able to understand why so many girls used them when they made their magic feel a little strange. But then, vanity had never been one of her vices.

"You look like a hairy man," Alassa said. She giggled, suddenly. "What do I look like?"

Emily frowned. Was Alassa going into shock? The coup had to be the most shocking event in her life, even more shocking—and terrifying—than the moment Emily had almost killed her. She *did* know that people could fall into shock as soon as they had a moment to reflect; God knew she'd certainly felt that way after Void had snatched her out of Shadye's clutches...and *he* had used a spell to keep her calm.

"Like there's two of you," Emily said. She *knew* the glamor was there, so it seemed like an insubstantial shadow concealing the girl below. The guardsman was only an illusion, after all. She took a breath, then transfigured Alassa's dress into something smaller, small enough that it wouldn't break the glamor. "Remember you have to walk naturally, not run. The last thing we need is to attract attention."

She pushed the door open and stepped out into the bright sunlight, wincing as the light stabbed into her eyes. Outside, a small group of guardsmen stood at the edge of the grounds, while others were heading into the building. Emily wondered just what they intended to do with the captives, before pushing the thought aside. There was nothing she could do for them now, apart from keeping Alassa safe and then...she didn't know. They'd have to work out some kind of solution or flee back to Whitehall.

"Stay calm," she muttered, as they headed for the gates. The sergeants had told her that you could get away with a great deal simply by acting as if you had a perfect right to do whatever you were doing. Someone who looked shifty, on the other hand, would attract immediate attention. "If anyone asks, we have been sent with an urgent message to the castle."

The sergeants had also hammered observation techniques into her head, reminding her that combat sorcerers and sorceresses were often called upon to spy. She counted upwards of forty guardsmen near the Assembly, a sizeable percentage of the force legally available to any of the barons. But if someone had determined on a coup, they wouldn't let little details like a ban on more than two hundred armsmen get in their way. None of the guardsmen wore anything that identified them, suggesting... what? Was their master still unsure of success?

She pushed that out of her mind as they reached the gates, silently cursing Whitehall under her breath. The tutors allowed the students to use glamors freely because it taught them how to sense their presence and peer *under* the illusion. If one of the guardsmen happened to be a magician, he might well realize that two people were trying to escape. Emily nodded to one of the guards as they walked through the gates and out into the streets. No one moved to stop them.

"Thank the goddess," Alassa breathed. "Back to the castle?"

Emily glanced up the long road towards the castle gates and shook her head. There were squadrons of horsemen patrolling the streets, with heralds bellowing commands for everyone to remain indoors and lock their doors. They didn't seem interested in giving explanations, Emily realized, although *that* wasn't too surprising. King Randor was a reasonably popular king—he was certainly more popular than any of the nobles, particularly the barons—and the populace might rise up in his support, if they knew what was happening.

"I think we'd be caught if we tried," she said. And even if they *did* get into the castle, what could they do? Just sit there and wait for the enemy forces to catch up with them? It probably didn't matter; by now, the castle had to be crawling with enemy troops. "Where else can we go?"

"The shrine," Alassa said. "The priestesses would give us sanctuary, but..."

She broke off. "They wouldn't help us fight back," she added. "They're not allowed to involve themselves in mundane matters."

Emily wasn't too surprised. From what Alassa had said, the sisters of the crone goddess lived on the very edge of acceptable society. It was easy to see their existence as a challenge to male authority, even if the very concept of male authority was thoroughly absurd. The temples could be closed down and the sisters scattered if they annoyed enough people in power, whatever defenses they might believe the goddess offered them. No, they'd be unwilling to assist openly. It was more likely that they would simply keep Emily and Alassa within their shrine, unable to leave.

"We can't stay here," Emily muttered. By now, the faceless enemy would probably have realized that they hadn't caught Alassa. They'd start hunting for her as soon as they had secured the castle and the garrison. If they worked along the same lines as Dragon's Den, they might well have secured the gatehouses leading out of the inner city too. "Come on."

She felt an odd flash of *déjà vu* as they slipped down the stairs where she and Imaiqah had been attacked, barely a week ago. "Stop here," she ordered, summoning charms Sergeant Miles had taught her. "We don't want them tracking us."

The simplest way to track someone, Sergeant Miles had said, was by using a trained dog. There were no shortage of huntsmen in the nobility, all of whom owned dogs; a simple spell broke the trail, making it impossible for the dogs to follow them any further. A second set of spells disrupted the link between Alassa and her father, at least to some extent. But then, Alassa was almost as unique as Emily. Given time, the Royal Bloodline could probably be used as a needle to point directly at her.

There were other ways. Sergeant Miles had tracked Emily and Jade through the forest near Whitehall so effectively that Emily had been *convinced* that he'd used magic. He hadn't; afterwards, he'd taken them back along their route and pointed out all the subtle hints they'd left that had shown him their path. It would be harder to leave a trail in the city, but…if someone could track them, they'd better be prepared to fight. Who knew *what* would happen once they fell into enemy hands?

They'll want Alassa alive, Emily told herself. *But they won't want me.*

"I'm going to alter the illusion slightly," she said, out loud. "We won't look like guardsmen, but ordinary citizens. Just remember to walk with your head slightly bowed."

"Understood," Alassa said. Her voice was uneven, but she was holding herself under control. "Where are we going?"

"We need help," Emily said. And Alassa needed a place to collapse for a few minutes. "There's only one place we can go."

"Imaiqah's," Alassa said.

Emily nodded, thinking hard. The problem was that their unknown enemy, if they knew *anything* about Alassa, would almost certainly draw the correct conclusion. Alassa didn't have any friends in Alexis apart from Imaiqah…who else would she run to? And Emily shared the same friend. If *she'd* been in command of the hunt for the missing princess, she would have staked out Imaiqah's apartment right from the start.

We could go to the warehouse, she thought, instead. *I could break in easily and then…what?*

Nothing came to mind. They needed help and Imaiqah's family were the only ones who could provide it.

They will be targeted too, Emily thought, although she wasn't sure if she really believed it or if she was trying to salve her conscience. The coup might well be aimed at reversing the changes Emily had brought to Zangaria before it was too late, in which case Imaiqah and everyone else associated with the new knowledge would be targeted for elimination. Maybe they had moved too far, too fast; maybe other guilds had feared their own destruction and decided to help the aristocracy strike back.

"Come on," she said, shaking her head. There would be time to unravel the mystery of who was behind the coup once they were safe. "We need to move."

They kept to the shadows as they walked away from the castle, heading down towards the docks. The streets were being patrolled by horsemen, who paused long enough to bellow instructions to the citizens, ordering the market sellers off the streets and back into their homes. Here, where people actually had to work daily for a living, there was grumbling and defiance, even outright resistance. The horsemen looked ready to draw their swords and lash into the crowds as Emily and Alassa slipped by them, hidden under the glamor. Passing through the market would also add some more confusion to their trail, Emily told herself. Thousands of people passed through it every day.

"They can't keep everyone off the streets forever," she muttered, as they slipped into a darkened alleyway. "The entire city would grind to a halt."

The thought was chilling. Alexis depended on a constant supply of food from the farms surrounding the city. If that supply line were to be broken for more than a day or two, the citizens would start to starve and then die. The new authorities would have riots on their hands.

Or is that what they want? She asked herself. *Do they want the entire city dead?*

She was tempted just to run into Imaiqah's shop, but held back, checking out the entire area first. There didn't seem to be any guards, or magical surveillance, apart from a handful of wards that had Imaiqah's signature. Bracing herself, Emily stepped into the store and saw Imaiqah sitting behind the counter, her eyes narrowing as she saw the glamor. Emily smiled, allowing the glamor to fade away into nothingness.

Imaiqah stared at them as she looked up. "Emily? *Alassa?*"

Chapter Thirty-Three

"YOUR HIGHNESS," IMAIQAH'S FATHER STAMMERED. "WHAT ARE...WHAT'S GOING ON?"

"I'm not quite sure," Emily admitted. She ran through a brief outline of the attack on the Assembly, concluding with their escape from the attackers and flight through the streets. "Do you have a place where you can hide us?"

Paren hesitated, studying Alassa thoughtfully. "Hiding you might be difficult, Your Highness," he said, finally. "You're quite recognizable."

Emily couldn't disagree. *She* could pass for a local, at least once she'd changed into more basic clothes and undone her hair. Alassa, on the other hand, was the result of a breeding program that had produced a stunningly beautiful girl. She'd draw eyes wherever she went, no matter what she wore. Perhaps they could give her a headscarf and claim that she was married, using the scarf to conceal her blonde hair, but her face would still be recognizable. And a glamor might well be noticed once the enemy started searching in earnest.

Lin marched over to her husband, pulled him to one side and started whispering to him angrily. Emily wondered what she was saying—perhaps insisting that her husband helped or perhaps urging him to get rid of them as quickly as possible—before looking over at Imaiqah, who had brought in a small pile of clothes.

"They're my size," Imaiqah stated. "But you should be able to wear them."

"I should have taken that class on clothing transfigurations," Alassa said, ruefully. She still sounded shaken and, from the glances she was directing at Imaiqah's parents, could hear too much of their conversation for her own peace of mind. "I could have altered them to fit."

"Get in here," Imaiqah ordered, pulling them into a small chamber. "Change into these clothes, then your old ones can be turned to dust. They can't be found here."

She hesitated as Emily started to strip off the dress the maids had given her...had it really only been a few short hours ago? It felt like years had passed since the coup had been launched. But then, Alassa and she had spent the night awake...she really needed to get some sleep. So did Alassa, or they'd be completely exhausted when the enemy finally caught up with them.

"Can you find Alassa a scarf?" Emily asked, as she finished pulling on the trousers and shirt. They felt uncomfortably tight, but it should help to convince any watchers that she was simply too poor to buy clothing in her own size. "Her hair is simply too recognizable."

"Here," Imaiqah said. She smiled brightly at Emily's expression. "I thought of that."

"Thank you," Alassa said, seriously. She took the scarf and tried to put it on. "How do you do it?"

"Like this," Imaiqah said, and demonstrated. "Remember, you're a married women and you cannot take the scarf off in public."

Alassa snorted as Emily inspected her. She didn't *look* like a princess any longer, unless one paid too much attention to her face and realized that it was inhumanly perfect. Emily wondered if they could find something that could be used to mar

Alassa's skin, perhaps creating the impression of a wart or even a simple pimple. But it would have to be done carefully...perhaps they could create two glamors, one to suggest a nasty birthmark on Alassa's face and the other to cover it up. Anyone who looked too closely would see the birthmark and hopefully not look any further.

Or we could just use dirt, she thought. *It would be completely undetectable—and cheap!*

Paren was waiting for them as they stepped back into the living room. "I've sent out messengers to the craftsmen to suggest that they go into hiding," he said. His tone suggested that he'd had a contingency plan for that all along. "However...Your Highness, I would like to know why I should risk my family to help you."

There was a long, uncomfortable pause.

"The only people who could make the coup work are the barons," Alassa said, finally. If she found the question offensive, she kept it to herself. "I don't understand how the duke could have risen against my father—if it is the duke—but both he and the barons have one thing in common. They both disapprove of the changes that have recently been introduced into the kingdom."

Her eyes sharpened. "You are one of the most prominent merchants involved with spreading new knowledge," she added. "Even if I'd never come here, you will be targeted. They will seek to make horrific examples out of everyone they can catch. If you help me restore my father to his throne, you will have his gratitude—and you will have safeguarded your own lives."

Emily nodded when Imaiqah's father looked at her. Alassa was correct, although it wouldn't make the knowledge any easier to bear. Lady Barb had been right, Emily decided; she *had* been careless when she started offering Imaiqah the benefits of her knowledge. If they'd moved more carefully, perhaps the coup would never have happened...but then, once certain items became common knowledge, they would have spread like wildfire. The arrogance and corruption of the Accountants Guild would have seen to that.

"True, Your Highness," Paren said, finally. "But how can we help restore your father to his throne?"

"I don't know yet," Alassa admitted. "There *will* be loyalists out there..."

"There's a place where you can hide for a few days," Paren said. "I'll be sending most of my children to other hiding places. Imaiqah will take you there."

"Thank you," Alassa said. "And I *will* see you rewarded for this."

Imaiqah led them both out of the room and into the store. "You'll need some food," she said, picking up a small knapsack. "The bread is freshly baked; father buys it from the baker just down the street. The apples are tasty; make sure you eat at least one a day. Everyone is eating apples right now. I'm not so fond of the cheese, but it will keep you healthy."

Emily concealed her amusement. It had been her suggestion to set up a convenience store, one where people could buy whatever they might want without having to search through dozens of stores. Admittedly it didn't work as well as it had on Earth, but it still brought in some additional money for Imaiqah's family. She added a couple of bottles of water to the knapsack, slung it over her shoulder and waited.

"I've wrapped up the swords," Imaiqah added. "If the guardsmen see you carrying them, they will certainly stop you and ask questions. Swords aren't permitted to commoners."

She gave Alassa a rather droll smile. "And what would have happened to the coup if they were?"

"Nothing," Alassa said. She still sounded nervous, almost unsteady. "Everything happened too fast for anyone to do anything."

Imaiqah frowned, then looked at Emily. "I could get you some potions," she offered. "One of them ensures dreamless sleep."

"No," Alassa said, before Emily could say a word. "We can't risk being caught while we're drugged."

Emily nodded. She'd used sleeping potions before when she'd had nightmares after Shadye's defeat and they tended to work *too* well. Being woken up before the potion had completely worn off had produced hallucinations and waking nightmares, bringing back uncomfortable memories of the time Shadye had used her own blood to manipulate her. He'd moved her like a puppet and only lost control right at the end. And if Sergeant Harkin hadn't sacrificed himself, she would still be his slave—or dead.

She tossed Alassa a puzzled look as Imaiqah opened the door. "When did *you* use them?"

Alassa made a face. "My roommates insisted after you hit me with those spells," she said, one hand touching her jaw. Emily had turned it into stone when she'd been too angry to think clearly, coming within a hairsbreadth of killing her. "I was having too many bad nights."

Outside, there was a new sense of tension on the streets. Most of the sellers seemed to have vanished, apart from a single hopeful-looking man pushing a wooden trolley that advertized sausages in a bun. Emily couldn't help wondering how he got any business at all—his hygiene seemed almost non-existent—before seeing the marked prices on the side. Even a small bronze coin was fantastic wealth to some of the poorer people in the city. She looked away as the seller started to pick his nose, hearing the sounds of arguing in the distance. It sounded as though not everyone had decided to tamely accept the coup plotters' orders to stay off the streets.

"Keep your heads down," Imaiqah muttered, as she guided them into a cramped alleyway. "We don't want to be noticed."

The city was normally clean—or maybe Emily had simply become used to the smell—but the alleyway stank unpleasantly. She saw a handful of people trying to sleep and looked away, granting them what privacy she could. It was a mystery what they ate until she saw the remains of fish bones by one of the sleeping vagrants and realized that they probably helped out at the docks in exchange for food. Fish was cheap here…there was no real danger of fishing the waters until the fish were driven into extinction. That might change in the future, she told herself, grimly. Who knew where modern technology would lead them?

I should start writing about the pitfalls, she told herself, and added it to her ever-growing list of things to do. *What will happen when they start producing factories?*

She hadn't studied the industrial revolution as enthusiastically as she had studied ancient history—it was closer to her own time—but she had read about cities draped in smog and the health problems it had caused. And factory owners had been just as bad, in many ways, as the aristocrats they'd displaced from the pinnacle of power. Who knew what Imaiqah's father would become when he no longer needed so many skilled craftsmen?

The stench grew stronger as they turned a corner and walked into a slaughter-house. A giant animal—Emily realized, to her horror, that it was a whale—lay on the ground, while fishermen cut and hacked at its body, slowly removing all of the flesh. She had no idea what whale meat tasted like, but they would be able to melt down the fat for oil and—if she recalled one of Thande's lectures correctly—probably use it for alchemy as well. Whales had been a protected species back home, but not here. But at least hunting them would be difficult.

She looked away as Imaiqah hurried them out of the far end and up a tiny flight of outdoor stairs. The buildings had become cramped boxy apartments, designed to cram as much living space as possible into a tiny area. Imaiqah knocked on a door, whispered something to the woman who opened it and then led the way inside. The woman gave Emily and Alassa a sharp look, but didn't seem to recognize either of them. Emily breathed a silent sigh of relief as she turned and beckoned for them to follow her. Inside, the corridor was dark, barely illuminated by light streaming in from a window at the far end. The woman stopped in front of a door and pushed it open.

"Ye have paid for ten days," she said, in a scratchy voice that sounded vaguely for-eign. "Should ye not pay for more days by the seventh, ye will be evicted. Ye may not bring guests here without ma permission."

Emily nodded and stepped into the room. It was tiny, barely large enough for the three of them to stand upright together, illuminated by a single flickering lantern. Emily closed her eyes and concentrated, sensing no trace of magic within the tiny compartment. The bed was barely large enough for one person, let alone two. At least the blankets appeared relatively clean. One look in the washroom told her things she didn't want to know about it.

Imaiqah closed the door and sat down on the bed. "I miss Whitehall," she said. "The rooms there were so much nicer than *this*."

Alassa had a more practical point to raise. "Who *was* that woman?"

"Madame Comfort," Imaiqah said, as if she expected the name to explain every-thing. It meant nothing to either of her friends. "She...runs this place as a boarding house for female visitors to the city. Most places refuse to take women unless they are accompanied by their male relatives—those that *do* take women are often rather unsavory. Just don't bring any men here."

"Oh," Alassa said. "Is she discreet?"

"She won't breathe a word about any of her guests to anyone," Imaiqah assured her. "And this is the last place anyone would look for a princess."

"I can see why," Emily said. A small cockroach was crawling across the floor. Whitehall was nearly free of such pests, but they would be epidemic in the cities. Professor Thande had told the class that cockroaches were useful in certain potions that granted increased resiliency. Given how hard they were to eradicate, Emily could well believe it. "Are you going to stay here?"

"Not now," Imaiqah said. She made a face. "Can you imagine what it would do to my father's reputation as a councilor if his daughter stayed here?"

She stood up and put her hand on the door. "Cast one of those personal wards we played with at Whitehall," she ordered. "I'll be able to come in; everyone else will have to break down the wards before they can get at you. Just...just be careful if you leave. This district is not safe."

Emily watched her go, then cast the first ward into the air. They'd experimented for hours at Whitehall, learning how to shape wards that were keyed to the three of them, without allowing others to pass without a struggle. Like so much else they'd been taught, it did have a practical application, although it hadn't been perfect. Emily's expanded wards had caught Imaiqah and Alassa—the other two who were supposed to have access—several times.

"Done," she said, finally. The privacy ward was low-power, but that wasn't a bad thing. Anyone who wanted to peek on them would still have to break it down, alerting her. "I should check the ways out..."

She hesitated as she realized that Alassa was shaking. The shock was finally getting to her. Emily reached out and enfolded her friend in a hug, feeling her trembling. Alassa had seen her uncle collapse—perhaps die—and her father blasted down by madmen with wands. Who knew what had happened to King Randor? Emily knew that the coup plotters would probably want him to surrender his authority peacefully—or as peacefully as possible, given that they would be forcing him to abdicate with a knife at his throat—but what would happen then? Had enough of the Confirmation been carried out to make Alassa his legal heir?

"They won't kill your father," she said, and prayed that she was right. "They can't do anything to him until they get their hands on you."

The possibilities kept spinning through her mind. The duke could take the throne if Randor and Alassa were dead—but if he took the throne now, he would only legally be regent for Alassa. On the other hand, if he controlled the army and had support from a majority of the barons, it wasn't likely to matter. However, if the true plotters were some of the barons, they'd need Alassa to use as a puppet queen. Even with the Royal Bloodline, there were plenty of ways to make someone do what you wanted.

"You need to sleep," she said, as she pulled back the cover. They might have to leave without warning, so there was little point in getting undressed. Besides, she had her doubts about how safe the tiny box-like room actually was. "I'll secure the wards and then sleep next to you."

"Don't go," Alassa said, as she lay down. "Please."

Emily nodded, although Alassa couldn't see her. "I won't," she said, out loud. "I'm going to be here."

But what were they going to *do*?

Getting back to Whitehall wouldn't be *that* hard, she suspected. With a little effort, they could catch a ship from Zangaria and sail around the Allied Lands until they reached Vonda, where they could hire a coach to take them the rest of the way. And once they got there, no coup plotter could hope to get at Alassa…but she'd become a prisoner, trapped within the wards. Whitehall's political neutrality would prevent it from offering overt support to the princess. All it could do was offer safety as long as she stayed there.

She could ask Void to help…but she didn't know how to contact him. All of their meetings had been organized by him, without warning; she wasn't even sure how to contact the grandmaster without risking detection. And the grandmaster might well refuse to pass on a message. God alone knew what he'd heard from Zangaria by now.

And she had no way to know what had happened to Lady Barb. A prisoner, perhaps, or simply dead. The coup plotters wouldn't want to keep a trained combat sorceress alive, not when they could simply cut her throat. She would be too dangerous to them.

Emily yawned and lay down on the bed, feeling Alassa pressing against the thin wall. She knew she should explore the building and make sure that she knew all of the possible exits, but she was just too tired. Staying awake all night had taken a toll out of her, even before she'd been forced to draw on so much magic just to survive. Her eyelids suddenly felt too heavy to keep open…

Snuggled against Alassa, she quickly fell asleep.

Chapter Thirty-Four

IT WAS PITCH BLACK WHEN SHE AWOKE, THE LANTERN HAVING LONG SINCE BURNED OUT. Emily started as she felt someone pressing against her, then remembered everything that had happened since the ceremony had begun. King Randor was a prisoner—she hoped - and Alassa and Emily were fugitives. Carefully, she pulled herself free of Alassa and cast a light ball into the air. It illuminated the entire room in pearly white light.

Emily's head spun as she sat upright. How long had it been since she'd eaten? There hadn't been any time for a snack at Imaiqah's, which meant that the last time she'd eaten had been the small breakfast before the ceremony. How long ago was that? She could have been sleeping for hours after spending the entire night awake. Shaking her head, Emily reached for the knapsack and retrieved the bread, tearing it into strips with her bare hands. It was messy and sent crumbs falling everywhere, but there was no choice. The bread and cheese tasted almost heavenly as she wolfed it down.

After testing the wards, she pulled herself to her feet and opened the door, stepping out into a dim corridor. There was no one around, as far as she could tell, but she cancelled the light ball anyway, instead using one of the spells Sergeant Miles had taught her to see in the dark. Silently, she padded down the long corridor and peered out the window at the end. The sun was just starting to rise over the mountains. It had been early afternoon when they'd arrived at the tiny room. They'd slept for nearly sixteen hours.

Alexis looked dim to her eyes, although that shouldn't really have surprised her. There were no such thing as streetlamps in this world, even primitive gas lamps; the streets were wrapped in shadow that even her night-vision spell couldn't penetrate completely. She could hear some chatter in the distance as the fishermen prepared for another day on the water, but she couldn't see any of them. And the window opened in the wrong direction to see the castle.

Shaking her head, she explored the rest of the floor as quickly as she could. There were no such things as emergency staircases in this world, she realized, after checking out both windows. If they had to climb out the window, they would have to drop down at least two floors before they hit the ground. There were spells that could help with that, if there was no other choice, but they were easy to disrupt. Sergeant Miles had told her about dozens of magicians who had loved to fly, until someone disrupted their spells and sent them plummeting to their deaths.

Returning to their room, she tested the wards again before opening the door. It had been bad enough being trapped by her own wards at Whitehall, where it had been humiliating, but here it would be disastrous. The wards allowed her entry and she stepped back into the room, closing the door behind her. There was a brilliant flash of light and she yelped in shock, covering her eyes. Alassa was sitting upright, her hand raised and ready to cast another spell.

"I'm sorry," she muttered, as she dimmed the light. "I woke up and found you gone…"

"I just needed to check out our surroundings," Emily explained, rubbing her eyes. "Can you remember how to levitate?"

"I also remember getting yelled at for going up too high," Alassa said. She reached for the knapsack and pulled out an apple, which she bit into thoughtfully. "Why do we need it?"

Emily explained, quickly. "We might be able to get out that way even if we weren't being chased," she concluded. "The woman who owns this place would never know that we were gone."

"Maybe," Alassa offered. "But few things are completely missed. There was a man in the court who liked"—she shook her head slowly—"something that I was too young to know about. Or so I was told. It involved magic and a skilled witch. But he thought it was a secret and yet everyone knew about it."

Emily rolled her eyes. There were five books on sex magic in the library at Whitehall—and they had all been *very* well thumbed. Lady Aylia had told her rather sarcastically that almost every known book on sex magic—and rituals that required any form of sexual activity—had been written by adolescent male magicians. Emily had glanced through one of them and hadn't been able to decide if she should be impressed by their ingenuity or shocked by some of the more perverse aspects of the rituals. They certainly didn't *seem* very magical.

They ate in silence, lost in their own thoughts. Anything could be happening outside, while they were confined to a tiny room that had become their entire world. Emily wondered if they dared try to walk outside later, before dismissing the thought. They'd need to hear from Imaiqah first…but what if they never saw her again? The coup plotters could have arrested her entire family by now and Emily would never know about it.

The wards sparkled with energy. Emily looked up sharply, then relaxed as the door opened to reveal Imaiqah. She looked tired and worn—and not a little fearful.

"Too many guardsmen on the streets," she said, as she sat down on the bed. "I had to befuddle one of them to escape."

Emily frowned. "They know they're looking for female magicians…"

"I befuddled him hard enough that he shouldn't know he was befuddled," Imaiqah said. "Besides, from the look in his eye, I don't think he was taking the search for you two very seriously at all."

"Never mind that," Alassa said. "What is happening outside?"

Imaiqah looked down at the wooden floor. "The heralds have claimed that King Randor has abdicated in favor of his brother, the Duke of Iron," she said. "Apparently, the duke has the complete trust and support of the barons…"

Alassa snorted, rudely. "They couldn't agree on jumping in the pond if their britches were on fire," she said. "And as for trust…"

Her voice trailed off. "Is it really him, then? My uncle?"

"I haven't seen him in person," Imaiqah said, gently. "He could be a prisoner too."

Emily gritted her teeth. The interrogated prisoners had sworn blind, under the strongest truth spells Lady Barb knew, that the Duke of Iron had given them their orders to kill Emily and Imaiqah. But the duke had also sworn that he had nothing to do with it–and *he* had been under truth spells as well. The only way to resolve the contradiction would be to assume that the prisoners had *thought* that the duke had given them their orders…

She looked over at Alassa. "Could the duke have been replaced by someone else?"

"I rather doubt it," Alassa said, sarcastically. "I could *feel* him; he shares part of the Bloodline. No one could fake that."

Emily nodded. At least Alassa wasn't falling into despair. "Imaiqah," she said, slowly, "what is the situation like on the streets?"

"There are plenty of guardsmen on the streets in the inner city," Imaiqah said. "There have been a number of fights between them and locals who want to move their stuff around…but for the moment, they have the streets under control. Father was at the council yesterday and he told me that the councilors can't make up their minds what to do."

"Right," Emily said. The sergeants had told her to gather intelligence, so that was what she would do. "How many of them are there in all?"

"We're not sure," Imaiqah admitted. "At least a thousand, perhaps more."

Emily considered it, tossing the thought over and over in her mind. Moving a vast army into Alexis without being detected would be difficult, to say the least. What if the enemy plotters were much *weaker* than they'd thought? Putting so many men on the streets could easily be designed to create the appearance of strength to mask true weakness. It wasn't something they could count on, but maybe it could be confirmed.

Alassa leaned forward, thoughtfully. "Who are they?" She asked. "The Royal Army? Or the duke's personal guard?"

"The Army," Imaiqah said. "Does it matter?"

"It might," Alassa answered. She studied her pale hands carefully, then looked up. "If it is the regulars, it does point to the duke."

Emily heard the bitterness in her friend's voice and shivered. The Duke of Iron was a stranger to her, but he'd been Alassa's uncle ever since she'd been born. It was easy to imagine him urging her mother and father to spoil her, just to make her easy to manipulate in later life, yet…he had been her uncle. She loved him. The thought of him betraying her had to be maddening.

And yet it wasn't unprecedented. Mary of Scotland had been betrayed by *her* uncles, a betrayal that had led to the collapse of her reign years later. How many other queens and princesses had been manipulated and betrayed simply for having been born female and then assumed not to have the strength to hold on to the throne? But then, male kings and princes were also the targets of intrigue. It just tended to be viler when women were involved.

"He was bound to his father, King Alexis III," Emily said, slowly. "Would that binding have passed to your father?"

"It should have done," Alassa said. "My father would have become the Prime, the linchpin of the entire Royal Bloodline. I don't think the duke could have avoided becoming bound to him."

She looked down at the floor. "He has to be stopped," she said. "Whatever the cost, he has to be stopped."

"My father wishes you to meet with some of the councilors," Imaiqah said, softly. "They are unsure who to support."

Alassa stared at her. "But…they're just councilors," she pointed out. "They don't have any soldiers…"

"They have city guardsmen," Emily said. And they'd had funds from taxes. "They might have more military power than you think."

Imaiqah stood up. "There's also a reward on your head," she said. "Apparently, you're being blamed for an attempted coup that crippled your father. Most people don't find that unbelievable."

Alassa put her head in her hands, her long golden hair falling down over them. *Of course* they believed that she would strike against her own father. Everyone would have known her as the royal brat who used magic freely, without consequences; the girl who used to make Imaiqah do her homework while tormenting her at Whitehall. How many commoners had ever *met* her? Imaiqah was the only person in Zangaria, outside the aristocracy, who might understand that Alassa had changed.

"My father believes me," Imaiqah added. "But the others…they don't know which way to jump."

"They'll stay on the sidelines until it is too late," Emily muttered. If the coup plotters had any sense, they would refrain from purging anyone until their grip on power was secure—*then* they'd start distributing terror and oppression. The duke probably had a handful of barons lined up behind him already…now, seeing they'd been taken prisoner at the Assembly, he was probably collecting their oaths of loyalty. "You have to talk them out of it before it is too late."

"I'll talk to them," Alassa said. "I take it we're not meeting in their chambers?"

Imaiqah shook her head. "They've been guarded since last night," she said. "The councilors, thankfully, do have other places to meet."

She led them out of the room, cautioning them to leave nothing behind. The locks were flimsy; a good kick could easily break one down, while the owner hadn't bothered to pay for a magician to protect the rooms. On the other hand, most of the people who stayed in the rooms wouldn't have anything worth stealing. Adding additional protection might convince potential thieves that wasn't true.

"There are few guards near the docks," Imaiqah offered, as they stepped onto the streets. "The fishermen didn't take kindly to their intrusion."

Emily considered it as they walked quickly away from the docks, up towards one of the inns that catered for wealthy visitors to the city. Holding an entire city under control was *not* easy, even with modern weapons; a thousand soldiers, most of them armed with swords and spears, would have real difficulty controlling anywhere outside eyeshot. On the other hand, if they held the gates and most of the main roads, they could probably bring up more troops against any rebellious district. And they did have magic.

But the attackers used wands, Emily recalled. *Does that mean they weren't strong magicians?*

The maid who'd tried to assassinate them on the first night had used a wand too—and no one had been able to find out who had given it to her. Or so Lady Barb had told her and Emily had grown to trust her, even though the woman seemed unable to decide if she liked Emily or not. Had the same person produced both sets of wands?

Imaiqah led them into the inn and up the stairs into a small room. Emily's nose wrinkled as she sniffed tobacco in the air, along with a scent she didn't recognize. Imaiqah's father stood up and bowed formally to Alassa, followed by the other men in the room, who watched her—and Emily—through shrewd intelligent eyes. Their faces were hidden behind simple glamors...

They're afraid, Emily realized. *What would happen to them if the monarchy turned on them?*

"We have been told that the king is crippled and his brother, the Duke of Iron, has assumed the throne until he recovers," one of the councilors said. The glamor added an odd hiss to his words. "And we have been told that you, Your Highness, are responsible for your father's injuries. Why should we do anything to help you?"

Alassa kept her voice under firm control. "You have magicians, I assume," she said. "One of them could cast a truth spell to verify my words."

There was a pause as the councilors looked towards an empty corner. It was several seconds before Emily saw the magician sitting there, cloaked behind a glamor so powerful that she hadn't even realized it was there until they'd pointed it out. The magician lifted his hand, cast the truth spell into the air and sat back, waiting to see what would happen.

"My uncle appears to have turned on my father," Alassa said. "I do not pretend to understand how he was able to keep his plans concealed for so long, but he seems to have succeeded. Right now, he controls the castle, the army—and, by holding the barons, he can prevent their families from interfering. Some of them will support him automatically. Given time, he can solidify his grip on power.

"My uncle is also highly conservative," she continued. "He is strongly opposed to the new learning"—she nodded to Emily, reminding them that Emily had helped many of them achieve wealth and power—"and he will certainly refuse to allow it to spread further. In this, he will have the heartfelt support of all the barons. You will find yourselves targeted and jailed, or executed. The wealth you have built up for yourselves will evaporate. Your families will be hunted down and killed."

There was a long pause. "My father wanted to embrace change slowly, believing that it would weaken the barons," she concluded. "If you help restore him to the throne, that will continue. You will be able to make money and reap the rewards of having supported the rightful king in his time of need."

"King Alexis III made an offer to the commoners," one of the councilors said, finally. "He promised them a share in power; he promised them legal rights that all would respect. Those rights lasted little longer than it took the ink to dry on the parchment. We showed the nobility that we could be a powerful force, then the king stood aside and watched as the nobles crushed those who dared try to claim those rights. Why should we do anything to help you, Your Highness? We have been betrayed once before."

He leaned forward, the glamor fading to reveal an elderly face. "If we help you, we will demand a steep price. You must bring the barons to heel."

Emily spoke before anyone else. "If we fight the barons at the same time as the duke, we could force them all into an alliance against us," she said. "Why not ask for the right to levy taxes instead, then you can deal with the barons later."

The old councilor smiled. "That would suffice, if Her Highness swears to grant us that right afterwards," he said. He looked up at Alassa. "*Would* you swear, Your Highness?"

Emily saw Alassa tense and felt a flicker of sympathy. Oaths were dangerous things when sworn by magicians. Deliberately breaking them would result in death— or worse. No doubt Alexis III had found a way to wiggle out.

"I will swear," Alassa said. Emily was perhaps the only one who saw her fear. "How do you wish me to phrase the oath?"

"Carefully," the old councilor said. There were some chuckles from the others. "We do have some ability to help you, but…"

Emily jumped as she heard a thunderous racket from downstairs. "Soldiers," someone shouted. "They're outside!"

One of the councilors pushed aside a curtain and gazed outside. "They're here," he snapped, as *something* rattled off the window. He looked over at Alassa. "They've come for you!"

Imaiqah grabbed Alassa's hand. "This way," she snapped. The noise from downstairs grew stronger, suggesting that someone was trying to break in. "Quickly!"

Chapter Thirty-Five

THERE WAS A DARK STAIRCASE HIDDEN BEHIND ONE OF THE CURTAINS. IMAIQAH YANKED Alassa through it and up a flight of stairs that were barely large enough to take the three girls. A man in armor would have real trouble climbing up unless he was prepared to undress, Emily realized, as the sound of banging and crashing grew louder. It sounded as though an entire army was trying to break into the inn.

"Your father," she said to Imaiqah. "What's he going to do?"

"There are other ways out," Imaiqah said. "They just wanted to make sure that you were safe."

Me, Emily thought. Not Alassa, not his daughter...Emily herself. It left her with an odd feeling in her chest. Was that what it was like to have a proper father? Or should she be angry that Imaiqah's father had put *Emily* first, rather than Imaiqah or even Alassa?

Imaiqah stopped as the stairway came to an end. "Hold on," she said, casting a light ball into the air. It revealed a wooden hatch set in the ceiling above them. "We just need to get this open..."

She levitated up and pushed the hatch aside, allowing bright sunlight to stream down into the stairwell. Emily tensed, realizing that they'd be caught like rats in a trap if the soldiers had already taken up positions on the rooftop, but no one moved to stop them as they climbed up and out onto the roof. The sound of angry citizens rose up from below and she realized that gangs of youths had moved to confront the soldiers. Emily hoped they would provide a distraction, then cursed herself a moment later. They'd be slaughtered by the soldiers if it came down to a fight.

"This way," Imaiqah said. "Hurry!"

She ran towards the edge of the rooftop and leapt to the next building, using a hint of magic to ensure that she covered the gap. Emily and Alassa exchanged glances, then followed, just as they heard shouting from down below. Someone had clearly seen them running for their lives. Emily landed on the next building and followed Imaiqah towards the edge of *that* rooftop. They had to keep running to get ahead of the men on the ground.

Alassa giggled, despite the situation. "Good thing we're not wearing skirts," she said.

Emily rolled her eyes.

"Keep moving," Imaiqah called. "We have to get out of here!"

The sounds from the ground were turning ominous. There were hundreds of youths now, confronting the soldiers and slowing them down. Emily heard someone cry out in pain, but there was no way to know if it was one of the soldiers—or one of the youths trying to slow them. People were hurling rocks at the soldiers now, along with rotting fruit and anything else they could throw as a missile, she guessed. Sergeant Harkin had told her that mobs could be the most dangerous enemy a soldier could face. It was funny that she'd never really believed him until now.

She landed on the fifth building and glanced up sharply as she saw a flock of birds moving through the air. The sight reminded her of some of the lectures from the sergeants covering the many ways that magic could be used for warfare. There were certain magicians who could form a blood-bond with animals and use them as spies; birds, for some reason, were particularly useful for such magic. And who would be able to pick out the right bird when the skies were full of them, assuming they ever suspected at all?

The birds—crows, she realized—hovered down in front of Imaiqah, blocking their escape. A moment later, they blurred together and became a man, wearing a long dark robe and hood that concealed most of his features. All she could see was pale skin, very dark hair and a beak-like nose. How had he done it? Animal transformation was normally into one animal, not over a dozen different creatures! But if he'd spread his thoughts out over the flock, he might have been able to keep his thoughts almost completely human.

"Princess Alassa," he said, gravely. His voice had an irritatingly screechy note that made Emily wince. "You have to come with me."

Alassa shook her head, stumbling backwards. Behind them, Emily heard the soldiers finally breaking out onto the roof and jumping after them. They had no magic, she assumed, to keep themselves from falling, but they were probably better trained and stronger. The boys in Martial Magic had almost always been able to outpoint Emily and the other girls over long exercises. No doubt they could leap over the gaps and reach them before they could escape.

"No," Alassa said, finally. "Who are you? A necromancer?"

Emily doubted it. Shadye had emitted an aura of power that had dwarfed that of every other magician, even the grandmaster and Void. But the newcomer didn't seem to be anything like as powerful. It was possible for a magician to conceal his strength by using his wards to shield himself, but a necromancer would find that tricky, if he even thought to try. Even so, that didn't mean the newcomer was less dangerous. If he could keep his thoughts together when in an animal form—multiple animal forms—he would be very focused, capable of using his magic more effectively than any of them.

"No," the newcomer said. "Come with me, now!"

He advanced towards Alassa, who threw a spell at him. It struck the newcomer's wards and faded out of existence. His face twisted into an ugly sneer as he threw a spell back, a draining charm that slammed right into Alassa's wards and started to claw them down. Emily cursed and threw her own set of spells at the newcomer, trying to push as much power as she could into the attack. Raw magic was the easiest to dispel, but it would distract him—she hoped.

"Drop your wards," she hissed to Alassa. No magician would do that easily, which was why the draining charm was so effective. "Quickly!"

Imaiqah threw a cutting hex at the newcomer, who ducked it rather than trying to absorb it and threw something of his own back. There was a massive gust of wind and Imaiqah toppled backwards, falling off the edge of the rooftop. Emily let out a shout of horror and threw the most lethal spell she had memorized at the newcomer.

He exploded in a sheet of black light which rapidly took on other forms—and crows swooped down to attack her. Emily ducked and tried to use her magic to swat them away, generating fireballs and throwing them at the birds. But they seemed to be very good at dodging...

"She fell!" Alassa yelled at the birds. "What did you *do* to her?"

One of the birds came too close—and Alassa caught it, holding it tightly in her hand. "What did you do...?"

The bird broke free, its sharp claws cutting at Alassa's hand. Alassa let out a curse and used a handkerchief to mop up the blood as the birds drifted away and gathered at the edge of the rooftop. The magician couldn't use magic in bird form, Emily realized. Most magicians had enough trouble keeping their human mentality in control, let alone trying to use magic. It was good to know that their unnamed adversary had some limits.

There was a crash as the first of the soldiers landed on the rooftop and advanced towards them. Emily swore to herself; she didn't feel like she could generate enough magic to overwhelm the armor they wore. If it *was* enchanted armor...but then, the duke had been one of the richest men in Zangaria. He could probably afford to buy enchanted armor from every kingdom in the Allied Lands. And if he was careful, it probably wouldn't even raise eyebrows. She cast around for alternatives and saw the pile of stones someone had left on the rooftop. Before she could think better of it, she shaped a spell in her mind and hurled the first stone at the soldiers with staggering force.

Sergeant Miles had told her that stone-throwing had its weaknesses. Most warded locations included spells that would automatically disrupt the spells propelling the stones through the air, causing them to fall harmlessly to the ground. Magicians accompanying armies could deflect stones before they crashed through the ranks, if they saw them coming. But the soldiers facing her had no defenses at all, apart from the enchanted armor. And while it worked well against magical attacks, it was almost useless against physical force.

Emily recoiled in shock as the first soldier seemed to disintegrate into a mass of bloodstained chunks. The others were slammed backwards, two of them toppling off the rooftop and falling to the streets far below. One more seemed to be dead; the other two badly injured. Even with the most powerful healing spells Emily knew, their survival would be in doubt. She hesitated, shocked at what she'd done. How could she inflict that much damage on *anyone*?

There was a hissing sound behind her and she spun round, just in time to see the birds merging together and revealing the newcomer. Alassa lifted her hand to throw a curse, but he got his spell off first, slamming a hex into her wards that sent her staggering backwards. The bloodstained handkerchief fell to the rooftop as Alassa fell over and landed on her rear, still trying to cast a spell of her own. There was a blinding flash of light, but the newcomer seemed unbothered. Emily couldn't have said what Alassa was actually trying to do.

She gathered her magic, shaped a cutting hex of her own and threw it right into the newcomer's wards. While he was dealing with that, she threw a second one, aimed at the rooftop below his feet. The rooftop shuddered and started to collapse inwards, forcing the newcomer to jump backwards before he fell into the room underneath. Emily took advantage of his distraction to summon up a wind of her own, shoving him over the edge of the roof. He fell, but a moment later a murder of crows rose up and hovered in front of them. It was easy to imagine that the sounds they were making were laughter.

Alassa picked up a stone and hurled it at the birds, using magic to shape its trajectory. Several birds were hit and sent falling down towards the ground, forcing the others to dive after their comrades and save them before they hit the ground. Emily couldn't help wondering what would happen if one or more of the crows were to die. They'd been warned, time and time again, *never* to split anyone into two or more pieces. The tutors just hadn't been very clear on what would happen if they did.

If we caught one of the birds, she asked herself, *could he return to human form? Would he be missing a leg?*

"Keep him busy," Emily ordered.

She moved quickly to the edge of the rooftop and peered down. Imaiqah lay on the ground below, staring up at them. She'd broken one of her legs, Emily realized, but the impact should have killed her outright. Emily breathed a sigh of relief and made quick hand signals, promising that she'd be down as soon as they'd dealt with the bird-magician. She just hoped that it wouldn't be before the soldiers reached Imaiqah. Sergeant Harkin had told them horror stories of what could happen when undisciplined young men discovered women who were apparently defenseless. And Imaiqah would be using most of her magic to hold back the pain.

The bird-magician shimmered back into existence, drawing all of the birds—even the stunned ones—back into his body. If it made the transformation harder for him, there was no easy way to tell for sure. Emily made a mental note to look it up when she got back to Whitehall; she'd never heard of a person transforming into more than one animal at a time. Maybe he could afford to lose a number of birds before he couldn't change back, or his thoughts were submerged within the bird mentalities. It didn't make logical sense, but so much else about transfiguration didn't make logical sense either.

Alassa threw a spell at him. He jumped to one side and advanced, firing off spells like they came from the barrel of a machine gun. He didn't seem to have the power Lady Barb had demonstrated when she'd been drilling Emily, she realized, but he didn't seem to be holding back at all. Alassa's wards started to stagger, then crumble under the endless series of impacts. Emily gathered herself and threw a handful of practical joke jinxes at the bird-magician. It was odd, but she'd learned that the practical jokes could sometimes catch more experienced magicians by surprise. They tended to prepare for the lethal hexes and curses.

The bird-magician threw a final hex at Alassa, knocking her to the ground, and then turned on Emily. She had barely a moment to realize that she might have made a mistake before he started throwing spell after spell at her, each one hammering into her wards. The pounding sent her staggering backwards, forcing her to abandon her own offensive just to keep her wards in place. Desperately, she picked up a stone with her bare hand and threw it towards him. For a moment, the bombardment stopped–his wards wouldn't have stopped the stone, as it hadn't been propelled by magic–and Emily used the opportunity to shape a lethal spell in her mind. Sergeant Miles had warned her never to use it unless she was in deadly earnest, but there was no other choice. She started to cast the spell…

…And the bird-magician threw a final hex into her wards. Bright green balefire flared around her, sending pain searing through her hands and arms. Half of the tutors at Whitehall had scarred hands, something that had puzzled Emily until she'd learned that most small magical accidents tended to burn hands. Hands were, after all, used for casting most spells, if only to indicate the target. The pain was so intense that Emily almost blacked out before it faded, leaving only a dull ache in her temples. Her hands looked undamaged, but they were shaking so badly she realized that it would be almost impossible to cast another spell for hours.

She'd been lucky. If her spell had been closer to completion, the backfire would have killed her outright. It had already been within her wards, almost part of her. She wasn't quite sure what the spell actually did–Sergeant Miles had once told the class that investigations into that topic were discouraged–but she knew it killed.

"Enough," the bird-magician said.

He threw a spell at her. This time, Emily couldn't even move, let alone deflect it. It struck her–and she froze solid, unable to move. There was a countercharm she could use to beat the paralysis charm–it was commonly used in Whitehall–but it required concentration and she could barely concentrate on anything. The headache was growing stronger. He could just walk over to her and cut her throat if he wanted. There was nothing she could do to stop him.

The bird-magician ignored her and stopped in front of Alassa. Emily watched helplessly as he touched the stunned princess's forehead with one long finger. Alassa shrank, clothes and all, until she was barely larger than one of the dolls Emily had played with as a child. The bird-magician stepped backwards, took one last look at Emily, and then exploded into a mass of birds. One of them swooped down and picked up Alassa, before the entire flock headed off towards the castle. They–he–had succeeded. Alassa was now a prisoner.

Emily felt strong hands on her paralysed form and realized that other soldiers had caught up with them. The bird-magician had left her alive simply so she could be carted off to the prison…raw anger flared through her mind as she saw the soldiers coming into view, poking and prodding at her body. Desperately, she reached into her mind and triggered the *berserker* spell. There was a rush of energy and the paralysis snapped. The soldiers had no time to react before Emily was lashing out at them with her fists.

Sergeant Miles had scorned the very idea of a fair fight. There was no such thing in war; anyone stupid enough to believe otherwise would very quickly learn better, or end up dead. He'd taught Emily and the other girls that they had to outthink their targets, or male strength would prove decisive. Her training, combined with *berserker*, made her lethal in close-quarter combat. The soldiers never knew what had hit them.

Emily staggered to one side and collapsed on the rooftop as the spell faded away. It was simply too dangerous to use for more than a few minutes, particularly when she was alone. The last time she'd used it outside training, Jade and the other Redshirts had been there to carry her to safety. Here, she was alone. Imaiqah was wounded, perhaps dead...and Alassa was a prisoner. Somehow, drawing on reserves she hadn't known she had, Emily stumbled to her feet and saw a white scrap of cloth lying on the ground. Alassa's handkerchief...

Shaking her head, Emily picked it up, took one last look at the soldiers, and headed for the hole in the roof. There was no way she dared levitate down right now. Her magic was simply too unreliable. One lapse in concentration and she would die.

She had to save Alassa, she told herself, but she just didn't know how.

But if she failed, the duke would win outright.

Chapter Thirty-Six

THE INHABITANTS OF THE BUILDING HAD VANISHED IN THE CONFUSION. EMILY couldn't blame them, any more than she could avoid a sense of relief that she wouldn't have to fight again. Her headache was returning in force, now that *berserker* had faded away; it was all she could do to keep going, step by step. Making her way outside, she found almost no one in the streets, apart from a handful of youths who eyed her with a mixture of concern and puzzlement. Emily ignored them as she stumbled into the alleyway and found Imaiqah lying on the ground.

"I didn't quite catch myself," Imaiqah whispered, as Emily collapsed beside her. "My leg..."

Emily nodded. They'd been warned never to use healing spells on themselves, but numbing spells were actually quite effective. At worst, they simply refused to work. Emily tried to focus her mind enough to cast a healing spell, then scowled as her headache grew stronger. She had to fight down the urge to vomit...her head spun so badly she was surprised that she didn't faint. The only thing she could do was sleep, but she didn't dare collapse into the darkness. God alone knew what would happen while they were helpless.

"They took Alassa," she mumbled. Speaking above a whisper only seemed to lead to more sparks of pain in her head. "What...what will they do to her?"

Imaiqah shrugged. "Use her as a puppet," she said, finally. "Or have her executed to make her uncle's throne safe."

Emily looked up as she heard a number of men entering the alleyway. Soldiers...? She relaxed, feeling an overpowering sense of relief, as she recognized the leader as Imaiqah's brother Johan. The men were wearing what looked like makeshift armor and carrying clubs and staves. Given some ingenuity, she decided, they might be able to produce weapons for themselves. Or, given that they were merchants, simply manipulate the records to ensure that no one noticed some extra weapons had been produced in the factories before being shipped to the army.

"By the God," Johan said. "Are...what happened?"

Emily felt her head spinning. "Get her a healer and get me to bed," she ordered. "And then get water..."

The blackness rose up and pulled her into its depths. Emily felt almost feverish, as if she were caught in the grip of waking nightmares, before something finally yanked her awake. A young woman was bending over her, gently pushing a straw against her mouth. Emily sipped gratefully, too thirsty to care that it might have been a trap. The liquid tasted vaguely like peppermint tea, but with the addition of some herbs that she didn't recognize.

"Stay there," the woman ordered. "You're safe now."

For the moment, Emily thought. Johan and his friends must have carried her and Imaiqah to a safe house, but they hadn't known to keep a watch for birds. Even if they had known, what could they have done about it? Come to think of it, *someone* must have tipped off the soldiers, or they would never have known about the meeting at the inn.

Her throat felt too dry to speak, but she had to try. "Who...who are you?"

"I'm Pat," the woman said. She gave Emily a reassuring smile. "I'm a healer, of sorts."

She passed Emily a gourd of water and helped her hold it until Emily had swallowed all of the liquid. "I've seen spell addiction before," Pat added. "I think you should stay away from whatever spell you used for several months, at the very least."

Emily blinked in surprise, then nodded slowly. *Berserker* could be addictive–she'd been warned of that when she'd first been taught the spell–and repeated use could have disastrous side effects. But it wasn't too surprising that a civilian healer had never actually heard of the spell. The combat sorcerers preferred to keep certain kinds of knowledge firmly under wraps.

"I'll do my best," she said. God knew if she'd be able to *keep* that promise. "What time is it?"

"Eighteen bells, thirty-two chimes," Pat said. Emily scowled. She'd been unconscious for at least ten hours. Long enough to recover, perhaps, but long enough for something truly awful to have happened to Alassa. What would her uncle do with her? "Your friend healed quickly, once I cast the right spells on her leg."

"Glad to hear it," Emily said, as she pulled herself upright. They'd been told, back at Whitehall, to go to the infirmary after using healing spells, no matter how successful the spell had seemed. She'd never been quite sure why. "How is she?"

"Worried about you," Pat said. "And her father is waiting for you to see him."

Emily swung her legs over the side of the bed and stood up, gratified to realize that she wasn't shaky. Her hands didn't *look* scarred, she decided, as she looked down at them, but there was a hint of a tremble as she held them in front of her face. She'd just have to hope and pray that she hadn't caused herself any permanent damage. Professor Thande's hand had been scarred so badly that Emily didn't understand how he could still use it.

Magic has a price, she thought, remembering one of her tutors saying that to her. *Sometimes the price is very high indeed. Even the necromancers pay a high price for their power. They lose their sanity.*

"Get me some proper clothes," she ordered, as she started to pull off what remained of the garment she'd borrowed from Imaiqah. Between the fight and stains caused by various potions, it was no longer wearable. Emily promised herself that she could buy Imaiqah a new outfit as soon as the whole affair was over. "And then find me something to eat."

Pat snorted. "Typical sorceress," she said. "Barely recovered from a life-threatening accident and she's already barking orders."

Emily flushed, realizing just how much she sounded like the old Alassa.

"Don't worry about it," Pat added, with a nasty grin. She picked up a dark bundle and passed it to Emily. "I believe that you will be eating with the others tonight."

Emily finished undressing and donned the new outfit. It was a black tunic, loose enough to hide the shape of her body and allow her to move properly, but not dramatic enough to call attention to her. Emily had picked up more than she wanted to know about courtly fashion, thanks to the princes, and knew that it was the type of outfit that would be worn by a very minor aristocrat. The soldiers should leave her alone as long as she didn't do anything too suspicious. Once she'd finished dressing, she went through the pockets of her old outfit and recovered Alassa's handkerchief. It was still stained with her friend's blood.

An idea occurred to her and she carefully folded the handkerchief before putting it in her new pockets. Pat gave her an odd look, then beckoned for Emily to follow her out of the room and into a larger room. It was almost empty, apart from Imaiqah, her father and two younger councilors, both wearing their chains of office. Emily wondered briefly how they'd managed to escape the soldiers who'd attacked the inn. But if the soldiers had been mainly concerned with Alassa, they might have ignored everyone else.

Imaiqah welcomed Emily with a hug, her eyes showing her relief. Emily couldn't help noticing that her friend was limping slightly, although her leg had definitely been healed. Healing spells didn't always compensate for the shock caused by physical trauma, she knew, if only because it wasn't very well understood by the healers. There wouldn't be any physical cause for her pains, but they would torment Imaiqah for days before finally fading away.

"It's good to see you," Paren said. Imaiqah's father looked deeply worried. "What are they going to do to the princess?"

Emily shook her head. "I have no idea," she said, "but I don't think it will be anything good."

The thought made her scowl. No one in the room knew better than her how easy it was to turn someone into a puppet. Shadye might have taken advantage of Emily's unique blood to control her, but Alassa had only a handful of blood relatives. The Royal Bloodline was supposed to provide some protection against mind control, yet...would it really stand up to a sorcerer who was quite prepared to do whatever it took to take control of the lawful heir to the throne?

Her scowl deepened as she remembered Zed's reaction to her questions about the Royal Bloodline. What if the Court Wizard, the same person who had carefully crippled Alassa's ability to learn magic, had been working on controlling the Royal Bloodline all along? If the duke had been manipulated by an outside force, would he have been *aware* of it? And, as Sergeant Miles had pointed out more than once, a truth spell wouldn't work if the person lying didn't *know* that he was lying. The Royal Bloodline couldn't do any better. If the duke had been unaware that he'd been used as a puppet...

...But if so, why bother with the coup at all?

On the other hand, most powerful magicians hated the thought of anyone meddling in their field of interest. Zed might have been furious because Emily had dared to question his work and encourage King Randor to bring in outside experts, rather than because he was trying to hide something. And, of course, she'd implied that his work had been less than perfect...few magicians would take that lightly. It wouldn't matter if she was right or wrong. He'd still be dreadfully upset at the mere suggestion.

Imaiqah's father tapped the table, drawing her attention to the map he'd placed on it. "The problem is that we cannot storm the castle," he said. "Do you have a spell powerful enough to break through their wards?"

"Probably not," Emily admitted. She looked up at him, suddenly. "You've been planning...*something*...for a while, haven't you?"

"Yes," Paren admitted, finally. "If the king decided to crack down on us..."

He shook his head. "But we couldn't storm the castle," he added. "The best we could do is lay siege to it—and that would take weeks, at least, before they had to surrender. In the meantime, other garrisons could march towards Alexis and reclaim the city."

Emily nodded. Unless they had a really powerful sorcerer on their side, the combination of the castle's wards and stone walls would make it effectively impregnable. Castles had been taken by storm before, according to Sergeant Harkin, but the attackers *always* suffered disproportionate casualties. Indeed, he'd added rather snidely, the attacking force had often won the battle only to lose the war. They'd been broken in the hour of their triumph.

We're going to have to invent gunpowder, she thought. But the early experiments had not proven successful. Pulling the basic formula out of her mind had taken a handful of memory spells, but the alchemists had been unable to get it to work properly. That might have been caused by the strict secrecy—she'd warned them that the aristocrats would explode when they worked out what gunpowder could do—yet it hardly mattered. Right now, there would be no cannons or rifles to help them take down the castle.

"So...what do you have?" She asked. "And what do *they* have?"

"They've been running patrols through the inner city, as well as reinforcing the gatehouses," Paren said. He tapped the map to illustrate his point. "We have a few thousand men with limited training, but some are trapped in the outer city. What do you want to do with them?"

Give the duke time to organise and he'll win by default, Emily thought. *We don't have much time to deal with him before he makes his position impregnable.*

"I'm going to sneak into the castle," Emily said, finally. "I need you to weaken the defenders as much as possible."

"I told you that we *cannot* storm the castle," Paren said, sharply.

"I don't want you to storm the castle," Emily said. The locals thought in terms of castle and other secure locations, which wasn't too surprising. But she knew that modern warfare was targeted on the enemy's army. "I want you to target their patrols."

She tapped the map. "How many of them could you attack at once?"

"Some," Paren said, doubtfully. "Maybe more if we didn't worry too much about coordinating it. What do you want us to do?"

"You hit the patrols and try to pin them down," Emily said. "The soldiers will scream for help from the castle. I think the duke will have to send out additional soldiers to back them up, or risk losing his men to us."

"Drawing down the defenses of the castle," Paren said. "And how do you plan to sneak in through the wards? There's only one way into the castle."

That settled one thing that had been bothering Emily; Paren *didn't* know about the tunnel network running under the city. She'd considered using it to sneak into the castle, perhaps leading a small assault force, but the wards would make that difficult. Lady Barb's warnings rang in her ears. It would be quite possible for them to walk in and lose themselves in the catacombs, never to be seen again.

"I've had an idea," Emily assured him. She didn't go into details. "But the fewer guards in the castle, the better."

"I can enchant some mirrors to allow us to communicate," Imaiqah said. "They won't last for more than a few hours, but we'd be able to coordinate our actions."

Paren nodded. "But tell me," he said, "what do you intend to do once you're inside the castle?"

"Rescue Alassa," Emily said, simply. "And then try and take down the wards, allowing you to walk into the castle."

"The wards aren't the only defenses," Paren reminded her. "Do you think we can take out enough soldiers to allow us to break into the castle, even without the wards?"

Emily frowned. "How many magicians do you have who are willing to help?"

"Not many," Paren admitted. "Most mages stay out of politics here. They don't entirely trust the council."

Emily looked at Imaiqah, who shrugged.

"There was an accusation that a magician who specialized in mental magic had used magic to convince people to vote for him," Paren said. There was a dark tone in his voice. "The magician eventually had to withdraw from the council chamber, which didn't sit well with the other magicians. Most of them are likely to side against the council if they have to make a choice."

"Even a handful of magicians could make the difference between success and failure if the wards were completely gone," Emily pointed out. She looked over at a large grandfather clock perched against one wall. "How long will it take you to get organized?"

"Perhaps an hour or two," Paren said. "Night will have fallen by then, Lady Emily..."

"Good," Emily said. She tried to project a confidence she didn't feel into her words. "It will make it easier to remain unseen."

"I'll have food brought in for the pair of you," Paren said, standing up. "And I'll let you know when we are ready."

He left the room, followed rapidly by the other councilors.

Imaiqah cast a privacy ward in the air as soon as the door had closed behind them. "Are you sure that you can get into the castle?"

"Yes," Emily said, and prayed that her friend wouldn't ask for details. "I think I can."

Christopher Nuttall

"Most of the magicians they have seem to need to use wands," Imaiqah said. "But the crow-faced magician who took Alassa didn't need one. Do you think he's a full-fledged sorcerer?"

"More experienced than me," Emily muttered. The bird-magician hadn't *felt* as powerful as Void or the grandmaster, but he could easily have been concealing his magic. But then, if he *was* that powerful, all three of them could have been taken prisoner easily. "And I don't think he will be holding back the next time."

"If he was," Imaiqah reminded her. "He came very close to killing me."

Emily nodded, silently promising herself that the bird-magician was going to pay for that.

"I could come with you," Imaiqah offered. "Or surely there must be someone else...?"

"No one we can call," Emily admitted. "If we had Jade here..."

She thought–again–about trying to contact the grandmaster and asking him to pass a message to Void, but it wouldn't be fair to him. And besides, it would take time for the message to reach her guardian even if the grandmaster forwarded it without hesitation. It was just another reminder that instant communications were very rare in the Allied Lands.

"You should have accepted his offer," Imaiqah said. She stuck out her tongue at Emily's expression. "If he'd been engaged to you, he might well have come with you to Zangaria, just to make sure that a handsome prince didn't sweep you off your feet."

Emily made a threatening gesture with her hand, then giggled.

"We'd better eat," she said, as a woman appeared with a large tray of food. "Tonight–victory or death."

Or death even if we win, she added, in the privacy of her own mind. There *was* one way to break through a set of complex wards, but it came with a price. And an automatic death sentence in some parts of the Allied Lands. If they'd worried about what she'd done to Shadye, they'd be completely horrified if they ever found out what Emily had in mind to break into the castle.

"You'll win," Imaiqah said. "I have faith in you."

Too many people have faith in me, Emily thought, grimly. *When will it stop?*

Chapter Thirty-Seven

EMILY HAD ONLY BEEN DIMLY AWARE OF THE STARS ON EARTH. SHE'D LIVED IN A CITY, after all, and even the poorer districts had had enough streetlights to make it hard to see the stars. If there had been a space program worth a damn, maybe she would have been interested, but as it happened she had rarely looked up at the night sky. It had only been after coming to Whitehall that she'd learned how to use the stars to navigate and by then she remembered almost nothing about the stars that shone down on Earth. She had no idea if the constellations that shone above Alexis were anything like the ones visible on her homeworld.

The thought provided a distraction as she slipped through the streets, relying on stealth and a simple glamor to keep from being noticed. If the stars were similar, did that mean that her new world was actually an alternate Earth? But the continents were completely dissimilar to the continents she remembered from back home, suggesting otherwise. Although…if this were a different world rather than just an alternate timeline, how had humanity even evolved here? Had there been prior contact between Earth and the Allied Lands?

She'd read all the theoretical books on magic in Whitehall's library and none of them had even *mentioned* anything reassembling the many-worlds theory. Emily had always assumed that she was the first interdimensional traveler in Whitehall's history, if only because she was sure that something would have been recorded if it had been commonplace. And Shadye didn't seem to have realized that his search for a Child of Destiny might have plucked one from an alternate world.

But there was no way to know for sure. Professor Locke had told the class—when they'd been working towards their exams—that history became legend very quickly. There were no shortage of stories about what had happened when the Faerie had been at the height of their power, or the early days of the first necromancers, but many of the stories contradicted one another. Emily knew that historians on Earth had faced problems in uncovering what had happened during the Persian invasion of Greece—the first event in western history to have been recorded properly, at least as far as she knew—and *they* hadn't had to worry about magic, or completely alien creatures with alien motives. All they'd had had to worry about was the Great King's understandable reluctance to dwell on his own defeat.

Emily pushed the thought aside as she reached a position where she could see the castle. It had been darkened, illuminated only by a single glowing ball of light hanging above the gatehouse, but it glowed in her mind's eye. The wards surrounding the castle were nowhere near as powerful and specific as the wards guarding Whitehall—King Alexis hadn't had the chance to build on a nexus of power—and in some ways, they were basic. But they were powerful enough to alert the defenders if someone broke in by force.

The books she'd read about wards had pointed out that the larger the ward, the less it could effectively do. A very small ward could tell the difference between a friend and an enemy; a larger ward couldn't do anything more complex than keep people out, or simply alert the guards if there was an intruder. Emily had been keyed into the wards when she'd arrived at the castle, along with the princes, but she suspected that the duke would have revoked her permission to come and go as she pleased. If it *was* the duke—and if he did have that authority. The only person with complete power over the wards was the King.

But the authority would pass to the duke if the king died, Emily thought, staring up at the castle. *Is that why they attacked before Alassa could be Confirmed?*

Carefully, she walked around the castle, studying the rocky mound that held it above the city. She could have climbed up to the walls if the wards hadn't been there, but scrambling up the walls would have been almost impossible even without the surprises that might have been buried into the stone. Stone could hold magic for years, she knew, and a small team of enchanters could have prepared it for almost anything. A climber might suddenly lose his grip and plummet to his death, or a ladder might slip and fall at entirely the wrong moment. No, the only way up was through the gatehouse—and *that* would be dangerous. If they were checking everyone who went in and out of the castle…

But there was no choice.

She felt the mirror Imaiqah had given her vibrate in her pocket. Emily carefully cast a privacy ward into the air and then pulled the mirror out, wondering if they'd finally made steps towards a magical cell phone network. If only the enchantments lasted longer…Imaiqah's face appeared in the mirror, looking grim. The fighting would have begun.

"They're attacking the soldiers now," she said, softly. "We haven't actually tried to kill them, just to trap them."

Emily nodded. The duke was supposed to be a skilled commander; he'd suspect that the whole affair was a diversion if his soldiers weren't actually being killed. But what was he going to do about it? If he abandoned his men, his remaining followers would start wondering if they were going to be abandoned next. Morale would fall like a stone—she hoped. It seemed an unwise thing to base a plan on.

"Good," she muttered. "I'll watch and wait here."

She didn't have long to wait. The sound of the gatehouse opening was clearly audible in the still night air, followed rapidly by hooves as horsemen charged out the gate and down the road. A small army of armored soldiers followed them, carrying whips and swords. Emily couldn't understand why they were bothering with the whips, until she realized that it would keep civilian casualties down. She would have felt happier about that if it hadn't proved that *someone* had decided to try to avoid a massacre which might have caused the entire city to revolt.

But the barons might actually consider that a plus, she thought, wondering just who was behind the whole plot. *Destroying most of the city and killing the productive population would cripple the monarchy, no matter who was on the throne.*

"They're coming," she muttered, into the mirror. "Good luck."

She waited long enough to be reasonably sure that no one else was going to come charging out of the gatehouse and then pulled Alassa's handkerchief out of her pocket. Her original plan, such as it had been, had involved using Alassa to gain access to the castle; there was no way she could be excluded from the wards, at least as far as Emily knew. But the bird-magician had made that impossible.

Emily hesitated, looking down at the bloodstained cloth. Blood Magic was *dangerous*—as she, more than anyone else, had good reason to know. She'd been warned, right at the start of her time in Whitehall, to make sure that she took good care of her blood, if only to prevent someone from using it against her. And all of her precautions hadn't been good enough to prevent Shadye from using a tiny sample of her blood to control Emily. If it hadn't been for Sergeant Harkin...

She pushed the thought aside. After the Battle of Whitehall, she'd used her access to the library to find and read two of the books on Blood Magic, both heavily restricted and charmed to the point that she was surprised that she hadn't been caught. Reading restricted books was grounds for more than a simple thrashing, they'd been warned. The wrong kind of book, read without permission, could lead to expulsion—or worse. But she hadn't really had a choice. She needed to know as much as she could before someone else tried Shadye's trick, with more success. Shadye had wanted a subordinate as much as he had wanted a slave. The next necromancer might simply want her dead.

"If this goes wrong, or even if it works," she muttered, very quietly, "Alassa may never want to see me again. And if it saves her life, I will accept that as the price for my decision."

In a way, Blood Magic was very like necromancy, close enough that Emily had wondered if one automatically led to the other. But she'd heard of Blood Magic users who were not necromancers...Blood Magic didn't impose immediate costs, unlike necromancer, but using it involved crossing a moral barrier. If one could work through a person's blood, gaining some measure of power over them, it was a small step to make the decision to kill for power.

Carefully, she reached out with her mind, feeling the hints of magic surrounding Alassa's blood. Even without the Royal Bloodline, or any spells to preserve it, it could be years before blood lost its potency as a magical tool. Skin barely lasted seconds, hair couldn't be relied upon for anything...but blood lasted years. The only thing that seemed to remain potent forever were bones, yet they created their own problems. None of the books she'd read had suggested that using bones for ritual magic was a good idea.

She could feel the faint link leading off towards the castle, to wherever they were keeping Alassa. Most Blood Magic users would reach out along the link and try to influence the person at the far end, but Emily had something else in mind. Alassa's personality, the core that made her what she was, lay over the bloodstain like a curtain. And it was suddenly very easy to draw that curtain over Emily herself. The wards would simply mistake Emily for Alassa...

...Or so she hoped.

If the wards had been smarter, like the wards at Whitehall, they might have noticed that the same person was in two different places at once. Emily knew that it was a gamble, all the more so if there was another warden, apart from King Randor himself. A mind supervising the wards would make detection almost certain. But she'd gone too far to back out now. Bracing herself, pulling an additional glamor over her form, she started to walk up towards the castle.

The buildings outside the castle were dark and cold, almost completely abandoned. Emily couldn't blame the occupants; they'd either been taken into the castle as honored guests–hostages, in other words–or had decided to suddenly move out to the edge of the inner city. Paren had told her that it had added to the confusion, making it harder for the duke's men to track the council and their followers. Emily felt an odd spurt of pain as she caught sight of where the Assembly building had stood. It was now nothing more than a pile of burned-out ruins.

They can rebuild, she thought, grimly. *And the next one will be stronger.*

She felt the wards brushing against her as she approached the gatehouse. Whitehall's wards would have repelled her, or frozen her in her tracks, if she hadn't had permission to enter the building. Here...what could they do? The wards might only be able to alert the guards, which would be bad enough. Emily would have to fight or run, losing the advantage of surprise. She clenched her teeth as the wards grew stronger, poking at the illusion covering her. And, a moment later, the wards seemed to fade away. It took her a long second to realize that she had just walked through without harm.

The main gatehouse was closed and barred, unsurprisingly. It was only opened to allow large numbers of troops or guests to pass in or out without impediment. Instead, she headed towards the smaller door and braced herself as two guards stepped out of nowhere, glaring at her. Emily prayed silently that the glamor would hold as they studied her, then waved her through into the outer courtyard. The combination of a safe passage through the wards and a compulsion woven into the glamor, suggesting that she was someone in authority, had worked.

In daylight, the courtyard had been bustling with life, but in darkness it was as still and quiet as the grave. Emily slipped across it, keeping to the shadows, and found one of the main entrances into the castle. It was unguarded, she realized in surprise as she stepped inside. She'd expected to have to use the glamor again...inside, half of the lights seemed to have been allowed to burn out, without replenishment. It didn't slow Emily down any longer than it took to cast a night-vision spell over herself.

But they did think that the council was involved in plotting resistance, she thought, as she headed onwards. *Maybe they intended to make it harder for their forces if they stormed the castle.*

She froze as she heard voices ahead of her, then leaned into the shadows and used another glamor to hide herself. Four people walked down the corridor and past her, one of them recognizable as Alassa's maid. She didn't recognize the other three, but from their garb she guessed that they were servants. It puzzled her why they'd been allowed to stay in the castle, before she guessed that they were still under obedience spells. As long as they didn't realize that King Randor and his daughter were prisoners, they would obey the duke without question. He *was* the King's official heir—and Alassa's regent—as the Confirmation had never been completed.

Emily slipped out of the shadows and reached the servant's staircase. It was nowhere near as ornate as the main staircases intended for the Royal Family, but it allowed them to move around the castle without actually being seen by *important* people. Their quarters were on the fourth floor, if Emily recalled correctly, isolated from the rest of the castle by a handful of wards. The Royal Family didn't want to have anything to do with their servants when they weren't actually working.

Servants are invisible, Emily thought wryly, as she stepped out of the staircase on the fourth floor. It was a matter of seconds to find a maid's closet and borrow a robe suitable for a young housemaid, someone who cleaned the halls, dusted the tapestries and generally remained unnoticed in the background. Emily was surprised to discover that the outfit was actually quite flattering, although in hindsight she should have expected it. Every ruler the country had had since its formation out of the ashes of the Empire had been male.

Smiling inwardly, Emily reached the end of the corridor...and then stopped as she felt the bloodstained handkerchief jerk in her hand. Pausing, she closed her eyes and concentrated...and gasped in surprise as she realized that there seemed to be *two* princesses at the far end. That was impossible...Alassa didn't have a sister and even if she did, the link wouldn't have reached the other girl. For a moment, Emily wondered if she was seeing the Blood Magic reflected back at her, before realizing that was unlikely too. Surely, she would have seen it the moment she'd sensed Alassa's presence on the other end of the link.

Controlling her breath, she concentrated again...and realized that one of the princesses was moving, head down towards the Court Wizard's lab. Emily hesitated, then made the decision to find out just what the Court Wizard was doing. Besides, it might be the real Alassa, being taken to a ghastly fate. Returning the handkerchief to her pocket, Emily walked out of the servants quarters and headed down towards the lab. A pair of young guardsmen leered at her as she passed, but did nothing to stop her. Emily kept her eyes on the ground and ignored their lewd gazes as they tracked her until she turned the corner.

There were more guards on the lower levels, but they ignored the housemaid, apart from one who tried to pinch her bum. His superior reprimanded him and motioned impatiently for Emily to hurry onwards, which she did. It took all of her determination not to smile until she was safely away from them; the duke must have picked noblemen to serve in his army. They *never* paid attention to the servants. God alone knew how many spies in history had posed as nothing more interesting than janitors or maids.

But then, they thought that she was under an obedience spell. Resistance was not only futile, but inconceivable. Why *not* let the servants try to clean up the mess?

She stopped as she reached the lab and glanced into the room. It had been devastated; the glass devices and test tubes Zed had been so proud of had been smashed, their remains left on the stone floor. The stench of hundreds of chemicals mixing together without restraint rose up to her nose as she stared at the destroyed work-room. It was easy to imagine Zed fighting to prevent outsiders from breaking into his private lab...

And then she heard someone ahead of her, in one of the rooms Zed hadn't shown her when she'd visited. Bracing herself, Emily crept forward and peeked through the door. The bird-magician stood there, his back to her, working on a vial of blood that he'd placed above a glowing fire stick. Emily gasped as she realized that he had to have taken the blood from Alassa. And now he was preparing to use it to take permanent control of the crown princess and future queen...

The bird-magician turned and their eyes met. Emily knew, beyond a shadow of a doubt, that he knew who she was. The disguise wouldn't fool another magician...

And then he threw a powerful curse right at her.

Chapter Thirty-Eight

EMILY JUMPED TO ONE SIDE AND THE BLAST OF BALEFIRE SHOT PAST HER, SLAMMING INTO the broken cabinets of alchemical ingredients against the far wall. She threw back a spell of her own, aimed at the vial of blood, then launched a cutting hex at the bird-magician's face. Both spells struck his wards and vanished. Emily cursed—destroying the blood had worked last time—and then smelled burning wood from behind her. She risked a glance and realized that the alchemical ingredients were starting to burn. Professor Thande had warned the entire class that randomly mixing chemicals could be very dangerous.

She parried another spell and then stepped backwards, towards the door. The flames were spreading quickly, changing color as more and more chemicals caught fire. Emily covered her mouth as green smoke started to billow up in the room, then ran for the door. The bird-magician came after her, using a simple spell to ward away the smoke. Emily scowled as she reached the door, then summoned up a final spell of her own. Why hadn't *she* thought of that?

Because Professor Thande taught you to keep magic to a bare minimum around the alchemical mixtures, her own thoughts answered. His lectures on safety had sunk in, particularly after watching one girl drink a shrinking potion and spend the rest of the lesson barely larger than Emily's finger.

Emily summoned fire and blasted the room, then turned and ran for the stairs. The bird-magician would have to deal with the fire before it spread further, she told herself; the stone walls were largely impossible to burn, but the flames and smoke could easily force the coup plotters out of the castle. And, if she were lucky, the chemicals would make it hard for him to simply summon water and drown the flames. If not...she pushed that thought aside as she reached the stairs and started to run up towards her quarters. By now, the entire castle would know that something was wrong. She needed a diversion.

Two guards stared at her as she approached, unsure of just what she was doing in the castle. Emily snapped off a pair of quick freeze spells and sighed in relief as they both froze in place, then tumbled down the stairs. If they'd been wearing enchanted armor, they could have caught her before she managed to overload the protective wards woven into the armor. She heard a yell of outrage from below her and turned to see another line of soldiers, led by one of the barons. Emily shaped the strongest light spell she could and triggered it, shining a blinding light right into their eyes. The baron staggered backwards, clutching at his eyes. His soldiers weren't in any better state. Magic could heal them, Emily told herself, but it would take time. Until then, they were blinded...Emily pushed the guilt aside and ran onwards.

A powerful spell struck her and she stumbled to her knees, feeling her entire body jangling with energy. She couldn't tell what the spell was actually designed to do, which made it harder to deflect. Somehow, she broke free and threw a kinetic spell of her own back down the stairs towards the bird-magician. The spell missed and shattered part of the railings.

Emily ran. She concentrated on warding herself as she reached the top of the stairs and fled towards her apartments. The sound of a man or men chasing her grew louder as she cancelled the ward she'd left on her own rooms, opening the door. It felt like she had left them a lifetime ago; had it really been three days? The world had turned upside down...she slammed the door closed and pushed the ward back into place. It wouldn't hold more than a few seconds when the bird-magician went to work—she knew that from Martial Magic—but it would keep him busy long enough. Her chest lay where she'd left it, right in the center of the room.

This could easily go badly wrong, a doubtful voice whispered at the back of her mind.

But there was no choice. The bird-magician was powerful and experienced. And he wasn't alone. Even if most of the magicians she was facing used wands—which meant that they were either very weak or didn't have any real magic at all—she was still badly outnumbered. She needed a diversion...she put her hand on the chest and sighed in relief as she realized that the charms worked into the pocket dimensions were still intact. After her unauthorized hacking and modification, it had been quite possible that the dimensions would snap out of existence completely.

The door exploded inward in a shower of dust and splinters. Emily looked up to see the bird-magician standing there, raw magic crackling over his fingertips. The ward shattered, sending jolts of pain flashing through her head, but she was used to ignoring such distractions. Instead, she stepped backwards—keeping the link to the chest—and tried to look like a cornered rat. It wasn't difficult.

"You are not very impressive for one who beat a necromancer," the bird-magician observed. "Could it be that Shadye was poisoned and your grandmaster decided to try to convince the world that you beat him in single combat?"

Emily said nothing, concentrating on the link to the chest. She was straining the enchantments still further, despite knowing the risk of breaking the chest completely. If Yodel's work had been less than perfect...but that hardly mattered. She'd screwed the warranty when she'd converted it into a makeshift prison.

"Not impressive at all," the bird-magician mocked. "I expected much better from the Necromancer's Bane."

Most of the tricks I have invented are too destructive, Emily thought. She could split atoms with magic—it wasn't very difficult, if one knew the basic concept—but doing it would destroy much of the city, as well as blowing herself up in the process. And if the necromancers learned how to make atomic bombs, they wouldn't hesitate before shattering the mountains and advancing on the Allied Lands. The only thing holding them back would be a reluctance to kill the people they needed for sacrifices, but she doubted they were sane enough to remember that indefinitely.

"Goodbye," he said, and lifted his hand.

"Goodbye," Emily said, and released the cockatrice.

The giant beast exploded out of the chest, slamming the bird-magician back against the stone wall. It's tail lashed out, smashing into Emily's bed and reducing it to firewood as it roared its outrage and confusion into the air. Time hadn't moved within the chest, Emily knew; the cockatrice had to be hellishly confused. From its point of view, it had been in the mountains one second and her rooms the next. And the stone walls were hideously confining...

The cockatrice roared again and blasted a wall of fire towards the bird-magician, who barely managed to shield himself in time. Fire cascaded around the room, sweeping over the hanging tapestries and reducing them to ash. A portrait of King Alexis II–bearing a surprising resemblance to Alassa–caught fire and burned with a brief, fierce light. The cockatrice couldn't turn in the confined space, Emily realized in relief. If it had been able to turn around, it would have come after her.

There was a flash of light and a wave of magic as the bird-magician threw the most powerful curse he could muster at the cockatrice. It howled in pain, but it didn't seem to have been really hurt; moments later, scaly claws lashed through where the bird-magician had been seconds ago. Black crows rose up and headed for the door, only to be caught in a terrific fireball as the cockatrice roared its fury. Emily saw the crows catch fire and fall to the floor, burning. She heard–or imagined–the howl of pain as the bird-magician died. The handful of crows that hadn't been incinerated fell to the floor and lay there, helpless. Moments later, the cockatrice snapped the birds up and swallowed them.

The beast roared again, shaking the entire castle, then blew fire out the door, down towards the soldiers Emily knew had to be coming to find out what was going on. They'd probably decide that discretion was the better part of valor, once they realized that there was a live cockatrice in the castle. She wondered absently just how long it would take them to comprehend what was going on. It was rare for cockatrices–or other large creatures–to pick fights with humans. Even if they did realize what was happening, it would take hours to assemble enough magicians to stun or kill the cockatrice. The flames alone would make it harder for them to do anything, but run.

She jumped backwards as the cockatrice lashed its tail about in Emily's direction. It knew she was standing behind it, all right...Emily ducked into the next room, avoiding the tail by a split-second, then ran over to the window. It had been spelled to make it harder to open, but a simple blasting hex shattered it, blasting the debris out into the night. Emily hoped that some of the enemy soldiers were underneath, before pushing the thought aside angrily. The cockatrice might have saved her life, but it was also blocking her way out of the apartment. Going out the window was the only other way to escape.

There was a fire in the distance, somewhere near the city walls. Emily felt a pang of guilt–she'd organized the resistance–and then pushed it aside as she cast the strongest night-vision spell she could on her eyes. It was a risk–a single flicker of light would be blindingly bright - but there was no choice. If she'd had proper equipment...she pushed the thought aside, then transfigured some of her spare clothes into rope, tying one end to the fireplace and attaching the other to herself. At least she'd have some security if she lost her grip. Pulling the handkerchief out of her pocket, she pulled the illusion of Alassa around herself and then climbed out the window. If she was right, the charms built into the walls wouldn't attack the crown princess.

Sergeant Harkin had been fond of forcing them to climb up cliff faces and buildings that Emily would have sworn were impossible to climb. The trick, he'd claimed, had been never to look down, at least until she was confident in her own abilities. Here, so high above the ground, there were plenty of hand and footholds, as long as she was careful. Emily felt dangerously vulnerable, almost naked, as she started to inch along the walls, trying not to think of the fall if she lost her grip. Cold wind seemed to bite at her as she pulled herself along, mockingly reminding her of the fall. And of the times she'd been abseiling and lost her grip. The sergeants might have had safety precautions in place to prevent anyone from actually injuring themselves, but they'd also been very sarcastic to those who made mistakes...

There was a dull roar echoing through the stone walls as the cockatrice scented humans nearby. Emily grinned to herself, guessing that the barons hadn't believed the first reports and had sent more men to check just what was going on. Those men had run right into the cockatrice and discovered that the beast was *furious*. It had to feel trapped inside stone walls...Emily wondered, suddenly, just how they were going to get it back to the mountains? How far could a cockatrice fly? Or maybe she'd be able to trap it again and take the beast to Whitehall, as she'd planned to do.

Wasting time, she told herself, as she reached a larger window. She'd memorized the castle's interior—at least the parts she'd been told about, which didn't include the secret passageways—but she'd never had to try to imagine how the outside windows corresponded with the interior. If she was right, the next three windows should be connected to Alassa's rooms...carefully, she pulled herself up to them and peered inside. The apartments certainly *seemed* luxurious enough. Emily summoned a small cutting hex and tried to use it on the window. It didn't work.

Emily swallowed a curse and tried again. Naturally, the security precautions on Alassa's windows were tougher than the ones on *her* windows. Maybe they took them down whenever the windows needed cleaning...Emily shivered, wondering if she'd made a dreadful mistake, then started to put a spell together from memory. The concept had been easy to imagine, once she'd sat down and worked out concepts from Earth she could bring to her new home, but very dangerous. If the necromancers ever realized that they could destroy something by absorbing the energy that held it together...

The window crumbled into dust. Emily coughed, clinging desperately to the wall, then flung herself into the room. She hit the carpet hard enough to knock the wind out of her, leaving her stunned and briefly helpless, but no one seemed to have heard her arrival. Pulling herself to her feet, she glanced around and realized that she was standing inside a nursery for young children. A large wooden cot, covered with gold and silver designs, stood against one wall. She felt an odd flicker of envy as she saw the toys scattered everywhere, from handmade dolls to board games, and realized that Alassa had to have grown up in this room. A large portrait of a chubby woman, glowing with life, hung above the cot. There was nothing to suggest who she might have been, or who had painted her picture. She didn't look anything like Queen Marlena, or Alassa herself.

Alassa had everything, Emily thought, *apart from friends.*

She lowered the night-vision spell, then touched the handkerchief long enough to get a sense of Alassa's location. The door leading out of the nursery was unlocked; she stepped through, ready to unleash a hail of spells at any target, only to encounter nothing apart from another darkened room. This one appeared to be a small bedroom, too small for Alassa or her mother. Emily guessed that it was where the nurse had slept every night; the royal family had probably hired a dozen nurses and nannies for their child. A portrait of the Royal Family hung on one wall; the child in the queen's arms looked around five years old. It was odd to realize that it had been painted at the same time as Emily's life was going downhill.

Pushing the thought aside, she stepped into the next room and saw the guards. They spun around to stare at her in disbelief—they had to have searched the rooms and *knew* that no one was there—and then opened their mouths to shout an alert. Emily froze them both before they could get a word out, then walked over to the door and listened, carefully. It sounded as though the cockatrice was still causing havoc.

The tug from the handkerchief pulled her towards Alassa's bedroom. Emily took a sword from one of the guards, braced herself and pushed open the door. The room was brightly lit, illuminated by a dozen glowing balls of light, with Alassa lying on the bed, staring up at nothing. Emily shivered as she realized that the bird-magician must have put her under a spell before taking her blood. How long would it have taken him to turn Alassa into a puppet? The books had suggested that it could take days to build up the spells and weave them through the blood, but they hadn't been very specific. And besides, Alassa had the Royal Bloodline. How long would it take to break the protections and enhancements that were worked into the Royal Bloodline?

Alassa looked peaceful as she lay on the bed, her hands folded on her chest. Emily took her pulse, then started to cast dispelling spells, one after another until she finally ran out of ideas. There were some curses and hexes that were resistant to standard dispelling spells...whatever the bird-magician had done to Alassa seemed to be one of them. Emily touched her finger to her friend's forehead, feeling...*something*...webbed over Alassa's mind, something so subtle that she wasn't even sure it was there. Maybe she was just imagining it.

Maybe I should just kiss you, she thought, grimly. There *were* spells that needed a kiss to break them, although they rarely lasted long when a trained sorcerer started to concentrate on breaking them down rather than humoring the caster. Emily *was* good at charms—it was her talent—but this was something different. It held Alassa's mind in thrall. A mistake could cause permanent damage.

Emily hesitated, unsure of what to do. If she left Alassa here, the coup plotters could just continue with their plan, even without the bird-magician. But if she risked using a spell to shrink Alassa to carry her out of the castle, what would it do to the spell holding her under control? She had to free her friend before someone else came into the room and discovered them. But how?

There *had* been a few suggestions in the books. But they had all been long on flowery language and short on actual detail, as if the writers had been too scared to write down precise instructions. Emily wasn't too surprised; the more she had explored the concept of Blood Magic, the easier it had been to see how it could be abused. And the more she used it, the stronger the temptations would become...

Bracing herself, Emily knelt down beside Alassa and unfolded the handkerchief. The link between Alassa and her blood was as strong as ever. For a long moment, Emily froze, unable to understand quite how to apply her thoughts in the right way...

...And then she plunged into Alassa's mind.

Chapter Thirty-Nine

NO BOOK HAD TOLD HER ABOUT DIRECT MENTAL CONTACT, OR PREPARED HER FOR THE experience. Emily understood why the moment she fell into Alassa's mind, the experience was indescribable. A howling storm rose up to greet her projection, blasting her with thoughts and memories that came from her friend's mind. Hundreds of thousands of disjointed impressions lashed out at her, each one distracting her for a split-second before vanishing again. Emily closed her eyes, but it was useless, naturally. She was navigating her astral projection within a person's mind.

"Alassa," she said, or thought. "Where are you?"

The storm seemed to part, just long enough to show her a direction—and the spell, holding Alassa firmly in a trance-like state. It represented itself as an evil green webbing floating through the storm, gripping parts of Alassa's mind and securing them in place. Emily stared, wondering how she was even going to *begin* untangling the knot. The charms exam she'd been put through at Whitehall—one more complex than any she'd expected—had been nightmarish, but this...? This was worse.

This is her mind, she reminded herself, as she started to float towards the core of Alassa's being. *A very subtle mind control spell might be very powerful here...*

Thoughts and memories blasted up at her, each one slamming into her projection before she could look away. Alassa, standing with her parents; Alassa, meeting her cronies for the first time; Alassa, laughing as a maid became a toad in a flash of light. A storm of emotion crashed over Emily as she pushed onwards, first a sly enjoyment that became shame as the memories grew older. Alassa hadn't realized just how much her cronies had taken advantage of her until she'd almost been killed by the Child of Destiny...

That memory rose up and swallowed Emily. She stood, facing herself, rage blasting through her mind. How *dare* this newcomer be so much better than her? Alassa had never questioned herself until after she'd come so close to death...Emily tasted her fear and shame and hatred, tempered by the sudden awareness that Emily was *important*. The meeting she'd had with the grandmaster, the brief eternity spent facing the Warden, the letter she'd had from her parents...Emily tried to look away, but the memories kept coming. Alassa had been forced to take a good hard look at herself and she hadn't liked what she'd seen.

And then Emily had saved her life.

"Alassa," Emily called again, trying to hear her friend. "Where are you?"

New memories surged around her. Alassa sitting on the bed, asking when her parents were going to come see her. Emily hadn't realized that Alassa had almost been abandoned for the first five years of her life, even by her mother. She'd been brought up by nannies and maids who had done whatever they were told, spoiling the little princess rotten. Emily had known, intellectually, that royal children were often given to others to raise, but she'd never really understood what it did to their minds. By the time King Randor had reluctantly accepted that there would be no other heirs, legitimate or illegitimate, Alassa had already been warped into becoming a brat. She should have been trained from the start...

The memories grew stronger. Zed, the Court Wizard, teaching her the first few spells. Alassa hadn't realized that he had been growing exasperated with her; Emily, seeing through her friend's eyes, understood perfectly why Zed had eventually given up. The royal brat just hadn't had the patience to understand what she was being told. Or maybe Zed *had* been convinced not to push any further. He had always been more interested in alchemy than in teaching unwilling students how to cast spells...

...Alassa's first meeting with the daughters of the barons and how they'd fawned on her, treating her like a crowned queen. Emily could see that they were taking advantage of her, but Alassa had honestly never realized it. How could she? She'd never been taught how to tell when someone was crawling to her because they wanted something. Alassa learned to throw tantrums to get what she wanted, egged on by her first set of cronies...

"Emily?"

"I'm here," Emily said. Her friend's voice seemed to be coming from all around her, but as she concentrated she saw the path to Alassa's soul. "What happened to you?"

"Not sure," Alassa said. "He took me, stunned me and then...everything went so strange."

"You're under a spell," Emily said. A final wave of memories struck at her, trying to force her back. She broke through and saw Alassa in front of her. Her friend seemed to be chained down, the force of the spell holding her in place. "You have to wake up."

"I don't know how," Alassa said, thickly. This deep in her core, the spell couldn't prevent her from slowly recovering the ability to think. "I don't..."

Idiot, Emily told herself. *You're in a mental representation, not reality!*

Alassa's voice was puzzled. "What's a mental representation?"

Emily flushed. Alassa had heard her thoughts? Of course, she reminded herself, tartly. This *was* a mental representation, not reality.

"I'm inside your mind," she said, finally. She concentrated hard, trying not to think about Jade or anything else she would have preferred to keep to herself. It wasn't easy. "The spell is holding you trapped inside your own mind."

Saying it out loud made it easy to visualise. "You have to take control back," she added. "Force yourself up and out of the spell's grip."

Alassa rattled her chains. "I don't know how," she protested. "I can't break free!"

"This is your mind," Emily reminded her. "The chains could be made of anything..."

Reality—or her perception of reality—shifted. The chains were suddenly made out of parchment, which started to tear as Alassa pulled herself free. Emily felt her friend's mind suddenly expanding, growing more and more powerful with every second, forcing Emily to travel back down the link into her own body. There was a sudden rush of energy and the world spun around her. When she opened her eyes—unaware that she'd closed them—she found herself looking down at Alassa.

"What..." Alassa coughed and started again. "What did you *do* to me?"

"I used some of your blood," Emily admitted. Part of her mind insisted that it wasn't wise to tell anyone, but Alassa would work it out for herself sooner or later—or tell Lady Barb, who would probably know enough to guess the truth. "It was the only way to find you."

Alassa rolled out of bed and stood upright. "I think I got some of your memories too," she said. "What were the dragon-things in your homeland?"

Emily stared at her. She hadn't realized there was a possibility that Alassa would pick up memories from her too—although it would be only fair. But dragons? There were no dragons on Earth, unless they were very good at hiding. *She'd* certainly never seen a living dragon until after meeting Void.

And how much had Alassa picked up from her thoughts?

"I think we'll have to discuss that later," she said. She passed Alassa one of the swords, then walked towards the door. "We have to deal with the duke and find your father."

The guards outside were still frozen, thankfully. Emily picked up the other sword and held it in one hand, trying to decide if she should attempt to interrogate one of the guards. It would have been easy to take some of his blood and scan his mind... angrily, she squashed the thought before it could tempt her any further. The whole concept of Blood Magic was terrifyingly easy to abuse.

"Coming," Alassa said. She glanced up as the roaring grew louder. "You freed the cockatrice?"

Emily grinned. "That should keep them busy for a while," she said. "Where do we go now?"

Alassa pushed one hand against a stone in the wall. There was a rumble as a stone slab moved to one side, allowing them to enter the secret passageway.

"No," Emily said. "If it is the duke, won't he know about the passageways? They'll expect us to use them and we'd be caught like rats in a trap."

"I don't know," Alassa said, hesitating. "The duke wouldn't share everything he knows with his people..."

"But it only takes a few guards to trap us," Emily reminded her. "Come on."

She walked to the door leading into the main corridor and stepped outside. Alassa followed her as she started to walk down the corridor, listening carefully for sounds of oncoming guards. It wasn't easy to hear anything over the roars that echoed through the castle; the entire city could probably hear the racket as the cockatrice fought for freedom. Could the beast actually break free? The cockatrice was strong, far stronger than a human...and the stories she'd read about dragons had talked about them tearing castles apart with their claws. Could the beast she'd unleashed do that?

Emily held up a hand to stop Alassa as they reached a corner. Two armed guards were standing in front of another door, backed up by a magician carrying a long wooden wand. Both guards wore enchanted armor, she realized grimly—and they were nervous. Whatever they were guarding had to be important. King Randor? Emily had assumed that the duke had put his brother in the dungeons, but King

Randor might have a secret way *out* of the dungeons. Why not? He could have easily had one installed that responded only to him.

"I'll deal with them," she muttered. "You just stay here and watch my back."

She walked around the corner and threw the strongest disarming jinx she could muster at the magician, then followed up by hitting him with a freeze charm. His wand shattered under the impact, releasing a flash of raw magic; he couldn't defend himself against the freeze charm at all. Not a real magician, Emily realized, as the guards turned to face her. The leers on their faces suggested that they might not take a girl carrying a sword very seriously, even though they'd seen her do magic. Emily smiled inwardly and triggered *berserker*.

The guards had almost no time to react as she ran forward and swung the blade with superhuman strength. One of them jumped backwards, crashing into the wall; the other staggered as the blade cut deep into his chest. He collapsed to the ground as his companion hesitated, torn between fighting or running, then struck out at Emily with his sword. To Emily, it seemed almost as though he were moving in slow motion. It was the easiest thing in the world to step to one side and skewer him through the throat.

She cancelled *berserker* and staggered, feeling the effects catching up with her. It was just too dangerous to use often, she reminded herself, even if she was stronger than she'd been when she'd started to learn the spell. Alassa came forward and put a hand on her shoulder, then looked at the door the guards had been watching. She didn't look as though she knew what was inside either.

"They won't have left my father here," she said, finally. "This is one of the bragging rooms."

Emily looked at her, puzzled.

"Big room for the guests," Alassa said. She found a key on one of the guards and inserted it into the lock. "They come here to tell lies about their great deeds…"

The door clicked open, revealing Prince Hildebrand. He stared at Alassa, then started to laugh. Beyond him, Emily saw the other princes, sitting in the room. None of them looked very happy. They'd been taken prisoner and held for nearly two days. Chances were that holding them like that was a declaration of war. Or was it? Had anyone ever gone to war because a prince had been held prisoner? She honestly couldn't remember.

Prince Hildebrand hadn't taken his eyes off Alassa. It struck Emily suddenly that they might feel ashamed of being saved by a woman, even though they obviously hadn't been able to break free themselves. Prince Hedrick looked as dull-eyed as ever; the remaining princes came to their feet slowly, staring at their rescuers. Emily couldn't think of what, if anything, they could say to them. Was an internal coup in Zangaria even their problem?

"My father is a prisoner," Alassa said, into the silence. "Will you help me to rescue him?"

"Yes," Prince Hildebrand said, simply.

The other princes agreed quickly. Emily wanted to roll her eyes; she'd forgotten that they'd come to court Alassa, the Crown Princess of Zangaria. If they *didn't* take part in the counter-coup, they'd have to explain their inactivity to King Randor, who would definitely not allow them to marry his daughter. Emily concealed her amusement as she motioned for the princes to take weapons from the guards, surrendering her sword to Prince Hildebrand. Alassa flatly refused to give her weapon to anyone else.

"Take the armor too," Emily ordered, after checking that there were no nasty surprises attached to the metal. "Hurry."

The princes hesitated. "Do as she says," Alassa said, sharply. "Now."

Emily didn't bother to hide her irritation as she led the way down the corridor. The roaring seemed to be fading away, leaving her wondering if they'd managed to do something about the cockatrice or if the beast was growing tired on its own. She'd ridden a dragon from Void's tower to Whitehall and she'd never had the impression that the trip had *tired* the dragon, but the cockatrice was smaller...perhaps it could be exhausted. Or perhaps it had eaten everyone sent to stop it and then settled down for a nap.

"There should be weapons in here," Alassa said, as they reached a small storeroom. "Take what you need, then we can inch downstairs to the Great Hall."

The princes rapidly armed themselves, then formed a bodyguard around Alassa as they moved down the stairwell. Emily found herself feeling dangerously exposed, but they reached the lower floor without problems. There was a faint tinge of smoke in the air, suggesting that parts of the castle were still burning. Emily glanced from side to side, then picked the direction that should have led to the Great Hall.

"Stop," a voice bellowed. "This is none of your concern."

Emily saw one of the barons standing there, surrounded by armed soldiers. He must have meant the princes, Emily decided. The whole thought of a coup in her country *not* being of concern to Alassa was ludicrous.

"You are a traitor to my father, breaking oaths you swore when he was crowned," Alassa said, very coldly. If she had any doubts at all, they weren't showing in her voice. "Surrender now and I promise that you will live."

But her father might not keep that promise, Emily thought. *Alassa* wouldn't suffer if her father was the one to kill the baron—come to think of it, the barons couldn't have sworn binding oaths to her father, or they would be dead by now. Unless the oaths had been neutralized somehow...she shook her head. Every time she thought she understood the rules, something changed.

The baron gestured and his soldiers ran forward, slamming into the princes as they pushed Alassa back and shielded her. Emily watched the fight for a moment, then joined Alassa in hurling spells at the baron. His enchanted armor rapidly overloaded, leaving him unprotected. Alassa's final curse tore off his head.

"And so perish all traitors," Alassa said, her voice shaky. The remaining guards threw down their weapon in surrender. "To the Great Hall!"

The big stone doors were shut and warded, but the wards couldn't keep out anyone who shared the Royal Bloodline. "Stay here and guard the entrance," Alassa ordered the Princes. "Come inside if I call, but not before."

She opened the doorway wide enough to allow her and Emily to step inside before Emily could ask if leaving them outside was a good idea. The throne room was dimly lit—the only source of light was a fading light ball, floating up above the throne—but it was bright enough to allow them to see someone sitting on the throne. Alassa generated a light ball of her own and pushed it towards the figure, revealing the duke. He didn't respond, even when Alassa hovered the light ball right over his head.

"Stay here," Emily muttered and walked up towards the duke. He didn't respond at all as she neared him, then touched his forehead very lightly. It reminded her of how Alassa had also been held in a trance, but it seemed to be stronger in the duke's case. He was a puppet whose strings had been cut. "I don't understand."

"Someone could have been controlling him," Alassa said. She shook her head in disbelief. "But that should have been impossible…"

"They intended to control you," Emily reminded her. What had the bird-magician intended to do with Alassa's blood? Maybe the Royal Bloodline simply required more work before it could be used to control the blood donor. Emily hadn't had any problems using the link between Alassa and some of her blood to find her, and then plunge into her mind. "What if…?"

She saw the shimmer, an instant too late. Someone was right behind Alassa…a second later, there was a sword at the princess's throat. Alassa froze, almost as if someone had cast a freeze charm on her. Emily stared as the invisibility spell faded away, revealing a young woman with red-gold hair.

"Welcome back, Your Highness," Duchess Lithia said. Her face twisted into a wry smile as she looked over at Emily. "I'd advise you not to move, or to try magic. I could slit her throat and…well, where would we be then?"

Chapter Forty

"Duchess," Emily said. Something in her mind yammered at her to keep the woman talking, at least until she could get the sword away from Alassa's throat. "What are you doing?"

"I'm taking control," Duchess Lithia said. She snorted, rather rudely. "You're really not very clever, are you? What does it *look* like I'm doing?"

Emily flushed. She'd discounted the duchess, everyone had. Duchess Lithia might have married the duke, but she'd never been part of the Royal Bloodline. King Randor had insisted on it, Emily had been told, just to ensure that Alassa wouldn't end up with cousins who might have a claim to the throne. Under the circumstances, it might not have been a very smart move.

"You had access to your husband's blood," Emily said, very slowly. The bird-magician had clearly thought that he could control Alassa. Why *not* the duke? "That's how he was able to lie to his brother. He didn't *know* that he was lying."

"He issued the orders to have you killed," the duchess confirmed. "You do seem to have a habit of surviving through dumb luck."

She smiled. "Crow was very unimpressed with you," she added. "He thought that you were madly overrated. But you did break into the castle..."

Stall for time, Emily told herself. "Why are you doing this? What's the *point* of it all?"

"Power," Alassa croaked. "She's the daughter of one of the barons. They could take control of the country using her as their weapon."

"And turning you into a puppet," the duchess confirmed. "Of course, you wouldn't last very long. The barons misread the threat from the Line of Alexis once before. They won't do it again."

"You'd be the last survivor," Emily said, slowly. "The king and queen would be dead. The duke would be dead. Alassa would be dead, presumably after nominating you her successor. You'd be all that was left of the Royal Family. The barons would acclaim you queen and then divide the country up between themselves."

"And destroy those who spread the new knowledge," the duchess said. "Didn't you ever realize, *Child of Destiny*, how much of this is your fault?"

Emily nodded ruefully, never taking her eyes off the duchess.

The duchess smiled, coldly. "They wanted to make sure that no one respected Queen Alassa," she added. "The girl who grew up here was a brat, with a reputation that they spread far beyond the castle walls. But then she met you and...I heard King Randor cursing, the day he realized just what you'd done. If he'd known that it would take a near-death experience to convince Alassa to grow up, he would have dropped her out of a window."

Emily frowned. "How can you trust the barons?"

She pushed ahead before the duchess could say a word. "They were willing to settle for having Alassa as a puppet ruler," she said. "Why would they not want to stick with that plan?"

"Because Zed did a very good job on her," the duchess said. "Controlling Alassa permanently would be difficult, perhaps impossible. And when she broke free, she might rise up against the barons. Now *that* would be tricky to manage."

Why? Emily thought, bleakly. *She'd be isolated, in a castle…in a castle where the wards would be tuned to her. Maybe they feared being unable to control her if her thoughts cleared.*

"I was the one who encouraged the king to get Zed to teach Alassa basic magic," the duchess said. "He is a great Alchemist, but a poor teacher. I knew that she would never be able to develop her magic…well, not until you came along. And having the spells she *did* have under her control, she would just become much more of a brat. Which she did."

"So Zed isn't part of your plot," she said, coolly. "You didn't control everything."

The duchess smiled. "I didn't *need* him to be part of my plot," she pointed out, mildly. "All I had to do was egg him on when it came to raging about a chit of a girl who questioned the work of a lifetime. He didn't even come to the ceremony because he was so angry at you, Child of Destiny. Wouldn't his presence have made the coup so much harder?"

"Very well done," Alassa said, sardonically. She twisted slightly, until the blade was pushed closer to her throat. "Except, of course, that the moment you let go of me, one of us will turn you into a slug and stamp on you."

"I have protections," the duchess said. She smiled. "No one thought anything of them, of course. A lady has to be careful, particularly when she's in a castle with a royal brat. Why, I heard that the magicians down in the inner city were doing a roaring trade in protective amulets when the servants heard that you were coming home."

Her voice hardened. "I may have no magic of my own, but you can't touch me," she added. "And I *can* slit your throat before your friend can push my protections aside."

Emily thought fast, but she couldn't come up with a solution. Even *berserker* wouldn't give her the speed necessary to kill the duchess before she murdered Alassa in cold blood. The barons would count it a victory if the princess died, Emily realized; if they worked together, they might be able to rule their private estates while sharing national authority. Or perhaps Zangaria would simply dissolve into a handful of smaller states that would be gobbled up by stronger neighbors. It would be pretty much inevitable if other states reaped the benefits of Emily's concepts while Zangaria tried to turn the clock back.

The duchess didn't give her any more time to think. "You can be a useful girl, I am sure," she said. "But trusting you would be difficult, hey?" Her face twisted into a smile. "If you want to see your friend live, you will swear an oath never to harm me—indeed, you will swear to obey me and protect me and help me rule this country to the best of my ability."

Emily winced. It *was* a logical solution to the duchess's problem.

"The barons just want you as a puppet," she pointed out, still playing for time. There had to be *something* she could do. "They're not going to let you *rule*, not if they were nervous about *Alassa* taking the throne. The best you can hope for is looking good on the throne."

"Ah, but I will have *you* helping me," the duchess said. "You do realize that King Randor seriously considered having you killed?"

She smiled, grimly. "You brought so many changes, even when you were thousands of miles away at Whitehall," she said. "Who knew what you would do when you were here?"

Emily didn't want to think about it, so she changed the subject. "Listen to me," she said, urgently. "What will happen when Zangaria collapses into anarchy? Because that is what is going to happen. You *know* there are people outside fighting your men. What happens when the country comes apart at the seams?"

She pushed on, desperately. "The fighting will draw in the other powers," she added. "All of the nearby kingdoms will see their chance at snatching territory for themselves. The fighting will grow worse as foreign armies invade, probably drawing in other powers that don't border Zangaria. And it will grow and grow until the Allied Lands disintegrate into chaos. And then the necromancers will just walk in and that will be the end.

"Think about what you're doing," she pleaded. "You're giving up wealth and power in exchange for chaos, chaos that will end with the complete destruction of civilization. Don't you *understand*? Everything will be destroyed!"

The duchess didn't understand, Emily saw. How could she? She was one of the most powerful women in the country and yet her horizons didn't stretch much further than Alexis and the duke's lands in the countryside. She was barely aware of the neighboring kingdoms, let alone the rest of the Allied Lands—or the necromancers. A threat so far away might as well have been on another world as far as she was concerned.

But it shouldn't have been a surprise. The White Council—and sorcerers like Void—had a global understanding; the rest of the Allied Lands simply didn't have anything of the sort. There was no internet, little in the way of long-range communications—at least without using magic—and no real interest in foreign affairs, at least outside the high nobility and monarchies. The duchess, a powerless woman without her husband, could hardly be expected to have a global outlook.

My fault, Emily thought, bitterly. *How much of this whole ungodly mess is my fault?*

"You prattle about nothing of importance," the duchess informed her. She didn't seem to care about the necromancers, or anything else apart from her power. "All that matters is power, power to secure my position."

Emily had wondered if a necromancer was behind the whole plot. Why not? The necromancers had good reason to want both Alassa and herself dead. But there was no necromancer hiding behind the curtain, just a woman who wanted power and security and didn't care who got stamped on in the process. She might have felt sympathy for the duchess, but she was threatening Emily's friend. *Both* of her friends.

She couldn't swear to serve the duchess. The consequences would be far worse than anything she'd done before, particularly once the duchess pushed her into talking about splitting atoms. She couldn't see the duchess hesitating over the use of nuclear weapons...

...But if she refused, Alassa would die.

Emily was sure she could kill the duchess seconds later, but it would be too late. She'd never really had friends before coming to Whitehall; she couldn't lose either of them. And without Alassa, Zangaria would have a civil war anyway, a civil war made worse because of concepts Emily had introduced. The duchess was right, she told herself again. Too much of the ghastly mess was her fault.

Shadye had thought that Emily was a Child of Destiny, never realizing that her mother's name had been Destiny. Now, Emily found herself wondering if she were a Child of Chaos. Was there such a concept? She didn't know.

Alassa was going to die. Imaiqah was going to die. It would happen whatever she chose, Emily knew, yet she couldn't make the choice. She *couldn't* sacrifice Alassa, even if it *did* mean peace in the kingdom—and it wouldn't. Her thoughts ran round and round in her head, unable to come to a decision. What could she do?

If it had been her...she'd braced herself to die, when she faced Shadye. But how could she throw away the life of a friend?

She opened her mouth...

Alassa spoke first. "Duchess Lithia... you don't have to do this," she said, twisting slightly. One hand dove into the loose-fitting trousers Imaiqah had given her. "I could keep you alive, exile you from the kingdom with a bag of gold...you'd be an exile, but you would be alive. You wouldn't even be a *prisoner.* You could go wherever you pleased..."

"As a *woman* in a world where we are expected to simper for men?" The duchess demanded. "Why should I walk away from the chance at real power?"

"Because the power wouldn't last," Emily said. She kept her eyes firmly on the duchess's face. "You'd be riding a dragon. One slip and you'd fall off. And if the barons decided to put you aside...what's to stop them? Alassa's offer is far more than you deserve."

"Her father will send assassins after me," the duchess snapped. Her voice hardened. "How stupid do you think I am?"

She glared at Emily, who flinched back from the sheer naked hatred in the duchess's eyes. "I thought that I would have power and respect as the wife of the Duke of Iron. Instead...I have nothing. My husband could have put me aside at any time. Why should I not make a grab for power? What do I have to lose?"

"Your life?" Alassa asked.

"I don't have a life," the duchess snarled. "And *you* should understand *that!*"

"Move the sword," Emily said, sharply. She could see a red splash where it was touching Alassa's throat. If she was wrong about what Alassa had in mind...everything was about to be lost, forever. "Move the sword and I will swear to you."

"You can't crack my protections in time to save your friend," the duchess sneered. "I can cut her throat in a second."

"I understand," Emily said, desperately. Blood was trickling down Alassa's neck and staining her shirt. One slip might cut Alassa's throat by accident, ending her life. "Move the sword and I will swear..."

The duchess moved the sword away from Alassa's throat, very gently. Emily tensed as the duchess turned her eyes to meet hers, inviting her to swear the oath. And then Alassa's right hand came up and caught the duchess's sword arm, holding the blade back from her throat. Her left hand stabbed the concealed dagger into the duchess's chest. Emily ran forward as the duchess struggled, gasping for breath, and pulled the sword right out of her hand. Alassa put one hand to her bleeding throat as the duchess crumpled to the floor, fighting for life.

"Give me the sword," Alassa said. Her hand was stained with her own blood, but she didn't look weakened at all. "Now!"

Emily blinked at the note of command in her voice, but obeyed. Alassa took the sword, tested it and then looked down at the duchess. The woman was still fighting...if she got to a healer, she might even survive.

"I am the Crown Princess of Zangaria, daughter of King Randor, heir to the throne," Alassa said, looking down at the duchess. Her voice was very cold, very clear. "The power of High, Middle and Low Justice rests with me. In the name of Alexis I, founder of the kingdom, I sentence you to death."

The blade sliced through the duchess's neck, beheading her in a single blow.

Emily stared, feeling a confusing mixture of emotions. Shock and horror warred with pride and understanding...and a droll awareness that she'd killed too. But she'd killed in self-defense and Alassa had sentenced her aunt to death. And yet who else could have executed the duchess without raising more issues that would need to be settled by force? It had to be Alassa, the crown princess who had yet to be Confirmed. Somehow, she doubted that the barons would appreciate the irony. By delaying Alassa's confirmation, they had created a legal gap between the unconfirmed and confirmed crown princess, even though they happened to be the same person.

There was a grunt from behind them.

"Uncle," Alassa said, and ran for the throne. "Uncle!"

The duke's eyes opened and he stared blearily at his niece. "Al... Alassa? What... what happened?"

Alassa looked down at him. "It's a long story," she said, finally. "A very long story. But it's all over now."

No, Emily thought, grimly. *It is far from over.*

They might have defeated the coup plotters, although some of the barons were still alive and would probably try to bargain for their lives. It had worked before, although the barons facing Alexis III had been in a stronger position than the ones who had tried to unseat King Randor. No doubt most of them would claim to have been misled, or tricked, or forced into going along with the *real* plotters, the ones who were safely dead.

But the problems Emily had caused wouldn't go away so quickly.

How could they?

She yawned as Alassa pulled her uncle to his feet and sent him to call off the guards. The duchess had used him to command the Royal Army—after all, he *was* their commander—and the soldiers would listen to him. After that, they could find King Randor and work out what to do next. Alassa seemed to believe that some of the barons had probably built up their own private armies. Avoiding a civil war might be impossible.

"Be careful where you go to sleep," Alassa said. "You never know what might be lurking in your room."

Emily stared at her, then burst out laughing. There was a *cockatrice* in her room! The entire section of the castle would have to be abandoned until they could get enough magicians in place to stun the beast, or simply wait for it to starve. How long would that take? The books had suggested that dragons could go *years* between eating...on the other hand, it would make a new form of cruel and unusual punishment to replace hunting transfigured criminals. Maybe the king would hurl the treacherous plotters into the rooms and watch as the cockatrice ate them.

"We have to deal with the rest of the plotters," Emily reminded her. She wanted to sleep—she hadn't slept for over twenty hours—but there was no time. "The others are still out there."

Alassa looked down at the bloodstained sword in her hand, then up at Emily.

"Let them come," she said, quietly.

Chapter Forty-One

"ARE YOU GOING TO THE CEREMONY?"

Emily looked up, rubbing her eyes. Lady Barb stood in front of her, her face bruised and battered after she'd been beaten into unconsciousness by the duchess's hired soldiers. Four days under the care of a watchful healer had saved her life, but not repaired her face. That would have to come later.

"I don't know if I'd be welcome," Emily said, finally. She'd barely seen Alassa since the coup had been defeated, let alone King Randor. The Royal Family had to secure their grip on power before they did anything else. "Do you think they'd want me?"

She looked back at the floor, wishing that Lady Barb would go away so she could finish moving her possessions into her new chest. The damage she'd done to trap the cockatrice had weakened the spells binding the pocket dimension badly, to the point where she could tell that they were definitely fraying. Thankfully, Zed had been able to recommend an enchanter who had sold her another chest for her to use, at least until she could have the old one repaired. If it *could* be repaired. The enchanter who'd produced it had warned her not to try to alter the spells.

"I think they're very grateful to you," Lady Barb said, dryly. "You should know that you saved their lives as well as their rule."

"After endangering them in the first place," Emily pointed out. She couldn't escape the nagging sense of guilt, that the entire episode had been her fault. Even removing the cockatrice and finding a new chest hadn't provided a distraction. "I should think they'd want to drive me to the border and push me into the next kingdom."

Lady Barb's lips twitched. "What did they do to deserve you?"

Emily flushed, angrily. "All of this was my fault," she said, flatly. "Why would they want me anywhere nearby?"

"Shut up and listen," Lady Barb said. "You're right; the ideas you introduced to this country *did* cause unrest, which encouraged the plotters to think that they needed to strike sooner rather than later. And you're right; helping Alassa to be a decent human being convinced them that they couldn't count on having an easily-manipulated puppet on the throne. But the original plot was in place a long time before you went to Whitehall and met the crown princess.

"Yes, you certainly contributed to the mess," she added. "No, it was not *all* your fault.

"The correct way to deal with a problem that is your fault is to do what you can to make amends. If the problem isn't your fault, the correct way to deal with it is to learn from it and get revenge when you have a chance. At no point is sitting in your room, indulging in self-pity, a valid option. Your friends need you."

Emily nodded, slowly.

"Now, I suggest you go see the princess," Lady Barb told her. "I think she needs to see you."

Emily looked away, over at the walls. They'd been burned and clawed by the cockatrice, yet they'd remained largely intact. It had taken seven magicians to help her stun the beast—it hadn't fallen for the mirror trick the second time—and then they'd had to transfer it to another pocket dimension just to get it out of the castle. And one of the magicians had made a joke about cutting the creature up for alchemical ingredients and Emily had almost bitten his head off.

"I'm surprised that she doesn't hate me," Emily admitted.

Lady Barb scowled at her. "What have I told you about self-pity?"

Emily stood up. "Tell me something," she said. "What happened between you and Void?"

"That is between me and him," Lady Barb said, tartly. "And really none of your business."

"It *is* my business," Emily snapped. "You seem to have decided to dislike me because of Void, right from the start. Why?"

Lady Barb gave her a long, considering look. "Your mentor is a poor example to any would-be sorceress," she said. There was something in her voice that dared Emily to press further. "There are better people to learn from…"

Emily glared at her, feeling hot frustration surging through her body. "What did he *do* to you?"

"The White Council had received a report that a sorcerer of great renown had started experimenting with a form of necromancy," Lady Barb said. Her eyes never moved from Emily's face. "They asked Void to investigate—and to take along a new combat sorceress as an assistant."

Emily blinked. "They asked Void to investigate?"

"They're quite happy to use him to do their dirty work," Lady Barb confirmed. "So they went to the sorcerer's tower and discovered that they couldn't get in—the sorcerer had devised wards so powerful that they couldn't sneak in without setting off the alarms. Luckily, Void had a plan. The sorcerer loved slave girls and owned almost a hundred of them. Void caught one of the girls at the nearby market and replaced her with that new sorceress. And he transferred the slave-spell from one to the other."

"He did…he did *what?*"

"He effectively turned me into a helpless slave and sent me right into the enemy camp," Lady Barb said. The rage and hatred in her voice was no longer hidden. "Oh, he had this grand plan; no one ever looks twice at an ensorcelled slave, because the slaves can do naught, but obey. I'm sure it sounded good inside his head. But he never even *asked* if I would consider doing it for the White Council. He just went ahead and did it.

"I spent two weeks there, watching the sorcerer while my body did as it was told," she added. "In the end, we concluded that one of the sorcerer's rivals had tried to get him into trouble, because we found no trace of necromancy. When it was my turn to go to the market, Void met me, removed the spell and sent the old maid back again. And that was the end…"

Emily stared in horror. She'd known that Void used servants who were under loyalty spells, but she'd never even *imagined* that he would push someone into servitude.

But that was silly…she couldn't imagine why *anyone* would volunteer to be turned into an obedient puppet, even though servants were meant to obey orders. Maybe it was a condition of their employment, she'd told herself; loyalty spells worked at their best when they were accepted voluntarily. And someone like Void would be able to offer the best wages.

But what he'd done to Lady Barb was *cruel.*

"If something had gone wrong, I would have been trapped there," Lady Barb said, quietly. "Or he might just have left the charm on me, out of fear of what I might do afterwards. He never even gave me the chance to decide if I wanted to take the risk or not."

She turned and marched towards the door. "Go see the princess," she ordered. "And then think about what I said."

"I will," Emily promised, too stunned to say anything else. How *could* Void have done that to anyone? "I'll go see her now."

She closed both chests, checked the security spells holding them closed and then followed Lady Barb out of the room. The outside corridors had been badly scorched by the flames, forcing a small army of maids to work for several days to scrub away the scorch marks and start replacing the destroyed portraits and tapestries. Emily couldn't help wondering how willingly the maids had accepted their own loyalty spells. Had they been pushed into it by whoever had hired them? There was no way to know.

Alassa's rooms were heavily guarded, even though King Randor knew that it was a case of locking the barn door after the horse had been stolen. The guardsmen relaxed slightly as they recognized Emily and stepped aside, allowing her to enter. There was no sign of Alassa until Emily glanced into the bedroom and saw her friend lying on her bed, staring up at the ceiling. She should have been surrounded by maids, but she was alone.

"Alassa?" Emily called, stepping into the room. "Are you all right?"

"I killed the duchess," Alassa said, without looking at her. "Why do I keep having nightmares about it?"

Emily remembered some of the nightmares she'd had and nodded in understanding. "It happens," she said, finally. The dream where they had been chased by orcs and goblins had haunted her for months after the incident itself. "There are potions for it, if you want to take them…"

"I don't think I do," Alassa said. She turned her head slightly, allowing her to look at Emily. "I didn't tell father about the Blood Magic."

Emily let out a breath she hadn't realized she'd been holding. Blood Magic was bad enough, but when it involved the heir to the throne…the bird-magician had wanted to use Alassa's blood to control her. King Randor would be furious with *anyone* who messed around with his daughter's blood, even her best friend.

"Thank you," she said, finally.

"But tell me," Alassa added. "What happened to the rest of the blood?"

"Here," Emily said, producing the handkerchief. "I thought you could dispose of it safely."

"I will," Alassa said, taking it. She smiled, rather faintly. "Half of your memories don't make sense."

"My *life* doesn't make sense," Emily grumbled. But she knew it wouldn't distract her friend for more than a moment or two. They'd been bound to talk about what Alassa had seen in Emily's mind, sooner or later. "What did you see?"

"I'm honestly not sure," Alassa said. "What *were* those dragon-creatures?"

"I don't know," Emily admitted. There were *no* dragons on Earth. Could she have seen a car? Or a massive truck? Or even a jet plane? "I don't know what you actually saw."

"Neither do I," Alassa said. They shared a smile. "I spoke to my father. He has pledged never to ask me about your past."

Emily felt her eyes narrow. King Randor would keep his word, but he'd know that there was something important about Emily's origins. Who knew what would happen in the future if he started to investigate her more thoroughly? And yet...if Emily told Alassa the truth ahead of time, it might convince them not to bother looking any further. As far as she knew, even the most powerful sorcerer in the world couldn't open a portal into another universe.

But if they can build pocket dimensions, she asked herself, *why not?*

"So you can tell me," Alassa said. "Where do you come from?"

Emily hesitated. She *wanted* to tell one of her friends, someone closer to her than Void or the grandmaster, but at the same time...Alassa would be queen. Who knew what her duty would compel her to do after she was crowned? But Emily *had* promised her that she would tell her the truth. Eventually.

"Another world," she said.

She had to smile at Alassa's expression. Her friend might have imagined that Emily came from another continent, one more advanced than her own, even though no such continent had been discovered. How could she have imagined an alternate world? But in hindsight, Emily suspected that it would appear obvious. Alassa, more than almost anyone else in the world, had deduced that Emily *wasn't* a genius who could invent a whole branch of science in an afternoon. It wasn't a big jump from there to realize that Emily had learned her knowledge somewhere else.

The whole story came tumbling out, from Shadye's decision to kidnap her to Void's rescue and her enrolment at Whitehall. Alassa listened, staring at her, as Emily calmly described parts of her world. Emily had wondered what she would make of Earth, if she ever had the chance to visit; in many ways, Earth was a paradise.

"I never even considered," Alassa said, finally. "Would you go back, if you could?"

Emily shook her head. Back home, she'd been a nobody with no prospects of a better life. Here, she had friends, magic...and money. Whoever had said that money was overrated had clearly never had to worry about being poor. Whitehall *didn't* have internet, or television, but it did have magic. Why would she ever want to go home?

"This is my home now," she said, seriously.

She shook her head. "I think those dragons you saw are actually *cars*," she added. "Given enough time, steam engines will eventually lead to internal combustion engines, allowing you to have thousands of cars on the road."

And there would be other changes too. By Zangaria's standards, even a relatively small country such as Britain or Ireland was grossly overpopulated. As medical care advanced, lives would be longer; as farming techniques improved, the population would grow rapidly...as knowledge spread, smart people would build on what they read to produce new ideas of their own. And to think that the barons had thought that change was already moving too quickly. They'd be horrified when they realized that it would only grow faster.

"You weren't happy there," Alassa said. "Is it something we actually want to emulate?"

Emily gave the question serious consideration. "I think that you need to find other ways to counter the necromancers," she said. "The next time Whitehall is attacked, we might not be so lucky."

"You might not be able to save us," Alassa said. She looked down at her hands for a long moment. "All of your memories of Shadye are *strange*. I cannot follow them."

"Probably for the best," Emily said. It was frustrating, sometimes, to have to keep so many ideas under wraps, but the consequences of losing control of some of them could be disastrous. "I still have nightmares."

Alassa snorted. "So would any citizen of the Allied Lands," she said, rather dryly. She looked up at Emily. "Will you be coming to the ceremony?"

"If you'll have me, I'll come," Emily said, as reassuringly as she could. "Where are you going to hold it?"

"In the Great Hall," Alassa said. "The Assembly won't be rebuilt–my father wants them to build a bigger and better building; the Assembly remained loyal when so many of the aristocrats hedged their bets. And there's gratitude for what Imaiqah's father did for us..."

Emily smiled. "You never had time to swear," she said. "Are you going to keep your word anyway?"

"No, I didn't," Alassa said. She shook her head. "I'll keep my word, even though... is your world really what we want to be?"

Emily tried to see Earth through Alassa's eyes. A dizzying blur of impressions, light and noise. Monstrous vehicles clogging up the streets, pollution in the air, litter everywhere...promiscuity and STDs running rampant all over the world, weapons that could destroy an entire city in a moment...terrorists, dictators with far more power than any monarch in the Allied Lands. Earth was far from perfect.

"I think you can try to do a better job," she said, finally. Who knew? Combining magic and science might produce all sorts of interesting results. "But the genie is out of the bottle now. You won't be able to stuff him back inside."

"The barons wanted to try," Alassa reminded her. She shook her head. "We'll just have to see how things go. My father always told me that patience was the best option when one wasn't sure what one should do. I never listened until now."

She swung her legs over the side of the bed and stood up, her expression hardening. "One other thing," she said. "*Don't* use my blood for anything, ever again."

Emily understood. *She'd* been manipulated—and, in some ways, her mental contact with Alassa had been even worse than using her body as a puppet. Some of Alassa's deepest thoughts and feelings were part of her now; Emily suspected that some others would emerge slowly, flashes of insight and knowledge that came from what she had absorbed. Who knew *where* it would end?

"And don't tell anyone else what you did, either," Alassa added. "It would only give them ideas."

"I won't," Emily promised. The duchess had believed that she could control Alassa, at least long enough to be declared her successor. It might well have worked…Emily still got the cold sweats when she realized how close they had come to disaster. "And you'd better make sure you destroy all that remains of your blood."

"Zed handed in his resignation after we liberated him," Alassa admitted. "Brain isn't really up to taking his place yet, so Father is going to hire a small number of alchemists to work on the Royal Bloodline. And pay Brain's tuition fees if he wants to go to Whitehall…his apprenticeship with an Alchemist has left him deficient in other matters, apparently."

She shrugged. "We should have time to make sure we destroy *all* the samples," she added. "We should be safe."

But they'd never be *certain*, Emily knew. There could be one final sample of Alassa's blood out there, ready and waiting for someone to find it and realize what it was. And, no matter what precautions they took, someone might manage to use it to influence the queen. Alassa would not have an easy reign, no matter what else happened; there would always be whispers that she wasn't entirely her own mistress.

She's going to have to marry, Emily reminded herself. *That was always true.*

She looked up. "Did you settle on a prince?"

Alassa giggled. "My father has decided that the whole selection process needs to start again," she said. "After all…they *all* fought for me, when the time came. How do we choose the bravest of them?"

"So we're going to have to do it all again next year?" Emily asked. "Do I *have* to come?"

"Yep," Alassa said. Her face sobered slightly. "Where would I be without you?"

Chapter Forty-Two

T HE GREAT HALL HAD BEEN CLEANED AFTER THE DUCHESS'S BODY HAD BEEN REMOVED, then decked out to match the destroyed Assembly Hall. Emily had watched the maids prepare the hall, transporting the thrones from the Assembly Hall into the castle while hiding the King's original throne behind one of the white curtains. The symbolism—a king and his heir—would be maintained, even if the ceremony was being held in the wrong place. Now, she watched from behind one of the curtains as the hall slowly filled with people, chattering happily amongst themselves.

King Randor had thrown open the castle to potential witnesses. Aside from the surviving nobles and princes, there were assemblymen and councilors—including Imaiqah's father—from the city below. Emily had heard that the guards had been worried about an assassin sneaking in with the crowds, but King Randor had dismissed their concerns. A show of bravado, he had said, would help convince people that the monarchy wasn't scared.

Emily looked over at Alassa, who was clearly nervous. It had been decided that she didn't need to remain awake for the vigil a second night before the ceremony, as she had already sat it in good faith, but not everyone had been happy with that decision. Too much of the original ceremony had been shortened for the second ceremony. Emily had heard two of the aristocrats complaining that the traditions were being mocked. She'd been unable to help wondering if they really *cared* about the future of the kingdom.

"Ready," Alassa said, as the trumpets began to blare. "Here we go."

Emily couldn't escape the sensation that she was escorting Alassa to her wedding as they walked up the middle of the Great Hall. She could feel eyes staring at them - some friendly, some hostile, some merely indifferent—and winced, inwardly. Whatever had happened in her life, she *still* didn't like being the center of attention— or even *close* to the center of attention. Alassa stopped in front of her father and went down on one knee, followed by the remainder of the hall. Emily stepped back until she was at the edge of the crowd and then joined them.

"There were those who believed that they could destroy the Line of Alexis," King Randor said, into the silence. "They believed that We could be kept prisoner, along with Our wife, and the kingdom would just fall into their lap. But they reckoned without Our daughter. Few sons have ever served their fathers so well."

Emily concealed her private amusement. The official version of the story credited Alassa with almost everything, including killing the duchess. She couldn't blame King Randor for wanting his daughter to receive most of the credit; after all, the barons would remember what Alassa had done and perhaps think better of challenging her. Besides, three of the barons were dead, two more were under arrest and the remaining four knew that they were on probation. They'd want to claw back as much power as they could before they tried anything overt.

"There were those who said that Our daughter had the body of a weak and feeble woman," King Randor added. He probably wouldn't credit Emily—or Queen Elizabeth

I - for the lines either. "But she has the heart of a king and a King of Zangaria too. Within her runs the blood of King Alexis I, who created our kingdom, and King Alexis III, who restored our control over rebellious factions. They thought they could remove her as easily as one might sweep out a cobweb. But she defeated them and executed the ringleader herself. She has more than proved herself in front of Us."

Emily wondered, rather sourly, what the discovery that the duchess had been behind the plot would mean for Zangaria. It would be nice to believe that they'd start taking women more seriously, but it wasn't too likely. No doubt they'd conclude that the duchess had been the puppet of her family and the other barons. It would certainly be more comforting than facing the truth.

King Randor stepped forward and helped his daughter to her feet. "It is Our wish that Alassa, crown princess of Our kingdom, be confirmed as heir," he said. "What do you say?"

The cheer was so deafening that Emily's ears rang for moments afterwards.

"We therefore confirm you, Our daughter, as Our Primary Heir," King Randor said. A young page came up to him, carrying a thin silver crown on a cushion. The king took it from him, held it up over Alassa's head and gently placed it on her golden hair. "You may take your seat."

Alassa sat down on the second throne and folded her hands in her lap. Emily was perhaps the only person in the room who could see her relief. From what Alassa had told her, many of the rehearsals for the ceremony Alassa had undergone before leaving for Whitehall had been disasters. Emily had never considered that there might *be* rehearsals, but she had to admit that they might well be useful.

She looked back at the audience, decked out in their finery, and smiled to herself. After everything that had happened over the last week, very few people would dare to cross the King. The remaining barons had loudly protested their loyalty, while the heirs of the dead or arrested barons had promptly disowned their fathers. It wouldn't be enough to save some of them. The arrested barons had been interrogated and confessed that their families had been deeply involved with the entire plot.

"It is traditional that we proceed to the feast," King Randor said. "But there are others whose behavior requires acknowledgement. Those who were loyal to Us and Our family in Our time of need shall not go unrewarded. Paren, son of Johan, Councilor of Alexis, step forward."

Imaiqah's father stepped forward, looking shocked. Emily had to smile; surely, he'd known that there would be some reward. Unless, of course, he'd also feared what the king would say when he realized that the weapons the council had been stockpiling could have easily been aimed at him. But then, without those weapons the plotters would have kept most of their armed force in the castle and the counter-coup would have failed miserably.

"Kneel before Us," King Randor ordered. "Paren, son of Johan, you were loyal to Our family. When all seemed lost, you convinced your fellow councilors to stand up against the usurpers who would take Our throne. Your loyalty will not go unrewarded."

He drew his sword and placed the flat of the blade, very gently, against Paren's shoulder. "We dub thee Viscount Paren, of House Steam," he said. "We trust that you will always remember your duties to Us as well as you have done in the past."

Emily had to smile when she caught sight of Imaiqah's expression. A viscount wasn't all *that* high a rank in Zangaria, but it would give Paren a degree of social prominence—and protection—that he could use to reform the city and challenge the remaining guilds. And it would also serve to bind him to King Randor. As a newly-minted aristocrat, his loyalty could be relied upon.

The king wants to co-opt the revolution, she thought. *Will it cushion the impacts to come?*

Absently, she wondered how he would fit in with the other aristocrats. Paren was wealthy—Emily had a private feeling that he'd kept more of the profits of their joint endeavors than he'd ever admitted—and with a title, poor but noble families would probably see his children as worthy partners for *their* children. Or would House Steam—a rather pointed name—be treated as little better than unwanted intruders, pretenders to true aristocratic glory? Who knew?

Paren rose, backed away from the king and returned to where he'd been standing. One by one, the other councilors were called out and rewarded, although none of them were promoted above the rank of knight. A handful of City Guardsmen were also knighted and offered commissions in the Royal Army. Given that a commission was the key to rising higher in social class, Emily doubted that any of them would refuse. Emily found herself growing impatient, wondering when the ceremony would come to an end. She had no idea how the rest of the guests were able to stand so still for too long.

"But there is one more person who should be rewarded," King Randor said. "One person who has performed a great service for Our kingdom and asked for nothing in return. Lady Emily, step forward."

Emily froze. She hadn't expected *this*. A hand pushed her gently and she stepped forward, feeling dazed. It was all she could do to remember to kneel before the king...for a moment, she caught a mischievous glint in Alassa's eye. Had her friend known what was to come and kept it to herself, hoping to surprise Emily? Surely the king would have consulted with his daughter, the person who knew Emily best, before deciding how best to reward her.

"You have done us a great service," King Randor said. His face was impassive, but Emily was sure that she could detect lurking amusement behind his eyes. *He* hadn't even asked her if she *wanted* a reward. "There have been few people in our kingdom's history who have been Children of Destiny, let alone performed such a service as yourself. For that, you must be rewarded."

Emily thought fast, trying to understand what he meant. He couldn't tell the court about Emily's role in stopping the duchess, even though most of them probably had some idea of the truth. It would destroy the myth they were trying to build around Alassa. And she doubted that he wanted to advertize the fact that *Emily* was behind all of the new concepts spreading through the Allied Lands. It would have made it harder for him to profit from them, particularly if she became a target for kidnap—or assassination—by just about every interested party.

And then it struck her. She'd helped Alassa reform into a decent human being, rather than a royal brat with more power than common sense. The king wouldn't want to call attention to that either. After all, the sense that Alassa could be manipulated had helped spur the coup plotters onwards...

"We thought long and hard about what reward would be suitable for you," the king said. "What could we offer you that would reward you for what you have done? And then it occurred to Us that the Barony of Holyoake is vacant. The baron and his sole heir were deeply implicated in the plot, as was his young daughter."

The duchess, Emily thought. The Duke of Iron had collapsed when he'd finally found out the truth about his wife, and then decided that he needed a long holiday. He hadn't even stayed around for the Confirmation...which might not have been a bad thing. It was removing him as nominated regent, in the event of the King's death.

"Holyoake will vanish from the kingdom," the king said. There was a mild edge to his voice that fooled absolutely no one. "In its place, there will be the Barony of Cockatrice—and you, Baroness Emily, will be its ruler."

Emily felt her mouth drop open. Her, a *baroness*? And a baroness with *real* power?

She found herself eying the king with new respect as she realized what he had done. No one could dispute that she'd earned a reward, so he'd given her one that came with a nasty sting in the tail. By accepting it, she would be binding herself to Zangaria, perhaps even accepting him as her overlord. She would have to be loyal to him, placing his interests above those of the Allied Lands as a whole. If she'd been asked, in private, if she would accept, she might well have turned it down.

And yet...it did have its temptations. A baron had absolute power within his barony, as long as he didn't plot rebellion against the king—or at least get caught at it, the cynical side of her mind added dryly. She could introduce all kinds of innovations in Cockatrice—she had to admit that the king had picked an appropriate name—without needing to worry about opposition. Hell, she could invite anyone who felt that their local aristocrats didn't approve of them to come *live* in her barony. Hadn't there been a ruler of the Ottoman Empire who had gloated when medieval Spain expelled the Jews? They'd enriched his country tremendously.

She needed time to think about the implications. Would she have to leave Whitehall and stay in Zangaria? What would the king want from her in the future? For her to be a friend to Alassa or something else? Would he insist on controlling her marriage? And what was she actually getting into...?

But there was no time to think. And she couldn't object here, not in front of the entire court. The king had planned that too, she realized. And once she'd accepted, it would be very hard to get rid of the title. He'd manipulated events with as much skill as the duchess, bending them to suit his own ends. No wonder he'd stayed on the throne for so long.

"I thank you, Your Majesty," she stammered, finally.

The king placed his sword upon her shoulder. "I name you Baroness Emily, of House Cockatrice," he said, formally. "And I welcome you to my kingdom."

He'd dropped the royal We, Emily realized, numbly. Barons were *important*.

"You may join your peers," the king said, nodding to the remaining barons. None of them looked quite happy to see Emily raised to their level, but they didn't dare object. Not publicly, anyway. Judging from some of the comments she'd overhead before the coup had been launched, the barons struggled against each other as much as they struggled against the King. The entire country was the Allied Lands in miniature.

King Randor sat back on his throne. "There will be changes to come," he said, once the cheering had died away. "But Zangaria will adapt; we will preserve the essence of what we are, no matter what becomes possible in the future."

He stood up, took Alassa by the hand and led the way out of the Great Hall. The barons followed them, forcing Emily—still numb from her sudden ennoblement—to walk after them. She shook her head tiredly, unsure of what it all meant, then stepped into the dining hall. Servants were ready to point them towards their seats; Emily's, she realized in some relief, was right next to Alassa's throne. They could talk.

"You could have warned me," she muttered, after casting a privacy ward into the air. "Why...?"

"Father wanted it to be a surprise," Alassa admitted. "He felt that you deserved a large reward."

She smiled, brilliantly. "You do realize what this means?"

"No," Emily said.

"You will be one of the most powerful people in the kingdom," Alassa said. "When I am queen, you will be my chief advisor. Your children will be marrying into the other noble families, building up your personal power and influence. There isn't a person in the kingdom who wouldn't want to change places with you right now."

She frowned. "But you don't like the idea?"

"I don't know what to make of it," Emily said, softly. "What does this mean for me personally? What does it mean for my life?"

"Nightingale is already looking forward to briefing you about protocol," Alassa said, with an evil grin. She knew how Emily felt about protocol briefings. "Just remember that House Holyoake no longer exists. You can make a clean sweep of their retainers if you choose or you can take them into your own service. I plan to do that now that I'm Confirmed."

Emily blinked in surprise. "Right now, we have a window of opportunity to get some changes made," Alassa said. "A number of hereditary posts are going to stop being hereditary. It seems that quite a few of them were actively disloyal or untrustworthy...so we can get a few changes made. You can help with that."

She reached out and gave Emily a hug, in full view of everyone in the hall. "If you don't want to stay and rule the barony, you can appoint someone to serve as your regent," she added. "You're going to have to do that anyway, unless you stay here instead of going back to Whitehall. Just make sure you pick carefully…Paren of House Steam wouldn't be a bad choice, if he were willing."

"I'll ask him," Emily promised.

"And after the banquet," Alassa said, "you and I are going to have a long chat about the future. Perhaps we can avoid future problems if we talk out the changes first."

Emily nodded. Alassa was right.

"We will," she agreed. She looked over at her friend and smiled. "And thank you for putting up with me."

Alassa elbowed her. "You saved my life, my father's life, my mother's life…we have good reason to be grateful to you," she said. "Stop feeling sorry for yourself."

Emily flushed. "I'll do my best," she promised. Lady Barb had told her the same thing. And yet it was hard *not* to feel guilty for her role in the near-catastrophe. "But thank you anyway."

She cancelled the privacy ward as the servants began serving the high table with roast beef, potatoes and a thick gravy that smelled faintly greasy to Emily. No doubt it was very unhealthy…but she could take more exercise in the morning. And Sergeant Miles would make her work hard in second-year. She wondered, absently, who would replace Sergeant Harkin before deciding that it didn't matter. There was too much else to worry about right now.

Wait till after the feast, she told herself. *You can talk to Alassa then.*

Chapter Forty-Three

FATHER HAS BEEN LOOKING FORWARD TO THIS FOR AGES," IMAIQAH SAID, AS THEY waited outside the modified warehouse. "I think it has actually been distracting him during meetings."

Emily shrugged. In the month that had passed since the duchess had been defeated and Alassa had been Confirmed, she'd been very busy. While Alassa oversaw the process of interrogating the remaining suspects and rooting out every last aspect of the duchess's conspiracy, Emily had taken a trip up to Cockatrice and inspected her new lands. The whole experience had been faintly surreal, even though most of the peasants she'd met had seemed pleased to see her. She'd had to keep reminding herself that they probably wouldn't say anything else to her face.

She hadn't intended to stay long, but the task of cleaning up the problems caused by the previous baron—no one spoke his name out loud now—had taken longer than she'd expected. Most of his appointed superintendents were either corrupt or thugs or both, forcing her to unceremoniously discharge them from office and exile them from her lands. The baron's legal system was appallingly bad; one afternoon spent reading a sample of the paperwork had convinced her that the laws contradicted themselves on at least a dozen different points. There was no way that it could be both legal and illegal to hunt wild boar on the edge of the forests. Eventually, she'd appointed a handful of superintendents who were willing to swear oaths to use common sense and promised to sort out the rest of the headache later.

"I don't blame him," she said. The barons might have been blocking large sales of iron ore, but *Emily* hadn't hesitated to order the ore sold from the mines she'd inherited. Indeed, she'd discovered that the previous baron had built up quite a stockpile of ore, leaving her wondering just what he'd had in mind. "I've been looking forward to this too."

Paren had taken advantage of his new rank to buy up a large chunk of the outer city, build a number of new houses and construct a factory right at the edge of the city. It had taken longer for him to impress the importance of sanitation on everyone—the houses outside the walls were so cramped that Emily was surprised they weren't more disease-ridden—but free baths and health advice had helped with that. He'd ended up with thousands of very willing workers, who'd started to learn how to work with iron ore. The blacksmiths hadn't quite realized what this meant for them in the future, but Emily suspected that wouldn't last long. Mass production would weaken their position. On the other hand, more metal meant more work.

"My father wanted me to give you this," Imaiqah said. She passed Emily a folded sheet of parchment. "They finally succeeded."

Emily opened the sheet and glanced at the formula written there. "Good," she said, although she wasn't sure if it *was* good. "They know what to do with it."

There was a whistle and the crowd turned to face the doors, which opened slowly to reveal a darkened interior. Imaiqah caught Emily's hand in her excitement as the steam engine slowly came into view, puffing smoke into the air as it moved along the iron rails. It didn't look very impressive, not compared to some of the early locomo-tives Emily had seen in history books, but it was a start. Besides, it was a great deal more impressive than any purely mundane device this world had ever seen.

It inched forward, slowly picking up speed. The crowd cheered as the driver waved to them, while the fireman kept shovelling coal into the boiler. Emily smiled as the crowd started to walk alongside the locomotive, pacing it. Not all of the crowd was so impressed.

"It's so slow," a man complained. By his outfit, Emily guessed that he was a wealthy merchant. "A man could outrun it easily!"

Emily gave him a wintery smile. "What use is a newborn baby, sir?"

The man smiled and clicked his fingers. Emily sensed the pulse of magic just before the entire world froze.

"Void," she said.

"None other," Void agreed. "Should I be calling you by your title?"

"I was wondering when you were going to show up," Emily said, ignoring the ques-tion. "How much of this did you know about?"

Void shrugged, making no pretense that he didn't understand the question. "We knew that the Kingdom of Zangaria was in trouble," he said, dryly. "Part of that was your fault–your influence on Princess Alassa, the ideas you introduced–and part of it was the barons struggling to reassert themselves against the Royal Family. I'm sure that King Randor wanted to cripple them and would have tried, even without your meddling."

Emily scowled at him. "And did you *want* me to meddle?"

"Whatever happens, happens," Void said.

"That isn't an answer," Emily snapped. "What did *you* want from all of this?"

"The Allied Lands have got to work together," Void reminded her.

"Hang together or hang separately," Emily said.

Void bowed his head to her in acknowledgement. "I believed that you coming here would give King Randor a chance to secure his grip on power," he said. "Without you, Alassa might have fallen back into her bratty ways, allowing her enemies the chance to manipulate her. The end result would have been chaos, which would have allowed the necromancers a chance to resume their assault on the Allied Lands. It could not be allowed."

Emily remembered his casual dismissal of how close Alassa had come to death–at Emily's hands–and shivered.

"Besides, you had friends there," he added. "I believed that you deserved a chance to try to deal with the matter yourself."

"Thank you," Emily said, sourly.

Void showed no reaction. "I had a few words with Zed," he said, instead. "He knows that you used Blood Magic to locate the princess. I... *convinced* him to keep it to himself."

Emily blanched. "He *knew?*"

"He is an expert in alchemy and Blood Magic is related to alchemy," Void said. "It would have been simple for him to deduce what you did, Emily. You're lucky that he was so mad at King Randor that he didn't say a word to him."

"Alassa knows," Emily admitted. "And she knows about Earth."

Void snorted. "I never assumed it would remain secret forever," he said. "Luckily, the only known way to *reach* your world requires a vast amount of power and bribes."

He reached into his pocket and produced a long scroll of parchment. "This spell isn't exactly classed as Dark," he said, "but there will be some eyebrows raised if you show it to anyone else. It's called 'The Secret That Cannot Be Spoken.'"

Emily couldn't help giggling.

Void eyed her, crossly. "Some senior wizards have an infinite capacity for pretension."

"Yes," Emily said, deadpan. "I've noticed that."

"The spell renders you immune to all manner of truth-spells," Void said, passing it to her. "If someone tries to read your mind, they will find it impossible. Given time, you will actually discover how to *lie* with your mind, once the spell is firmly in place. It cannot be removed without killing you."

"Thank you," Emily said, doubtfully.

"The grandmaster was prepared to respect the Sorcerer's Rule," Void said. "Other magicians might not share his scruples."

Emily eyed the scroll, taking his point. Leading magicians—and sorcerers—was like herding cats, with the added danger of being turned into something unpleasant. By the Sorcerer's Rule, anyone who came up with a new spell or technique couldn't be forced to disclose it to anyone else, unless they wanted to share. It was all that had protected her from being forced to tell everyone just what she'd done to Shadye.

"And there are others who will try to force you to talk," Void added. "This spell will prevent you from being drugged, hypnotized or simply tortured for information. You simply will not be able to pass on the information without making a considered—and free—decision to talk. I think you need to learn it as soon as possible."

Emily stuck the scroll in her handbag and scowled at him, but he wasn't finished.

"You might also want to consider making the princess forget," he said. "There are…*dangers* involved in growing too close to a local monarchy."

It was on the tip of Emily's tongue to point out that he'd dismissed the matter earlier, but she held back.

"I will not wipe my friend's mind," she said, flatly. Taking a gap out of Alassa's mind would be wrong, even if she never found out. And if she did, their friendship would be gone forever. "I won't."

"Glad to hear it," Void murmured.

"I have a question for you," Emily snapped. "Why did you do…what you did to Lady Barb?"

"Do you find it hard to put into words," Void asked lightly, "or are you fishing, hoping that I would assume you know everything?"

Emily just stared at him, refusing to back down.

"The White Council wanted me to fix their little problem," Void said, after a long moment. "Typical, really–they let the problem fester for years, then they expect me to solve it for them. And Dubcek was a strong sorcerer. Any overt approach would have resulted in a fight even if he hadn't been starting the slide down into necromancy. So I did what was necessary to find out the truth before it was too late."

"By turning Lady Barb into a slave," Emily said, evenly.

"I did what I had to do," Void said. "She was a young sorceress, just graduated from Whitehall, with almost no actual experience. What *else* could I have done?"

"You could have asked her," Emily said, keeping her voice under tight control.

"She would have said no," Void countered, blithely.

His eyes narrowed. "Do you like Alassa's father?"

Emily nodded, staring at him in horror.

"Every king on a throne must get his hands dirty if he wishes to *keep* his crown," Void said. His voice hardened, making Emily flinch and step backwards. "I have far less blood on my hands than King Randor, whatever...*questionable* choices and bargains I might have made. Just keep that in mind."

He eyed her for a long moment, then stepped back and vanished, collapsing the temporal bubble as he left. Emily looked back at the steam locomotive, then touched the two pieces of parchment in her pocket, wondering where they would both lead. Both of them would change the entire world.

One would protect her mind from all intrusion, if Void was telling the truth...

...And the other held a working formula for gunpowder.

END OF BOOK TWO

Emily will return in

Study in Slaughter

About the author

Christopher G. Nuttall is thirty-two years old and has been reading science fiction since he was five, when someone introduced him to children's SF. Born in Scotland, Chris attended schools in Edinburgh, Fife and University in Manchester before moving to Malaysia to live with his wife Aisha.

Chris has been involved in the online Alternate History community since 1998; in particular, he was the original founder of Changing The Times, an online alternate history website that brought in submissions from all over the community. Later, Chris took up writing and eventually became a full-time writer.

Current and forthcoming titles published by Twilight Times Books:

Schooled in Magic YA fantasy series
  Schooled in Magic book 1
  Lessons in Etiquette book 2
  Study in Slaughter book 3
  Work Experience book 4
  The School of Hard Knocks book 5

The Decline and Fall of the Galactic Empire SF series
  Barbarians at the Gates book 1
  The Shadow of Cincinnatus book 2

If you enjoyed this book, please post a review
at your favorite online bookstore.

Twilight Times Books
P O Box 3340
Kingsport, TN 37664
Phone/Fax: 423-323-0183
www.twilighttimesbooks.com/

Lightning Source UK Ltd.
Milton Keynes UK
UKOW06f1841161117

312843UK00001B/188/P